PUFFIN BOOKS

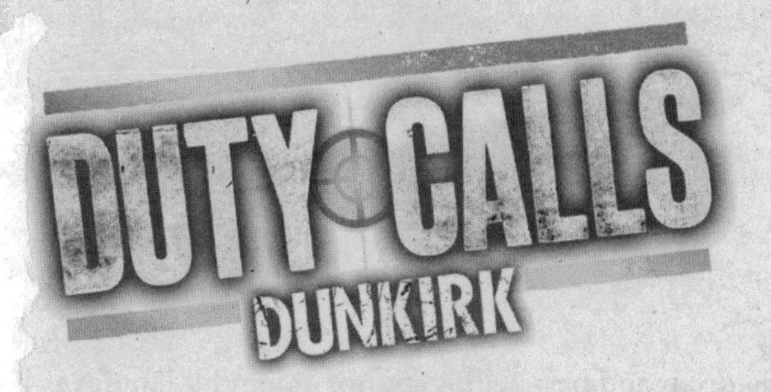

Historian and best-selling author James Holland was born in Salisbury, Wiltshire, and studied history at Durham University. He is the author of numerous historical non-fiction titles and the Jack Tanner fiction series, and presented *Battle of Britain: The Real Story* on BBC2.

A member of the British Commission for Military History, his many interviews with veterans of the Second World War are available at the Imperial War Museum and are also archived at *www.secondworldwarforum.com*. *Duty Calls: Dunkirk* is his first novel for younger readers.

*www.dutycallsbooks.com*

# JAMES HOLLAND

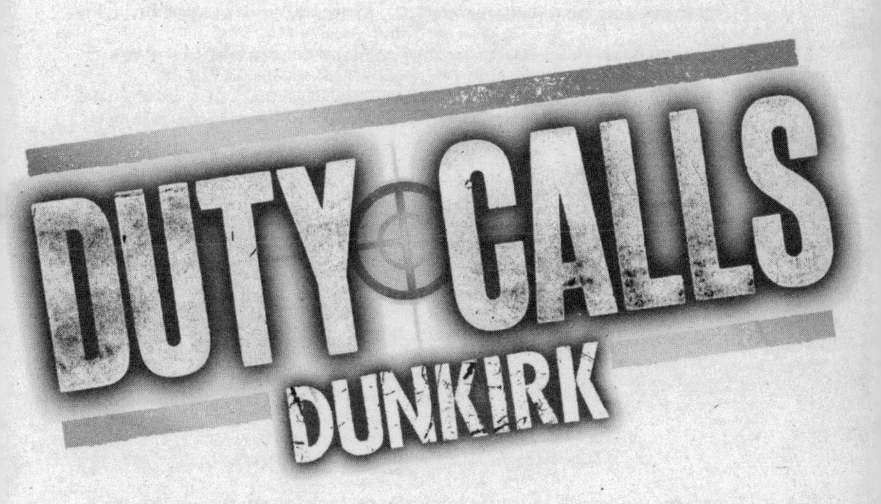

PUFFIN

PUFFIN BOOKS

Published by the Penguin Group
Penguin Books Ltd, 80 Strand, London WC2R ORL, England
Penguin Group (USA) Inc., 375 Hudson Street, New York, New York 10014, USA
Penguin Group (Canada), 90 Eglinton Avenue East, Suite 700, Toronto, Ontario, Canada M4P 2Y3
(a division of Pearson Penguin Canada Inc.)
Penguin Ireland, 25 St Stephen's Green, Dublin 2, Ireland (a division of Penguin Books Ltd)
Penguin Group (Australia), 250 Camberwell Road, Camberwell, Victoria 3124, Australia
(a division of Pearson Australia Group Pty Ltd)
Penguin Books India Pvt Ltd, 11 Community Centre, Panchsheel Park, New Delhi – 110 017, India
Penguin Group (NZ), 67 Apollo Drive, Rosedale, Auckland 0632, New Zealand
(a division of Pearson New Zealand Ltd)
Penguin Books (South Africa) (Pty) Ltd, 24 Sturdee Avenue, Rosebank, Johannesburg 2196, South Africa

Penguin Books Ltd, Registered Offices: 80 Strand, London WC2R ORL, England

puffinbooks.com

First published 2011
001 – 10 9 8 7 6 5 4 3 2 1



Set in 10.5/15.5 pt Sabon MT
Typeset by Palimpsest Book Production Limited, Falkirk, Stirlingshire
Made and printed in Great Britain by Clays Ltd, St Ives plc



British Library Cataloguing in Publication Data
A CIP catalogue record for this book is available from the British Library

ISBN: 978–0–141–33219–2

www.greenpenguin.co.uk

*For Ollie Mills*

# CONTENTS

# GLOSSARY

| | |
|---|---|
| adj | Adjutant – effectively the battalion administration and operations officer |
| angels | RAF terminology for height in thousands of feet. Angels 10 = 10,000 feet |
| bandits | RAF terminology meaning enemy aircraft |
| Bren carrier | Small-tracked vehicle for carrying infantry |
| B Echelon | Support troops, including mechanics, cooks, transport, etc |
| BEF | British Expeditionary Force |
| bipod | the same as a tripod, but with two legs rather than three |
| Blighty | Nickname for Britain |
| blood wagon | Slang for a squadron transport truck |
| Boche | Slang for German, used mostly in the First World War |
| char-wallah | Anglo-Indian slang for tea maker |
| clobber | Anglo-Indian slang for kit and clothing |
| CO | Commanding Officer |
| debus | get off a bus, truck, lorry, etc. |
| dekko | Anglo-Indian slang for having a look around |
| div | Short for Division |

| | |
|---|---|
| DLI | Durham Light Infantry |
| DR | Despatch rider |
| embus | get on a bus, truck, lorry, etc. |
| entrenching tool | a small pick and shovel – part of every soldier's kit |
| field glasses | Binoculars |
| frog | British nickname for the French |
| GHQ | General Headquarters |
| housewife | a small cotton holdall, containing needles, thread, spare buttons, patches, etc. which rolled up with a tie-pull and was issued to every soldier |
| howitzer | Field artillery gun |
| Huns | Old-fashioned British name for Germans |
| *iggery* | Anglo-Indian slang meaning to get a move on, to hurry up |
| in the bag | Taken prisoner |
| IO | Intelligence Officer |
| *Jaldi* | Anglo-Indian slang meaning the same as *iggery* |
| Jerry | British term for Germans |
| little jobs | RAF terminology for enemy fighter aircraft |
| Mae West | Inflatable life-jacket worn by the RAF |
| magazine | A chamber for holding ammunition – from the French word '*magasin*', which means 'store' |
| MG | Machine gun |
| MO | Medical officer |
| mole | a narrow jetty |
| M/T | Motor transport |
| NCO | Non-commissioned officer |
| panzer | German name for a tank |

| | |
|---|---|
| picquet | Sentry, or guard, keeping watch for the enemy |
| pom-pom | a quick-firing anti-aircraft gun, either twin or four barrels |
| port | Left-hand side |
| POW | Prisoner of war |
| RASC | Royal Army Service Corps |
| R/T | Radio transmitter |
| sangar | Defensive post built up from the ground when the ground is unsuitable for digging. Usually made from stone |
| sapper | Common name for a member of the Royal Engineers |
| small arms | Pistols, rifles, machine guns |
| Spandau | British name for a German machine gun |
| starboard | Right-hand side |
| stonk | A sustained attack by artillery, which can include field guns and mortars |
| subaltern | Name for a second-lieutenant or lieutenant. Subalterns could also be referred to as 'Mister', while a second-lieutenant would also usually be addressed as simply 'Lieutenant' |
| tiffin | Anglo-Indian slang for lunch, adopted by men who had served in India |
| Tommy | Slang for a British soldier |
| vics | an inverted 'V' shaped formation of three aircraft |

Visit *www.dutycallsbooks.com* for more information.

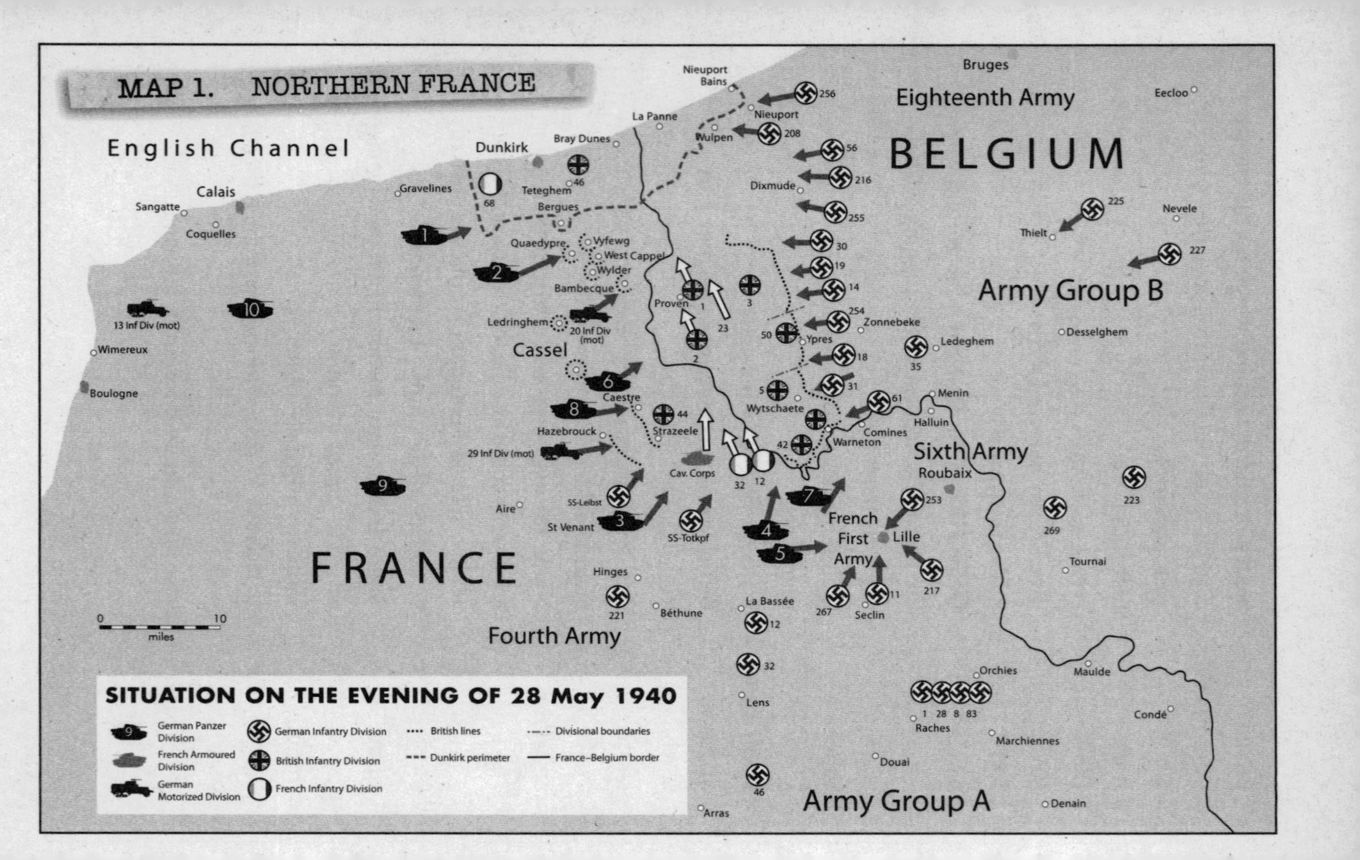

MAP 1. NORTHERN FRANCE
English Channel
BELGIUM
FRANCE
Eighteenth Army
Army Group B
Sixth Army
French First Army
Fourth Army
Army Group A
Bruges
Eecloo
Nevele
Thielt
Desselghem
Ledeghem
Menin
Halluin
Roubaix
Tournai
Condé
Maulde
Denain
Orchies
Marchiennes
Raches
Douai
Lille
Seclin
Comines
Warneton
Zonnebeke
Ypres
Wytschaete
La Bassée
Lens
Arras
Béthune
Hinges
Nieuport Bains
Nieuport
Wulpen
Dixmude
La Panne
Bray Dunes
Dunkirk
Teteghem
Bergues
Quaedypre
Vyfewg
West Cappel
Wylder
Bambecque
Ledringhem
Cassel
Proven
Caestre
Strazeele
Hazebrouck
Cav. Corps
SS-Totkpf
SS-Leibst
St Venant
Aire
Gravelines
Calais
Coquelles
Sangatte
Wimereux
Boulogne
13 Inf Div (mot)
20 Inf Div (mot)
29 Inf Div (mot)
0
10
miles
SITUATION ON THE EVENING OF 28 May 1940
German Panzer Division
French Armoured Division
German Motorized Division
German Infantry Division
British Infantry Division
French Infantry Division
British lines
Dunkirk perimeter
Divisional boundaries
France–Belgium border

# MAP 2. CASSEL

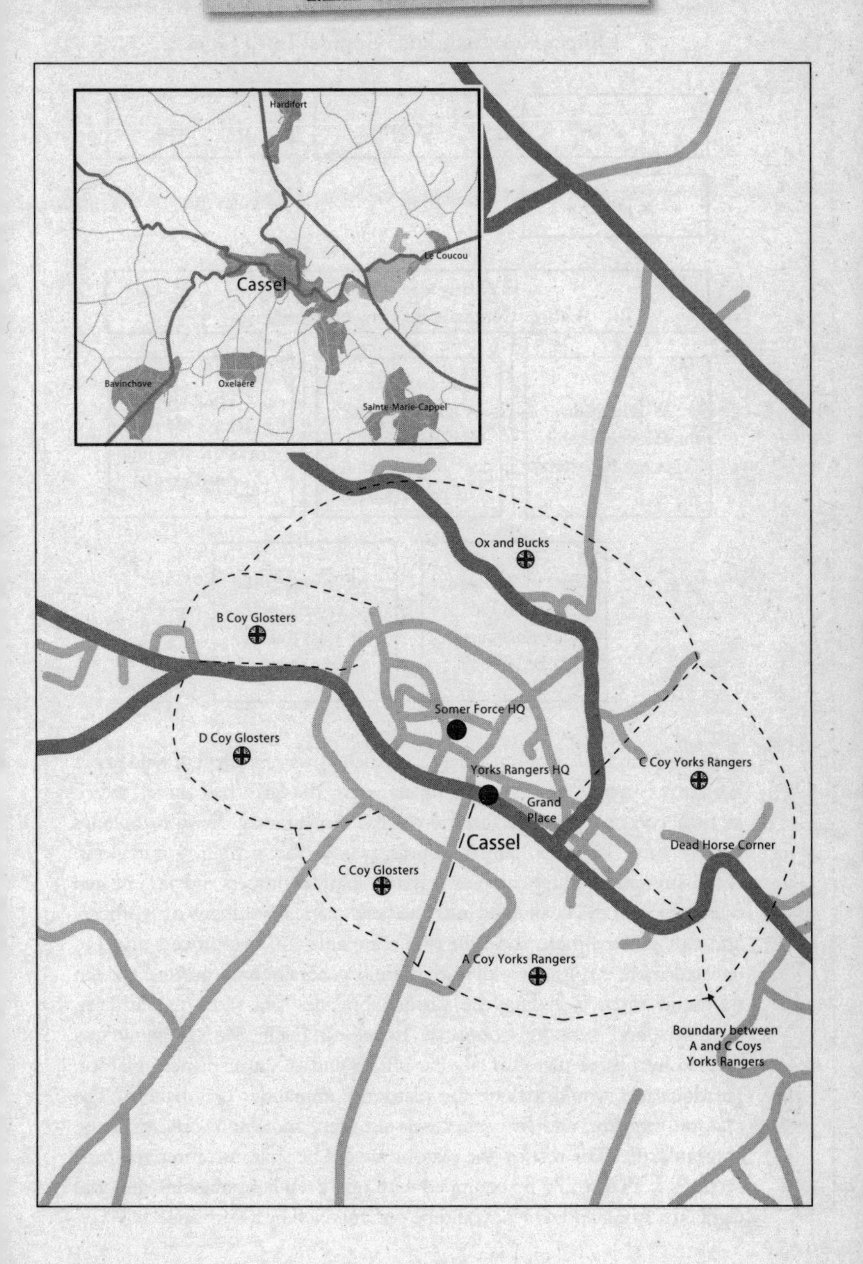
Hardifort
Le Coucou
Cassel
Bavinchove
Oxelaëre
Sainte-Marie-Cappel
Ox and Bucks
B Coy Glosters
Somer Force HQ
D Coy Glosters
Yorks Rangers HQ
C Coy Yorks Rangers
Grand Place
Cassel
Dead Horse Corner
C Coy Glosters
A Coy Yorks Rangers
Boundary between A and C Coys Yorks Rangers

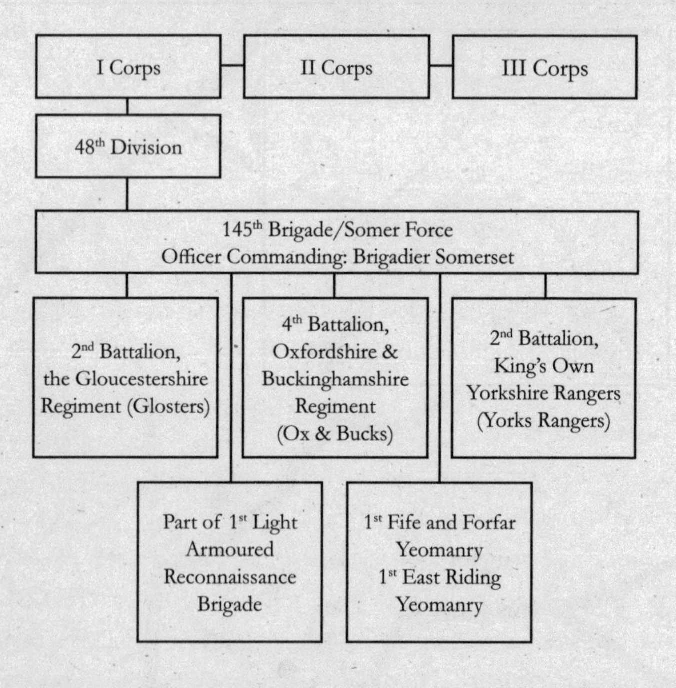


Although the BEF was not labelled as such, it was, in effect, a field army. An army is made up of two or more corps (the BEF had three), which in turn comprise two or three divisions. An infantry division includes two or three brigades, which include two or three infantry battalions. A full-strength infantry battalion is made up of 28 officers and 724 enlisted men, which would be divided into one headquarters company of 8 officers and 248 enlisted men, and four rifle companies of five officers and 119 enlisted men. An infantry division would generally have around sixteen thousand men, including the various brigades plus attached artillery, engineers and support troops (B Echelon). Each rifle company was divided into three platoons of one officer and 36 enlisted men. Platoon Headquarters would include the platoon commander (a subaltern), the platoon sergeant, and five other enlisted men, and one mortar and one anti-tank rifle. The rest of the platoon would be split into three ten-man sections, which would be equipped with one Bren light machine-gun and eight .303 rifles, and which would be commanded by a corporal.

# 1

# THE ROAD TO CASSEL

A little after 7 a.m., Friday 24 May 1940. The sun was already clear in the sky, shining brightly across the flat Flanders landscape. The road from Steenvoorde wound east to west so that as they left the small town the morning sun shone directly into the back of the truck, the sudden brightness jolting a young soldier from his sleep. A very young soldier – only just sixteen, although he was tall for his age and with a few hairs already on his chin that needed shaving, could just about pass for man two or three years older. If there were anything about him that betrayed his age, it was his eyes – deep brown under a mop of thick dark hair that suggested an innocence and lack of worldliness that was very much the case.

Private Johnny Hawke yawned, rubbed his eyes, then, squinting, looked out. The air was fresh and crisp after the rain, the water glinting on the grassy verges either side of the road. Somewhere to the south, desultory artillery fire was booming, dull and heavy, and Hawke felt a lurch in his stomach at this renewed proximity to the front line. Already refugees were trudging alongside the road, most heading towards Steenvoorde. Several cars had been left on the grass verge, evidently out of fuel. Hawke caught the eye of a young boy standing with his family beside a small wooden cart laden with suitcases and belongings, his expression one of exhaustion and resignation. Hawke nodded at him, but the boy just stared back as the truck trundled slowly by. The boy's father, sleeves rolled up already, pushed his hat back on his head and wiped his brow. Hawke could not help wondering what would happen if the Germans invaded Britain. He thought of his home in Leeds, in Yorkshire. Would the population really all leave their homes with just a few possessions, like these people had? Where were they going, anyway? Surely, he thought, it would be better to stay put. Certainly that's what Tom – Sergeant Spears – and the rest of the lads seemed to think. All that the refugees were doing, Sergeant Spears had said, was making matters worse – getting in the way, and clogging up the roads, and making it difficult to move troops around.

And, God only knew, it had been a hell of a job getting them this far. Corporal McLaren had told him that it was only around forty miles from Carvin to Cassel, but when they had embussed the previous evening, no one had thought it would take them all night to make the journey. Hawke looked at his wristwatch – one his father had worn in the last war. *Oh-seven-ten*. Nearly twelve hours! Twelve hours of stops and starts, of complete gridlock as they crossed routes with other British and particularly French units, and endless refugees. And they still hadn't reached Cassel – not quite.

It had rained the day before and although Hawke had followed the lead of the others and taken his gas cape out of his large pack he had still got damp, particularly on the sleeves and legs of his battledress. As the youngest and newest member of the platoon, he was the last on to the truck and so had to sit nearest the tailgate, where the canvas surround was open to the elements and the cold night air. It had made sleep difficult. Since joining the battalion four weeks earlier, he had noticed how some of the older hands seemed able to sleep anywhere and at any time, but he found it difficult – especially on the hard wooden bench of a truck, in full marching order, being jolted as the Bedford rumbled over every stone, bump and pothole on the road. Eventually, though, his exhaustion had got the better of him. After long hours crawling across the back roads of northern France, he'd somehow drifted off.

How long he had been asleep, he wasn't sure. Three hours, maybe? Not enough; his eyes stung, and he had a slight, dull headache. Even now his battledress felt damp. He had got used to the thick wool serge but when it was wet it itched and chafed more than usual. Hawke sighed and rubbed his eyes, then gripped his rifle between his legs – a Short Magazine Lee Enfield No.1 Mk 3, with its hard, wooden butt and barrel casing, and ten-round magazine. Eight pounds it weighed and with the best part of sixty pounds worth of kit he was grateful to have been made a rifleman and not one of the three men in the section's Bren gun team – the machine gun was three times as heavy as the rifle. Hawke liked to think of himself as strong for his age, but carrying full kit was tiring, and even more so when they'd had such little sleep over the past week.

Hawke looked across at Charlie Drummond sitting opposite him, who at eighteen was the second-youngest in the platoon, and saw his head lolling in sleep as the truck rumbled slowly forward. Next to Drummond was Bert Hebden, who caught his eye and smiled, then delved into the top pocket of his battle-dress for a packet of cigarettes. Hawke liked Hebden. Unlike most of the lads, who nearly all came from Leeds and Bradford, Hebden was a farmer's son. He could have avoided joining up, since farming was a reserved occupation that exempted him from front-line duty, but Hebden had an older brother and, in any case, explained to Hawke that he felt it was the right thing to do. 'I don't want that Hitler chappie coming anywhere near Yorkshire,' he'd told Hawke, 'so I thought I'd better do my bit to make sure he don't.'

Hawke looked out of the back of the truck, and at the rest of the column. There were some twenty trucks in all, a mixture of Bedfords and Morris Commercials, carrying the three remaining companies of the 1st Battalion, the King's Own Yorkshire Rangers, a little over four hundred men. He brought a hand to the semi-circular black cloth badge on his shoulder, and felt the green stitching that said 'Yorks Rangers'. Few other regiments had such a distinction on their uniforms; it marked the Rangers out – a Yorkshire regiment with a proud history. His stepfather, Richard, had told him about some of the Rangers' battle honours. They read like a roll-call of most of Britain's greatest victories: Blenheim, Ramillies, Quebec, Mysore, Corunna, Talavera, Badajoz, Salamanca, Vittoria, Toulouse, Waterloo – so it went on. Anywhere the British Army had fought during the last two hundred and fifty years, it seemed, the Yorks Rangers had been there too. It was the same regiment his father, John, and stepfather, Richard Mallaby, had fought in during the last war. And it was the regiment of which he, too, was now a part.

Hawke's thoughts were suddenly interrupted by the faint whirr of aero engines. Another artillery shell exploded dully to the south, momentarily blocking out the noise, but then he heard the sound more distinctly, and saw Hebden cock an ear too. Leaning out of the back of the truck, Hawke craned his neck. The whirr of engines was louder now and, as he shifted his position, he saw one of the men in the cab of the truck behind them also hoist himself up and crane his neck at the sky.

'There!' said Hawke, suddenly spotting a number of dark dots heading towards them from the north-east. He pointed and now Charlie Drummond had woken and was looking too.

''Ere,' said Corporal McLaren, hurrying towards the tailgate and pulling a pair of field glasses from his haversack, 'mind out the way, lads.' He peered through his binoculars but already Hawke could see the approaching aircraft were Stukas, their distinct gull wings and fixed undercarriage clearly visible now against the pale blue morning sky.

'There's a bleedin' two dozen of the beggars,' muttered McLaren, then yelled to the front, 'Sir! Sarge! Stukas!'

The truck jolted to a stop.

'Everyone out!' shouted Sergeant Spears from the front of the Bedford. 'Quick!'

Hawke jumped down as Spears appeared from the front of the vehicle. He glanced at him, but Spears scowled and said, 'Go on! 'Op it, or I'll kick you off the road!'

The whole column had by now come to speedy halt, the trucks all at a standstill as men poured out and clambered up on to the grass verge and across the culverts running either side of the road, then across the fields of young, green corn. Above, the first of the Stukas were peeling off to begin their dives. Soldiers were frantically running, and so too were the civilian refugees. Hawke was conscious of a young woman trying to soothe a screaming child and paused, only for a hand to roughly grab his shoulder.

'I said, move it!' snarled Sergeant Spears.

The Stukas screamed down towards them, their sirens whining, rising to a deafening crescendo, one after the other, and then the first bomb exploded and Hawke flung himself on to the ground, brittle young wheat stalks scratching his face, and his gas-mask pack winding him as it was pushed against his chest. He gasped and the earth shook with powerful pulses that lifted him clean from the ground as repeated detonations erupted nearby. Another explosion now ripped the air apart and as grit and soil and bits of stone pattered down on him Hawke dared to glance back at the column. One truck towards the rear of the line was engulfed in flames, while the Bedford in front of it had also caught fire, the grey-green canvas livid with angry orange flames and thick, black smoke billowing into the sky.

The Stukas appeared to have gone, but as Hawke tried to breathe more easily again he heard more of the dive-bombers screaming down on another target a few miles away. His legs felt weak as he shakily stood up. Others were getting to their feet too, and now that he was away from the long line of trucks he saw what the Stukas were bombing. Ahead, up the road, rising out of the softly rolling Flanders countryside was a hill – the only significant hill that could be seen at all in this relentlessly flat countryside. And on top of the hill, just visible amidst the mass of woods around it, stood a town.

'Will you look at that,' said a voice and Hawke turned to see Charlie Drummond standing beside him. 'You know what that place is, don't you, Johnny?' A ripple of bombs exploded and the two of them watched the hilltop town disappear under a cloud of rolling smoke and dust.

'Cassel?'

Drummond nodded, then dusted himself down. 'No wonder Jerry wants it. Must be the best view for miles and miles – when it's not covered in smoke, that is.'

Spears ordered them back to the truck, but then, as they made their way through the wheat, a flight of four Messerschmitt 109 fighters suddenly roared towards them, low and out of the sun. Barely before a warning could be shouted out, the four planes had opened fire, long lines of soil were punched from the ground as the bullets tore towards them. Hawke had barely thrown himself on to the ground a second time when the aircraft were past them.

He clambered to his feet and watched them climb and bank away to the north, towards the coast. One man from the platoon had been hit – Lance Corporal Bellamy from 3 Section. Spears and Lieutenant Farrish kneeled beside him, Spears hurriedly pulling field dressings from both his and Bellamy's packs. Hawke watched, mesmerized by the amount of blood streaming from Bellamy's stomach and by the lance corporal's waxen-looking face, now drained of colour, except for the blood already running from his mouth. He hardly looked like Bellamy at all.

'Stop staring, and get over to the truck,' Spears snapped.

'Sorry, To– I mean, Sergeant,' said Hawke.

Spears glared at him.

'Corporal!' called out Farrish, seeing McLaren picking up his Bren and slinging it on to his shoulder. 'Organize the platoon, will you, Corporal? See what help we can give, but get the men over to the truck ready to move out.'

'Sir,' said McLaren.

Along the road, frightened refugees were moving forward once more. Hawke noticed how much more tightly parents now held their children to them. A little further back down the road, someone was wailing, a woman, her body rocking as she crouched on the verge. Beside her a man was shouting at the sky, clutching his face in despair. Hawke recognized him immediately – the rolled-up sleeves, the felt hat on his head – and began running towards them, past a dead mule and an abandoned car with a line of bullets running across it. Ten yards from the man, he stopped abruptly. There on the ground was the boy he had seen just a few minutes earlier. The same wide, staring eyes looked up at him, but they were now lifeless, and then he saw the woman's hands, covered with blood, her sobs of grief and incomprehension jarring the air that was now thick with the black, whirling smoke of the burning lorries.

For a moment, Hawke thought he might vomit. He paused, bent over, his hands on his knees, then, breathing heavily, glanced around. Down the road, the last trucks in the column, those behind the burning lorries, were already reversing clear of the wrecks, while those ahead were starting their engines once more.

'Johnny!' he heard someone shout, and looked up to see Charlie Drummond hurrying towards him. 'Johnny,' he said again, 'come on, we're moving out. Quick!'

Hawke glanced back at the man and woman, then turned and ran, his rifle in one hand, his heavy haversack thumping against his hip. At the tailgate, Bert Hebden offered a hand, which Hawke clasped and then he felt himself being pulled back up on to the truck just as the engine coughed into life.

‘Right,’ said Spears, appearing from round the side of the Bedford. ‘Everyone back on?’ He was wiping blood from his hands as he spoke, his rifle slung over his shoulder. ‘Still feeling brave, then?’ he said, eyeing Hawke keenly.

Hawke swallowed. Anger and humiliation welled deep within him and he felt his cheeks flush.

Spears shook his head. ‘This is no place for kids,’ he muttered, then turned back towards the front of the truck.

Hawke sat there, unable to speak, his fingers clenched ever more tightly round the barrel of his rifle. He was conscious of the eyes of others on him, so turned away, determined they should not see the tears he could feel welling.

# 2

# DEAD HORSE CORNER

Firing continued to the south as the column trundled on its way, the road leading them past several old brick farmhouses and barns and a couple of tall wooden windmills perched on low ridgelines. A mile or so further on, the road began to climb and weave through thick woods of chestnut, oak and plane. Hawke gazed out, unwilling to look any of his comrades in the eye. Tom was such a changed person. He could not understand it. Last summer, he had been so friendly, so open, always laughing and smiling. He had come to think of Tom Spears as his friend.

He felt a nudge in his side and turned to look at Hebden.

'Don't worry about the sarge,' said Hebden quietly. 'It's only that he's got a lot of responsibility, you know.'

Hawke nodded silently.

'I mean, it's quite a big deal being platoon sergeant, particularly with men like Mr Farrish as platoon commander. Don't get me wrong, I'm sure Lieutenant Farrish will be just fine, but he's not got the experience of the sarge. We all know it's Spears who is really running this platoon.' He scratched his chin, then looked back to where they had come from. From beyond the trees, the smoke from the still-burning trucks was clearly visible. 'And he did just lose a man, an' a good one at that. Doesn't put anyone in the best of moods when one of your men dies on you, you know.'

Hawke nodded and smiled weakly. 'Thanks, Bert.'

'And you are a young 'un,' added Hebden, 'but I'm sure you'll do fine. We all admire you for what you've done – joining up before you had to and coming out here. Shows a lot of guts, I reckon.'

'You don't want to take it personal,' added Charlie Drummond. 'He's sharp with everyone. Just his way.'

Hawke nodded again. It wasn't true – Spears was not sharp with everyone. Firm and tough, yes, but as willing to share a laugh and a joke as anyone. *But just not with me*, thought Hawke. Even so, he was glad about what Hebden and Drummond had said.

'So what does anyone know about this place?' Hebden asked the rest of the men in the truck.

'It's where the Grand Old Duke of York went up the hill,' said Corporal McLaren.

'What the 'ell are you talking about, Corp?' asked Chalkie White, one of the section's Bren gunners.

'You know – the nursery rhyme.'

'The Grand Old Duke of York,' Hebden sung softly, 'he 'ad ten thousand men. He marched 'em up to the top of the hill and then he marched 'em down again.'

'That's the one,' said McLaren. 'Mr Farrish told me. It really happened.'

'Really? When?' asked Jack Ibbotson, the section lance corporal.

'I dunno. Way back. The olden days sometime.'

'And when 'e was up 'e was up,' continued Hebden, louder

now, 'and when 'e was down 'e was down, and when 'e was only 'alfway up 'e was neither up nor down.' He grinned then raised his arms, as though pretending to conduct an orchestra. 'Oh, the Grand Old Duke of York,' he sang out, and first Drummond joined him then suddenly everyone was singing too, even Hawke, the humiliation of earlier put to one side. As they sang the rhyme again, they all began to stand up, then crouch down, but on the third time the Bedford turned a sharp corner and they all fell over, cursing and laughing.

'You bunch of idiots,' grinned McLaren. 'Johnny might be the nipper among us, but you all act like bloomin' eight-year-olds, if you ask me.'

The truck now rumbled to a halt and everyone looked at each other expectantly. Hawke peered out of the back of the truck. They were on a short, straight stretch of cobbled road, tree-lined, which climbed steeply towards the edge of the town. To their left, on the slopes, he saw there was a cemetery: rows of dark tombs – some particularly ornate – densely packed. Hawke sniffed and smelled the sharp, acrid stench of smoke and explosives – and something else too, something sweeter, almost sickly. The Stukas had gone, but their handiwork was still heavy on the air.

Sergeant Spears appeared at the back of the truck. 'All right, you lot,' he said. 'We're debussing here. Grab all your kit and form up in sections. We're walking the last bit.'

'Why's that, Sarge?' asked Hebden.

'Trouble up ahead. The M/T can't get around it just yet.'

The men clambered down, blinking and squinting in the bright sunlight after the heavy shade given by the dark olive-green tarpaulin over the back of the Bedford. In just a few minutes, however, they were formed up and ready to march. Hawke slung his rifle over his shoulder, adjusted his webbing and, on command, moved off, his sense of pride returning as he listened to the rhythmic drum of B Company's hobnailed boots on the cobbled stone road.

Yet no sooner had they started than they were halted.

'Bleedin' typical,' muttered Corporal McLaren. 'Can't even get going on foot without stopping and bloomin' starting.'

Already the stench was worsening. Hawke watched Lieutenant Farrish and Sergeant Spears conversing with Major Strickland, the B Company commander, and then there were shouts from up ahead. Spears hurried back towards them.

'All right, lads,' he said. 'We've pulled the short straw, I'm afraid. Headquarters and A Company are going on ahead to help set up Battalion HQ and to see what's here in the town, but we've got a bit of a clear-up to do first.'

The men groaned.

'A French artillery battery,' Spears continued. 'I'm afraid those Stukas hit them a bit harder than they hit us.' Spears glanced at Hawke. 'Hope your stomach's stronger than it was back on the road, Private,' he said.

The smell grew ever stronger as they moved forward, although the first houses on the corner betrayed nothing. Only as they followed the road round was the carnage beyond revealed to them. Hawke could not help but gasp. Along the road the remains of guns, wagons, men and horses were strewn haphazardly. The road was cratered, while beyond, a hundred yards further, a six-wheeled lorry was burning ferociously. Either side several houses had collapsed, rubble spewing on to the street.

'Jesus, will you take a look at that,' muttered Bert Hebden. 'Dead horse corner.'

Hawke's stomach lurched as he spotted a mule, its teeth bared and eyes wide with terror. Beside the animal, a young French gunner had his arm across its head, as though trying to calm the beast. Both were quite dead, the mule with a huge gash in its side and its innards spread out on to the road. A few yards away lay the torso and legs of another Frenchman, the arms and head completely vanished. Others lay with limbs twisted grotesquely, large stains of blood streaked across the cobbles. Another horse, down on its side, its rear legs trapped by an overturned cart, suddenly began whinnying, and Hebden called to Hawke and Charlie Drummond.

'We've got to put it out of its misery,' he said.

Hawke followed, nearly slipping on the blood as he hurried after Hebden.

'All right, girl, all right,' said Hebden, crouching down beside the terrified animal. He stroked her cheek and she let her head drop. 'Just stroke her, Johnny,' said Hebden. 'Stroke her nose.' He turned to Drummond. 'Charlie? Put your rifle to her head, right between the ears and fire, all right?'

Drummond nodded and did so, the crack of the rifle sharp and loud, and the report ringing around the narrow street. The horse sighed and went limp.

Hebden shook his head. 'I find the animals worse than the men,' he said. 'It's not their ruddy war, is it?'

Hawke stood up and clutched his handkerchief to his mouth. He could not help thinking that it could have been them. The men and animals here had been alive just twenty minutes earlier, but now they were gone, ruthlessly torn and mangled. Not men at all, but meat, like that on the slab in a butcher's. He swallowed hard and felt the bile churn in his stomach. *Please don't let me be sick*, he prayed.

'Hey, you three!' shouted Spears from beside a mass of overturned guns and their carriages. 'Get over here!'

Hawke hurried, grateful for the distraction. The men were trying to right a gun carriage, and Hawke, along with Hebden and Drummond, joined in, heaving at a large upended metal wheel and trailer. Grimacing and straining they at last managed to heave the howitzer upright. Hawke wiped his brow and looked across at the men of C Company as they collected the bodies of the French soldiers and placed them on sacking laid out across the far side of the road. Suddenly, squeaking and the rumble of engines could be heard from up the road towards the main part of the town. For a brief moment, Hawke thought it was the enemy and felt a flush of panic, but then a moment later a Crusader tank appeared round the corner, followed by another and two Bren carriers.

'Now that's a sight for sore eyes,' said Corporal McLaren, pushing back his helmet and wiping his brow.

'Hooray for the cavalry,' agreed Ibbotson. He turned to Sergeant Spears. 'When did this lot get here, then, Sarge?'

Spears shrugged, but Lieutenant Farrish answered for him. 'They're from the 13th/18th Hussars, Lance Corporal. They're part of Macforce too – accompanied General Mason-Macfarlane here last night. Reassuring sight, isn't it?'

'Too right, sir,' grinned Ibbotson. 'Does that mean we can leave the rest to them, then, sir?'

Farrish smiled. 'Not quite, but I'd say we shan't be among this ghastly mess for as long as I'd first feared.'

The lieutenant was right. The tanks and carriers made light work of the carnage, dragging the horses, wrecked wagons and artillery pieces clear of the road, while the Rangers loaded the dead on to the carrier and, with their entrenching tools, did their best to load rubble and earth back into the cratered road. By a little after 9.30 a.m., the grisly task was done and, by now hungry and not a little exhausted, the men of B Company continued on their way at last, marching down a long, narrow street before emerging into a large cobbled square at the heart of the town.

Several buildings in the town square – or Grand Place as it was called – had been hit too, rubble tumbling out on to the cobbles, but although distant shelling to the south could still be heard, Cassel, for the moment at any rate, was quiet.

The men stood restlessly, looking around them. The square was several hundred yards long, but quite narrow, lined by various tall, high-gabled houses. At one end, raised above the houses beneath it, stood the church, while above the square, standing sentinel, was another large timber-framed windmill. There were still civilians in the town, which surprised Hawke – he had assumed almost everyone in northern France was on the move. Or perhaps people were coming here, to Cassel. Maybe they felt safe high on this hill in the middle of the plains. But then he looked at the rubble and timbers of one of the collapsed houses across the square, and shrugged to himself.

Nearby, next to a well in front of an ornate stone building, Lieutenant Farrish and a number of other officers and senior NCOs were conferring. Hawke watched Sergeant Spears among them then saw him stride back towards them.

'We'll wait here for a moment,' he told the platoon. 'It looks like we'll get some proper hot grub tonight, but in the meantime some rations will be handed out. Once we've had a brew and something to eat we'll know what positions we've got to move into.'

'Any idea where Jerry is, Sarge?' asked McLaren.

'Hammering Hazebrouck still. But he's not far to the south.' He nodded in that direction. 'So make the most of this. I reckon we'll be busy before the day is out.'

In the couple of weeks since the Germans had first launched their attack, Hawke had been amazed by the speed with which the more experienced men could produce both food and endless cups of tea. Even before rations had been handed out, Bert Hebden and Chalkie White had produced small Primus stoves, and had lit them right by the side of the square and begun boiling mess tins of water, into which had been added generous amounts of tea leaves and sugar pulled from their packs. Johnny watched the water slowly darken. The tea leaves slowly sank, but floating around the water were bits of grass and even tobacco from Hebden's pocket.

Seeing Hawke peering at it, Hebden grinned. 'All adds to the flavour,' he said, then smacked his lips. 'I'm gasping for a wet.' He gave the brew a stir with the end of his seventeen-inch sword bayonet.

Soon after, B Echelon men from Battalion Headquarters arrived with boxes of rations in thick cardboard cartons, two cartons per section, each containing an assortment of tins of bully beef, Machonochie's tinned stews, bars of chocolate, packets of plain biscuits, condensed milk and more tea, sugar and cigarettes. Using the marlin spike of his clasp knife, White quickly stabbed a hole in the top of one of the cans of condensed milk and added a generous amount to both mess tins of brewing tea. Meanwhile, two more Primus stoves were produced, lit and tins of bully beef opened. Added to the corned beef were crumbled dry biscuits and a bit of water. In under a quarter of an hour, the whole section not only had an enamel mug each of hot, sweet, tea, but also a thick dollop of bully beef hash in their mess tins.

Hawke had thought he was both hungry and thirsty. The hot tea was instantly soothing but after one mouthful of the hash he stopped. It tasted all right – salty, like all corned beef – but it was the colour and texture that now made him pause. As he was about to put another spoon of the stuff into his mouth, images of dead and dying mules and French gunners came into his mind. All he could think of were the entrails of that first black mule and the severed torso he had seen. He wiped his brow and closed his eyes, dropping the spoon of hash back in his mess tin.

'You all right, Johnny?' asked Drummond, squatting down next to him.

'Yes, yes – fine,' Hawke replied. Conscious that the others were now watching him, he lifted his spoon again and this time put the pink mashed-up hash into his mouth, chewed briefly and then swallowed.

'Feeling better now?' asked Hebden.

Hawke nodded and took a third mouthful, but almost instantly knew that had been a mistake. Once more the dead mule and Frenchman flashed across his mind and at the same time he looked down at the fleshy mush. Bile and nausea welled up in his stomach and he now hurriedly got to his feet, ran across the square and at the edge of a parked carrier, vomited.

As he gasped and retched, doubled up, his hands on his knees, he heard catcalls and whistles from the men, then a sharp, 'Hey!'

Looking up, dabbing the sick and spittle from his chin, he saw an officer from the 13th/18th Hussars striding towards him.

'What the devil do you think you're playing at?' snapped the captain.

'I'm so sorry, sir,' mumbled Hawke.

'If you're ill, go and see the MO. Don't vomit all over my machines.'

Hawke saw the captain's small black moustache bristle.

'Sorry, sir,' Hawke said again, conscious of the laughter of his fellow Rangers behind him. He raised himself, dabbed his mouth again with his sleeve and saluted.

'Bit young, aren't you, to be playing at soldiers?'

'Wanted to do my duty, sir,' said Hawke. The smell of the vomit wafted unpleasantly under his nose.

The captain now turned as another soldier approached. Hawke followed his gaze and saw Spears walking towards them.

'I'm very sorry about this, sir,' said Spears, snapping to attention and saluting. 'I'll make sure Private Hawke here clears it up and that it never happens again.'

'Hm,' said the captain. 'Well, make sure it doesn't. And I suggest you try getting men not boys into the Rangers in future.'

'Yes, sir,' said Spears.

'All right. No great harm done, I suppose. Carry on.' He turned and left them.

Spears glared at Hawke. 'What the hell did you go and do that for? Are you ill?'

Hawke shook his head.

'Or was that all too much for you back there?'

Hawke looked down.

'It was, wasn't it?' Spears chuckled mirthlessly. 'For God's sake. That captain was right.'

'I'm really sorry, Tom.'

'It's not Tom,' snarled Spears, prodding a finger into his chest, 'it's Sergeant Spears to you, Private. Now get some water and clear this up.'

Spears left him, and for a moment Hawke stood where he was, too miserable to move. Tom Spears had been one of the main reasons Hawke had joined up. He had liked him immediately, from the moment his older sister, Maddie, had brought him home for the first time – nearly a year ago. He had thought Spears had liked him too, but now it was as though the sergeant could hardly bear to speak to him. Hawke could not understand it. He tried to swallow the hurt he felt, the tears he knew were not far away. He'd felt humiliated earlier, but this was far worse. He wondered how he would ever be able to look at the others again. Miserably, he took out his water bottle and poured it over the vomit, dispersing it between the cobbles, then hurried to a water trough beneath one of the square's buildings to refill.

Hawke had barely reached it when a loud boom rang out from the south followed by the express whistle and whine of an incoming shell. The effect was instant. Men shouted out and a split second later they were all flat on the ground as the shell detonated a few hundred yards to the west of them, followed by the crash of falling stone and timber. A moment later, another shell hurtled over, this time beyond them.

Hawke scrambled to his feet and hurried over to the others, now up and crouching against the walls of the buildings to the south of the square. Orders were being barked: they were to fall in quickly. Engines were starting up; a despatch rider roared into the square. Hawke saw Major Strickland talking urgently to one of the Macforce staff officers and pointing south, then looking at a map. Around him, food and stoves were being hastily packed away as a further shell screamed over, this time closer, and landing just beyond them next to a house near the crest of the hill. As it collapsed with a deafening roar, smoke and dust rolled into the air.

Hawke stood beside Drummond and Hebden against the edge of a long stone building, helmet down over his eyes, rifle in his hand, as Lieutenant Farrish and Sergeant Spears hurried towards the platoon.

'Sorry Jerry's cut short our breakfast, chaps,' said Farrish, 'but it seems he's a little bit closer than we thought. There's not a lot of us here and I know we haven't had much chance to prepare our defences but that can't be helped. We need to get moving quickly and do the best we can to keep the enemy at bay.' He glanced around at the men and, apparently satisfied that they had all been listening, continued. 'The Battalion is going to defend the town from the south, which is the direction from which Jerry's approaching. A and C Companies are going to start digging in just to the south of the ramparts, which I've been told are right behind this building here, and they run all along the southern edge of the town.'

A loud boom rang out from behind them to the north, making them all instinctively flinch, followed almost immediately by a second blast.

'Ah, good,' smiled Farrish. 'That's our chaps. So, as you see, we've got some artillery support.'

'What about B Company, sir?' asked McLaren.

'Mr Farrish is coming to that, Corporal,' said Spears.

'Yes, thank you, sergeant,' said Farrish. 'We're going to be the first line of defence.' There was another groan from the men.

'Why are we always picking the short straw at the moment, sir?' said McLaren.

'Some would consider it an honour, Corporal,' replied Farrish. Like the rest, the lieutenant was a young man, only twenty-three, something his light brown moustache could not hide.

'Some might, sir,' grumbled McLaren, 'but I can't think who.'

'That's enough, Mac,' said Spears.'

Farrish cleared his throat. 'Well, this is what we've been given and we must make the best of it. Now, intelligence on the enemy's strength and dispositions is a bit shaky, so we're to probe forward and see what we can see, so to speak.' He held up a map, stroked his chin, then said, 'There are two villages near the foot of the hill, Bavinchove and Oxelaëre. Fifth Platoon is going to go to Bavinchove, we're going to Oxelaëre and Seventh Platoon is going to cover the Hazebrouck road. Any questions? McLaren, any other thoughts you'd like to share?'

'No, sir. Thank you, sir,' muttered the corporal. The others remained silent.

'Good,' said Farrish, 'then let's get going.'

Hawke felt Spears grab his arm.

'Sir?' said Spears, shoving Hawke towards the lieutenant. 'I'm wondering whether Private Hawke should remain here, sir. He's not well.'

Farrish looked up and down at Hawke. 'Looks all right to me. Are you ill, Private?'

'I was a bit, sir, but I'm fine now, sir,' mumbled Hawke.

Farrish smiled. 'Good man.' He clapped Hawke on the shoulder. 'It's right that you worry about the men, Spears, but just now we're going to need every man we've got.'

'Men, yes, sir, but I'm not so sure about boys.'

'Come on, Spears,' replied Farrish, smiling ruefully, 'we haven't really got time to worry about that now.'

They hurried on, jogging down a narrow alleyway that led down to the ramparts the lieutenant had mentioned a moment before. Through men already frantically digging in, they ran on, down the terraced slopes, and joined a track that led through woods towards a cluster of farm buildings, houses and a church.

No one spoke much, chests heaving from running in full marching order, and, Hawke guessed, with the thoughts of what was to come swirling around their heads. As they emerged through the woods and saw the village ahead of them, he was conscious of Spears running beside him.

'I'm sorry about what happened earlier,' said Hawke. 'Really I am.'

'Forget it,' growled Spears. 'Mr Farrish is right. We haven't got time to worry about it. After all, we've got to try and stop the whole bleedin' German advance – and with only about six hundred men, a handful of guns and tanks, and a limited amount of ammo.' He turned to Hawke as they ran. 'We haven't got a prayer, Johnny boy, not a bleedin' prayer.' He shook his head. 'You wanted to see some action – well, you're going to get it now. You're going to get it now all right.'

# 3

## THE DOGFIGHT

Pilot Officer Archie Jackson was amazed by how little time it had taken to cross the Channel. That morning, 629 Squadron had taken off from Northolt, landed a short while later at Rochford on the south Essex coast, refuelled, then soon after taken off again. From there they had climbed up to fifteen thousand feet, the whole of the Thames Estuary, Kent and southern England spread before them looking green and way smaller than it could possibly be imagined from the ground. Then the CO had led them in formation – four flights of three beautifully maintained tight vics – out over the Channel.

Even with England just behind them he had been able to see the continent stretching endlessly beyond, but then they had flown into some cloud and the bright morning light had changed into that strange milky glow and all sense of speed had stopped. Then the cloud thinned once more, the huge power of the Spitfire obvious again as the knife-like wings scythed through wisps of white.

And then there it was: Dunkirk and the French coast, a huge column of thick, rolling smoke rising high into the sky, obscuring much of the town and beaches below. In fact, the smoke was so high it had dispersed into a kind of dark shroud that seemed to lie just beneath them.

'My God,' muttered Jackson to himself, and he felt his heart lurch and then begin to hammer once more in his chest. He was nineteen, had joined the squadron just a month before, and the only war he'd seen so far was what they showed on the newsreels at the cinema; and now here was the evidence of it, stark and real. *But what were you expecting?* he asked himself. After all, the men from 74 Squadron at Rochford had already been over several times, and had warned them of the smoke at Dunkirk – the oil depots there had apparently been hit several times already by the Luftwaffe – but somehow he felt unprepared for what he now saw: a vivid marker that he was on a combat sortie, after months of training and then sitting on his backside waiting for things to happen. For so long he had been champing at the bit, itching to have a crack at the enemy, but now that that moment was almost upon him, he felt consumed by an urge to flip his Spit on its side, bank hard and head for home.

Crossing the coast, Jackson heard Squadron Leader Dix, the CO, say over the R/T, 'Keep your eyes peeled, chaps.'

Jackson craned his neck, glad to feel the soft silk of his new scarf brushing against his neck rather than the tight buttoned shirt and tie he had always worn up until now. He'd bought the scarf only the day before, in London. It was bright orange and at first he had thought it rather dashing. Now he was not so sure. The other pilots had ribbed him mercilessly, and although he was glad of it he determined that when he next had a chance he would buy a more sober-coloured one: navy blue, perhaps, or maroon.

He was still looking around keenly when suddenly he saw them, a dark formation of he guessed around thirty Stukas, and above them the same number of fighters, twin-engine Messerschmitt 110s.

'There!' he shouted out, 'below us!' Then remembering he was supposed to use the correct code added, 'Bandits, angels twelve!' Already he could see the Stukas beginning their dives, peeling off one after the other.

'Roger, I see them,' crackled Dix. 'Red and Yellow sections head straight for the Stukas, Blue and Green go for the fighters. Number One Attack, go!'

Jackson dropped into line astern behind Blue One, his section leader, Sergeant Dennis Cotton, then saw the CO peel off and dive down, leading Red and Yellow Sections. Following Dennis, he pushed the stick forward and to the right, and felt his body thrust back into his bucket seat as the engine whined louder and the Spitfire hurtled down. Fifteen thousand feet to just twelve in a matter of seconds, the Messerschmitts suddenly looming larger so that he could now clearly see their grey mottled camouflage and the stark black crosses on the wings. It seemed unreal, and for a moment Jackson felt as though he were somehow not himself at all, but a spectator watching the scene unfold. He glanced at his speedometer – almost four hundred miles per hour! – and eased the stick back towards him.

The enemy fighters appeared not to have seen them yet and Jackson felt a surge of adrenalin – although his heart was still pounding, his earlier fear had gone, replaced by excitement, ecstasy even. Flicking off the gun safety catch, he held his thumb poised. Dennis, he saw, had picked out a 110 on the right of the formation, but Jackson decided to go for one in the middle and carefully lined himself up. He was gaining on the Messerschmitt.

*Wait*, he told himself. *Let him fill the gunsight*. He was now just seven hundred yards away and still rapidly closing, but that was not yet close enough. Four hundred yards was the prescribed distance, but he had never forgotten what his instructor had told him at flying school – that a fighter pilot should always get as close as he possibly could before firing. Jackson had listened to that advice – Mick Channon had been an ace in the last war.

Six hundred yards, five hundred, and then the formation spotted that they were about to come under attack. The Messerschmitt in front of him began to weave then bank to port and at the same time the rear gunner opened fire. Jackson saw orange sparks of tracer arcing towards him, slowly it seemed, but then suddenly they seemed to flash wide past him.

'He's firing at me!' Jackson said out loud. He opened the boost, felt the Spitfire surge forward as he swept across the sky, the Messerschmitt still in his gunsight. Four hundred yards, three hundred, two hundred and fifty. *Now!* Jackson pressed his thumb down on the tiny red button. A long burst of his eight Browning machine guns and the Spitfire shuddered from the recoil, jolting Jackson in his seat. The Messerschmitt ahead seemed to wobble and now within just two hundred yards, the 110 huge and close, Jackson opened fire again, his mouth set in a determined grimace as he did so. The return fire stopped immediately and he saw from his own lines of tracer that he had raked the fuselage.

*Have I killed a man?* he thought, but then a puff of dark smoke came from the enemy aircraft and it banked to the right and stalled, and for a split heart-stopping second, Jackson thought he was going to collide with it. Instinctively, he ducked his head – not that it would do him any good – as his Spitfire flashed past a huge grey wing, missing it by what seemed like only inches.

*Boy, that was close*, thought Jackson, gasping heavily, his chest hammering. But he'd shot down an enemy plane – his first combat sortie and he'd scored already! A wave of exhilaration consumed him, and he glanced around and saw a Stuka diving down away to his right, a long stream of smoke following behind. Jackson banked and began to climb once more, thinking he should try to rejoin the fray, but he was amazed by how far away they already seemed – distant specks towards the coast. He watched another plane dropping from the sky – another Stuka he thought, and so pulled back on the stick and began to climb towards them.

Orange flashes whipped past his cockpit and he heard machine-gun fire crackling in his ears. Momentary panic gripped him as he frantically looked behind him – but there was nothing. Then a moment later he saw two Messerschmitts diving at him from the north, and more tracer curling towards him. And these were not twin-engine 110s, but single-engine fighters, Me 109s.

Jackson cursed, the words of the station commander at Northolt ringing in his ears: 'Watch your back!' he'd said, which was precisely what Jackson had forgotten to do. Another piece of advice now came to him, the words of Mick Channon: 'Always turn in towards your attacker.'

His breathing heavy, his heart hammering, Jackson now did so, and felt his harness cut into his shoulders and his goggles slip down from his helmet, partially covering his eyes. Frantically, he pushed them back, and saw he was now heading straight for one of his attackers. He pressed down on the gun-button, the Spitfire jerked, and to his utter amazement the Messerschmitt belched a gush of black smoke and dropped out of the sky. Jackson quickly glanced around again, only to see a third 109, this time attacking from the right.

'Oh my God!' he said out loud as more tracer hurtled past him. There was a clatter, the Spitfire jolted and he saw a line of bullet holes across the wing, but his machine still seemed to be flying all right.

A Messerschmitt now thundered over him, its pale underside streaked with oil, the black crosses vividly clear, the wash of its passage jerking his Spitfire with sudden turbulence. But no sooner had it gone than more tracer whipped past him. Jackson banked again, as tightly as he dared, and felt himself pressed hard into his seat, his vision blurring and greying, yet as he emerged from the turn, sweat now pouring down his face, he glanced in his mirror and saw the 109 still doggedly on his tail.

'Damn it! Damn it!' exclaimed Jackson. More tracer curled towards him, and Jackson flung his Spitfire one way then another, radio static and chatter still crackling in his ears, the horizon sliding back and forth. Frantically, he kept glancing back but no matter what he did the Messerschmitt still kept on his tail. Jackson felt helpless, unsure what he should do, but then there was an ear-splitting crack, and the Spitfire jolted.

'Christ!' whispered Jackson. Where had he been hit? Another punch as a cannon shell tore into his plane, so hard it was like a giant fist ramming into him. Smoke now burst from the engine and flooded into the cockpit. His Spitfire was knocked upside down and he was spinning, the control column limp in his hands. He was falling out of the sky, his plane out of control and smoke billowing behind him, the sky and the ground spiralling, his altimeter spinning backwards too fast to read. *I'm going to die*, he thought to himself.

A moment later the control column hit his leg and, clutching it once more, Jackson felt the stick respond after all. Pushing it forward and applying the left rudder hard, he was amazed the Spitfire miraculously recovered from the spin. He gasped and opened the canopy so that the smoke whipped out. Wiping his brow, he pulled off his oxygen mask, pushed his flying helmet back off his forehead and glanced upwards. Two 109s were still circling, but they were several thousand feet above him.

He sighed and briefly closed his eyes, but then with a splutter and a cough his engine died and Jackson was left gliding. After the constant deafening roar of the engine, there was now a startling silence, save for the wind whistling through the cockpit.

'Damn it!' he exclaimed again. Where on earth was he? Away to his left he could still faintly see the coast, but was that Allied or enemy land below? He glanced at his altimeter – eight hundred feet, too low to bail out.

The Spitfire was losing height steadily. For several moments he sat there, unable to think clearly, but then realized there was only one option. He would have to crash-land somewhere. Sweat ran down his neck and his back. His free hand was shaking. Five hundred feet, the ground getting ever closer. To the north, he saw a town on a high promontory that stood out from the largely flat surrounding countryside, but before it the ground looked level enough. If he could just find a big enough field . . . but his sense of scale and proportion was warped by the height he was at. Below there were a couple of villages and then further to the south puffs of smoke – guns? – and suddenly a renewed sense of dread swept over him as he realized that even if he did survive he would probably find himself in the middle of a battle.

'Please God,' he said aloud, 'if you're out there. Help me.' Banking the Spitfire, he lowered the flaps, praying he'd judged it correctly. Just three hundred feet now, the village away beneath his port wing, but there was a field, a lush grass field, and about as flat as he could hope for. At one end was a wood, and to the left a thick hedge and a barn, but it looked to be long enough. He hoped it was long enough.

He pressed down the undercarriage lever, but nothing happened. The hydraulics must have been damaged. He cursed, but there was nothing for it: a belly-landing it would have to be. Checking the buckle on his Sutton harness and tightening the straps, he watched the ground loom towards him. Moments earlier he had thought he would die, then he'd thought he'd been spared. Now he wondered whether he would die after all, or be horribly maimed for life, or shot at the moment he clambered from his stricken aircraft. Over some trees, a hedge, grass rushing towards, and then *CRACK* . . .

# 4

## THE RESCUE

Private Hawke and the men of 1 Section had watched Pilot Officer Jackson's dogfight in the skies above them from their position on an old farm at the southern edge of the village of Oxelaëre. Corporal McLaren had been following the action through his binoculars, standing at the window in the clapper-board windmill, which stood beside the barn, and providing a breathless commentary. They had all cheered when the Me 109 had plummeted into the ground a couple of miles away, and had then watched in silence as the Spitfire screamed out of the sky in a horrific spin. But then it had miraculously pulled level in the nick of time, although as it approached a field up ahead of them even McLaren had stopped talking, instead watching open-mouthed as it drifted down, its undercarriage still up.

And then with a loud crash it hit the ground, slewed and eventually came to a halt.

'He's alive!' called out McLaren a few moments later. 'He just moved his arm.' But then the pilot remained still, motionless, refusing to unstrap himself and get out.

'What's he doing, Corporal?' asked Farrish, hurrying from one of the barns across the yard to the windmill.

'I can't see, sir. He doesn't seem to be doing anything.'

'Is he dead?'

McLaren strained to see. 'I don't think so, sir. Maybe he's injured. Or concussed or something.'

Lieutenant Farrish stood where he was a moment, then took a few steps up the wooden staircase that led into the windmill. Since they'd arrived at the farmstead a little under an hour earlier, more enemy artillery shells had been fired towards the town behind them, but in the last half hour mortar rounds had been directed towards the village and even towards the farm itself from the wood beyond. The roof of the main house had been hit. From the same direction, vehicles had been heard – the telltale squeak of tank tracks, the revving of engines. The enemy was not very far away – not very far at all. An attack was surely only a matter of time, and the Spitfire stood right between the two forces, between their small defensive position around the farm and the enemy massing in the woods beyond.

'Has he moved again, Corporal?' called out Farrish.

'Not that I can see, sir,' McLaren replied.

'Let me have a look,' said Farrish, climbing two more steps and taking out his own field glasses. From the open windmill door at the top of the wooden steps, Hawke strained his eyes to see any flicker of movement from the Spitfire. It stood, he guessed, about six hundred yards away – not in the field immediately in front of them, but in the one beyond, in the far corner.

'Well, we can't just leave him,' muttered Farrish. He stroked his chin again, and then he added, as though thinking aloud, 'and yet it's not going to be easy getting him out with Jerry over there.'

Hearing this, Hawke called down, 'I'll go, sir. I'll go and get him.'

Next to him, Hebden and Drummond looked at him in horror, but already Farrish had turned and now looked up at him. 'You, Private? But I thought you were ill?'

McLaren grinned. 'I think that was dead Frenchmen and bully beef hash not quite mixing for Private Hawke, sir.'

'Ah,' said Farrish.

'I'm fine now, sir. I'd like to volunteer, sir.'

'Johnny,' hissed Drummond, 'what are you thinking? Don't you know you never volunteer for anything?'

Hawke ignored him. 'Sir, please let me go and get him.'

Farrish nodded. 'All right, well done, Hawke. You'll need a couple of others, though.'

'I'll go,' said Hebden, standing beside Hawke at the windmill's door.

Behind him, Hawke heard Drummond sigh.

'And me, sir,' said Drummond. 'I'll go too.'

'No,' said a voice, and Hawke turned to see Spears striding across the yard. 'I've done a similar kind of thing before, sir. I'll go. Me and two others, preferably men with experience.' He shot a glance at Hawke.

'All right, Spears, you can lead, but take Hawke and Hebden – they put their hands up first.'

Spears looked as though he were about to protest, then scratched his brow, sighed and said, 'Very good, sir. Hawke and Hebden it is.'

He called them down, shooting another angry glance at Hawke, and with a stick quickly drew a rough map in the dirt. 'I think we can get to the field the aircraft's in without being spotted. Here's where we are,' he said, marking the small rectangular outline of the farm. 'We can crawl through the wheat in the field in front of us, then make the most of the hedges. At least he's in the corner of the field, and beyond it looks to me like a small brook that cuts back across the front of the wood. There's quite a lot of cover along it – some willows and shrubs and tall grass.'

Farrish nodded. 'All right. And we'll get the Brens to cover you.'

'Thank you, sir, although I'll take one of them.'

'If you think you need it.'

'Hopefully not, sir. But you never know.' He threw away the stick. 'Take your packs off,' he said to Hawke and Hebden as he quickly headed up the steps of the windmill. 'Webbing and ammo stays, but otherwise we want to be carrying as little as possible.'

Hawke nodded and began fumbling at the canvas straps and buckles.

'And make it snappy,' added Spears as he took the Bren from Ibbotson. 'We need to get that bloke out as quickly as we can.' He hurried back down the steps, thrusting two curved Bren magazines at Hawke.

Drummond took Hawke's pack from him. 'Good luck,' he said.

Hawke nodded, took a deep breath and, clutching his rifle in his hand, followed Hebden and Spears out of the gate at the side of the farm.

Half crouching, half running, they crossed a track and stepped into the young, dark green corn and long grass at the edge of the field. Droplets of water from the previous night's rain clung to the shoots, which then brushed off on to the serge of their battledress.

Two mortar shells whined over and Hawke flinched. They landed wide of the farm, but then an artillery shell followed, screeching through the air and up to the town behind them, exploding with a dull crash.

Spears glanced back. 'Come on. Let's keep going,' he muttered.

By continuing to half run in a crouch they managed to reach the far end of the first field. Spears stopped and raised a hand, cocked his head and listened, then set off again. Some of the shrubs and young trees dividing the two fields were high enough for them to stretch up and run freely, but as they neared the Spitfire, there was a gap of around thirty yards where there was no hedge or trees at all. Spears halted them again. For a moment they all listened. There was birdsong nearby and several crickets, but otherwise the air was strangely still.

'Right,' whispered Spears. 'We're going to have to crawl here. We'll cut into the wheat for a few yards then get on our hands and knees. All right?'

Hawke nodded. His mouth was dry and the nausea in his stomach had returned.

Spears was off, and Hawke followed closely, with Hebden behind. Light, loose soil, freshly dampened by the rain, stuck to Hawke's battledress, while water from the wheat clung to him as he slithered through the field. A rich, earthy smell filled his nose, clearing the stench of death and smoke that had been with him ever since Dead Horse Corner.

They had nearly crossed the gap in the hedge, when from the woods, now just three hundred yards away, came a sudden and deafening eruption of mortar and machine-gun fire. Hawke pressed his face into the ground as mortars fizzed over towards the village and bullets zipped through trees and hedgerows away to their left, branches snapping as they did so.

His heart pounding, he looked up and saw Spears already through the wheat and now beside a small oak at the corner of the field, frantically urging him and Hebden on. Wide-eyed, his mouth as dry as chalk, Hawke scrambled forward.

'What were you waiting for?' hissed Spears as more bursts of machine-gun fire sputtered from the woods.

'Sorry, Sergeant,' said Hawke. 'I wasn't expecting it.'

'Use your loaf,' said Spears. 'They're firing either side of us. Now stay here a moment.'

The Spitfire was now only twenty yards away, just the other side of the trees and hedge in the field beyond, but Spears moved to the left of the oak tree then, crawling on his belly, seemed to peer towards the brook and the wood beyond.

'What the hell's 'e doing?' asked Hebden, leaning towards Hawke's ear so he could be heard above the din.

Hawke shrugged, but then saw Spears inch back and scurry over to them again.

'As I thought,' he said. 'They've sent a patrol out to get our man. There's five of them that I can see. They're approaching the brook now.' There was a moment's pause in the firing and a short distance away Hawke heard voices – German voices.

*The enemy*, he thought. *Actual Germans.* He tried to swallow, but couldn't.

'What do we do now?' asked Hebden, worry etched across his face.

'Keep our heads. There are a number of young willows at the edge of the brook which partially cover the Spitfire from the wood. When I give the signal, I want you to go straight through the gap here, at its edge, and get him out.'

'But won't they see us?' asked Hebden.

'Just do it,' snarled Spears.

'And what about you?' asked Hawke.

'Don't worry about me. Just go and get him and bring him back here. Go – now!'

Hawke felt his whole body tightening. There was sweat running down the side of his face, but he was not hot. He was vaguely conscious of Spears heading towards the brook with the Bren, and then he was running himself, his body low, round the edge of the hedge, waiting for a bullet to strike and knock him down. Across the grass, his mind churning with the sound of whining mortars and the chatter of machine-gun fire, and up on to the wing of the Spitfire, his studded boot clattering on the metal. Fumbling fingers felt for the catch on the half door at the side of the cockpit and to his relief it dropped open. The pilot had his eyes closed and there was a trickle of blood running from his forehead down his nose, but then he groaned and Hawke was now aware of Hebden beside him.

'Come on, Johnny boy,' said Hebden, his voice breathless, 'let's get him out quick.'

'There's so many straps,' said Hawke, panic beginning to grip him.

Hebden yanked the radio and oxygen leads and pulled them clear as Hawke found the clip of the pilot's harness. With a click, it unfastened.

'He's free!' Hawke exclaimed. Pulling the straps off the pilot's arms, they grabbed his shoulders and heaved him over the small door, Hawke slipping and staggering backwards as the man's weight fell clear. The pilot groaned again, and then, at that moment, a burst of machine-gun fire rang out close at hand, a man screamed and Hawke momentarily froze.

Another burst, but while Hawke was amazed to find himself still alive Hebden had hoisted the pilot over his shoulder and was turning and running back to the gap in the hedge. Hawke turned to follow but, in another brief silence in the gunfire, heard a sound and turning towards the brook saw a German scrambling through the tall reeds. Without thinking, Hawke drew his rifle to his shoulder and pulled back the bolt. His finger hovered over the trigger as he looked at the man. The soldier had a young face too, but, seeing Hawke, instinctively brought his own rifle into his shoulder as he crouched there on the stream's bank.

*You've got to do it*, Hawke told himself, but something held him back, and then he saw the German draw the bolt of his Mauser and Hawke felt his finger press against the cold metal of the trigger and then squeeze.

The rifle cracked, the butt of the rifle thumped into his shoulder and the German was flung backwards into the reeds.

Hawke watched, stunned, then sped towards the gap in the hedge.

Spears was waiting for him and, grabbing him, thrust a grenade into his hand. 'Quick!' he said. 'Chuck it at the Spit.'

Spears pulled the pin from one he was holding and hurled it towards the plane, then threw a second. Moments later they exploded in turn, but neither were close enough to the engine to make it catch fire.

'Damn it,' cursed Spears, 'I'm going to have to place one of them in it.'

'Wait,' said Hawke, his grenade in his hand. It was heavy, heavier than a cricket ball. Taking careful aim, he took a deep breath and then threw it. The dark lump of iron and explosive flew through the air and Hawke watched, not daring to breathe, as it landed directly in the cockpit. A second later, it exploded and immediately the Spitfire erupted into flames as the fuel tank caught fire. In moments, the whole aircraft and engine cowling was engulfed, thick, black smoke billowing upwards.

'Good shot,' said Spears, wiping his brow.

Hawke staggered backwards, gazing at the burning Spitfire. He felt strange and lightheaded, as though he were somehow looking down on the scene, not part of it at all.

*I just killed a man*, he thought. It seemed unbelievable – one moment the German had been alive, raising his rifle, the next moment – *bang* – and he was gone. It had been so easy. Hawke felt for his water bottle and, taking it from his waist, pulled at the cork. His hand was shaking violently.

Next to Hawke, at the edge of the hedge, Hebden had placed the pilot on the ground and was squatting down beside him, catching his breath.

'I thought we were going to be goners then, Sarge,' he said. 'What happened to that Jerry patrol? And what were you firing at Johnny?'

Hawke was about to reply, when suddenly the mortaring stopped and machine-gun fire rang out once more, this time the bullets zipping through just above them.

'Down!' shouted Spears as twigs and branches snapped and fell, and bullets hissed and zipped just above their heads.

Pilot Officer Jackson groaned and opened his eyes.

'Where am I?' he said, grimacing, then touched his face. 'My head.'

'You're in no-man's-land, sir,' said Spears. More bullets fizzed above them.

'How are we ever going to get back, Sarge?' asked Hebden. 'We're completely pinned down.'

'I'm not sure, Hebden,' said Spears, raising his head slightly. 'I'm really not sure.'

# 5

## PULLING BACK

'I'm so sorry,' said Jackson. 'I just saw a field. I was only thinking of getting down without killing myself, not getting stuck in no-man's-land. And now I've damn well gone and put you all in danger.'

'Don't worry, sir,' said Hebden, 'at least we've missed out on being shelled. Those big guns have been hammering Cassel while we've been out here and they've been mortaring the village where the rest of the lads are.'

Jackson smiled weakly, but Spears rolled a few yards into the field, raised himself up and then looked around and back towards the farm, as though making mental calculations.

'What are you thinking, Sarge?' asked Hebden.

Spears put his finger to his mouth, indicating to him to be quiet, then waved the others over towards him. Jackson looked around anxiously then crawled over, followed by Hawke and Hebden.

'The oak and those willows give a bit of cover just here,' said Spears in a quiet voice as they joined him, 'and the smoke is hiding us completely. They won't keep firing at nothing forever. So long as they don't attack out of the woods, I reckon we might just be all right. We'll wait here a minute and see if those Jerries decide to quieten down.' Another burst of machine-gun fire spat out, but then it was quiet once more, the only sound the still-burning plane.

Spears turned to Jackson. 'How are you feeling, sir?'

'I've got a hell of a headache,' said Jackson. 'But otherwise I'm all right. I can't quite believe I'm alive at all, to be honest.'

'That spin looked nasty,' said Hebden. 'We all saw it.'

'I was terrified,' admitted Jackson, then brightened. 'Did you see my 109?'

Hebden grinned. 'Yes, sir. We all cheered.'

'Did you?' Jackson smiled now. 'It was my first combat sortie. Got two, though.'

'Well done, sir,' said Spears. Another burst of machine-gun fire, but shorter this time.

'Those Germans,' said Hawke now, 'did you get them, Sarge?'

'I thought I had,' said Spears. 'But it seems I may have left one for you.'

Hawke said nothing. His face was close to the ground again and he breathed in the smell of damp earth once more. A good smell, but all he could think about was the man he had just killed: a young man, probably only a few years older than himself, the body flung backwards.

'Seems you were right, Sarge,' said Hebden. 'Those Jerries have stopped firing.'

'Shh!' said Spears, turning his ear towards the woods. 'Listen.'

Hawke did so. He could hear voices from the wood, indistinct, and then the revving of engines and once again the squeaking of tank tracks.

'The attack?' said Hebden.

'I don't think we should hang around to find out,' said Spears. 'Come on, let's get out of here.' He looked at the others. 'I'll go first. If I don't get hit in twenty yards, then you all follow, all right?'

He pushed himself up on to his feet, crouched a moment, listening, then set off, running with his body as low as possible through the young wheat. Hawke watched, chest thumping, barely daring to breathe, waiting for the sound of machine-gun fire to tear the air apart once more.

But none came. And now Spears was turning and beckoning them to follow. Hebden first, then Jackson, and then, with another deep breath, Hawke was on his feet and running, running through the wheat, along the line of the hedge, the farmhouse getting closer with every yard.

'What on earth is Jerry playing at?' said McLaren from their vantage point in the windmill. 'I swear that squeaking of tank tracks is getting further away.'

'It seemed like it was getting closer when we were pegging it back here, didn't it, Johnny?' said Hebden.

Hawke was sitting on a dusty pile of hessian grain sacks at the far side of the windmill. After the surge of adrenalin, he now felt exhausted. The lack of sleep, the arrival at Cassel, throwing up, then the rescue of Jackson – it was incredible to think so much had already happened that day and yet it was not even noon.

'I was just running, Bert,' said Hawke. 'I was thinking more about those Spandaus opening up again and praying they wouldn't.' He rubbed his eyes, then closed them.

'Ah, the boy's tired himself out,' said McLaren.

Hawke opened his eyes again and sat up. 'Sorry, Corp,' he said, blinking.

McLaren waved a hand at him. 'Only joking – go on, you get a bit of shut-eye, Johnny. I still haven't the foggiest what Jerry's playing at, but I don't reckon that attack is coming any time soon.'

When he awoke, Hawke could smell wafts of cooking drifting up from outside in the yard, and noticed how quiet it was. The shelling had stopped.

'You're awake, then,' said Chalkie White, manning the Bren from the windmill's window.

'How long have I been asleep?'

'Oh, about an hour. You should go and get some grub.'

Hawke staggered down the steps into the yard. A number of small stoves had been set up, several men crouched and standing around them.

'Johnny,' called out Drummond.

Hawke looked and saw Drummond, Hebden and Ibbotson standing around a Primus to one side of the windmill's base.

'There's a brew for you here and some bully beef,' said Drummond as Hawke wandered over. 'You must be starved after chucking up that last lot.'

'I am,' Hawke admitted. He took off his tin helmet and ran his hand through his hair. It felt tangled and dirty, but then again they were all dirty. The last time he'd washed himself was when they'd first got to the River Scarpe to the west of Arras. When had that been? The nineteenth – *five days ago*. Five days! It seemed like a lifetime already. They'd been hot and filthy when they'd arrived at that river. For nine days they had done nothing but move – up to the front along roads clogged with refugees and troops.

They had been in reserve, kicking their heels for a couple of days somewhere to the west of Brussels while either side of the British front the Belgians and French had begun to crumble. Suddenly they were ordered into their trucks and back they went again, this time along roads even thicker with men and civilians. It had been chaos. Hawke had never realized how quickly the order and efficiency of an army could disintegrate.

On the morning of 19 May, they had reached the Scarpe to the east of Arras. It had been a Sunday, not that days of the week made any difference to anything. They had dug in – making two and three-man slit trenches back from the banks of the river, digging out the dark clay soil with their entrenching tools: short, wooden handles with a detachable head with a pick one side and a shovel the other. They were convenient and easy to carry, but, as Hawke had discovered, were too small, and the moment too much effort was made, the iron head might fly off. It had been hard work, but eventually, in the evening and with no sign of the enemy, they had been allowed to strip off and jump in the river.

As Hawke passed his mess tin and mug, he glanced at his hands. They were dark with grime – a mixture of sweat, mud and oil; his fingernails were chipped, with black lines underneath. When he'd joined up, he had thought only of excitement and glory. In the stories he'd been told, in the books he'd read, no one had mentioned how exhausting it was fighting a war, or how filthy a soldier became. Or that it wasn't really very glamorous at all.

Hawke took a mouthful of warm bully beef hash, then a

gulp of hot, sweet tea and felt his strength returning immediately. A bit of food and some sugar – he'd needed it.

'That feel a bit better, Johnny?' grinned Hebden.

Hawke smiled and nodded. 'I didn't realize how hungry I was.'

'Just don't think of those dead horses, now,' said Drummond.

'He wouldn't have done if you'd kept your trap shut, Charlie!' said Ibbotson.

'It's all right,' said Hawke. 'Honestly. I'm fine now.'

'And don't go and think of that Jerry you shot either,' said Drummond. Ibbotson cuffed him round the back of the head.

'Ow!' said Drummond. 'What did I say?' He was laughing.

'Leave the poor kid alone,' said Ibbotson. 'At least he's shot a bleedin' Jerry, which is more than can be said for you.'

Hawke smiled and caught Hebden's eye, who winked at him.

'I'm only having a laugh with you, Johnny,' said Drummond. 'You know that, don't you?'

Hawke nodded, and tried to put the image of the falling man out of his mind. He did not want to think of the German lying there, sprawled out, dead, while he was still alive, joking and eating his lunch.

'Have you nearly finished?' It was Sergeant Spears. Hawke turned and saw him stride towards them.

'Hebden, Drummond and you, Hawke, finish your tiffin and then I want you to take Pilot Officer Jackson up to Battalion Headquarters.'

'Do we have to, Sarge?' asked Hebden. 'I'd have thought Johnny and me had done our bit this morning.'

'Yes, Bert, you do. Battalion might want to ask you and Hawke some things about what you saw out there.'

'Sarge, what's going on?' asked Ibbotson. 'I don't understand what Jerry's playing at.'

'You and me the same, then, Jack,' said Spears. 'Looks like he's fallen back.'

'But why? I was bracing myself for an almighty scrap and now 'e's scarpered. It doesn't make sense.'

Spears smiled. 'You sound almost disappointed, Jack.'

'Seriously, though, Sarge,' said Ibbotson, 'what do you think they're up to?'

Spears shrugged. 'Dunno. Perhaps they're preparing to attack from a different approach. Or maybe they've only fallen back a short way. Perhaps what we came up against this morning was just their forward units, and they're waiting for more to catch up. Does it matter? The point is we thought we were in for it, and now they've given us a breather – a breather that gives us a chance to prepare some better defences.'

'Gives us a chance for some kip, more like,' said Hebden.

'We need to keep on our toes here, Bert, not go to sleep,' retorted Spears. 'Until we know what Jerry's up to, we've got to stay alert. If it's still quiet later, we'll send out some patrols. That'll give us a clearer picture.'

Hebden turned to Hawke and prodded him. 'And no more volunteering, Johnny, all right?'

Soon after, Hawke, Hebden and Drummond set off with Jackson, back up the hill to Cassel. The pilot had had his head bandaged, although he still needed stitches for the gash in his forehead.

'How are you feeling now, sir?' Hawke asked him.

'All right, thanks. I mean, the head still throbs a bit, but otherwise I don't feel too bad, all things considered. A bit of food helped, and the whisky and sweet tea.' He grinned. 'I've never had so much sugar in my tea before, nor condensed milk, but actually it's rather good, isn't it?'

'The army couldn't function without it, sir,' said Hebden. 'I reckon we'll be all right here, just so long as the tea ration gets through.'

It was by now a clear, early summer's day, with just a few white cotton wool clouds floating through an otherwise deep blue sky. It was warm too, and as they climbed the track towards the town Hawke's battledress began to steam as the last of the damp in his wool uniform evaporated.

'Look at me!' said Hawke. 'I wish we had more comfortable uniforms. A bit of silk would be good.'

Jackson grinned. 'This is my own, though,' he said, fingering the orange silk scarf round his neck, 'although I'm wondering whether it might have brought me bad luck. I'm thinking of changing it.'

'Or good luck,' said Hebden. 'You're alive aren't you?'

'In any case,' said Hawke, 'silk is much nicer than serge.'

'So is fine wool,' added Drummond.

'I've always thought these uniforms were pretty bad,' laughed Jackson, patting his blue service jacket, 'but I must admit that serge looks horribly hot for weather like this.' He still wore his Mae West life jacket, but he was now carrying his heavy sheepskin flying jacket and leather flying helmet over his other arm.

'It's good in winter, though, sir,' said Hebden. 'It was perishing cold this past winter out here, I can tell you. We were glad for some thick wool then.'

'We could have done with a few jackets like yours, sir,' added Drummond. 'One lad in our section got frostbite in his toes and fingers. You never saw anything like it. They went blue then purple. The MO took one look and packed him off to hospital. Apparently they took some of his toes off.'

'Really?' said Hawke.

'Yes. Amputated them. And all because he got too cold.' Drummond shook his head. 'You wouldn't believe it now, would you?'

'What happened to him?' asked Hawke.

Hebden shrugged. 'Back in Blighty, I suppose. Why do you think we needed you, Johnny? We lost a few good men over the winter – to the cold, to accidents. All sorts.'

'Well, I take my hat off to you,' said Jackson. 'I don't think I'm really cut out for being a soldier. I prefer flying.'

'Even after today?' asked Hebden.

'I admit it was terrifying, and I wouldn't wish it on anyone, but I can promise you that flying is the most exhilarating experience you could imagine. And especially in a Spitfire. The speed and power of the thing is incredible, and it's such a beauty too – a real thoroughbred. On my first flight, I couldn't stop grinning. I thought I could die a happy man after that – although obviously I'd rather not.'

'I'd love to fly,' said Hawke. 'The world must look an amazing place from up there.'

'Oh, it does,' said Jackson.

'You wouldn't get me up in one of those things,' said Drummond. 'No chance. I prefer being on my own two feet. I don't like heights anyway.'

Jackson laughed.

'What, sir?' said Drummond. 'What's so funny?'

'I'm sorry,' said Jackson, 'but you've got to admit it's strange: you face danger every day being a soldier and you don't turn a hair, and yet you've a fear of flying.'

Drummond looked sheepish. 'I don't like the sea, neither, sir. Suppose I must be a bit of a landlubber, that's all.'

They were quiet for a moment and then Hawke said, 'What are they saying back home, sir? About what's going on over here, I mean?'

'I think everyone's a bit shaken up, to be honest,' said Jackson. 'No one can believe it's all going so badly wrong. The papers are blaming the French.'

'With good reason,' said Hebden. 'We've barely fired a shot, have we, lads?' He looked at Drummond and Hawke in turn. 'We march all the way up to the Dendre, just as we'd agreed with the Frogs and the Belgians, and then, before we know it, they're in full retreat. We've got to keep our line with them intact, so then we have to withdraw too. I haven't a bleedin' clue what happened on their fronts, but it doesn't seem to me like they put up much of a fight. Ever since then it's been one rumour after another, but I know what we've seen with our own eyes, and I can tell you, sir, it's not been pretty.'

'It's been chaos, sir,' added Drummond, 'absolute chaos. You never saw anything like it. Those Frogs have been a disgrace. Discipline gone to pot, the roads clogged with refugees. No one seems to know their backside from their elbow.'

'No one tells us anything, sir,' continued Hebden. 'We're only blinkin' soldiers after all – but it's not looking good, is it? Jerry's to the north and the south. He's trapped us. I just hope you can get out of here and back home before it's too late.'

Jackson sighed and adjusted the bandage round his head. 'It's incredible, isn't it? And here we are, walking up a track and there's barely a sound, except the birds in the trees. You can hardly believe it.' He paused and looked back. Out in the field beyond Oxelaëre, the remains of his Spitfire were still smouldering. 'You know, everyone at home thinks the Germans are going to invade Britain at any moment. They've formed Local Defence Volunteers to watch out for German parachutists.'

'Local what?' asked Hebden. 'What's that?'

'Farmers, old men, anyone really. Anyone not already serving. They man road blocks and keep a lookout for anyone suspicious – Fifth Columnists, that sort of thing. We got stopped the other night by a load of them. We were on our way back from the pub and all a bit boozed up, I suppose, and we were told to halt and get out of the car. They had shotguns and old rifles and demanded to see our papers. The CO got a bit shirty with them, to be honest.'

'Blimey,' said Hebden. 'I'd no idea. We haven't really heard much from home, you see. There's been no post since all this kicked off.'

'Bert's a farmer,' said Hawke.

'Really?' said Jackson. 'Then why are you out here?'

'Thought I'd do my bit, sir,' he said. 'My old man's still running in any case. They can manage without me for a bit.'

'I take my hat off to you,' said Jackson. 'Really.'

They were now nearing Battalion lines on the southern ramparts of the town. Soldiers were busily digging in and building barricades, but, as they passed through, a subaltern from A Company offered to take them to Battalion Headquarters. Stepping along the old ramparts, they then turned up a narrow street and under an archway – once an old town gate – and followed the road back to Grand Place. There on the corner stood a brick building, crooked with age. It had large iron numbers nailed into the brickwork above the second-floor windows that made up the date '1631'.

'Here we are,' said the lieutenant, leading them round the side of the building to where a sentry snapped to attention. 'As of three hours ago, our latest Battalion HQ.'

Inside, clerks were already hammering away at typewriters on makeshift trestle tables, while in one room a staff officer was talking loudly and slowly into a field telephone.

'Do-you-know-the-latest-enemy-positions?' he said, then muttered under his breath, 'Ruddy Frogs, why can't they speak English like the rest of us?'

Hawke looked around, fascinated by the speed with which the Battalion had occupied this old building. The A Company lieutenant left them with a wave and a 'cheerio' and so they stood waiting on creaking wooden floorboards in the hallway listening to the movement of people and chairs on the floor above, and to the continuing hammer of typewriters. After a few minutes another staff officer appeared. He looked older, with greying hair and moustache, and had a pipe wedged into the side of his mouth.

'Yes?' he said, pulling out his matches to light his pipe, then looked up and saw Jackson. 'Ah, yes, of course, the pilot. Saw you get one of the Huns.' He held out his hand. 'Major Carter,' he said. 'I'm the adj around here.' He then glanced at the other three.

Jackson shook his hand. 'Two of the men here rescued me from my Spit, sir,' said Jackson, 'and between them killed a number of Jerries.'

'Ah, good show,' said Carter.

Hebden cleared his throat. 'We were told you might want to speak with us, sir.'

'Yes, absolutely, absolutely.' He looked at his watch, then glanced back into the room. 'Let me just speak with the colonel and I'll be right back.'

He reappeared a few moments later, and said, 'Yes, the colonel will see you now. Come through all of you.'

They followed Carter into a long, narrow room, and at the far end Hawke saw Lieutenant-Colonel Beamish, commanding officer of the 1st Battalion, leaning over a table on which was an old road map.

'Colonel?' said Major Carter.

Beamish looked up as the three Rangers snapped to attention and saluted. He was around forty, with a lean, clean-shaven face and sandy hair.

'At ease,' said Beamish, then leaned forward and shook Jackson's hand. 'I hear you bagged a couple this morning?'

'Yes, sir,' said Jackson.

'Good work, but we need you in the air again, not here. Major Carter is organizing a despatch rider to take you straight to Dunkirk – sorry it's not a car, but it'll be quicker by motorbike. Happy with that?'

'Of course, sir.'

'Strictly speaking, I should send you to see General Mason-Macfarlane, who would hold on to you for another couple of hours. Then you'd be sent to GHQ, but it would probably take you another day just to get there and when you finally did you'd probably find it had already moved. So you'll head straight for Dunkirk. They're already sending home the wounded and base troops so there are plenty of ships heading back to England. With a bit of luck you'll be in Dunkirk in a few hours and flying again tomorrow.'

Jackson brightened. 'Thank you, sir.'

'How's the head?'

'It needs stitches, but I'm all right, thank you, sir.'

'Can it wait, do you think?'

'Definitely, sir.'

'Good man. Then I think you'd best get going.'

'The despatch rider is waiting outside, sir,' said Carter.

Jackson nodded, then turned to the three Rangers. 'Hebden, Hawke – I can't thank you enough,' he said. 'You saved my life. If it weren't for you and Sergeant Spears I'd be either dead or a prisoner of the Nazis.'

Hawke smiled. 'Glad to have met you, sir.'

'Good luck, sir,' said Hebden. 'And if you fly over us again give us a wave.'

'I'll do that. My squadron letters are BW – look out for us. And here,' he said, pulling off his bright orange silk scarf and handing it to Hawke. 'Have this. Maybe it'll bring you luck.'

Hawke took it. 'Thank you,' he said.

Jackson grinned, saluted the colonel, then turned and left.

'Well done, chaps,' said the colonel as the sound of a motorbike starting up drifted through into the building. 'You did well. God knows, we're going to need every one of those pilots.'

'Excuse me, sir,' said Hebden, 'but do you know what's going on?'

Beamish sighed. 'Not really. But it seems Jerry has pulled back. God knows why. But it gives us a chance to strengthen our position here. Between you and me, we're getting reinforcements.

Macforce is being dissolved and General Mason-Macfarlane is heading back to GHQ, while we're getting 145 Brigade. I'm afraid it means we lose our two companies of the Yorks and Lancs, but we're getting two more battalions instead – the Glosters and the Ox and Bucks. They'll be here overnight. With luck Jerry won't attack between now and then. Might give us a chance after all. How are you all doing down in Oxelaëre?'

'Very well, thank you, sir,' said Hebden.

Beamish nodded. 'Good. You've done well this morning. You can be proud of yourselves. Took some guts doing what you did and by saving a pilot and preventing his Spitfire from getting into enemy hands you performed a great service. Well done. Now get back to your positions and keep on your guard. Jerry might have called off any attack for the moment, but we don't know when he might try and strike again.'

Outside, Drummond patted both Hebden and Hawke on the back. 'Quite the colonel's favourites, aren't you?'

'A great service!' grinned Hebden. 'That's what he said. How about that Johnny? From the bleedin' colonel himself too.'

Hawke smiled. 'It was the sergeant really, though,' he said. 'We just did as he told us.'

'You're too nice about Spears,' said Drummond. 'Too nice by half. He's always having a go at you and then you go and stick up for him like that.'

'But it's true,' said Hawke. 'He planned the rescue and he killed most of those Germans. And he told us to destroy the Spitfire. If it wasn't for him, we wouldn't have got Jackson out.'

Hebden said, 'I think you did all right, though, Johnny. You proved a point to Spears, and if it weren't for you we wouldn't have been stood there listening to the nice colonel telling us what splendid fellows we are.'

Hawke smiled again. 'Thanks, Bert.'

'But now we all know you've got some guts just try and keep your head down from now on, all right? Because I'll tell you one thing about heroes – they nearly always wind up dead, and I'd hate that to happen to you.'

'And God knows what we've got coming in the next few days,' said Drummond. 'Jerry might have pulled back for the moment, but he'll be back, as sure as anything. And there's no getting away from it: Jerry's broken through to the north and he's lining himself up against us to the south. We're almost completely surrounded now. I tell you, it don't look good. It really don't look good at all.'

# 6

## THOUGHTS OF HOME

Although the Germans seemed to have disappeared entirely, Farrish had received orders from Battalion HQ, via a note hand-delivered by Hebden, that the platoon was to maintain a rigorous watch on its front to the south of Oxelaëre. Even so, this did not require the entire platoon at one time. Farrish was fortunate: he had lost just four men so far since 10 May. One had fallen off a lorry and been hit by the vehicle behind, while a further three from Platoon Headquarters had been killed when a shell landed close by as they unloaded ammunition boxes from a truck. That left thirty-two; compared with many infantry companies in the British Expeditionary Force, B Company was still in good shape. Had it not been for the unfortunate disappearance of D Company, lost as they fell back from the Brussels-Charleroi Canal to the south of Brussels, the entire Battalion would have still been only fractionally under-strength.

Farrish therefore ordered his three ten-man sections to rotate their watch, five men on, five men off, two hours at a time. It meant that by the middle of the afternoon, Hawke had joined Hebden, Chalkie White, Foxy Foxton and Corporal McLaren in a secluded orchard at the back of the farm. It was quiet out there, despite a cockerel crowing nearby. The farm had been abandoned by its owners, although chickens and a half dozen cows remained. When the Rangers had reached it, the cows had been lowing pitifully, their udders swollen because they had not been milked. Hebden had relieved them with the help of two others from 3 Section.

'I thought cockerels only crowed in the morning, Bert,' said Foxton.

Hebden chuckled. 'No, as that chap's proving, Foxy. I used to have a fabulous cockerel back home. A brute of a lad – he had these huge spurs a good two inches long. Not only did he crow all day, he'd go for anyone who came near his girls – anyone but me. He was putty in my hands. Used to like a good cuddle.'

'What happened to him?' asked Hawke.

'Fox got him. But he saved a lot of the hens. He put up a hell of a fight – we could hear it going on, but unfortunately we got out there too late. I like to think he put those spurs to good use, though.'

Hawke smiled to himself, listening to Hebden. He had always lived in the city – the country was new to him, but he liked the sound of it. He liked this farm. *One day, maybe*, he thought. Lying beneath a tree with his greatcoat for a pillow, with the sounds of the men and the cock crowing and insects buzzing peacefully nearby, he soon drifted off to sleep.

A little more than an hour later, he awoke, his sleep interrupted by the clatter of a billy can and the sound of Hebden and White noisily brewing yet more tea.

Hawke stretched, yawned, ran his hands through his dark mop of hair and sat up.

'Want a brew, Johnny?' asked Hebden.

Hawke nodded, and rubbed his eyes. Gentle, dappled sunlight shone down through the apple trees, while the thick grass beneath him was soft and dark, lush with the renewed life brought by early summer. A blackbird sang nearby, while from the farm he could hear the soothing cooing of doves.

'Here you go,' said Hebden, walking over to him with a billy can of tea. Hawke held out his enamel mug, thanked his friend, then sipped at the hot, sweet liquid. Feeling revived, he delved into his haversack and pulled out the pad of light-blue letter-writing paper he had brought with him, then an old pencil. He sharpened it with his clasp knife and, leaning his back against the tree and the paper on his thigh, began to write a letter.

*24 May 1940*, he wrote at the top, then *Dear All*, and then stopped. He had been about to write that he was now in Cassel, but then remembered that it was strictly forbidden to mention place names in letters. In fact, the censors were so strict he now struggled to think what he could say, and absent-mindedly tapped the end of his pencil between his teeth for a few moments, then began again.

*I hope you are all well and in good spirits. I am fine. The battle has been going on for some time now, but we seem to have missed most of it. There are a lot of people running from the Germans. We see them on the road, sometimes whole families, struggling with suitcases or with carts piled high. I hope the Germans never get to Leeds – they won't if I have anything to do with it!*

*This morning we had to rescue a Spitfire pilot who had crash-landed (after shooting down two of theirs). I shot a –*

Hawke paused, thought a moment, then crossed it out, repeatedly covering the words so they became completely illegible.

*I threw a grenade at the Spitfire to stop the enemy getting their dirty hands on it and managed to score a direct hit, lobbing it into the cockpit so the plane would catch fire, which it did. The smoke enabled us to get back to our positions without the Jerries getting a clear crack at us. Tom seemed quite pleased with me for that one.*

Hawke paused again, thinking about what Spears had said to him. Just two words: *Good shot*. They were the first words of praise he had said to him since Hawke had joined the battalion. He sighed and took another sip of his tea, and thought about the first time he had met the sergeant.

He remembered it well. They had all sat down to lunch in the kitchen of their small terraced house in Headingley. It had been quite a squeeze: Hawke and his three sisters, his mother, Uncle Richard and Tom Spears, all crammed around the old wooden table. Maddie had been both proud and self-conscious, which had made her unusually quiet.

It had been Uncle Richard, Hawke's stepfather, who had come to the rescue, prompting Tom to tell them something of what it had been like out in India. It turned out Tom had seen his fair share of action along the North-West Frontier and with Uncle Richard's encouragement had told them a number of stories of fighting Pashtuns, of expeditions into the mountains, and of the sights and smells of the ancient cities of Lahore and Rawalpindi.

Hawke had been mesmerized. He had always loved adventure

stories and it was as though he were face to face with one of the heroes from his *Chums* magazine.

Tom Spears had looked the part too, the campaign medal ribbon above his tunic, his face tanned and healthy. Later, after lunch, when Hawke had suggested they play cricket in the alley behind the house, Tom had eagerly agreed, leaving Maddie and their mother and two other sisters, Molly and Joan, inside. Not only had Tom complimented him on both his batting and bowling, he had later shown great interest in Hawke's collection of cricket cigarette cards. And, although they had argued good humouredly about some of the great Yorkshire players, both had agreed that Hedley Verity was the greatest spin bowler ever.

'I've got his autograph,' Hawke had told him. 'Here,' he said, showing Tom his autograph book. Apart from his cricket bat, it was his most prized possession.

'That makes two of us,' Tom had grinned. 'It was at a match at Scarborough back in 1932. He got seven wickets that day. I'll never forget it.'

From that day, Johnny had hoped that Tom and Maddie might eventually get married. At last there would be some male company in the family other than Uncle Richard – someone closer to his own age, who liked the same things he did. When, a few weeks later, Tom and Maddie had become engaged, Johnny had been as pleased as any of them. He had looked forward to having an older brother.

*I think I have already told you that Tom is greatly respected here and a great figure in the platoon. I was certainly glad he was leading us when we rescued that pilot.*

He paused, tapping the end of the pencil between his teeth again. He imagined them all at home: their terraced house in Back Headingley Mount in Leeds, with its familiar smell of polish, cooked food and Uncle Richard's pipe smoke, and with the photograph of his father on the mantelpiece above the grate and the small carriage clock beside it. This time last year, the cricket season had just begun, the summer stretching before him: matches for Kirkstall in the league, and long holidays spent watching Yorkshire at Headingley. A wave of sadness swept over him. He had been in such a rush to escape the factory, to emulate both his father, and, if truth be known, Tom Spears, that he had joined the army when still only fifteen. Making the most of his height, he had lied about his age and been taken on. But in doing so he now realized for the first time that his childhood had gone forever.

*It seems odd being out here in France where they don't play cricket and it now being the start of the new season. I wonder whether there will be any matches this summer at Headingley? I miss you all and home, but don't worry about me. I'm all right and keeping fine. Things might not be going too well just at present but I'm sure we'll sort out these Germans eventually.*

*My love to you all,*
*Johnny*

Hawke folded the letter carefully, placed it in an envelope and wrote the address, then asked Hebden the time.

'Twenty to six,' Hebden replied. 'Twenty minutes left until we're on. Just time for another brew. Johnny – I reckon it must be your turn to be char-wallah.'

Hawke smiled. 'All right, Bert,' he said, getting up and moving over to where Hebden had set up the Primus.

'Good lad,' said Hebden. 'You're catching on, Johnny. We'll make a soldier of you yet.'

# 7

## RECCE PATROL

A little after 8 p.m., the same day. There had been no further sign of the enemy that afternoon. As the men on duty had stared ahead, not a flicker had been seen, not even a faint clang heard. Above, formations of enemy aircraft had flown over, but they all seemed to be headed south or towards the coast.

Now, however, as dusk was beginning to settle, Lieutenant Farrish ordered a reconnaissance patrol and chose Sergeant Spears to lead 1 Section. In the yard, the men gathered around the platoon commander. Packs and excess webbing had been left behind, but otherwise the men were fully armed.

'I don't want you to think that after this morning's escapade I'm picking on One Section,' said Farrish, 'but the fact is Sergeant Spears here and Privates Hebden and Hawke have already been forward of our positions and so know the ground.'

'Don't worry, sir,' said McLaren, 'I'm glad just to be doing something rather than staring into space.'

'Less of the backchat, Sid,' said Spears.

Farrish smiled. 'Glad to hear it, Corporal. Now, there are two things I need you to do. First, see if you can find the Germans we killed earlier and try to discover if there's anything useful on them – any papers, unit details, that sort of thing.

Second, push forward and have a look at the positions Jerry held earlier. You never know, we might be able to pick up something that gives us some kind of clue as to what the devil he's playing at.' He turned to Spears. 'How long do you think you'll need, Sergeant?'

'Do you want us to bury the dead, sir? Might not be too pleasant if it's another warm and sunny day tomorrow.'

Farrish nodded. 'Yes, perhaps you'd better, then.'

'Then an hour, sir. Perhaps a bit more.'

Farrish nodded. 'All right, good. Don't let it get too dark, though. Password will be "Knaresborough".'

They set off straight away, advancing in an extended line, sticking to the same approach Spears had used earlier. Despite the quiet, and despite the enemy inactivity that afternoon, Spears was cautious, pausing at the end of the first field and listening, before signalling them to move forward once more. At the gap in the hedge by the wrecked Spitfire, they paused again, but there was still no sign of the enemy up ahead, just birdsong and the delicate rustle of freshly budded leaves as a gentle evening breeze ruffled them. Satisfied the coast was clear, Spears ordered the Bren team to move forward, cross the brook and provide cover while the rest of the section looked for the dead Germans.

'Where was your one, then, Johnny?' asked Drummond.

'Through there, in front of the Spit, wasn't it?' said Hebden.

'Yes,' said Hawke. He led the two men forward through the gap in the hedge. The Spitfire had stopped burning. Just its blackened carcass remained. The engine cowling had burst off, revealing an engine seared clean, while the canopy had melted completely. A stench of burned rubber pervaded the air. Hawke stepped forward gingerly, the reeds sprouting up from the banks of the brook right before him. His heart had begun to pound once more, and he was overcome by a sense of dread.

'Come on, Johnny,' said Drummond. 'We haven't got all night, you know.'

Hawke swallowed, and stepped closer to the reeds. He could see where they had been flattened, but paused again, dreading what he would find, fearing that he would be repulsed by what he saw. Then Drummond pushed past him and shouted out in triumph, 'Here he is.'

Hawke watched, rooted to the spot, as Drummond leaned over and grabbed the man. He yanked him up, then dragged him back and laid him at the edge of the field on some grass unsinged by the burning Spitfire.

At first he saw only a glimpse of the dead man's face and limp arms. The skin seemed white, like wax, but now he stepped forward and stood over him.

'Look at that,' said Drummond, pointing to a dark stain on the German's tunic. 'Straight in the chest. Right through the heart, I'd say. Good shot, Johnny.'

Hawke squatted down beside the dead man. His eyes were closed, his face milky white. Hawke breathed a sigh of relief that the man he had killed looked so peaceful, and the bullet had made such a neat and inoffensive wound.

'Well done, Johnny,' said Hebden. 'He wouldn't have felt a thing, you know.'

'Go on, then,' added Drummond, impatience creeping into his voice. 'Check his pockets.'

Hawke glanced at Drummond, then felt the man's pockets. There was a packet of half-smoked cigarettes in the left-hand breast pocket, and a couple of packets of field dressings in the lower pockets. Then, carefully, Hawke undid the silver-coloured button on the right breast pocket. The field-grey wool was still damp with blood – blood that stained Hawke's fingers – but he felt inside and his fingers touched two pocketbooks. Carefully pulling them out, he prised them apart and wiped them on the grass then opened the first.

It was a diary – with a soft green leather binding. At the back were several letters and photographs, which Hawke now looked at. The dead man was smiling with his comrades in one, jackets off, sleeves rolled up. In another he was sitting in a small rowing boat with friends – or were they brothers? – presumably before the war. A third was a picture of him with his family – a formal studio photograph. He recognized the man's parents in a further picture – a middle-aged couple arm in arm, standing outside a house. Hawke felt a lump rise to his throat, then opened up the front of the diary. There was a name, written in ink: Rudi Wittmann.

Hawke now looked at the second pocketbook. It was dirty and dog-eared, with the word *Soldbuch* written on the front in gothic writing. Inside was a photograph of the man and his name and army number. Hawke flicked over a page and saw what he assumed were Rudi Wittmann's personal details, including a date: 1.v.21.

*His birthday*, Hawke thought to himself. That made him just nineteen.

'Will you look at these jackets!' exclaimed Drummond. 'Blimey! You can undo the cuff-buttons and everything. And nice lining too – what do we get? A bit of rough old wool and canvas.'

'I quite like our battledress,' said Hebden. 'Easier to move about in than that bulky great tunic they're wearing.'

Hawke paused, gripping the dead man's belongings tightly in his hand. This was not how he had imagined war to be. In his imagination, the enemy had always been faceless, almost inhuman, the Nazis especially. But here before him was a boy only a few years older than himself – a boy whose parents and family would soon be ripped apart by the news that their son was dead.

'Come on, Johnny,' said Drummond. 'He's just a Nazi. One less to worry about.'

Hawke stuffed the pocketbooks into his own top pocket then stood up once more. Hebden put an arm on his shoulder.

'Don't take it so personally, Johnny,' he said. 'What would have happened if you hadn't fired?'

'I know,' muttered Hawke.

'He'd have shot you instead. You didn't kill him. It was the war.' He shook him gently, then leaned over and hoisted the dead man over his shoulder. 'Let's go and find the others.'

There were ten in all – ten men, all dead, and, Hawke realized, Sergeant Spears had killed nine of them, mowing them down with the Bren. Most had fallen in the brook, a narrow and quite shallow stream, but, Hawke realized, Spears had been canny to wait until the men were crossing, their balance wavering as they waded through the water and stepped on stones and rocks, before opening fire. They were now laid out side by side on the far bank.

'Jump to it, you three,' Spears said as Hawke, Hebden and Drummond crossed the brook themselves. 'We need to get a move on.'

'I thought we had to bury them, Sarge,' said Hebden, laying Wittmann down beside his dead comrades.

'We'll do that on the way back. It's darker in the woods than out here. We're going to need all the light we can get.'

They set off again, this time in a wide arrowhead formation across the field towards the wood. There was still no sign of the enemy, but on reaching the trees they found plenty of signs of activity: spent ammunition cases, vehicle and tank tracks, and old ration packets. Spears led them along one set of tracks until they reached the far side of the wood, then halted them once more. The tracks headed away from them, following an old road that ran south.

'All right, boys,' he said, 'I think we've seen enough. Let's get those Jerries buried and head on back.'

'Sergeant?' said Hawke, standing beside Spears.

Spears turned and looked him.

'Why would the Germans up stumps and fall back like that?'

Spears pushed his helmet on to the back of his head and rubbed his brow. 'I don't know. I really don't. It makes no sense to me. No sense whatsoever.'

# 8

## REINFORCEMENTS

As Sergeant Spears and his patrol of Yorks Rangers were following the tracks made earlier by the enemy, a Humber Snipe staff car and two Morris Commercial trucks wound their way round the now cleared Dead Horse Corner, then, with a grind of gears, rumbled on along the cobbled road as it straightened towards the centre of the hilltop town.

Sitting in the back, anxiously watching the road, was Brigadier the Honourable Nigel Somerset, and his Chief of Staff, Major Harry Bullmore. The brigadier was forty-six, and, until nine days earlier, had been a lieutenant-colonel and a commander of 2nd Battalion, the Gloucestershire Regiment. But then 145 Brigade's commander was sent home – officially, because he had fallen ill, but unofficially because he had simply not been up to the job. In a trice, Somerset had climbed two ranks and been made acting brigadier. With the jump in rank came the jump in responsibility: instead of commanding a single battalion of eight hundred men, he was now commanding three battalions as well as artillery, engineers and other units that made up a brigade.

It had been a bewildering and exhausting couple of days. Two nights earlier, the brigade had been manning positions along the River Escaut in Belgium, on the northern front, but then orders had arrived to retreat to what was now called the Gort Line, named after the commander of the British Expeditionary Force, General Lord Gort. They had reached their new positions some miles back along the French-Belgian border in the early hours of 23 May, and had debussed and begun digging in, only for new orders to arrive telling them that French troops would be relieving them immediately. But, far from arriving within the hour, the French had not appeared until later that afternoon.

It had been a shock to see them as they trundled down the road past Brigade Headquarters, dressed in all manner of uniforms, and any semblance of marching discipline completely gone. Some were pushing small carts and even babies' prams. Somerset had watched appalled as on several occasions men had stepped out of rank, entered houses and reappeared with stolen bicycles and once even a chicken.

As the French had moved in, so the brigade had pulled out, ordered into reserve, where Somerset hoped his exhausted men might be given a day or two's well-earned rest. It had been another long and difficult journey, through the night, all the way to the village of Nomain, just to the south of Lille. Somerset had been given a new billet in a house in the village, but had barely put his head down on his bed when new orders had arrived telling him to hurry with his brigade to Calais, where the British garrison there was being besieged. His task was to try to relieve it.

Troop transports had not arrived until late that afternoon. All day, they had been hanging about, waiting to get going to Calais. It had given the men a chance for a rest, but then, just as the RASC men had arrived with transport, a staff officer from 48th Division had appeared at Brigade Headquarters and personally handed Somerset a note from Major-General Thorne, the division commander, overriding the orders to try to relieve Calais.

'You are to proceed to Cassel,' the note told him. 'We do not know where the enemy are, but we hope you will get there first.'

'What about Calais?' Somerset had asked the captain from Division.

'Calais's not expected to hold, sir,' the captain had replied.

Somerset had nodded, dumbfounded. This was dire news. If Calais was about to fall, then the whole of the BEF would soon be completely surrounded. And if that happened – well, it did not bear thinking about.

Since then there had been yet another change of orders – or an amendment, at any rate. His brigade was now not only to defend Cassel, but Hazebrouck too. Well, now he was here – or, rather, he and Brigade Headquarters. God only knew how long it would be before the rest of them arrived. Travelling under cover of darkness meant they were spared any aerial attack, but the roads were even more clogged than they were in daytime.

The town seemed quiet enough, but whether that was because the Germans had not reached them or because they had already overrun the town, he could not know. Brigadier Somerset sighed.

'What do you think, Bully?'

'Can't see any Jerries yet, sir.' He craned his head out of the window. 'No swastika on top of the church.'

Somerset sighed again and quietly shook his head. 'What a mess. What a damned mess.'

A couple of hundred yards further on, a British soldier – easily identifiable in his helmet – stepped out into the road.

'Thank goodness,' muttered Somerset. 'So we've got a place to defend, at any rate.'

His driver slowed and the soldier waved them towards an open gate in a high wall. The Snipe turned into a small courtyard, which was dominated on three sides by a substantial and elegant townhouse. As the Snipe came to a halt, the brigadier's door was opened, and when he stepped out on to the gravel he was confronted by a young lieutenant snapping smartly to attention.

'Welcome to Cassel, sir,' said the lieutenant. 'If you'd like to follow me.'

The brigadier glanced at Major Bullmore, now getting out of the other side of the car, raised an eyebrow and said, 'Ready to face the music, Bully?'

'I think so, sir,' said Bullmore.

Passing through the chateau's entrance, they entered a hallway from which a wide staircase wound its way to the next floor, but the lieutenant led them to their left, into a large, high-ceilinged drawing room. At the far end, near some open French windows, several men stood around a large mahogany table on which had been laid several maps.

'Brigadier Somerset, General,' the lieutenant announced.

General Mason-Macfarlane looked up and, seeing Somerset, smiled and strode towards him.

'Brigadier – my dear chap.' He held out his hand and gripped Somerset's firmly.

'General,' said Somerset. 'I'm afraid I'm only the advance party. The rest of the men won't be here for a few hours yet.'

‘Battling through roads heavy with refugees and French soldiers, no doubt,’ said Mason-Macfarlane. ‘No one predicted just how hard it would be to manoeuvre through Flanders. After all, it’s flat, and has an extensive road network. Just goes to show that you can plan all you like but something vital always seems to be overlooked. Anyway, what about a drink? I’ve got Scotch or there’s a rather good Calvados.’

‘Scotch, thank you, General,’ said Somerset, ‘and one for Major Bullmore here too, thank you, sir.’

Mason-Macfarlane nodded to a junior staff officer then led Somerset over towards the table. The brigadier glanced around him. Large portraits dating back several hundred years hung from the walls, although there was also a painting of Marshal Foch, French commander in the last war, hanging above the fireplace. Elegant settees and ornate armchairs filled the room, while through the open windows was a stone balcony and beyond clear views to the countryside stretching far to the south.

‘Hell of a view, isn’t it?’ said Mason-Macfarlane. He was lean-faced, in his fifties, with neat hair silver at the sides and an equally silvery and trim moustache. Dark, keen eyes followed Somerset’s gaze. ‘The saying goes that one can see a hundred villages and twenty towns from up here in Cassel. I haven’t had a chance to count, but actually I can well believe it. Of course, it makes this place a great defensive position.’

Somerset nodded and stepped out on to the balcony. He really could see for miles. The general was right – this *was* a fine defensive position. No enemy could arrive without being spotted clearly beforehand, that was for sure, despite the number of woods and trees that lay at the hill’s base and beyond.

'Am I to understand that I will be serving under your command, sir?' said Somerset, stepping back inside.

'Good Lord, no.' Mason-Macfarlane chuckled. 'No, I'm needed elsewhere. Macforce is being disbanded, but although I'm taking some of my units I am leaving you the First Yorks Rangers. They're a three-company battalion – one of their companies got separated as they fell back from the Brussels-Charleroi Canal a few days ago, which has apparently now been attached to the DLI in Fifth Div.'

'Any chance of getting them back, sir?' asked Somerset.

Mason-Macfarlane raised a dubious eyebrow. 'What do you think? But the three companies you've got have barely fired a shot yet – although they had a small exchange earlier this morning – and they're about ninety per cent strength. So far they've been mainly to-ing and fro-ing across Flanders.'

'And any idea where the Germans are, sir? I have to admit, it was with some trepidation that we climbed the road up to the town. I was half expecting to be halted by Huns.'

'Really?' said the General. He looked surprised. 'You have been told about the halt order, haven't you?'

Somerset frowned. 'Halt order? Er, no, sir – what halt order?'

Mason-Macfarlane shook his head. 'That's ridiculous – I'm so sorry, Somerset. I just assumed – but then how foolish of me. I should know by now that lack of information is proving our fatal flaw in this damned battle.' He sighed and rubbed his forehead. 'This morning, just before eleven-thirty hours, we intercepted a German signal ordering all German panzer troops to the south to halt and remain behind the Le Bassée Canal.'

'What? That's incredible. But why? They've got us absolutely where they want us.'

'Quite – I know. It's an extraordinary decision. It's even more extraordinary when one considers that a lot of their troops had already advanced beyond the Le Bassée Canal. It's meant they've actually had to fall back.'

Somerset chuckled. 'So the Germans are retreating. Well, well.'

'In a manner of speaking, yes. It was incredible. This morning we were being stonked quite heavily and then suddenly it stopped as they packed up and fell back south.'

'But *why*?'

'I know – they could have rolled us over here if they'd attacked in strength today. It may be a good place to defend, but there's only so much one can do against superior fire-power and when they hold the skies. I suspect they're getting cold feet. Surprised by the speed of their own advance.'

'Have you told your men?'

'No, and Gort wants to keep it that way. It's a matter for senior commanders only. Obviously they know the enemy have fallen back but they don't need to know any more.'

Somerset shook his head in wonder. 'It still seems incredible. They must think we're stronger than we really are.'

'Maybe, because our situation is certainly pretty dire. The fact of the matter is we have almost no tanks whatsoever, ammunition is getting low, rations are running out and we're almost completely trapped apart from a narrow strip of coastline. The Dutch have surrendered, and the Belgians have already ceded two-thirds of their country – no one expects them to hold out for too much longer. If they throw in the towel, then we'll be left with Dunkirk and that's about it. And the French – well, the speed and level of their collapse has been astonishing. It's terrible to admit it, but their commanders have lost all control. They're too old – relics of the last war. They'd planned for a repeat of the trenches and attrition of 1914 to 1918 – I suppose we all had, to a degree – and now that it's not happened, they're lost. They're like rabbits caught in headlights. I saw General Georges the other day and it was as though he were suffering from shell-shock. The fellow broke down in front of us and started weeping.'

'Good Lord,' said Somerset.

Mason-Macfarlane sighed. 'I'm sorry, Somerset, I'm not trying to depress you, but it's important you know the real picture. On the other hand, we have been given a breather. France is finished, but there's hope yet for the BEF. In fact, it gives us a chance to escape. I'm not sure whether I should be telling you this, but the commander is preparing to evacuate. They're already sending back the useless mouths.'

Somerset nodded. 'I see,' he said.

'Gort has got a continuous line along the northern flank but not enough men for the south. So he's doing the next best thing and establishing a series of strong points. The idea is that these will hold while the bulk of the BEF falls back to Dunkirk.'

Somerset nodded slowly as the reality of the task began to sink in.

'Do you know how long we need to hold out here?'

Mason-Macfarlane took a sip of his whisky. 'Just as long as you can.' He paused and eyed Somerset carefully. 'We don't know how long this halt order will be kept in place. You don't need me to tell you this, but you have to make the most of it.'

Somerset nodded again and stroked his chin. 'When do you leave, sir?'

‘Now – that is, this evening. You’re here now, your men are on their way, and I know I can leave Cassel in very capable hands. I know you won’t let your country down, Brigadier.’

‘No, sir.’ Somerset drained his glass. ‘But it seems we don’t have a minute to lose. With your permission, sir, could you spare one of your staff officers to show me around first?’

‘Absolutely.’ He beckoned over a young captain with bright ginger hair and a trim moustache. ‘Captain Stratton will do so. Stratton,’ he added, turning to the captain, ‘I want you to brief Brigadier Somerset.’

‘Yes, sir.’

‘Stratton is a sapper by trade – a good fellow. He’ll be able to give you a decent ground brief.’

‘Thank you,’ said Somerset. ‘In the circumstances I would certainly appreciate an engineer’s judgement.’

Stratton bowed his head slightly in acknowledgement, and then the general cleared his throat, patted his pockets and said, ‘Well, best of luck, Somerset.’ He held out his hand and Somerset gripped it firmly.

‘Thank you, sir. You too.’

Somerset saluted then turned and left, with Stratton and Bullmore in tow. Outside in the courtyard, dusk was falling. A dove cooed soothingly nearby. The air was fresh and cool. It was quiet too. Quiet now, thought Somerset, but for how much longer? He turned and smiled at Bullmore and Stratton, clapping his hands together and rubbing them vigorously.’

‘Right, chaps, we’ve got work to do. Stratton – lead on. Should we walk or take the car?’

‘It’s not a big place, sir, but in the interest of time, the car might be helpful.’

'Absolutely.'

His driver saluted and opened the rear door of the Snipe for the brigadier. Somerset stepped in and sat back in the seat, his mind racing. He knew he needed to convey a sense of confidence to all his men, but it was something he did not feel himself. Mason-Macfarlane's grim picture of the situation had shocked him. He had known things were not going well, but he had not appreciated it was quite so bad. But far worse was the stark reality of the task his new force here at Cassel had been given. They were the sacrificial lambs, given an impossible task of holding off the enemy. There could be no question of cutting and running. They would have to stand and fight, but eventually they would be able to stand and fight no longer.

And by that time, if they weren't already dead, they would inevitably be taken prisoner.

# 9

## SERGEANT SPEARS

After the patrol had safely returned, Sergeant Spears had reported to Second-Lieutenant Farrish, armed with a collection of *Soldbuchs*, letters and even a fold-up map of the area. Farrish had been delighted – maps were in short supply, and they had been relying on French motoring maps that the battalion commander had bought in a shop in Lille before the offensive had begun.

'The writing is a bit hard to decipher on some of these,' said Farrish as they sat around an old wooden table in the kitchen of the farmhouse. Above them, a large part of the plaster had fallen when a shell had landed on the roof above earlier. The remains of the plaster had been roughly cleared up from the stone floor below but the whole room was covered in a thin film of dust, apart from the table, which the two men had lightly wiped with a rag.

'Ah,' said Farrish, holding up a letter. 'This chap is in confident mood. *The French have been surrendering in droves and are in full flight. The battle to cross the Meuse was a hard one, but since then they have been advancing fifty kilometres a day.* Fifty kilometres? What's that – thirty-odd miles?'

'About that, sir,' said Spears. 'I didn't know you could read German, sir.'

'Yes, well – a bit. I studied it at school and did an exchange with a boy from the Black Forest. Andreas Deichmann. God knows what happened to him. For all I know he's fighting against us now.'

'What was it like? Germany, I mean?'

Farrish thought for a moment. 'Actually, for the most part it wasn't so very different from home. The family were decent enough and we boys came and went as we pleased. It's a beautiful part of the world and Andreas and I went hiking in the hills, or we'd go canoeing, or out on our bicycles – all outdoor kind of pursuits – and really had a splendid time. I liked him – as straight as you or I really. But then you'd go into the town – they lived near Freiburg, which is a picture-postcard Black Forest town – and you'd see all these swastikas all over the place and Nazis left, right and centre and that made you sit up a bit. It was quite intimidating.'

Spears smiled ruefully. 'A bit different from England.'

'You can say that again,' agreed Farrish. 'At home you see the odd bobby in his inoffensive odd-shaped helmet and armed with nothing more than a truncheon, but over there you'd see soldiers and police with all sorts of firearms. The swastika just looks sinister too.'

'I suppose it does,' agreed Spears. 'Blood red and that strange black symbol.'

'Apparently it's an old Norse rune,' said Farrish. 'Or so my German family told me. But it wasn't just the flags, to be honest. There were also posters up all over the place, with anti-Jewish proclamations and occasionally you'd see a shop that had been forcibly shut down and you'd realize the owners had been Jewish. That made you feel a bit uncomfortable too. And then there was the radio – Nazi marches blaring out and all this propaganda. Andreas's family liked what Hitler had done in terms of building up employment and improving things, but I wouldn't say they were die-hard Nazis or anything. Andreas used to call the radio "Goebbels's Gob" after the Nazi propaganda man.' He chuckled at the memory.

'He's still shooting his gob off now,' said Spears.

'Yes. Most Germans seemed to believe every word he said, but coming from Britain where we're all a bit more questioning, I couldn't help wondering how much he was saying was actually just hot air.' He paused and scratched his eyebrow. 'Although, having said that, they seem to have lived up to their boasting so far.'

He put down the letter and rifled through the collection of *Soldbuchs*.

'Anything of any interest, sir?' asked Spears.

'Not much. These are their paybooks. They were all from the Fifty-seventh Panzer Pioneer Battalion. *Pionere*,' he pronounced. 'That's what the Jerries call engineers. These chaps were all sappers, Spears.'

Farrish bundled them together. 'I should get these up to Battalion.' He looked out of the window. 'It's getting dark but we should probably do that tonight. Send Braithwaite, will you?'

'Yes, sir.' Spears paused a moment then added, 'I know he's the platoon runner, sir, but do you think we should send someone else with him?'

'Yes, good idea. Sort that out, then I suggest you try and get some kip. Jerry might have pulled back today, but I doubt that's the last we'll see of him. We all need to get what rest we can while we can.'

Spears nodded, and pushed back his chair.

'And, Sergeant?' said Farrish as Spears stood up.

'Sir?'

'Well done today. You did well. Really well. We're lucky to have you in this platoon.'

Spears nodded again in acknowledgement then took his leave and stepped back out into the yard.

It was only when he had found Braithwaite and Stubbs and was about to give them the bundle of German papers that he realized there were nine rather than ten *Soldbuchs*. He thought for a moment, but then decided to send the two men on their way immediately. There was still some light but not much and it would help the men to make the most of what still remained without delay. However, having sent them off, he then went looking for Hawke.

He found him in the orchard at the back of the farm. As he approached, Hawke saw him and quickly tried to hide what was in his hands.

'Give them to me,' said Spears, holding out his hand.

'What, Sergeant?' said Hawke.

'What you took from the German you shot earlier.'

Hawke paused for a moment, his young face downcast, then slowly held out the collection.

Spears looked through them briefly then took out a box of matches and, cupping his hands, struck one and set the flame against the bundle.

'What are you doing?' said Hawke in alarm.

Spears ignored him, watching the flames rise and carefully holding the collection between his finger and thumb. The photographs curled and blackened. Then he said, 'I'm doing you a favour.' He glanced across at Hawke who was now standing beside him, an expression of anguish across his face.

'First,' said Spears, 'you were supposed to hand these in. I could have you put on a charge for that. Second, it'll do you no good looking at these things.' He let go of the burning booklets and dropped them on to the grass, then turned to face the boy. 'Look,' he said, 'the first one is always the worst, but you've got to forget him now. You wouldn't be here now if you hadn't killed him.' He clapped Hawke on the arm. 'Go and find the others. Talk to them, put what happened out of your mind and then get some kip.'

Hawke nodded.

'Good lad. Now, be off with you.'

Hawke turned. 'Thank you, Tom.'

'Thank you, *Sergeant*.'

Spears watched him go and sighed, then ran his hands through his hair and rubbed his eyes. *That boy*, he thought. He had better things to think about than to be wasting time worrying about Johnny Hawke. Spears tramped through the orchard, the scent on the air fresh and crisp, then checked the sentries. Tobacco smoke and the faint whiff of food drifted across the yard. Men were huddled in the outbuildings or talking quietly. Spears looked up into the sky now twinkling with the first stars, then headed back into the farmhouse.

'Ah, Spears,' said Farrish as he entered the kitchen. 'You're still up? Well, I'm going to turn in myself, if that's all right with you.'

'Of course, sir,' said Spears. He was quite relieved. Farrish was all right – he liked him well enough and he was certainly better than some subalterns he had served under. He made sure everyone knew he was the officer and commander of the platoon, but at the same time he was not too proud to take advice. Spears was grateful for that, but at the same time, it did mean that the lieutenant leaned on him heavily, dependent on his greater experience. That meant that for so much of his time Spears had to make sure the men were all right, and that Lieutenant Farrish was all right, and that everyone knew what they were supposed to be doing and that morale was as good as possible and that no one was shirking. It was a relief to have a few moments to himself at last. A few moments in which he could reread his letters from Maddie and then write a few lines to her himself.

The last mail had come on 9 May, a day before the battle had begun, and there had been five for him then, written over a week. Most talked of life at the farm where she was now working as a Land Girl. Spears had been brought up in the country, within shouting distance of the sea at Scarborough, but Maddie's family were townsfolk. It made him smile to think of her on a farm and to read about her wonderment at the sights and sounds and smells she was facing daily. Her freshness – her genuine goodness – was one of the things that had attracted him to her in the first place. She was appreciating the seasons more, she told him – and who wouldn't after the winter they had just had? By God, Spears thought to himself, it had certainly been cold, but it was summer now, and although the nights were still chill, the days were long and mostly warm. There had only been a couple of days' rain since the Germans had attacked.

He thought of Maddie and wished he could be with her – wished he could see her gentle oval face with her deep brown eyes and dark, almost black hair. It was uncanny how much her young brother looked like her, but in many ways that just made it worse. Maddie was closer to him because of Johnny and yet tantalizingly as far away as ever. Worse than that, having him in the platoon reminded him of just how beloved the youngest member of the Hawke family was. How they would never forgive him if anything happened to Johnny. Oh, he knew they would never openly blame him, that Maddie would say that it was their fault that he had joined up in the first place, but they *would* blame him all the same. Of course they would. It would be impossible not to. No one would ever mention it, but it would be there, lurking underneath, gnawing away at them all.

They had put him on a pedestal, he knew: Maddie, then Johnny, then the rest of the family, just like they had their long-dead father. Spears tried to be a good person, to do the best by his family, his men and Maddie, but he did not believe he was the hero that Hawkes seemed to think he was.

And yet he did feel partly responsible for Johnny's joining the army. If only he had been more discreet, and had talked less of his adventures in India and elsewhere. Johnny had lapped up every word – and he, the older man, had enjoyed it, glad to have an appreciative audience. How could he have known then that Johnny would run away, and with a new name and a packet of lies behind him, to join the army? And not any old regiment but the Yorks Rangers. Spears shook his head – it had never occurred to him last summer that a fifteen-year-old would do such a thing.

He had been on his way to France by the time he had learned what had happened. Johnny had sent them a letter, which had arrived after two days of mounting panic back at their home in Headingley. Once in France there had been little Spears had been able to do. Maddie had appealed to him as though he alone possessed the ability, wherewithal and influence to get their little brother home, but, without a name or even a hint of where he was, that had been impossible.

And so it had continued through the autumn and winter. While neither Germany nor the western powers had seemed prepared to make the first move, the war had developed into a waiting game – and that was all he could tell Maddie and her family to do too. So long as Johnny was training and the war was quiet, they had nothing to worry about. *But what if the fighting begins?* Maddie had written to him. *It hasn't yet*, Spears had replied sometime in the middle of April. *They're not going to send boys like him over here, so try not to worry.*

But then they had. A savage winter in tented accommodation had taken its toll on the battalion. Three men had been invalided out with a combination of pneumonia and severe frostbite in B Company alone. That had been back in February and March and then, weeks after the requests for replacements had been made, three new recruits had arrived out of the blue, straight from training down in Kent. It had been 1 May and suddenly there was Johnny Hawke, one of the new boys, clambering down from a fifteen hundredweight truck, a big grin on his face and saying, 'Tom, hey, Tom!'

It made Spears wince to think about it even now. Seeing Johnny like that had made him freeze. For a moment he'd been barely able to move or speak.

'Johnny,' he had said at last in a low voice, 'what the hell are you doing here?'

'I joined up, didn't you know?'

'Oh yes, I knew all right, but I didn't know you'd join the Rangers. And I didn't know you were coming here.'

Hawke had still been grinning from ear to ear. 'A stroke of luck, though, joining B Company. I really hoped I'd be with you and now I am. I can't believe it!'

'Johnny, you're *fifteen*! What the hell were you thinking?'

The boy's face had suddenly looked crestfallen. 'I'm not. I was sixteen yesterday. Aren't you pleased to see me?'

'No, Johnny, I'm not. Your family have been worried sick. We're at war here – this is no place for boys.'

He could see Hawke swallowing hard, the hurt etched across his face.

'But I've proved myself,' he said. 'I went through training just like anyone else. I've worked hard. I'm a good shot. I'll prove it to you, Tom.'

'No you won't,' Tom told him. 'You're coming with me. Training doesn't mean anything – it's experience that counts and you haven't got any – not of life and certainly not of being a soldier.'

'What do you mean? Where are we going?'

'I'm taking you to see the platoon and company commanders and then I'm going to make sure you get put on the first boat home.'

'No!' Hawke exclaimed. 'No, Tom, you can't! I'm old enough now. Please, Tom, please, let me stay – I won't let you down, I promise I won't.'

'Don't make promises you can't keep. You're not old enough.' He turned and looked at him. 'You don't know anything,' he growled, 'and it's not Tom – it's Sergeant Spears to you, Private, and you'll do as you're damn well told.'

Lieutenant Farrish had been of much the same opinion as Spears, as had Major Strickland, but the adjutant had insisted on referring the matter to the Battalion commander, Lieutenant-Colonel Beamish. However, the colonel had not been available to see them until the following afternoon, by which time Hawke had been allotted to McLaren's section – after all, that was why the replacements had been sent in the first place – and with a sinking heart Spears could see which way the wind was now blowing.

The interview between Major Strickland, Lieutenant Farrish and the Battalion commander was then put back a further day, by which time both men, although still broadly of the same opinion as Spears, had already got used to having Hawke around. It did not help that although Hawke looked young he was taller than most and, with his dark brows and the first signs of hair on his chin, certainly could pass for someone two or three years older. Yet whenever Spears looked at the boy all he saw was those deep brown eyes and an expression of enthusiastic and wide-eyed innocence.

*Damn it*, he had thought, *he doesn't stand a chance.*

On his return from meeting the colonel, Farrish had taken Spears aside, away from the collection of bell tents where the company was bivouacked, although the sergeant already knew what he was going to say.

'Look, I'm sorry, Tom,' Farrish told him.

Spears had closed his eyes and pinched his brow, worried that the anger and frustration welling within him would boil over if he spoke.

'We did point out that Hawke was young, that he had lied about his age and that he had also given himself a false name, but I'm afraid instead of taking a dim view of this, the colonel seemed rather taken by the lad's determination and pluck. He also told us that Brigade is expecting the Germans to launch an attack in the next month or so. He said that if we sent Hawke back, the chances are we'd simply be one man less, as getting replacements seems to be such a palaver – and you have to admit he has a point. It took the best part of two months for the last lot to turn up. He also pointed out that Hawke was desperate to do his duty and he told us he was inclined to repay that kind of determination. When Major Strickland pointed out that the lad was just sixteen, he laughed and said the army had a long history of taking on boy soldiers.'

Spears nodded silently.

'Most of them *are* young, Spears,' said Farrish. 'We all are. I'm only twenty-one myself. A lot of the chaps are only eighteen. Does it really make any difference whether he's sixteen, seventeen or eighteen?'

'He doesn't know anything,' muttered Spears.

'Do any of those other lads? They're brought up in the backstreets of Leeds and Bradford and that's the only world they know and then they join the army. They know how to crawl, climb six-foot walls, how to march, how to strip and fire a Short Magazine Lee Enfield. They know how to obey orders. We're all new to this, Spears – yourself and a precious few others excepted. Hardly anyone in this platoon has fired a weapon in anger. Private Hawke is really no different.'

Spears sighed. 'No, I suppose not, sir.'

'And when Colonel B asked us whether we wanted to lose one of our platoon I'm afraid to say that we both admitted we did not. He said that in that case we should accept him and leave it at that. The lad is of legal age now and none of us feel that prosecuting him for lying is much use if the Germans really are about to attack.'

'He's my fiancée's younger brother, sir. If anything happened to him . . .' He let the sentence trail.

Farrish put a hand on Spears's shoulder. 'I'm sorry, Tom, but he's staying. I could try to swap him with one of the other companies' new chaps if you like . . .?'

Spears shook his head, as Farrish well knew he would. If the boy was not to be sent home then of course he had to remain in B Company. At least Spears could *try* to keep him out of trouble.

'All right, sir,' said Spears at last. 'If that's the colonel's decision, I'll just have to live with that. I just hope the day never comes when I have to tell his family that their boy is not coming home.'

'We none of us want that for any of the men. But we're not conscripted men here, Sergeant. All of us volunteered. We chose to answer the call to duty, and that applies to Hawke too.'

Now, three weeks on, the battle had begun, and so far Hawke had survived – he had lived through a few artillery barrages, several attacks by enemy aircraft and, earlier that day, when face to face with the enemy not ten yards from him, he had not frozen as some might well have done, but had shot first and killed a man. He'd done well – Spears had to admit that to himself, but the boy should never have volunteered to get that pilot in the first place. He knew Hawke was only trying to prove himself, but Spears wished to God he would not. If he had to be part of this platoon, then why the hell couldn't the boy keep his head down and try to survive, like most of the lads?

Spears stood up, grabbed the bottle of Calvados standing on the dresser against the wall and poured himself a generous glass. Leaning one hand on the dresser, he drank, and the spirit fired down his throat. He gasped, ran his hands through his hair, then poured himself another generous inch and sat back down at the table. Feeling inside his battle blouse, he delved into the deep pocket and pulled out the bundle of Maddie's letters. No doubt there were many more now, waiting in some sack in a depot somewhere, or maybe sitting in the back of a truck, but there was no chance of delivering them at present, not when they barely knew what day it was or where they were themselves. Instead, he would have to make do with looking at his one photograph of her, taken the day they'd become engaged, and the last letter he had received, dated 6 May. It had arrived on the morning of Friday 10 May, the day the Germans had attacked and just before they'd left to move up towards the River Dyle. Carefully, he tugged the thin blue paper from the envelope, unfolding the sheets and turning to the end first: *All my love and more, Maddie*, written in that by now so familiar, slanting loop.

He had, of course, written immediately Johnny had joined the company and with unusual swiftness it had taken just nine days for her reply.

> *I don't know whether to feel relieved or that our worst fears have been realized. Uncle Richard seems convinced that the Germans will attack now it's May. It looks like Mr Chamberlain is going to have to stand down as prime minister. I managed to speak with home today and Uncle Richard was convinced that Hitler will make the most of the mess the*

*government's in and attack, and now Johnny's going to be caught up in it, and you too, my darling. I've dreaded it for so long. I worry about you constantly but at least you know how to look after yourself. Johnny is just a boy. I'll never forgive myself if anything happens to him. Never.*

Spears sighed again, then banged his fist down hard on the table. *Damn him!* he thought. He looked back at the letter.

*Try to keep him out of trouble, won't you? I know you have all the other men to look after, but with you to watch over him at least he might have a chance. The thought of little Johnny being confronted by those evil Nazis makes my blood run cold.*

She ended the letter by telling him how much she was missing him, more than ever. She wondered where he was, what he was doing.

*When I'm out in the fields, or lying in my bed at night, I dream of the future, my darling Tom. A future that will be shared with you, and a time when there is no more war.*

Spears looked forward to that day too. When the war was over, he had already made his mind up that he would leave the army. More than anything in the world he wanted to be with Maddie, to look after her properly and to raise a family together, not drag her to godforsaken army camps or to far-flung corners of the Empire. No, he would buy a small farm, somewhere near the Yorkshire coast, with the sight of the sea and the green of the moors. Ever since Maddie had told him that she had joined the Land Army, it was a fantasy he had clung to – one he had not shared with a living soul.

God only knew whether he would survive the war – whether they would ever get out of Cassel – but Johnny Hawke's arrival, it seemed to him, had lessened the odds of that future being realized, and he resented him for that. He could not help it. Before Johnny had turned up, Spears had had one person to look after, one person to keep alive, and that was himself. Yes, he had a responsibility to all the men, but that was not the same thing. But since Johnny had turned up, his eager face smiling with excitement, that had changed. And while Tom Spears reckoned his own odds of survival were better than most, he could not say the same for a sixteen-year-old straight out of training.

Tom Spears rubbed his eyes, sipped his Calvados and then folded the letter and put it back in its envelope. Brooding would not help, however. The lieutenant was right: he should get some kip. He took himself into the sitting room, lay down on an old settee and closed his eyes.

*He hasn't got a chance*, he thought to himself. *Not a damned chance.*

# 10

## SHATTERED DREAMS

Sunday 26 May, around one o'clock in the afternoon. Half of 1 Section lay beneath the apple trees in the orchard, the warm early summer sun bearing down upon them, so that they had shed their battle blouses and rolled up their shirt sleeves. The five men had been stood down from picquet duty half an hour earlier, swapping with the other half of the section, and had wasted no time in preparing some food and tea. Rations had been officially cut by half the day before, but the platoon was better placed than most to supplement the now meagre supplies handed out by B Echelon. Hebden and a few others had organized regular milking teams, while one of the beasts had been slaughtered and its skinned and gutted carcass now hung in neatly sliced sections in a shed at the back of the farmhouse.

Now, Hawke was serving up large chunks of beef that he had fried and roughly hacked into five individual slices, along with a slab of what Hebden called his 'finest Yorkshire pudding' – a concoction he had made with fresh milk, some flour from the mill and a couple of eggs he had found under the chicken shed, and then fried, rather than baked, on the Primus.

'There you go,' said Hebden, a large grin on his face, 'Sunday best. A meal fit for kings: steak, Yorkshire pud and a cup of char. What could be finer?'

'A glass of beer wouldn't go amiss,' said McLaren.

'And some gravy,' said White.

'Never happy, are you?' said Hebden. 'What a miserable lot.' He took a bite of his beef and Yorkshire pudding and rolled his eyes in mock ecstasy. 'What d'you reckon, Johnny? I think we've done ourselves proud.'

Hawke grinned. 'I agree, Bert. I've not had a finer meal since I set foot in France.'

'Since last Monday, then,' said Drummond. Everyone laughed.

'I meant since leaving England,' said Hawke, 'and probably before that, now I think about it.'

'You know what?' said Hebden. 'Between us we've got quite a lot of skills, haven't we? I mean, I know we're all regular soldiers, but most of us wouldn't be if it weren't for the war.'

'Speak for yourself,' said McLaren. 'I've been in seven years.'

'All right, you excepted, Corp,' continued Hebden, 'but I grew up on a farm, Wainwright in Three Section used to be a butcher – he made a good job of that cow, didn't he? Chalkie was a builder, weren't you, Chalkie?'

'A brickie really. I couldn't do plastering or anything like that.'

'Actually, now I think about it,' said McLaren, 'I used to work in a garage before I joined up. Four years I did. In a little garage out on the Harrogate Road.'

'Whereabouts?' asked White.

'Potternewton. It was a great little place. A bit cramped but you got to work on all sorts: cars, motorcycles, trucks. The lot – although it was bikes that I liked most. The boss was all right too, and there was another lad who I'd been at school with. We had quite a laugh really.'

'Why aren't you in the RASC, then, Corp?' asked Drummond.

'Because I thought that if I joined the army I should be a proper soldier in a proper regiment.'

'So what made you join the army in the first place, Corp?' asked Hawke.

'Because I was young and stupid,' grinned McLaren. 'I was getting a bit restless and sick of cars and being covered in oil all the time. I thought I'd like to see something of the world. To get away.'

'But you could still be a mechanic if you had to be?' said Hebden.

'Course,' said McLaren. 'I'll have you know I could strip an engine and put it back together by the time I was Johnny's age.'

Hawke glanced at McLaren.

'Just making a point, Johnny,' said McLaren. 'Blimey, anyone would think you were a bit sensitive about your age or something.'

The men laughed again and Hawke felt his cheeks flush.

'Anyway,' said McLaren, 'did you have time to have a job before you joined up, Johnny? Got any skills we should know about.'

'No – not really,' said Hawke. 'I did have a job after school, though. I worked at a textile machinery factory in Leeds.'

'Why d'you end up there?' asked White.

'My stepfather was foreman there. He got me the job. I hated it.'

'So you thought you'd join the army instead,' said McLaren.

Hawke nodded. 'Pretty much.' He wondered whether he should say more, but something made him go on. 'My father used to be in the army. Or, rather, he was in the last war.'

'Like everyone else,' said White.

'What happened to him?' asked Hebden. 'If you don't mind me asking?'

'He died before I was born,' said Hawke. 'He was gassed at Passchendaele – only it took a few years to kill him.'

'Living in Leeds can't have helped,' said White. 'God knows, the air's bad enough there.'

'It's worse in Bradford,' said Foxton.

'I'm sorry,' said Hebden. 'My old man avoided it, being a farmer, but I know there was a lot of lads from the village didn't make it back.'

'Jack Ibbotson's dad was killed in the last war too,' said McLaren. 'He doesn't talk about it, though.'

Hawke wondered whether to tell them about what his father had done, and the hero he had been. But then Hebden said, 'But you do have skills, Johnny,' and Hawke looked at him quizzically.

'Cricket,' said Hebden. 'You're a good cricketer, aren't you? Play in the leagues.'

Hawke smiled bashfully. 'I don't know that you'd call it skill.'

'Course it is,' said Hebden, then, looking at the others, said, 'He's already played for Kirkstall firsts last summer. Got a fifty and two five-wicket hauls too.'

'It wasn't much,' Hawke mumbled.

'Stop it, Bert,' said McLaren. 'You're embarrassing the lad.'

'I'm just saying he's obviously got some talent.' He clapped

Hawke on the back. 'You'll have to play for Yorkshire one day, Johnny. When this is all over.'

'Would you want to?' asked Drummond.

'Of course he would,' said McLaren. 'What a stupid question, Charlie. More to the point, do you think you ever could, Johnny?'

Hawke looked sheepish. 'I don't know. It's a big leap from playing in the Yorkshire League to playing for the county. I'm not sure I'll ever be good enough.'

'And now there's this ruddy war,' said McLaren. 'Still, we've all got to have dreams.'

It was a dream Hawke had cherished ever since first falling in love with the game as a seven-year-old. Ever since watching his first match at Headingley. He had Uncle Richard to thank for that.

'And he lives right next to Headingley,' added Hebden, as though reading Hawke's thoughts.

Hawke nodded.

'Oh, well, of course he's going to love cricket, living right next door to one of the world's finest cricket grounds,' said White, then added, 'What about you, Bert? What's your dream? What do you want to do when this is over?'

'I don't know. Probably go back to the farm. I like making things, though, so maybe I'll become a furniture maker.' He smiled. 'Yes, that's what I'll do. That would be a respectable and worthwhile way to spend my life.'

'That's another one,' said McLaren. 'Another skill in the platoon.'

'A skill that would need honing,' Hebden smiled.

'What about you, Chalkie?' asked Hawke.

White shrugged. 'I don't know. I can't think that far ahead. I love football, but I could never make it as a professional.'

'I want to play for Sheffield United,' said Drummond. 'That's my dream. Don't get me wrong, Johnny, I like cricket well enough, but for me it's always been football. Bramall Lane, not Headingley.'

'Are you any good?' asked White.

Drummond shrugged.

'That means he is,' said McLaren. 'Come on, don't be modest, Charlie.'

'I think I might be all right,' said Drummond. 'At least, I nearly had a trial anyway.'

'That's amazing, Charlie,' said Hawke. 'I knew you were a United supporter, but I didn't realize –'

'Hang on a minute,' interrupted Hebden. 'You nearly had a trial? Why didn't you, then?'

'I joined the army. You see, I didn't think I was going to get one so I took the King's shilling and then the letter arrived after I'd already gone to Pirbright.'

'Why didn't you do a runner?' asked White.

'I thought about it, honestly, I really did. But it would have got me in all sorts of trouble, and if they knew I'd run away from the army I thought they probably wouldn't take me anyway.'

Hebden shook his head in wonder. 'Blow me, Charlie. How long have we been together? You kept that one quiet.'

'Bit of a dark horse, isn't he?' said McLaren.

'To be honest,' said Drummond, 'I try not to think about it too much. It's too depressing. What might have been.'

'What position did you play?' asked Hawke.

'Midfield,' said Drummond, then he grinned. 'I once kept a football off the ground for two hundred and fifteen kicks.'

'Really?' said Hawke, impressed. 'Maybe you'll get another chance, Charlie.'

'Maybe,' said Drummond. His brow knotted. 'We've got to get out of this place first and then win the damned war.'

'I think I prefer dreaming,' said Hebden.

'But that's all it is, isn't it?' retorted Drummond. 'A dream.' He sighed. 'I can't tell you how often I wish I hadn't ever joined up. Or that this stupid war hadn't ever started.'

'But then you wouldn't have met us,' said Hebden. 'And that *would* have been a tragedy.'

Everyone laughed, and Hawke thought how glad he was that he had joined 1 Section, with men he already liked to think of as friends – Hebden and Drummond in particular. He couldn't imagine the platoon without those two.

They were quiet for a moment as they finished their meal. A bee buzzed lazily nearby, while house martins chirruped as they darted in and out from the eaves of the barn roof and swirled around the sky above the farm.

'Ah, this is the life,' said McLaren, pushing his mess tin to one side and lying back down in the grass. 'Can someone please tell Jerry to stay away. I'm not in the mood for fighting.'

'I can't imagine Jerry ever coming back now,' said Hawke. The day before, they had begun the morning still on edge, expecting the sound of artillery any moment, but as the hours had passed so the mood had relaxed. As Hebden had pointed out, they could not be on edge *all* the time. Another night had passed with no telltale sounds of revving engines or squeaking tank tracks, and still none all that morning. Picquet duty had been a stultifying affair – ahead of them, the French countryside had been relentlessly still. An occasional deer, a few rabbits and the melodious sound of birdsong and that had been all they had seen or heard to their front. Overhead, enemy aircraft had passed and just occasionally, when the breeze changed, they could faintly hear guns to the north, but otherwise it was as though the war, so violent and explosive just a couple of days earlier, had melted away.

'I know what you mean, Johnny,' said White, 'but I can promise you something: he will be back. We ain't done with fighting yet.'

At that, the now familiar lurch in Hawke's stomach returned.

A moment later, Hawke heard a rumble and the sound of squeaking tracks and immediately sat up, feeling for his rifle.

Drummond laughed. 'Bit jumpy, eh, Johnny?'

'Tank tracks,' blurted Hawke.

'Carrier tracks,' replied Drummond.

Hawke breathed a sigh of relief. 'That made me start,' he said, standing up. The rumble became louder and then down the track through the orange clay dust, a Bren carrier appeared. They were all getting to their feet now, even McLaren.

'Curse him,' said the corporal. 'I was just nodding off there.'

The carrier cut through the lane to the edge of the orchard and squeaked and rumbled on into the yard. Hawke and the others followed, curiosity getting the better of them.

Lieutenant Farrish and Sergeant Spears were already beside the vehicle as the driver cut its engine. One of the men jumped down, went round to the back, opened the rear door and took out a single wooden ammunition box.

'Is that it?' said Farrish.

'Sorry, sir,' said the man, a corporal.

'What happened to the rest of it?' said Spears. 'Don't tell me you've come down with just one box of ammo for each platoon.'

'It's with the rest of your lot,' replied the corporal.

'That's hardly fair, sir,' said Spears.

'No,' said Farrish. 'No, it's not.' He turned to the corporal. 'Are you heading back up to town?'

'Yes, sir,' said the corporal.

'All right, then let me come with you. You can take me to Company HQ first, and then if Major Strickland can't divvy out the wares a bit more evenly, then we'll have to try with Battalion.' He turned to Spears. 'Happy to hold the fort here for the moment, Sergeant?'

'Yes, sir,' said Spears.

Farrish looked around him. 'I need a few volunteers,' then seeing McLaren and his half-section, said, 'Corporal, since you're stood down, you can give me three of your men.'

'I'll go, Corp,' said Hawke quickly.

'Come on then, Charlie,' said Hebden to Drummond, 'we'd better keep the boy company.'

'Privates Hawke, Drummond and Hebden, sir,' said McLaren.

Farrish nodded. 'Thanks, chaps. Right, let's go.'

Since the arrival of Somer Force, B Company had been redeployed. While 6th Platoon had stayed at the farm, the remaining three platoons had moved from Bavinchove and the Hazebrouck road to the village of Oxelaëre, and it was in a house near the church that the company now had its headquarters. The driver started up the engine once more as the four Rangers clambered into the back, and then in a swirl of dust, growling engine and squeaking tracks, headed back out of the yard.

They reached Company Headquarters a short while later, which had been set up in brick-tiled house opposite the village church.

'Just wait here a moment, will you?' said Farrish to the driver, then turned to the others. 'You stay here too. I won't be a moment.'

Hawke looked up at the church and saw the muzzle of a Bren poking out from a narrow window in the belfry.

'Looks like they've got it covered here,' said Hebden, following his gaze. 'At least we'll all have a bit of warning when Jerry decides to make his move.'

From a horse chestnut at the corner of the church, its pink blossom bright against the deep green of the newly emerged leaves, a wood pigeon cooed. The bird's rhythmic song was suddenly cut out by the arrival of a motorbike, which pulled up beside them outside Company Headquarters. With barely a glance at them, the rider got off and hurried inside.

'He's in a bit of a rush,' said Drummond.

'DRs,' said Hebden. 'It's their job to be in a rush. Don't ever be a despatch rider, Johnny.'

'Why not? I'd have thought riding a motorbike all day would be fun.'

'Dangerous,' said Drummond. 'Very dangerous.'

'No one ever really knows where you are, you see,' said Hebden. 'So, if you get into trouble, you're on your own. Much better to have your mates around you.'

A short while later, Farrish reappeared, putting on his cap as he strode towards them.

'Damn it all,' he muttered.

'On up to town, then, sir?' asked the corporal.

'Yes,' said Farrish. 'Straight to Battalion HQ.'

'What did Major Strickland say, sir?' asked Hebden.

'He hadn't realized that Fifth, Seventh and Eighth Platoons had taken the lion's share, but apparently it was not very much anyway. He's given me a note to give to Colonel Beamish pleading for some more.'

'Is there any chance of that, sir?' asked Hebden.

'In a fair world, yes, but it's not is it?' Farrish snapped. 'We're all in it together, Hebden, but everyone's still looking after their own. The fact of the matter is that we're very probably going to be the first to face Jerry when he attacks, so I'm damned if we should be the last to get any more ammunition. I'm afraid our supplies have always been inadequate – that was understandable before reinforcements arrived, but I'm not going to let our platoon become lambs to the slaughter if we don't need to be.'

The three others were silent for a moment, then Hawke said, 'Is it as bad as that, then, sir?'

'I don't want to alarm you, Hawke, but, since you asked, let me put it this way: when Jerry attacks, he'll probably have a division or more. That's some fourteen or fifteen thousand men. And our company is one of the first lines of defence – just over a hundred men. I'd call that quite bad, wouldn't you?'

Hawke felt the blood drain from his face. He swallowed hard and looked at Hebden and Drummond.

'That's not *bad*,' muttered Drummond. 'That's suicide.'

# 11

## FORTRESS CASSEL

In the two days since the three privates had last been in Cassel, the town had been turned into a fortress. Approaching roads had been blocked with stone and rubble and blasted with explosives to create anti-tank ditches. Wire had been laid too, and trees felled, so that of the five roads that had led into the town, only one now remained open to traffic. That way involved passing through a narrow access way along which further defences lay ready to be implemented the moment the need arose.

From the houses that rose around the edge of the town, narrow firing slits had been hacked out of the walls. Hawke looked around him, amazed at the transformation. The words of both Lieutenant Farrish and Drummond were still sharp in his mind. He wondered whether, if they ever had a chance to fall back from the farm at Oxelaëre, they would be able to get back behind the walls of the town, or whether they really would be sacrificed. He tried to put the thoughts to the back of his mind, but the sudden realization of the overwhelming odds that were stacked against them had descended on him like a heavy, dull shroud of dread that he could not shrug off. Just half an hour earlier he had been sitting in the orchard about as content as at any moment since joining the army. He wished he could return to that moment of oblivious innocence, but it was gone. Gone forever.

The only open approach led them back up around Dead Horse Corner, where a twenty-five-pounder had been set up looking back down the hill, as well as two machine-gun posts. Sentries waved them through, the carrier belching a cloud of thick, choking exhaust fumes as the driver put it into gear and opened the throttle. In the back, the four Rangers were jostled and jolted as the machine rattled over the cobbles. At the next corner, another mound of rubble lay across most of the road. On they went, down a narrow, straight road and then they finally reached the main square, now busy with a number of light tanks, carriers, trucks and other vehicles. There was still rubble in the square from where several buildings had been damaged earlier, but of the civilians they had seen when they'd first arrived two days earlier, there was now no sign. Hawke wondered what had happened to them.

As the carrier finally stopped outside Battalion Headquarters, firing could be heard from several directions and even a burst of Bren fire.

'I'm glad someone's got enough bullets to spare,' muttered Farrish as they stepped out of the carrier. The lieutenant hurried into Headquarters then half a minute later reappeared.

'Typical,' he said. 'The colonel's not here.'

'Shall we wait, sir?' asked Drummond.

Farrish looked at the corporal from Headquarters. 'Can you wait, Corporal?'

'Sir,' came the reply.

They did not have to wait long. Less than five minutes later, Colonel Beamish appeared from the road behind them that led up to the mount, the summit of the town, with several other officers beside him.

'He looks senior, sir,' muttered Hebden, nodding to the man beside the colonel now striding towards them.

'A brigadier,' said Farrish.

'Now's your chance, then, sir,' said Hebden.

Farrish smiled. 'Nothing ventured, eh, Hebden?'

'My thoughts precisely, sir.'

As the small delegation neared, Farrish stepped forward, blocking the doorway into Battalion HQ, and smartly saluted. 'Excuse me, Colonel – and, Brigadier,' he said, 'but I've just come from Oxelaëre.'

'What is it, Lieutenant?' said Beamish, a touch of irritation in his voice.

'We're very low on ammunition, sir,' said Farrish.

Beamish chuckled mirthlessly.

'It's just that, sir, we're going to be the first to face the enemy, and yet we seem to be last in the pecking order for extra ammo. So far we've received just one box of point three-oh-three.' He cleared his throat. 'It's demoralizing, sir, to think we're being thrown to the wolves. To think we don't have a chance in hell.'

The brigadier stepped forward. 'What's your name, Lieutenant?'

'Lieutenant Farrish, sir, commander of Sixth Platoon, B Company, the First Battalion, King's Own Yorkshire Rangers, sir.'

The brigadier held out his hand. 'I'm Brigadier Somerset,' he said. 'As of last night, I'm in command here. B Company is occupying Oxelaëre – that's right, isn't it?'

'Yes, sir,' said Colonel Beamish. 'A carrier with a supply of ammunition was sent down there earlier.'

'But not very much, sir,' said Farrish. 'Major Strickland asked me to give you this, sir.' He passed Strickland's note to the colonel.

'These are some of your men, Lieutenant?' Somerset asked Farrish, looking at the three privates now standing to attention behind their officer.

'Yes, sir,' said Farrish. 'Privates Hawke, Hebden and Drummond.'

The brigadier shook their hands in turn. 'Bit young, aren't you?' he said, looking at Hawke.

'Private Hawke has a strong sense of duty, sir,' said Farrish. 'He killed a German two days ago and helped rescue a downed RAF pilot.'

'Did you indeed?' said Somerset. 'Good for you.' He turned back to Farrish. 'We're all short of ammunition, I'm afraid. But you're quite right – you should not be expected to face the Huns without your fair share, so we'll see to it you get some more. But I don't want you thinking you're being thrown to the wolves. You're there to check the enemy advance and buy us some time. That's the essence here: time. But at the point when you think you are about to be overrun, you pull out of there, you understand? Don't wait for DRs that may or may not get through. Use your initiative.' He turned to Beamish. 'Isn't that right, Colonel?'

'Absolutely, sir.'

'Good,' said Somerset. 'Now, what is it you think you need, Lieutenant?'

'Bren ammunition, sir,' said Farrish. 'And more two-inch mortars.'

'Might struggle with the mortars,' said Somerset, 'but we can get you another couple of boxes of Bren ammunition.' He turned to one of the staff officers beside him. 'See to it, will you?'

'Thank you, sir,' said Farrish.

'I like a man who fights his corner,' said the brigadier, 'and shows a bit of initiative. Good luck, chaps. I know you won't let anyone down.'

As Brigadier Somerset turned and stepped into the building, Beamish paused and winked. 'Wait here a moment, Farrish,' he said, 'and I'll give you a note for Major Strickland. Just remember what the brigadier said: don't leave it too late before pulling back. Judge the moment, all right?'

Farrish nodded, then, when the party had all stepped inside, breathed out heavily.

'Well done, sir,' said Hebden. 'It's always worth going straight to the top, I always find.'

'Yes, well, I suppose it's better than nothing. And at least our orders are a bit clearer.'

But they did not seem that much clearer to Hawke. He could not imagine how they would know when the right moment to pull back had arrived. If the full force of the German advance was bearing down upon them, they might physically be unable to move at all. And, judging from the lieutenant's expression, the platoon commander was just as unsure.

'Told you,' muttered Drummond quietly. 'We've been dealt the short straw, all right.'

Having consulted with Colonel Beamish, Brigadier Somerset headed back across Grand Place, and up the cobbled road to

Mount Cassel, where he had moved his headquarters. It was true that the Châtellerie de Schoebeque, where he had first met General Mason-Macfarlane, had been a wonderful building with fine views to the south, but there was another building on the Mount, formerly the gendarmerie, that served his purposes better. From there, he commanded an almost perfect all round view – not just to the south, but to the north, east and west as well. The facilities were certainly more spartan in the new HQ, but that was no matter: practicality was more important.

When he reached the building, he was met by Bullmore, a taut expression on his face.

'What is it, Harry?' he asked.

'A message from GHQ, sir.' Bullmore held the thin piece of paper out to the brigadier.

Somerset took it silently and walked on into the command room, a long gallery with views to the south. 'So we've got a date now,' he said to Bullmore. 'We're to hold out until the thirtieth.'

'Another four days. Somerset leaned on a large dining table, covered with maps and other papers, and drummed his fingers. He had spoken the truth when he'd told that subaltern from the Yorks Rangers that they were all short of ammunition – not just Somer Force, as his new command had been christened, but the entire BEF. After all, they were now almost completely surrounded, except for the port of Dunkirk, and preparations were being made to evacuate through there, not bring more supplies in. No, Somerset knew that there would not be any more ammunition coming their way. His force had to hold out with what they had – God willing, for another four days. It still struck him as incredible that the Germans had issued that extraordinary halt order. It defied all military logic – surely they cannot have thought the battered and beleaguered BEF posed much of a threat? British forces in France and Belgium amounted to just ten divisions. Ten! Compared with the hundred and forty-five the French had begun the battle with and the more than a hundred divisions the Germans must surely have!

The speed and brilliance of the Hun attack had certainly taken everyone by surprise but now the enemy troops to the south were frittering time away, and with every passing day – every passing hour – Somerset knew his chances of helping the rest of the British forces escape back through the narrow corridor behind them to the coast were improving.

'What's your hunch, Bully?' asked Somerset. 'Will the Huns hold off another day, or do you think we're already into borrowed time?'

'Do you want an honest answer or one that will improve your mood, sir?'

Somerset smiled and patted his tunic for his cigarette box. Finding it, he opened it and discovered he had just one cheroot left. Cursing to himself, he lit it all the same, the grey-blue smoke swirling around him.

'I fancy you're right,' he said at length.

'The defences look good,' said Bullmore. 'The men have worked hard. The remaining civilians have been moved out, cellars and ceilings strengthened. Cassel is more like a fortress than ever it has been since the Grand Old Duke of York's day.'

Somerset looked at the map again, complete with coloured pencil markings denoting the deployment of his forces. He now had three infantry battalions, albeit all under-strength to varying degrees. The Glosters were dug in and holding the west of the town, the Ox and Bucks the east, and the Yorks Rangers the centre. In addition to outposts at Oxelaëre, a company had been placed in each of the other villages to the south and west, at Bavinchove and Zuytpeene, and there was a platoon holding a French blockhouse on the flat ground a few miles to the north. Somerset tapped a pencil on the spot on the map. *Should he recall them*? he wondered. And yet that concrete blockhouse was holding the road to the north. The Germans might have large numbers of panzers, but an army still needed roads. Without roads for all the rest of their transport, they could make little progress. No, he would keep them where they were, he decided.

In addition to his infantry, he also had the carriers and light tanks of the Fife and Forfar Yeomanry and 1st East Riding Yeomanry, brigade engineers and a battery of nine anti-tank guns and fifteen two-pounders. These were hardly the most destructive of guns, but they were better than nothing and, handled well, they would be able to knock out some of the enemy tanks at least.

Brigadier Somerset stood up and stretched his back. 'I think we're safe for today,' he said. 'Jerry always likes to attack in the morning. But we've got to expect an attack tomorrow. It would be too much to hope for another day of quiet.'

'I agree, sir.'

'Do you think we can hold him, Bully?'

'I honestly don't know, sir.'

'One thing's for certain. It's going to be hard fight. A damned hard fight.' He wandered over to a sideboard and poured himself and Bullmore two stiff whiskies. 'Here's hoping we get through it, Bully,' he said, raising his glass, 'although I can't help feeling like a condemned man.'

'Your great-grandfather survived the Charge of the Light Brigade, sir.'

Somerset smiled. 'What? Are you suggesting I might have lucky genes?'

'Here's hoping, sir.'

'Luck,' said the brigadier and downed his whisky. 'We're going to need a barrelful of it.'

# 12

## THE ATTACK

Shortly after 7 a.m. on Monday 27 May, a formation of nine Stuka dive-bombers arrived in the skies over Cassel. From their positions at Oxelaëre, the men of 6th Platoon watched the aircraft circle, faint black dots in the sky at first, then peel off and dive, the engines whining and sirens screaming. Growing in size as they fell from the sky, they then pulled out of their dives, one after another, as a series of bombs fell over the town. In moments the bombs were exploding, the detonations causing trembles in the ground that could be felt even a mile away from where the Rangers were watching.

'I always thought we'd pulled the short straw being stuck out here,' muttered McLaren, watching from the back of the windmill, 'but now I'm not so sure.'

Hawke was standing beside Hebden at the top of the steps of the mill, by the open door. Since arriving at the farm they had been able to clearly see the town behind them, up beyond the line of woods and trees, perched on the top of the hill, standing sentinel over them. Now, however, it was disappearing behind a swirling, rising cloud of smoke. Another bomb exploded, a particularly loud crack. Hawke jerked a little.

Hebden grinned at him. 'That was a big one, Johnny, I'll admit.'

A loud crash of tumbling masonry could now be heard drifting down from the hill.

Hawke pulled his tin helmet a bit closer over his head.

Inside the windmill, McLaren counted off the Stukas one by one. In just a few minutes, the attack was over, the enemy planes turning and droning away eastwards until they were out of sight and then out of earshot too. Smoke continued to shroud Cassel, however.

'I wonder if this is the start of something,' said Hebden, turning back to face the woods away to their front.

As another pair of shells screamed overhead, Spears now strode across the yard towards the mill and began climbing the steps. 'All right, boys,' he said, 'the show's over. Let's keep watching the front, all right?'

No sooner had he said this than a shell whooshed overhead with a thunderous scream and exploded on the lower slopes of the town. Hawke instinctively ducked, then, with Hebden, quickly stepped back inside the mill, as though the wood-framed structure would give them any protection against such a missile. More shells followed in rapid succession, the charge of the field guns firing them reaching the ears of the men a couple of seconds later.

In the yard and the orchard to the rear, men were quickly getting to their feet, looking to the sky anxiously, grabbing webbing and rifles. Lieutenant Farrish had emerged from the farmhouse and rushed into the long barn facing south, while Sergeant Spears had run from the mill and was hurrying among the men, telling those off duty to quickly stand to. Returning a short moment later to the mill, Spears clambered up the stairs, stepped inside and, with his binoculars, moved to the window beside Ibbotson, who was manning the Bren.

'Do you think this is it, Sarge?' asked Drummond. 'D'you think Jerry's about to attack?'

Spears continued to peer through his binoculars, then eventually said in a quiet voice, 'Jerry's bombed Cassel from the air and now he's shelling the place. Now what do you think?'

The shelling continued, the guns firing from a broad front to the south.

Lieutenant Farrish appeared in the doorway, then ducked himself as another shell hurtled above them.

'Damn it,' he muttered, 'I could even see that one fly over.' A moment later it crashed into the hill behind them. 'They've not quite got the range yet.'

'They will, sir,' muttered Spears.

'Can you see anything, Sergeant?' asked Farrish.

'No, sir, but can you hear that – between the shells?' He cocked his ear slightly towards the direction of the woods to the south.

Farrish listened. So too did Hawke, standing up now behind Ibbotson and Spears. A faint squeak and a dull rumble. Hawke felt his mouth go dry.

'Tanks?' said Farrish.

'Yes, sir. Those field guns are firing over the advance. It won't be long now.' He looked at his watch. 'We shouldn't keep too many men up here, sir. A Bren team and someone keeping watch, but that should be it. A direct hit on this, and there won't be a lot left.'

Farrish stood still, his brows knotted, as though unsure what to do. 'Yes – yes, you're right, Sergeant,' he said at length. 'Let's keep a half-section here, and get the rest of the men into position around the barns and farmhouse.'

Spears nodded, then turned to McLaren. 'Sid, get Fletcher up here with White and Ibbotson, the rest of you down to the barn.'

McLaren nodded. 'Come on, you lot,' he said, 'you heard what the sarge said.'

Hawke followed the rest mutely out of the mill and across to the barn, his hands gripped tightly round his rifle. Firing slits had been cleared along the barn's long southern wall – the cement chipped away with their bayonets and the bricks pushed out. Sun was already streaming through these embrasures, highlighting the many dust particles floating idly in the still barn air. There were wooden cattle stalls along this far wall, and in the opposite corners lay a mass of old farming machinery and tools. It was from this barn that two days earlier they had pulled two wooden carts and, turning them over on to their sides, had used them as barricades across the main entrance into the yard.

Hawke stood beside a loophole in the wall and peered out. Nothing. Ahead stretched empty fields and the woods beyond. The cockerel crowed and somewhere from a tree nearby a wood pigeon cooed. As the minutes passed, so the nervous tension that had gripped them gradually melted away. Desultory artillery fire continued, but of the enemy there was not a sign.

The men soon became restless. After an hour, the lieutenant gave permission for one man in each section to prepare a brew of tea for the rest. After two hours, Hawke was struggling to stay awake. Staring out of his loophole, waiting for an enemy who seemed never to appear began to be mesmerizing. The sun was high and bright, the sky clear, and contrasted starkly with the gloom of the barn, so that he found it increasingly hard to focus on the outside world to their front.

But then, a little before 10.30 a.m., he was sure he saw something move in the woods some five hundred yards away.

'Bert, Charlie,' he hissed to Hebden and Drummond either side of him. 'Did you see that?'

'What?' said Drummond.

'Movement – in the wood,' said Hawke.

Drummond squinted through his hole in the wall. 'You're imagining things, Johnny.'

Just then they heard the hollow clunk of mortars being fired in rapid succession, followed by the whistle of the mortar shells hurtling through the air and then a rapid burst of machine-gun fire.

'Blimey!' exclaimed Drummond. Hawke instinctively ducked again, but most of the mortar shells landed away to their left, towards the main part of the village.

Yet more mortar shells followed and this time they were directed at the farm. The first two landed well forward of the farm, and were followed by another burst of raking machine-gun fire, which this time clattered against the barn, the bullets pinging and zipping as they ricocheted off the brickwork. More mortars came, this time much closer, while the third round hit the farmhouse and the roof of the barn with a deafening crash. Two men at the far end screamed, dust and smoke poured through the hole and wood and tiles clattered to the ground. Men began coughing and spluttering, while a corporal in 2 Section cursed, and yelled at his men to help those hit. Hawke glanced down the barn and saw one man sprawled on the floor, spotlighted by the shaft of bright sunshine pouring down through the now gaping hole in the roof.

For a moment, Hawke just stood and stared, unable to comprehend the speed with which that man had been cut down. His fingers tightened round his rifle. Glancing at Drummond, he saw his friend swallow hard. The barn reeked of cordite and smoke. Men were coughing and spluttering, and swearing angrily.

'Th-this is a hopeless position,' stammered Drummond. 'We haven't got a chance.'

'All right, steady, boys,' said Spears, now entering the barn. More mortars whistled down and Hawke was amazed to see that as they landed, this time behind the farm, Spears did not even flinch.

'Keep watching forward,' called out the sergeant.

Hawke peered through his loophole again, straining his eyes towards the woods. He could not see any movement at all now, but between the short, sharp bursts of machine-gun fire and the whine and crash of falling mortars, the squeak and rumble of tanks and heavy machinery could be heard ever more clearly.

The mortars were falling further towards the village again and Hawke allowed himself a brief sigh of relief. Wiping his brow, he was surprised to discover his head was damp with sweat and yet he did not feel especially hot. His mouth felt parched, so he took his water bottle from his belt. His hands were shaking.

*Come on*, he told himself, *get a grip on yourself.* He glanced at Hebden, whom he saw had noticed his unsteady hands. Hebden winked at him reassuringly.

'So we've just got to stand here and watch those Jerries march towards us,' said Drummond. 'What the hell is the point of that?'

'Ours not to reason why,' said Hebden cheerfully.

'Well, it should be,' snapped Drummond. 'What on earth can we hope to achieve here?'

Minutes passed, but still there was no sign of the enemy, just the whistle and crash of artillery and mortar shells and the chatter of machine guns. In the brief lulls, they could hear further firing away to the east and west.

'That settles it, then,' said Hebden. 'This is a proper attack all right.'

One of the wounded men was groaning, then cried out as two others lifted him from the rubble and put him on a stretcher. Hawke turned and watched as he was carried past, his face ashen with dust but streaked with dark blood.

'Look!' said Drummond suddenly, and peering back through his loophole Hawke saw them too: tanks away to their left, emerging through the woods in the direction of the village. Behind them, soldiers followed, tiny stick-like figures, half crouching. Several bursts of Bren gun fire chattered and Hawke saw some men fall. Were they hit or just ducking out of the line of fire? He wasn't sure, but he continued watching, mesmerized. He had seen newsreel footage of the Germans in Poland, but now here they were for real, and not in monochrome, but full vivid colour. Although he was now witnessing a battle for himself he still felt as though he were merely an observer, watching it as he had the newsreel, and was not a part of it at all.

*

Sergeant Spears had seen the tanks too, and now ran across the yard to the farmhouse. He knew their own role was to slow down the enemy advance and to gain precious minutes, but one company was simply not enough and a single platoon even less so. Braithwaite, the platoon runner, had already been sent off to get instructions from Company HQ, but it had been twenty minutes and there was still no sign of him. If they left it much longer, it would be too late.

Clambering up the old wooden staircase, he found Farrish beside the Bren gun team in a bedroom at the front of the house. The bed had been pushed out of the way, the rug rolled up, while a stool from the dressing table had been moved to the window and was now being sat on by the Bren gunner.

'Sir,' he said, 'can I have a word?'

Farrish turned and nodded. 'What is it?' he said, walking over to Spears.

'There's still no sign of Braithwaite.'

Farrish sighed and looked at his watch. 'No.'

'And there are Jerry tanks advancing towards the village.'

Farrish rubbed his face, then looked at Spears. 'We can't fall back yet. Not without word from Company HQ and not without having fired a shot.'

Firing could now be heard further to their left. Spears moved to the window overlooking the yard and beyond, towards the village of Bavinchove.

'It looks like the Ox and Bucks are coming under attack in Bavinchove,' he said. 'If we're not careful, sir, we're going to be completely cut off and no use to anyone.'

'Well, what the devil do you suggest?' snapped Farrish.

'Send two more runners and tell them to be back here within

twenty minutes at the absolute latest. It should only take around five minutes to reach Company HQ if they're quick.'

Farrish nodded. 'All right. God, what a mess.'

Spears hurried back out of the farmhouse and across the yard to the barn. 'Hawke, Drummond – here, quick.'

Spears saw the startled expression on Hawke's face, the eyes wide with a combination of apprehension and disbelief. He understood because he'd been a boy soldier once himself.

'Yes, Sarge?' said Drummond.

'Listen carefully,' said Spears as another shell hurtled overhead. 'I want you to run to Company HQ – and I mean *run* – and find out whether there are plans to pull back, then run as fast as you can back again. If you can't get through for any reason, then come straight back.'

The two nodded.

'And if this place is being overrun by the time you get back then turn and head for Cassel. Understood?' Another nod of the head. 'Now go!'

Spears watched them tear out of the yard. He hoped he had done the right thing. Instinct told him they should all leave now, before it was too late, but he hoped that if they were overwhelmed sooner than expected then at least the boy would have a sporting chance of getting back to Cassel. On the other hand, where the hell was Braithwaite? Not for the first time, he wished Hawke was back in England – safe, and where he would no longer be an unwanted millstone round his neck.

Hurrying across the yard, he ran up the steps into the windmill.

'What can you see, lads?' he asked.

'Jerries, Sarge,' said Ibbotson. 'Look – heading for the

village, and over there to our right. I reckon they're hitting Bavinchove. Maybe Zuytpeene too.'

Spears stood at the edge of the window and looked out. Tanks and infantry were pressing forward, slowly inching their way across the fields. He saw a section of men crouching along the hedgerow some four hundred yards south from the centre of Oxelaëre. A mixture of rapid-firing German guns and the slower chatter of the Bren rang out, while the dull crumps of field guns and the whine of the shells and subsequent explosions sent reverberations through the wooden floor beneath him. He looked out again and this time saw grey figures emerging from the woods directly ahead of them.

'There're Jerries in front of us now too,' he said.

'Good God,' muttered Chalkie White.

Ibbotson pulled back the cock on the Bren with a sharp click.

'Steady, Jack,' said Spears. 'They're still more than five hundred yards away.'

'The Bren's got the range, though, Sarge.'

'Not effective range, though. A big difference. If you fire now, your bullets will drop short and all you'll do is alert them to where you are. Wait until they're four or even three hundred yards, allow a bit of height and then mow them all down.' He patted Ibbotson lightly on the back and hurried back out, hoping he would reach the men in the barn before they opened fire. In training he had always preached the importance of waiting, of holding fire until the maximum effect of their bullets could be achieved. But battle made men impetuous, and once one fired he knew the rest would follow.

To his relief the men seemed to be holding their nerve. Corporal Bradley, 2 Section commander, had been badly wounded when the mortar shell hit the roof and he was pleased to see McLaren standing by the Bren crew.

'Hold off, boys,' he said, then peering through a loophole next to McLaren realized they could barely see the enemy from ground level. 'Hold your fire until Jerry gets much closer,' he said. 'Make every bullet count.' He turned to McLaren. 'Good work, Sid.'

'Jerry's going to get a nasty shock here, Sarge,' said McLaren.

Spears grinned, then moved down the line. Fifteen men, waiting, poised, rifles at the ready. He could see the tension etched on their faces. The fear too. He watched Private Miller, one of McLaren's boys, trying to open his magazine pouch, his fingers quivering.

'Not long now,' he said. 'You'll forget your nerves once the firing starts. Trust me.' He looked at his watch – nearly eleven o'clock – then paused to look back out through a loophole. He couldn't really see – not well enough, at any rate. 'All right, I'm going back to the mill,' he said. 'I don't want anyone firing until One Section's Bren opens up. Clear?' Nods and a few mumbled, 'Yes, Sarge,' and Spears slipped out of the barn again. Hurrying into the farmhouse, he told Lieutenant Farrish what he had instructed the men in the barn.

'Yes, very good, Spears,' said Farrish. 'We'll wait on your signal here too.'

Spears paused to look out of the window. Yes, the enemy were getting closer – a number were now crossing the brook. Excusing himself, he ran back down the stairs, across the yard and back to the mill.

'They're getting closer, Sarge,' said Ibbotson.

'I know,' said Spears. 'Just give them a bit more.' He stood at the edge of the window, staring out, then brought his binoculars to his eyes. There were no tanks directly in front of them, just men, spread out and moving in depth, but although they were still half-crouching, they were beginning to present a clear enough target. Scanning the row of field-grey troops, he looked for an officer, and then spotted him, his trousers the old-fashioned baggy pantaloons and clutching a pistol rather than a rifle. Spears smiled grimly to himself, then brought his rifle to his shoulder. He had had his Enfield zeroed to four hundred yards, but he reckoned the leading enemy troops were a little less than that now. Aiming just a fraction low – at the officer's crotch rather than his chest – he steadied his aim, then breathed in deeply and held his breath. The steel of the trigger was cold as he felt his finger press against it.

*One*, he counted to himself, *two, three.*

Spears squeezed the trigger, heard the deafening tinny crack in his ear, and felt the butt press hard into his shoulder.

And he saw the German jerk backwards and fall to the ground.

# 13

## OVERRUN

Hawke and Drummond had run as fast they could out of the farm, and down the track alongside the edge of the orchard and on along the long lane, lined with hedgerows of bracken and brambles that led into the village. The high hedges had given them a sense of security, but as they neared the first few houses a strong stench of smoke and cordite – the acrid-smelling propellant used in shells and mortars – filled the air, while up ahead wisps of smoke shrouded the cottages. And as they broke out of the lane and on to the main village road, they saw a small crater in the road and on the far side, flung against a brick wall, the inert figure of Braithwaite.

Both Hawke and Drummond paused then approached the body. His right leg had been twisted grotesquely while from his chalky, bloodstained face, wide eyes stared lifelessly.

'Blow me,' muttered Drummond, then looked up. Bren and rifle fire was cracking and chattering nearby, while more machine-gun fire was answering in reply. A sudden whistle and Drummond said, 'Look out!' and flung himself flat on the ground. Hawke did the same, the grit of the road painful on his hands and knees. A moment later, two mortar shells landed close by, smashing into the roof of one of the houses. Hawke clutched his hands over his ears and gritted his teeth, as an artillery round smacked into the same building. Hawke heard shards of brick and stone whistle above his ear and then a deafening crash of falling masonry and timber.

'Johnny!' hissed Drummond as the roar of falling stone subsided. 'Are you all right?'

A high-pitched whistle rang in his ears, and his mouth was dry with dust, but Hawke looked up and said, 'I think so. Are you?'

Drummond was getting back on his feet, dusting himself down. 'I think so too. We need to keep going.'

'What about Braithwaite?'

'We've got to leave him. Come on, Johnny. Jerry's almost overrun the village as it is.'

They ran on. Bullets spat over their heads as they passed between two houses. Hawke ducked, tripped, lurched forward, but just managed to recover his balance. The firing was even louder now. Even closer. Where were the enemy? Hawke couldn't tell, but they had to be close. Up ahead was the church and, opposite, Company HQ. More mortar shells hurtled over, this time landing further on, but artillery rounds were now being punched into the houses all along the road – houses which backed on to the fields across which the enemy was advancing.

As more bullets fizzed in a mad ricochet nearby, Hawke and Drummond reached the house, gasping. From inside the sound of small-arms fire was tinnily loud, the air thick with a cloying sulphurous stench. In a room off the hallway, an officer was tending two wounded men.

'Sir,' called out Drummond. 'Where's Major Strickland, sir?'

The captain waved his arm vaguely, then flinched as another artillery round smashed into a neighbouring building.

Drummond and Hawke pushed on, past two men staggering with another wounded or dead soldier – Hawke could not tell – then climbed the stairs. Bits of chipped plaster covered the carpet on the staircase, and smoke and dust swirled making Hawke cough and rasp. Two Bren gunners were hammering away from the bedrooms at the back of the building and after pushing past another stumbling Ranger, Hawke, with Drummond following, finally found Major Strickland. The company commander had a gash on his forehead that had been roughly bound and he barely glanced at them as Hawke saluted.

'Keeping firing!' he yelled as one of the Bren gunners stopped.

'She's overheating, sir!' the gunner replied. 'I need a new barrel here!'

Beamish yelled at another man. 'Get that spare barrel, damn it!'

'Sir,' pleaded Hawke. 'Sir!'

Strickland now looked at them impatiently. 'What is it?' he snapped.

'Sir, Lieutenant Farrish sent us from Sixth Platoon at the farm,' said Drummond. 'He wants permission to pull back, sir.'

'We're about to pull back ourselves,' said Beamish. They all ducked as a flurry of mortar shells landed just in front of the house. Shrapnel and shards of stone clattered against the walls. 'Yes, tell him yes. My God!' A further mortar hit the roof behind them, plasterwork crashing to the ground.

Ducking, Drummond and Hawke turned and scampered back down the stairs, only for a soldier in the hallway to suddenly shudder and jerk as a volley of bullets hit him through a hole in the wall at the back of the house. Hawke and Drummond pressed themselves against the wall as the man crashed to the ground, then when the shooting stopped ran for the door and back out on to the street. Ahead, where they had left Braithwaite, a house was now on fire, livid angry flames dancing as billowing clouds of smoke rose into the air.

'The smoke's too thick!' exclaimed Drummond.

'But at least it's giving us some cover,' said Hawke. He stopped, quickly poured some water over a handkerchief and, tying it round his face, saw that Drummond was doing the same.

'Ready?' said Hawke. Drummond nodded.

They ran again, through the thick smoke. Hawke felt his eyes watering and his throat catch, but then they were quickly through and speeding back down the lane towards the farm, the firing and explosions still close but no longer as near as they had been.

Reaching the yard, they gasped and coughed. Hawke saw Spears through the open door of the mill, firing out over the fields. The sergeant glanced at him – *Well?* – and Hawke moved towards him only for several bullets to thump into the wooden staircase. He wondered how on earth Spears, Ibbotson and Chalkie White would ever get out of there.

Farrish now ran from the house, his approach covered by the long barn. Drummond was bent double, his hands on his thighs, but straightened as the lieutenant reached them. 'We're t-to pull out, sir,' he stammered.

'How bad is it in the village?' asked Farrish.

'Bad, sir,' rasped Hawke. His throat burned; his lungs felt tight. 'Braithwaite's dead.'

'Braithwaite? My God,' said Farrish.

'Sir,' shouted out Spears as a round of machine-gun fire peppered the mill.

'We're to pull out,' Farrish called back.

Spears scanned the yard briefly, then said, 'Sir, we need to torch the cart. Me and the lads up here can break out once we've got some cover from the smoke.'

'I've seen some oil, sir,' Hawke told Farrish. 'In the shed by the house. There are a couple of cans.'

'Good,' said Farrish. 'Get them quickly.'

Hawke did so, returning with two tins, one of which he gave to Drummond. The rest of the men were still firing off sporadic rounds of rifle and Bren gunfire as Hawke and Drummond scampered to the upturned cart and began pouring the thick fluid over the main body. Far heavier return fire was being directed at the farm, bullets fizzing as they ricocheted off the brickwork or smacked into wood. Hawke was breathing heavily, his heart hammering, sweat running down his face and back. He flinched as a number of bullets hit the cart, but was aware that most of the heaviest fighting was taking place either side of them. He wondered whether the rest of the company was managing to get out of the village.

'Are you done?' Spears shouted down to Drummond as McLaren and several others emerged from the barn.

'Yes, Sarge!' Drummond called back, then, grabbing Hawke and stepping away, lit a match and threw it at the cart. Cursing as it went out, he lit another and this time the oil caught and in a moment the cart was enveloped in flame and crackling, and the burning oil causing thick black smoke to billow up and cover the windmill like a veil. Coughing and spluttering, Spears, with Ibbotson and White in tow, hurried down the steps as the can of oil was thrown inside the barn.

'We've got to get out of here fast, sir,' said Spears to Farrish. 'Jerry's only about five-hundred-plus yards away.'

Farrish nodded. 'What about a covering force?'

'Leave the three Bren gunners until last, but get the rest out now. You should lead the men, sir, and head back through the orchard and make for that line of trees behind.' He turned and pointed to a thick row of horse chestnuts. 'Behind them there's a field then a small wood and beyond that a track that leads up to the town.'

'And we've got two wounded men. Corporal Bradley and Private Thornley. Thornley's in a bad way – I don't want to leave them . . .'

'We can make two stretchers,' said Spears. 'Button a great-coat together and put a rifle either side.'

'All right. We can try. And what about you, Spears?'

'I'll stay with the Brens, sir. We won't be far behind.'

Farrish nodded. 'Make sure you're not.'

'Sir,' said Spears.

A couple of minutes later, Farrish led the men out through the yard and into the orchard, half running and half crouching. Hawke looked around him, saw Hebden and Drummond nearby, then glanced across towards Bavinchove, where a company of the Ox and Bucks still seemed to be fighting. Several fields away he could see the turrets of two tanks moving forward, almost level with them. He guessed they were five hundred yards or more away, but felt another lurch in his stomach at the proximity of the enemy. He looked behind him. The Bren gunners were still firing off short, sharp bursts. Smoke from the cart had shrouded the whole yard, so that only the top of the windmill could be seen above it. Not for the first time that day, Hawke was struck by the unreality of the situation. It was as though he were merely an observer watching the mayhem and chaos that was unfolding before him.

At the farm, Spears had retrieved a further can – of petrol rather than oil, which he had spotted and hidden when they'd first arrived there. This he took into the farmhouse and poured liberally over the back room on the ground floor – over old oak and pine furniture, over the curtains and rugs on the floor, and the armchairs in front of the hearth. Above, Merryweather and Grimshaw, the 1 Section Bren team, were still firing – short, sharp bursts as they had been instructed – but Spears now called them down.

'Get out into the yard,' he barked. Waiting for them to clatter down the stairs, Spears then stood in the doorway of the back sitting room, struck a match and threw it in. With a loud whoosh the petrol ignited and in moments the room was ablaze. Spears smiled grimly then sprinted back out into the yard and to the barn. Crouching, he ran over to one of the loopholes and peered out, only for a burst of machine-gun fire to spit across the wall in front of him.

'How far are they now?' he called out.

'About three hundred yards, Sarge,' said Ibbotson. Smoke from the house was already rolling towards them, wisping in through the loopholes.

'Right, lads, time to go,' said Spears. 'One at a time. Ibbotson and White, you go first, head straight across the orchard and then stop and set up, covering our left flank towards Bavinchove.'

Ibbotson pulled the Bren out from its slit in the wall, folded back the bipod and slung it over his shoulder with a grunt. Following him into the yard, Spears said to Merryweather and Grimshaw, 'Give Ibbotson and White a minute then follow them and make for the line of trees over there.' He pointed again. 'And then stop and set up facing the open ground to the west.'

Livid flames were rising from the house, and from the yard Spears saw that the second storey had now caught alight. Thick clouds of smoke enveloped the whole farmstead and, with his throat rasping, Spears urged Merryweather and Grimshaw on their way.

He had just stepped back into the barn to call out Collier and Ostler, the last pair, when a burst of enemy machine-gun fire raked the barn and both men fell backwards. Hurrying over, Spears saw that they were dead, killed instantly, their faces a bloody pulp. Sickened, he snapped the string of their identity tags, pulled out their remaining magazines, grabbed the fallen Bren and ran.

Behind the small wood, Farrish halted the platoon. The trees bordered a track that led up to the town, and there, in the sunken lane, the men rested. One of the wounded men, Thornley, had died. Hawke passed him, lying on the greatcoat at the side of the road, his battledress dark with blood, his face splintered from the blast. Three days earlier he'd not seen a single dead body in his life, yet he now felt he'd seen enough to last a lifetime. In the films he had seen and in the books and magazines he had read, men were always killed cleanly – a bullet to the heart, or collapsing neatly to the ground. There was never any mention of the distorted limbs, the large quantities of blood and innards hanging loose, the wild staring eyes or the ashen, wax-like skin. He had been struck by how much dead people *looked* dead – the skin starved of colour, all vitality gone. And they were nearly always filthy – filthy uniforms, filthy hair, hands muddied, nails black, blood and dust covering them.

Hawke swallowed hard. His throat was sore, his mouth dry. He wondered whether he would share the fate of Thornley – his body blasted, a burden to his friends, his last moments breathed at the side of an unknown road, in who knew what pain and discomfort. And a long way from home.

Hawke pulled out his water bottle and drank the last of his metallic, now warm liquid. Before he'd arrived in France, he thought to himself, he would not have considered drinking such stale water – but now he was happy just to taste the fluid in his parched mouth.

A shell hurtled over on its way to the town, its passage through the air whining malevolently. Moments later it landed, exploding with a loud crash half a mile beyond.

'Have you had a look at this?' said Hebden, peering over the top of the bank above the road.

Hawke turned and inched himself up. They were already quite elevated. Smoke and flames were still billowing from the farm, but much of Oxelaëre seemed to be hidden by smoke too. Tanks were pushing across the fields, but the village looked to have been already overrun.

'I can't believe it,' mumbled Hawke.

'Believe it,' said Drummond, next to him. 'And we need to get our skates on or we're going to be overrun ourselves.'

'Skipper's waiting for the Brens,' said Hebden, then added, 'Here's the sarge now – with Chalkie and Jack. Good on 'em.'

Hawke followed his gaze and saw Spears with Ibbotson, White, Merryweather and Grimshaw emerge from the woods. Spears had the third Bren slung over his shoulder. He was grimacing, short of breath.

'You all right, Spears?' said Farrish. 'Where are Collier and Ostler?'

'Sorry, sir,' gasped Spears, 'they didn't make it.'

'Damn it,' muttered Farrish. 'Well, we'd better get going.'

'Yes, sir,' said Spears. 'Jerry's overrun the village, sir.'

They moved on, hurrying up the track. The shelling of the town continued intermittently. There was still firing from Bavinchove, where the Ox and Bucks seemed to have held up the enemy's advance briefly, but as they passed an old farmhouse to their right the road cleared its banks and looking back down the hill they saw three German tanks emerge from the larger wood to the north-east of Oxelaëre.

'Blimey, that's all we need,' said Drummond.

But Hawke now noticed that running from the farmhouse was a low hedge, already thick with new foliage, leading to a small copse.

'Sarge,' he said to Spears, 'couldn't we try to get to those trees? Maybe we could get the tanks from there?'

'What, you think a few three-oh-three rounds will have any effect against tanks?'

Hawke looked crestfallen. 'I don't know, I just –'

'But hang on,' said Spears, cutting Hawke short, 'we could distract them. You said we had anti-tank guns in the town?'

'Yes, Sarge,' said Hawke.

'I saw them,' added Drummond. 'Two-pounders and some others as well.'

Spears nodded. 'All right, let's put it to Mr Farrish.'

As they sheltered briefly behind the farmhouse, Spears outlined his plan. 'We've got to try and take them on, sir,' he said, 'or we'll get caught out in the open. They'll mow us down if we're not careful. The copse will give us some cover and hopefully the gunners in the town will knock them out.'

'It seems to be leaving an awful lot to chance, Spears,' said Farrish.

'I don't think we have much choice, sir. If we push on up this track, those tanks are going to see us and get us with their machine guns. They're faster than us. At least in the wood we can lie low.'

Farrish sighed and rubbed his eyes. 'You're right, Sergeant. All right, let's make for that copse.'

They moved on, crouching along the hedge until they reached the copse, a mixture of chestnuts and oaks. Below, the undergrowth was thick and the men lay on the ground in their sections. The three tanks were advancing steadily. Several artillery rounds had been aimed at them, but so far all had missed. Two of the tanks suddenly swung off the track along which they had been advancing, and turned towards the copse.

'Would you believe it, Hawke?' said Spears, grinning. 'They're heading straight for us.'

'Sorry, Sarge,' said Hawke. 'I-I didn't think that they'd –'

'No, no,' said Spears. 'That's good, trust me. They're thinking the same thing: they see this as cover.'

'But won't they kill us all, Sarge?' said Hebden.

'Not if they don't know we're here. And I don't think they do, because if they did they'd have opened fire already.'

Hawke glanced across at Spears then back at the tanks.

Steadily the two vehicles rumbled towards them, tracks squeaking and groaning, their grey bodies jolting across the field at around twenty miles per hour.

Hawke barely dared watch. In moments, he thought, the tanks' machine guns would open fire and then that would be the end.

# 14

## PANZERS!

It had already been a frustrating morning for Brigadier Somerset. The early Stuka attack had been as clear an indication as any that the Germans were preparing to renew their attack, but as he had been dictating messages to his various subordinate commanders, a runner had arrived with a message summoning him to the Hotel Sauvage in Le Grand Place where, he learned, senior British and French generals were holding an unexpected meeting.

Somerset had assumed there must have been some mistake, but having hurried down the hill to the town square he had been astonished to see several staff cars and accompanying outriders outside the old hotel, even though the place had been hit and damaged several days before. Inside, he had been ushered into the hotel's dining room, where standing around a side table were General Adam – commander of III Corps, and Major-General Pakenham-Walsh – the BEF's Commander of Engineers, as well as the French General Fagalde and an assortment of staff officers. Somerset recognized none of them except Colonel Bridgeman from Gort's staff.

'Ah, Brigadier,' said Bridgeman.

'Forgive us for descending on you like this,' said General

Adam, extending his hand. 'But Cassel was the one place we could all get to with comparative ease. You've heard the news, I take it?'

'Which news, General?' Somerset replied. He wondered what was coming next. Would it be another change of plan? Or perhaps Somer Force was about to be redirected somewhere else.

'We're evacuating through Dunkirk. The order was issued last night. Operation Dynamo has begun.'

'I see,' said Somerset. *So*, he thought, *it really is happening*.

'General Adam has been commanded to set up the perimeter defences around Dunkirk,' Bridgeman explained, 'but General Fagalde here commands XVI Corps. Both French and British troops will be defending Dunkirk.' He smiled amiably. 'We just need to establish which troops are going defend what.'

Somerset looked across at Fagalde, who gave a forced smile. The brigadier noticed the Frenchman's jaw muscles clenching. The man was seething with anger, Somerset thought.

Somerset coughed. 'I should warn you, gentlemen, that we have recently been bombed and that we're expecting the enemy to attack at any moment.'

'I'm sure this won't take long,' said Adam. 'I think we're all agreed on the principles.'

Fagalde turned to Somerset. 'It seems you and I have much the same job, Brigadier. We will hold the line while the rest of the British escape.' He smiled thinly.

General Adam was about to reply when they all heard the screech of a shell hurtling over. For a moment they looked at each other in silence and then the shell exploded somewhere behind them. The building shook, the bottles still lining the bar chinking together. At the far end of the room, a chunk of plaster fell from the roof.

'I think you should hurry,' said Somerset.

Bridgeman nodded and quickly outlined his thoughts. The perimeter would make use of the extensive canals that lined the coastal area. The French would hold the western part of the perimeter from the town of Bergues as far as Gravelines, while the British would hold a line along a canal that ran from Bergues, some seven miles inland, all the way to Nieuport, fourteen miles down the coast.

Another shell hurtled over, this time landing further away, but, Somerset thought to himself, the beginning of the enemy barrage was doing wonders for the Allies' willingness to cooperate. Fagalde may have been furious to discover the BEF was leaving, but he nodded readily enough at Bridgeman's suggestions. In less than ten minutes, an agreement had been reached.

The meeting had broken up immediately after, the generals speeding off as more shells crashed into the town. Somerset envied them. As he'd hurried back towards Brigade Headquarters, he'd felt overwhelmed by how alone he and his force now were. He doubted any more supplies would reach them, or whether there would be any further contact with the rest of the BEF. They were marooned, isolated on this hill. And facing an unenviable future. He wondered how it might end – were these his last days, or would he soon be a prisoner? Or could they possibly still escape? That seemed unlikely.

It had been with a heavy heart that he'd arrived back at Somer Force Headquarters, although, as more shells screamed over, his maudlin thoughts of earlier quickly evaporated: the men had been looking to him for leadership, and the time for defeatist thoughts had passed. At HQ, now shared with the Ox and Bucks, the mood had been tense, yet Somerset had busied himself looking at the map, getting confirmation of dispositions and making half-hourly trips to the top of Mount Cassel to scan the south for any signs of enemy movement.

Everyone at Brigade had replaced caps with tin helmets and Somerset had noticed how with every screech of a shell the men would stiffen and visibly flinch at the resulting explosion. Headquarters had thankfully been spared, although one shell had landed close by, hitting a house just a stone's throw away. Half the lower storey had survived, but the rest of the building now lay strewn across the road, a pile of stone, brick and collapsed timbers.

When the news arrived that the ground attack had begun, the brigadier had felt something close to relief, and had once more hurried up to Mount Cassel and with his field glasses had watched the enemy advancing to the south. Returning soon after, he quickly realized that the best intelligence he was likely to get would be what he saw with his own eyes, and, as the smoke of battle quickly filled the ground below the town, that was not a great deal. Staff officers and clerks were frantically trying to make calls on both field telephones and the local network, but most information was arriving by despatch rider or runners from the various companies. It was patchy and, the brigadier knew, often out of date by the time it arrived.

Inside Headquarters, the rooms were filled with a faint haze and a stench of dust, smoke and cordite, mixed with tobacco. Typewriters chattered, runners came and went, but despite all this apparent activity the brigadier could not help feeling both cut off from higher command and his men on the ground. When a runner from the Glosters arrived to report the news that Zuytpeene was under attack, Somerset had been unable to hide his exasperation.

'I know the outposts are under attack,' he snapped, 'I can see that with my own eyes. But what is the situation there?'

'I don't know, sir,' replied the man. 'It's hard to tell, sir.'

Somerset sighed and looked down at the map spread out on the table. With a crayon he marked the enemy advance from the south, then stood up again. 'This is hopeless, Bully,' he said. 'It's impossible trying to run a battle with runners and DRs. Why the hell haven't we got more radio sets? That's what I want to know. It's ridiculous.' He sighed again, then said, 'I'm going to get out and see the men. At least that way we can talk and make decisions immediately. I'll see the Glosters first, then head over to the Yorks Rangers.'

'All right, sir,' said Bullmore. 'Will you take anyone with you?'

'Yes – Captain Dillon can come.'

'And some runners, sir?'

The brigadier gave a wry smile. 'Yes, Bully, and some runners.'

Around forty minutes later, at around eleven, the brigadier reached Battalion HQ of the Yorks Rangers, where he found Colonel Beamish in a state of considerable concern about the fate of his B Company.

'It's impossible to know what's going on, sir,' said Beamish as he led the brigadier through to the rear of the building. 'We had a field line running down to them but that's obviously been cut because the line's dead.' At the back of the house they passed through an old oak door, down several stone steps and out on to a terraced garden above the old town ramparts.

As at the Châtellerie de Schoubeque, the brigadier reflected, further along the southern edge of the town, the view to the south was superb.

'We've sent several runners as well,' said Beamish, pausing with his field glasses in his hand, 'but so far none have come back.' He peered through his field glasses. 'It does seem as though the village has been overrun, though, sir, but there's so much damned smoke it's hard to say. We're obviously praying the chaps managed to do the sensible thing and pull back.'

Brigadier Somerset looked through his own field glasses. Away to the south-east he could see tanks and men moving across country, and beyond, behind the woods a couple of miles to the south, he spotted the muzzle flash of an enemy field gun. Further west, too, enemy troops and armour were pressing forward. From Zuytpeene, fighting could be heard, the crack and splutter of small-arms resounding clearly. But directly in front, towards Oxelaëre, it was indeed hard to see much. The village itself was lost in smoke, while further to the south-west he could see a farm burning fiercely.

'Communication – or the lack of it – has been the story of this campaign,' said Somerset. 'It's more than frustrating. The modern army needs radio. We're learning that rather too late.'

'What news of Zuytpeene and Bavinchove?' asked Beamish.

'It seems the company of Ox and Bucks have pulled back from Bavinchove, but we can't make contact with the Glosters at Zuytpeene. Judging from what we can see and hear, though, it seems they're still there.'

'Brave men,' muttered Beamish.

'Yes.' They were silent a moment. Somerset had hoped he'd made it clear to all his commanders that the small forces in these outlying villages were to put a brake on the enemy advance and nothing more. They were not to sacrifice themselves, and yet it seemed a company of his old battalion was doing exactly that, while Beamish's company of Yorks Rangers at Oxelaëre appeared likely to have similarly left it too late. The losses were mounting. His old battalion had suffered particularly. A week earlier, the battalion had been bombarded from the air near Tournai. Because of the congestion, the men had been trapped. They had lost nearly two hundred men that day. And now it seemed likely another company was about to be lost. Somerset cursed silently to himself.

'Look, sir!' said Beamish suddenly, pointing towards the woods in front of the village. 'Enemy tanks!'

Somerset followed with his field glasses and saw three enemy tanks emerge from the trees perhaps fifty yards apart. One took the main track that led from Oxelaëre directly up to the town, while the other two sped across the fields in front of them.

Several rounds from a two-pounder anti-tank gun rang out, fired from its position on the barricaded road just in front of them, but the range was too long. The tanks now moved to their left, away from the track, and briefly disappeared behind a fold in the hill. Somerset lowered his field glasses and then saw a small column of platoon strength a few hundred yards to the south-west.

'Look,' he said to Beamish, 'are they some of yours?'

'Good God!' muttered the colonel. 'Those damned panzers are heading straight for them.'

The men were disappearing into the cover of a copse as the

three enemy tanks reappeared, cresting a rise and hurriedly making towards the cluster of trees.

The two-pounder fired again, but once more missed.

'The question is,' said Somerset, peering through his binoculars once more, 'do those Hun tanks know our chaps are in that copse, or are they simply looking for cover?'

'I think, sir, we're about to find out,' Beamish replied.

The lead German tank was now just twenty yards away, and positioning itself towards the edge of the copse. A short way behind were the other two. From the undergrowth beneath the trees, Hawke watched, mesmerized. He could feel the rumble of its engine pulsing through the ground, and whenever it moved its tracks squeaked and rattled like a giant angry beast. Painted on to its side was a black and white cross, the white vivid against the dark blue-grey of the hull. He noticed now that the one closest was different from the other two – it had a small narrow gun and single machine gun in its turret, while the other two appeared to have machine guns only in the turret. What began to worry him now was the ease with which these three panzers could crush them all, should they move towards the wood itself.

One of the men moved, crunching a twig, and Hawke froze. A moment later, a head appeared from the turret of the nearest tank. With his rifle ready in front of him, Hawke felt his finger brush the cold metal of the trigger, and as the German scanned the town above with field glasses Hawke thought, *I could hit him – I could hit him now.* But then what would happen? One German dead but three enemy tanks would bear down upon them and then they really would be finished.

A bead of sweat trickled down Hawke's face, tickling him,

and he desperately wanted to move and wipe it, yet dared not flex so much as a muscle. The German shouted over to his colleagues now pulling up alongside. Another figure appeared, similarly dressed in a black jacket and large beret, and for a moment the two men spoke, pointed, then, much to Hawke's relief, both withdrew into the bellies of their tanks once more.

Spears was now whispering to McLaren and then suddenly both men were up and running in a crouch. Hawke watched open-mouthed as Spears sped low towards the second tank while McLaren slid down beside the tracks of the first and then, pulling the pin from a grenade, stood and pushed it through the open viewing vent. Desperate shouts came from within the tank, then first one and then a second explosion rang out, bits of shrapnel flew from the forward and side vent followed by wisps of smoke. Another explosion, then a third and fourth in quick succession and the turret of the nearest tank came apart with a burst of fire, shooting into the air and landing several yards behind. McLaren, crouching beside it, arms clasped over his head, now sped back to the safety of the trees, followed by Spears.

From the second tank, machine-gun ammunition had caught fire and was pinging manically inside the metal hull. The third tank now reversed frantically, the gears grinding, but no sooner had it pulled back from the cover of the trees than two anti-tank shells smacked into it one after the other, the first disabling the tracks, the second striking the turret. Moments later, a crew man emerged.

'Hold your fire!' shouted Farrish, then said, '*Hände hoch! Hände hoch!*' The German looked at him, his eyes wild and terrified, and thrust his arms into the air.

'Sergeant Spears,' called out Farrish, 'get those men.'

'Sir!' replied Spears. Having recovered his Bren and rifle and pointing the machine gun towards the enemy tank crew, he said, 'Sid, Hebden, you come with me.'

McLaren and Hebden followed him, as the three stunned German tank crew clambered down, hands high.

'Sarge!' said Hebden, pointing back down towards the woods below, 'look!'

Spears pushed the three men forward towards the copse, then turned. More enemy panzers were emerging from the trees, but now accompanied by troops as well.

'Sir!' called out Spears, 'Jerry's pushing out of the woods!' Pushing the three prisoners forward with a jab of his rifle, he hurried over to Farrish. Just as they reached the edge of the copse, a volley of mortar shells whined over.

'Take cover!' cried Spears, diving to the ground. The mortars landed well short, but Hawke still clutched his hands over his helmet. His ears were ringing, the air was once again thick with smoke, this time from the burning tanks, but then Farrish was yelling orders for them to fall back. His senses numbed, Hawke had barely registered the command when around him the men were scrambling to their feet and pushing their way back out through the undergrowth and clear of the trees. As he got up himself he saw Spears running forward with the Bren, reach the crest of the ridge and then pour several long bursts of fire down towards the enemy.

Without thinking, Hawke ran towards him, diving down beside him, and handing over several magazines from his pouches. Spears barely looked at him, but snatched them, deftly pulling one magazine out, tossing it to one side and slotting in another, and then opening fire again. Hawke saw several men drop, then pulled his own rifle into his shoulder, aimed, held his breath and squeezed the trigger. An enemy soldier jerked backwards and fell. Hawke now pulled back the bolt, rammed it forward again and fired, missing his target. He pulled the bolt back a further time, steadying his aim and firing again, this time seeing a second man tumble. A further mortar shell whined over, but Hawke barely flinched as it landed forty yards behind them among the trees. In no time at all, he'd fired all ten rounds in his magazine and was fumbling in his pocket for two more clips of five when Spears was tugging at his battledress.

'Time to go,' he said, shuffling backwards on his knees and elbows. Hawke nodded and they both turned, crouching, getting themselves clear of the narrow ridge, and then they were running past the burning tanks towards the track, so that Hawke gasped, his eyes streaming from the sting of the smoke. Not far ahead of them the rest of the platoon were running too, spread out in a long line as more mortars crashed into the copse behind them. Artillery shells hurtled overhead and from the town the rattle of small-arms rang out.

# 15

## REDEPLOYMENT

Enemy mortars followed them all the way to the town's edge, and although most fell short, one landed near enough the leading Rangers to knock down two men. Hawke, running with Spears at the rear of their column, saw the men fall, and heard Farrish pause, but urge the rest of the men to keep going. Hawke looked back and saw that, for the time being at any rate, the German advance to the south had faltered.

'Keep going!' Spears yelled at him. From the town several artillery rounds were fired from the eighteen-pounders, fizzing overhead and crashing down into the woods below. Hawke's chest burned, his legs ached and his shoulders rubbed. It was, he discovered, one thing making a short, sharp dash across open ground with thoughts of firing on the enemy coursing through his veins, but quite another slogging uphill with a full haversack and pack, and with his entrenching tool, water bottle and bayonet slapping against his thighs and tugging on his belt, and with gas-mask bag, ammunition and rifle to carry as well.

The two men down, were, he saw as he passed them, O'Connell and Trimble from 3 Section. Lieutenant Farrish and Bristow, the 3 Section commander, were crouched down beside them. O'Connell, Hawke saw, was dead, his entire back torn open. Trimble was alive, gibbering, with wild, darting eyes, but half his left leg lay several yards away, still booted and putteed. The stump was quivering, a bloody, shredded pulp. Hawke looked briefly, but moved on past. Just fifty yards ahead, clambering over a barricade across the track at the town's edge, were two medical orderlies with a stretcher.

*Nearly there*, he told himself. *Forty yards, thirty, twenty*, legs aching in a way he had never known possible during all those runs during training, his chest tight, and lungs unable to gasp enough air, but then he was looking at a two-pounder gun and a barricade of rubble and wood and waiting to help him across were a number of men from the Glosters.

'Well done, sonny,' a soldier grinned at him, and offered a hand as Hawke scrambled over the piled-up barricade. 'Saw what you did down there. Showed guts.' He winked.

'Thanks,' Hawke gasped. Hebden and Drummond were beside him now, and then there was Spears too. An enemy shell whooshed over and Hawke flinched as it landed with a deafening crash a hundred yards or so inside the town. He bent over, hands on his thighs, grimacing and fighting for breath, and looked back down the track. The stretcher bearers were lifting Trimble, while Farrish stood over O'Connell, grabbed the dead man's tags and papers, and then turned and hurried on up the lane with Bristow and the two orderlies in tow.

'What about O'Connell?' said Hawke.

'He's dead,' said Spears. 'He'll be picked up later. It's the living we need to worry about.'

As Farrish clambered over the barricade, Hawke turned to Spears.

'Tom – I mean, Sergeant,' he said, 'that was amazing what you did – destroying those tanks.'

Spears looked at him. 'Not really. They hadn't seen us. A lot of blind spots on a tank.' He turned to Farrish, 'All right, sir? We should move on into the town. Rejoin the battalion.'

Hawke noticed the lieutenant had blood on his hands and across his battle blouse, and that his hand was shaking as he raised it to adjust his helmet.

'Yes – yes, you're right, Sergeant,' Farrish replied, his voice strained. Hawke thought to himself: *This is getting to the lieutenant*. In a way, it made him feel better. It was natural to feel scared.

'And, er, well done back there,' Farrish added, looking at Spears. 'You and McLaren – you did a brave thing.'

Spears shrugged. 'Thank you, sir. Shall I order the men forward?'

Farrish nodded and rubbed his brow so that a streak of blood ran across it. 'Yes – if you wouldn't mind.'

'All right, let's keep moving, boys,' Spears called out, taking the lead, and moving off up a cobbled road into the heart of the town.

The road led them into an open square in which there were already several large craters and a burnt-out carrier. From the square another narrow street took them to the western end of Grand Place. It looked a desolate place. An upturned car and another wrecked carrier and a tank, blackened and ugly, stood as a reminder of the day's fighting, while even more of the houses had been hit, rubble and debris spewing out on to the cobbles. A stench of smoke and fumes and cordite hung heavily on the air and Hawke began coughing, his throat as dry as sandpaper. He felt for his water bottle but then, with dismay, remembered that it was empty.

'Here,' said Hebden beside him, unclasping his own bottle. 'I've a glug to spare.'

Hawke took it gratefully and drank. 'Thanks, Bert,' he said.

They pulled up outside Battalion Headquarters as two more enemy shells whistled over, one crashing at the far end of Grand Place. Hawke barely flinched as with a cloud of swirling dust, part of a wall collapsed on to the ground with a tremendous and resounding crash.

'Stand easy, chaps,' said Farrish, then headed inside to Battalion HQ.

Hebden and Drummond squatted down and Hawke followed, gasping with relief as he sat himself down on the cobbles.

'Ahh!' sighed Hebden. 'I never knew sitting on stone could bring such joy.'

'My legs are dead,' said Drummond, then grinning at Hawke and Hebden added, 'Is it just me, or are we actually still alive?'

Hebden leaned across and pinched his leg.

'Ow!' cried Drummond.

'Then we must be,' said Hebden.

McLaren wandered over and cuffed Drummond lightly over the back of his head.

'What was that for, Corp?' said Drummond.

'Do I need a reason?'

'Good work on that tank, Sid,' said Hebden.

McLaren's face creased into a wry smile. 'I have to admit that when the sarge suggested it to me I thought he'd gone mad.

But, actually, he was absolutely right – so long as we crept up to them below their eye line, they weren't going to see us. It couldn't have been easier popping in a grenade.'

'I'm glad I'm a rifleman and not a tank man,' said Hawke.

'You and me the same,' said McLaren. 'Engines get hot, very hot, and lots of horrible flammable oil and fuel runs around them. It's one thing having your head in an engine in peacetime when you're trying to repair the beggar, but quite another with bullets and bangs going off all around you.'

'Oh, I couldn't agree with you more, Sid,' said Hebden. 'No escape from that thing. And even if the grenade didn't kill them their shells detonating did. It would have become an inferno in there.' He shuddered. 'No thank you.'

'D'you see what happened to O'Connell and Trimble?' said Drummond. 'I'm not sure having shrapnel rip open your guts or tear off a leg is any better than being blown up inside a tank. No, I'm not glad I'm a rifleman.' He took out a cigarette from his top pocket.

'What would you rather be, then?' asked Hawke.

'Playing football?' grinned Hebden.

'Yes I would,' replied Drummond. 'No, I reckon I should have joined the RASC – that must be a bit more of a cushy number. B Echelon stuff – out of the firing line.'

'And you know what would happen, Charlie,' said McLaren. 'You'd get a transfer and you'd be going back to some depot to pick up rations and a big fat Jerry fighter plane would fly over and open fire and you'd get a bullet right through you and then you'd wish you'd stayed where you are now – with one of the finest regiments in the entire British Army.'

They all laughed – even Drummond.

'One of the finest?' said Hebden, a look of mock indignation on his face. '*The* finest, surely.'

'Not with the likes of you three in it,' said McLaren.

'Surely you can't mean Johnny here,' said Hebden. 'Didn't you see him firing away with the sarge as we all scarpered?'

Hawke looked down, embarrassed. 'I wasn't really thinking, I just –'

'Had to have a pop at some Jerries,' said McLaren. 'Did you hit any?'

Hawke shrugged. 'I saw a few drop. The sarge hit loads, though.'

'We're lucky to have him – I've always thought so,' said Hebden.

'You weren't saying that a few weeks back when he put you on prowler guard for three nights in a row,' said Drummond.

'Well, no,' admitted Hebden. 'I was cursing him to hell, and I still think he was a bit harsh – and I wasn't the only one who had had too much to drink anyway. But I'm a forgiving bloke and I won't hold it against him. Anyway, there's no denying he's a good soldier.'

'He's got experience, you see,' said McLaren. 'He's been in a long time, and although I've been in a few years now I hadn't seen any action before this show. The sarge saw quite a bit in India, you know.'

'He told me some of his stories,' said Hawke.

'Did he?' said McLaren, surprised. 'I thought he barely ever spoke to you?'

'Johnny's sister is the sarge's fiancée,' said Drummond. 'Didn't you know?'

Hawke now wished he had never opened his mouth.

'Well I'm blowed,' said McLaren. 'How did that one pass me by?' He shook his head in wonderment. 'That explains a lot. Well, well.'

'I can't believe you didn't know,' said Drummond.

'Talk of the devil,' muttered Hebden as Spears now walked towards them.

'Boys,' said Spears, pausing beside them. 'All right, Sid?'

'A bit knackered, but otherwise we're all in one piece,' said McLaren. 'Which is more than can be said for O'Connell and Trimble. Any news on Trimble?'

'Doesn't look good,' said Spears. 'If we could get him to a proper hospital and quickly, that would be one thing.' He pushed his helmet back and wiped his brow. 'No, Three Section are four men down, and Two Section have one dead and Corporal Bradley wounded.'

'And we lost Braithwaite and Stubbs,' said McLaren.

'We'll probably have to combine Two and Three Sections under Bristow,' said Spears. 'It's been hard fighting so far.'

'We've been lucky in this section,' said McLaren.

'Sarge, can I push my luck a bit further?' said Hebden.

Spears smiled. 'Probably not, no.'

'We could really do with a brew. Have we got time? We're all parched here.'

'You might have to wait, Bert,' said Spears. 'Lieutenant Farrish will be out in a moment, I'm sure. We'll be deployed and, assuming Jerry hasn't reached the town, perhaps you can have a brew then. Things are still a bit hot out there, you know.'

As if on cue, another shell hurtled over, this time crashing into a building only sixty yards behind them, on the rise of Mount Cassel. Even Spears ducked and held his hands over his helmet. Fortunately, the row of buildings facing out on Grand Place stood in between, but a deep rumble resounded around the town as part of a building collapsed. The men watched as another cloud of dust and grit mushroomed into the air.

At the far end of Grand Place, a dozen soldiers staggered into view.

'Look, Sarge,' said Hawke. 'Tommies.'

'They look spent,' muttered Hebden. 'Where've they come from?'

'I could hazard a guess,' said Spears.

As the men drew near, the dark black arc of cloth on their shoulders could be seen – which with its green writing marked them out as Rangers.

'That's Alf Addington,' muttered Spears, 'Fifth Platoon.' He hurried towards them. 'Alf!' he said.

Sergeant Addington raised an arm in acknowledgement.

Spears undid his water bottle and passed it to his fellow sergeant, then called back to his own platoon. 'Some water! Quick!'

A number of 6th Platoon got to their feet, Hawke included, gathering around the new arrivals, offering them water bottles and patting them on the back.

'You lot are a sight for sore eyes,' said Addington. He was older than most, perhaps thirty, Hawke guessed, and had scratches across his face and hands. So did the others.

'What happened?' asked Spears.

'We pulled back too late,' said Addington.

'By which time the village was already almost overrun,' said another.

'Where's Major Strickland?' asked Spears.

'In the bag,' Addington told him, 'along with most of the company. All rounded up and taken Jerry prisoner.'

Spears shook his head. 'Damn it all.'

'We wondered what had happened to you lot. You all got away?'

'Most of us.'

'That's something,' said Addington. 'We did only just. We managed to hide in those woods for a bit and then Jerry was pushed back a bit and we made our escape. We lost a few lads but us lot managed to make it. We worked our way up, eventually getting into the town at Dead Horse Corner. The C Company boys told us to make for Battalion HQ.'

'You'd better go and see the IO,' said Spears. 'He'll want to speak to you. The rest of your lads can stay here, if you like.' He patted Addington on the shoulder. 'I'm sorry, Alf – that's a big blow.'

Soon after, Lieutenant Farrish reappeared with the battalion adjutant – Major Cartwright, and Captain Astell – the A Company commander.

'All right, men,' said Cartwright, 'continue at ease.' He cleared his throat. 'You've done a superb job so far, but as I'm sure you are now aware we have lost most of B Company this morning. The Hun has overrun our outposts, but we still have a key role to play here in Cassel and even with his tanks and apparent control of the skies, taking this place from us will be no easy task for him. It's a superb defensive position and we intend to fight for every yard of it.' He paused. 'Now we need every one of you to help with that defence and so we are attaching you to A Company under Captain Astell here.'

There were a few mutterings and a shuffle of feet as Cartwright stood back and offered a hand to Captain Astell. He was young, barely thirty, and, unlike most of the officers, clean-shaven, with a round, kindly face.

'I'll be honoured to have you chaps fighting under me,' he said, his accent betraying a faint trace of the Yorkshire accent. 'We're currently deployed on a two-hundred-yard front just the other side of these buildings here.' He turned and pointed to the Battalion HQ behind him and the row of buildings that ran along the southern edge of Grand Place. 'I don't know how much of the town any of you have had a chance to see, but behind these buildings are rows of walled terraced gardens, and beyond that the town ramparts. These have long ago collapsed, but we are manning the soft ground in front and have prepared defences both behind the walled gardens and in the houses themselves. We are also being helped by gunners from the Worcestershire Yeomanry, who have deployed two eighteen-pounders and three two-pounder anti-tank guns in our section.' He paused, cleared his throat, then said, 'Now we need to get you in position quickly. Jerry's advance seems to have stalled for the moment, largely thanks to your efforts earlier taking out those panzers, but we're expecting him to attack again at any moment. I also know you haven't had much food. Rations are short, I'm afraid, but as soon as you're in position, if Jerry hasn't begun his attack again, you can make a brew then. So follow me.'

'Seems like a good sort,' muttered Hebden to Hawke and Drummond.

'It's odd not being part of B Company, though, isn't it?' said Hawke. 'I can't believe the company's no more. What do you think Jerry does with his prisoners?'

They began marching down along the southern edge of Grand Place. Hebden shrugged. 'Sends them to Germany, I suppose, and puts them in a prison camp.'

'They wouldn't shoot their POWs would they?' asked Hawke.

'Oh, no, I'm sure not.'

'I don't intend to find out,' said Drummond.

'But what if we can't ever get out of here?' said Hawke. 'What if the Jerries decide to surround this place and besiege us? That's what they would have done in the olden days.'

'Maybe they'll pull us back tonight,' said Hebden. 'The brigadier might be prepared to lose a company or two, but no one in the top brass is going to want to lose an entire force like this. There's more than a brigade here.'

'I've long since given up trying to work out what the hell is going on,' said Drummond. 'None of it makes a lot of sense to me. But I hope you're right, Bert. If they've got any sense, they'll pull us back tonight.'

Captain Astell now led them off the square and down a narrow brick alleyway.

'Anyway,' added Drummond, 'we've got to get through today yet. I've a feeling the captain's right – we've got more fighting to do before the day's over.' He glanced at his wristwatch. 'And it's barely past noon. Blimey, we're not even halfway through the day yet.'

# 16

## THE MORTAR MEN

As the remnants of 6th Platoon reached the ramparts, there was still no further movement from the woods below, just intermittent but regular artillery and mortar fire. Of the old ramparts there was now little more than an imprint – a path that led round the edge of the town, but the long brick wall that divided the ramparts and the walled gardens of the buildings behind had been well prepared with loopholes knocked out of the brickwork. Forward of the ramparts, on the kitchen gardens and allotments on the ground immediately in front, slit trenches had been dug, and a small amount of wire had been laid across their front. There were a few trees, chestnuts and horse chestnuts, which offered a certain amount of protection and cover, but the allotments overlooked a shallow lip, which gave the position both a degree of concealment while at the same time providing a good view of the woods and surrounding villages below.

It was along this area in front of the ramparts that the company's two-pounder anti-tank guns and mortars were positioned, dug into the ground between the newly tilled vegetable patches and fruit cages, and between which, straddling a fifty-yard front, 6th Platoon were now deployed.

Between them, Lieutenant Farrish and Sergeant Spears positioned their men, now made up of two sections – Alf Addington and the remainder of B Company had been allocated to A Company Headquarters. The platoon had a forty-yard front, covering two houses behind them. 1 Section was positioned just to the right of the alleyway down which they had arrived, on the open ground in front of the ramparts.

'I don't understand, Corp,' Hawke said to McLaren as they were retrieving new boxes of ammunition from the cellar of the house behind. 'Why are we positioning ourselves in front of the ramparts? Wouldn't it make more sense to place them here, in the gardens or the houses themselves?'

McLaren passed Hawke a metal tin of twelve Bren magazines.

'It's a balancing act,' said McLaren. 'You see, the problem with buildings is that for the Jerry gunners these provide a much bigger and more obvious target. Say you're firing from the first floor and a shell hits the roof, you have the whole ceiling collapse on you. If a shell lands on the ground, on the other hand –'

'It absorbs much of the blast,' said Hawke.

'You're learning, Johnny,' said McLaren. 'Although only as long as you're below ground level, which is why the lads occupying this ground before us very kindly dug us some nice deep slit trenches.' They both climbed the steps of the cellar. 'It was different at the farm. That was an outpost and, although we were getting a little bit of mortaring, most of the heavy stuff was being aimed at the town. Brick and stone is good for defence against small-arms, but nothing much bigger. Trust me, when a shell hits, it's not just the bits of shrapnel from the exploding shell casing that causes the problem, it's a thousand jagged shards of stone and brick too. Clods of soil are a pain in the backside, but they rarely rip your guts open.'

Hawke carried his magazine box down through the walled garden and out over the ramparts on to the ground below. A three-inch mortar crew was sitting in a round pit, about eight feet wide and long, and four feet deep, the excavated earth all around them. Three men sat in the pit, their battle blouses discarded and draped over mortar ammunition boxes.

'You the corporal who helped take out those Jerry panzers?' one of them asked McLaren.

McLaren nodded. 'And this lad here took out a fair few Jerry soldiers.'

Hawke felt himself redden.

'Oh yeah,' said another, 'with that mad sergeant.' He held up a pair of binoculars. 'We were watching it all. Grandstand view from here, see.'

'I reckon that's given us a bit of a respite, so we owe you one.'

'Cheers,' said McLaren.

They moved on a further twenty yards to where Ibbotson, Chalkie White and Fletcher were already in their own machine-gun nest, a similar sized pit, the Bren positioned on its bipod over the lip.

'Here you go, boys,' said McLaren as he put down a tin of magazines, and squatted beside them. 'Hm. A good field of fire from here.' He looked out towards the south and Hawke followed his gaze. From the woods below there was still no sign of any activity, but beyond the still smoking village of Oxelaëre, small clouds of dust could be seen moving across the endlessly flat landscape.

'Look at all that dust,' said Hawke.

'Probably the enemy moving up.'

There was still heavy firing going on to the west and east of the town. From the direction of Zuytpeene it was particularly loud, the chatter of small-arms cutting across the still midday air. Hawke looked either side of him, at the line interspersed with weapons pits, Brens and mortars pointing outwards, down the hill, and a little further on, on the road leading into the square near Battalion HQ, a two-pounder anti-tank gun, protected by a screen of rubble.

'Come on, Johnny,' said McLaren, 'we've positions to prepare.'

Around two o'clock in the afternoon, Hawke sat next to Hebden in the slit trench they were sharing, the soil piled around them and compressed at the front into a lip over which they could look down the hill. They had inherited the pit, but, with their entrenching tools, had deepened it and created seats at either end and at the back so that they could sit in reasonable comfort. They had eaten too, each pair taking it in turns to heat the last of their rations over a Primus set up in the walled garden of the house behind them. The whole platoon was now well spaced out: three Bren teams, with pairs of riflemen in between, and with the company's mortar crews behind them.

Hawke had picked up some more five-round clips of ammunition and had cleaned his rifle – it was now the only part of himself and his equipment that was clean. His battledress was filthy – mud-stained, blackened and beginning to stink of sweat and grime. It was starting to itch too and he shuffled and wriggled in his earth hole.

'It's probably lice,' said Hebden. 'I found a few of the beggars on my jacket earlier.'

'That's all I need,' muttered Hawke.

'Here, take it off a moment.'

Hawke undid the buttons on his shoulder straps, eased the webbing down over his arms, then unbuttoned the serge jacket and passed it to Hebden, who peered at it intently.

'Yes – here you are,' he said, pointing to the seams along the shoulders and under the arms. 'Not too bad – I've seen worse.'

Hawke looked closely and saw several tiny mites crawling along the line of the seams. 'No wonder I'm itching, then,' he said.

'Don't worry – I can sort that out for you.' Hebden pulled out a box of matches, lit one and ran the flame along the edge of the seams.

'Don't set fire to it, Bert,' said Hawke.

Hebden winked. 'I won't.' He lit a second match, repeated the procedure, then passed the jacket back. 'Now give me your shirt.'

Hawke had just taken it off and passed it to Hebden when Spears appeared beside them, crouching down at the edge of their slit trench.

'What the hell do you think you're playing at?' he demanded.

'He's got lice, Sarge,' said Hebden before Hawke could answer.

'I can see what you're doing, Hebden,' Spears snarled, 'but I want to know why this couldn't wait until later. Jerry might attack at any moment.'

'It won't take a moment, Sarge – I'm nearly done.'

Spears looked at Hawke. 'I'd be surprised if you didn't blind the enemy.'

Hawke looked at his white-skinned torso. The ribs were showing at his sides – he'd not noticed that before.

'Just put your uniform back on – now!'

Hebden flicked away the match and passed back the shirt. 'All done,' he grinned. 'You wouldn't want us to be distracted by itching lice, would you, Sarge?'

'Just concentrate on what's in front of you,' said Spears, then hurried back to his own slit trench.

The smell of singed wool now mingled with the odour of sweat and dirt, but Hawke quickly forgot all about it, for no sooner had he dressed again than the Bren next to him opened fire and Spears shouted out, 'Enemy at eleven o'clock!'

Hawke slapped his helmet back on his head and, hastily grabbing his rifle, quickly scanned the ground ahead of him, his heart hammering in his chest. Soldiers were flitting between the trees that extended from the woods and making their way along the low hedgerows that divided the field below them. He felt his hands tighten round his rifle and his mouth go dry. Dull nausea filled his stomach. Behind, a row of trees covered the road that linked Oxelaëre to the eastern side of the town and the sound of tanks and vehicles could be heard rumbling along.

Hebden fired off a single shot and cursed. The Bren spat out another burst, while behind them mortars began firing, the shells falling into the barrel with a dull clunk and then discharging with a louder crash. From below, the faster-firing enemy machine guns were rattling, while their mortars began raining down on the Ranger's positions.

'Damn mortars!' muttered Hebden. 'You can never tell where they're going to land.'

One mortar shell crashed into the houses behind them,

another fell just in front of their positions, and Hawke ducked and then felt grit and soil clattering down on his tin helmet. The stench of cordite and explosive charge was sharp and acrid on the air, and again Hawke felt his throat catch. He spotted a German running between the trees, aimed, allowing plenty of lead, but the man disappeared behind some thicket. The noise was immense. Enemy artillery shelling began again, the missiles hurtling over and exploding behind them.

Suddenly, Spears was up and darting from slit trench to slit trench. 'Don't fire unless you're sure you're going to hit,' he said as he reached Hebden and Hawke. 'Save your ammo. Leave the firing to the MGs and mortars.' He scuttled off once more, but then another mortar shell landed some twenty yards away and to his horror Hawke saw Spears fall flat, as though hit.

'*No!*' he called out, but then once the debris had landed Spears was up again and dashing for his own slit trench. Hawke briefly closed his eyes. His heart was still pounding, his hands shaking.

'It would take more than an enemy mortar to knock out the sarge,' said Hebden. 'I reckon that one's got some kind of guardian angel protecting him.'

Four tanks were now making another attempt to storm the hill, the squeaking and grinding of their tracks audible between the crash of mortars and rattle of small-arms. Three were the slightly larger models, with a narrow gun in the turret, while the fourth was, Hawke saw, the same as the smaller ones with machine guns they had knocked out earlier.

Behind them, the two-pounder positioned at the mouth of the alleyway opened fire. Hawke could see its tracer base and thought the shell would hit the lead tank, but at that moment the panzer lurched into a small trough in the land and the shell passed over it and landed in the ground beyond. Unfortunately, the tracer had given away the gunners' position and the enemy tank now adjusted its direction, swivelled its turret and opened fire. The shell smacked into the wall above the ramparts only ten yards from the two-pounder, but the two-pounder fired again, and this time the shell hit the tank, but bounced off its armour below the turret.

'Did you see that?' exclaimed Hawke.

Hebden nodded, but then both ducked again as another mortar crashed not ten yards away.

'Urghh!' cried out Hebden. 'They're getting closer!' More grit and soil rained down on them, but then they raised their heads and peered out. In the Bren pit, they were changing magazines, while a little further along, just in front of a lone horse chestnut, were Drummond and Foxton. Hawke saw Drummond now look across and run a finger across his throat.

The enemy panzers were getting closer. The lead tank now opened fire again, this time the shell crashing into the building above the covered alleyway, but the two-pounder responded again. The tank moved off, and then a second rumbled up in line. The gunners continued their duel, the tanks moving, stopping, then firing, and the two-pounder somehow continuing unscathed, even though the panzers' shells seemed to be crashing perilously close. One even exploded in the mound of rubble and sandbags stacked up in front of it, but although the gun disappeared briefly behind a cloud of dust and smoke, when it settled, the gunners replied with another round.

'By God, it's getting close,' mumbled Hebden. The mortaring had lessened momentarily. The Bren teams were firing again, their bullets pinging off the tanks. Another duel had begun between one of the other panzers and a two-pounder further along to the right, while the third had pressed further east, towards C Company's lines, and the fourth had begun to open fire with its machine guns, raking the ground in an arc. Hawke saw an A Company Ranger stand up in his slit trench and fire a Boys anti-tank rifle. The .55-calibre bullet hit the turret but the panzer's machine guns replied immediately and a second later the Ranger fell backwards, his arms splayed as the bullets cut him down.

The lead panzer was now just a hundred yards away. A strange calm settled over Hawke. His heart-rate had dropped and, although his ears were ringing, his hands had stopped shaking. With the enemy machine-gun fire, most of the men had ducked below the surface but he now leaned out of his slit trench, his head as low as he could make it, and aimed his rifle at the larger vent to the side of the turret. The gunners fired again, this time aiming lower, and at last the shell caused some damage because the track snapped and unravelled and the tank lurched to a standstill. Hawke's aim had altered, and as he readjusted the tank fired another shell towards the two-pounder. Hawke felt his finger stroke the trigger. Breathing in, he held his breath and, having allowed enough aim-off, fired.

The Enfield pressed hard into his shoulder. There was no sound of any bullet strike and for a moment Hawke thought he must have missed altogether.

'Did you get it?' asked Hebden.

'I'm not sure,' Hawke replied.

The two-pounder fired again, hitting the tank in the wheels a second time. The metal beast jolted and then the hatch opened and two of the crew clambered out. Immediately, the Bren opened fire. One of the tank men tumbled off the hull with a cry, while the second managed to get a few yards before also being cut down. From A Company's lines, the men cheered, but now the second of the larger tanks opened fire again, hitting the rubble protecting the two-pounder positioned on the right on the road below Battalion Headquarters. Dust and grit rolled into the sky and the tank moved forward, heading straight towards 6th Platoon's positions, the third panzer close behind.

Hawke aimed again, focusing on the open viewing vent. The panzer paused, swung its turret a few yards so that it seemed to be pointing directly at them. Hawke squeezed the trigger but his shot was too high, and then the tank fired. Hebden had already ducked, but Hawke felt the whoosh of the cannon shell just inches above his head, then immediately it exploded behind him. Someone cried out, but at the same time the two-pounder at the alley's entrance fired again, hitting the tank, now no more than fifty yards away, and penetrating the metal shell between the hull and the turret. The upper half of the tank exploded, the turret fragmenting into a thousand pieces of lethal metal. Hawke ducked again and shards of metal fizzed into the soil mounded up around them. Gingerly, he lifted his head again. A man was screaming behind him and, turning, Hawke saw the mortar crew had gone. The barrel of the 3-inch mortar lay twisted some yards behind, one of the men had lost both his legs and was sprawled, dead, beside the blackened pit, while a second man lay half out, his eyes wide.

Without thinking, Hawke scrambled out of his slit trench.

Hebden called him back, then, cursing, followed, but as Hawke neared the wounded man he felt his stomach lurch. A dark hole in the man's stomach glistened, while in his reddened hands were his entrails. It was the mortar man who had spoken to them earlier. He had been cheery then, his grin revealing several missing teeth, but now his mouth was covered with blood and wild eyes were staring aghast at his guts spilling out from him. Fully conscious, he was desperately trying to hold them in.

'Help me,' the man stammered.

'What do we do? What do we do?' Hawke asked Hebden.

'All right, mate,' said Hebden, swallowing hard, 'we'll get you help.'

Hawke glanced around. The fourth tank was reversing, but another shell from the two-pounder smacked into its wheels and the track rolled off. The tank veered. Spears was now hurrying, crouching, towards the smashed mortar pit.

'Get back, you two!' he shouted. 'Get back now!' He pulled Hawke by his shoulder. 'Damn it, Hawke! Do you want to get yourself killed?'

'He needs help!' Hawke burst out.

'I can see that, Private!' snarled Spears. 'Now do as I damn well say!'

Hawke scurried back as the stricken panzer opened fire in a wide arc. Flattening himself on the ground, he felt momentary panic but then two shells, fired from both two-pounders, one after the other, smashed into it and exploded, knocking the turret clean into the air. A moment later, Hawke heard a single pistol shot behind him. Turning, he saw Spears look up, defiance in his eyes, the man beside him now dead.

Hawke tumbled back into the slit trench, his mind reeling. Hebden was now tumbling in beside him, his face ashen.

'I've seen some sights since I've been out here,' he jabbered, 'and I thought my stomach was pretty hard. But that . . .' He let the sentence trail.

Hawke said nothing. His hands were shaking again, his heart pounding and his ears were ringing. Directly in front of them, not thirty yards away, were the smouldering remains of the leading panzer. Along to the right, stood the second, while further down the hill was the third. Three out of four tanks destroyed. Behind him, the bloody remains of the mortar crew lay dead and mangled. The air was heavy with the smell of smoke and death. Where was the enemy? Suddenly everything had gone quiet, so that all he could hear was the shrill ringing in his ears.

Hebden was shaking him by the shoulders, and Hawke stared as his friend's mouth opened, but it seemed no words were coming out. Then, as though a cork had been popped, noise flooded back – the sound of mortars and machine-gun fire, the scream of artillery shells overhead, and Hebden saying, 'Johnny! Johnny! Can you hear me?'

Hawke jolted, blinked and said, 'Yes – yes, I can now.'

'You scared me then,' said Hebden, breathing out heavily.

'I couldn't hear a thing – it was strange.' He looked at his friend. 'Spears shot him. He actually shot him.'

'At least someone was prepared to put him out of his misery,' said Hebden. 'Poor bloke. Scared witless and no chance of surviving. The sergeant did the right thing.' He patted Hawke on the shoulder. 'I'm sorry you had to see that, though. God knows, I'm sorry I had to see it.' He half turned his head. 'I'm sorry they're still there. Why did I ever leave the farm, eh, Johnny? Why did I ever join up?'

Hawke sighed and rubbed his eyes. He was beginning to ask himself the same question.

# 17

## SURROUNDED

For a further hour, A Company was pinned down by enemy mortar and machine-gun fire, but the men of 6th Platoon, by hunkering low in their slit trenches, managed to survive unscathed, the missiles falling all around them but not directly on top of them. Then, at around four o'clock, a mortar shell landed within a few yards of Drummond and Foxton's slit trench, and when the dust and earth and grit had settled, Foxton was crying out in agony with a piece of shrapnel stuck in his shoulder.

'Get me out of here!' he cried. 'Please! Arghhh!'

Hawke could see him writhing in agony, with Drummond trying to calm him. 'What should we do, Bert?' he asked Hebden.

'Hey, Charlie,' Hebden called out, 'How bad is it?'

'I can't see,' Drummond replied. 'The stupid beggar's moving too much. But he needs help all right.'

'We'd better get over there and help,' said Hawke. 'I've got some dressings.' Without waiting for Hebden to reply, he hoisted himself up and scampered the twenty yards to Foxton and Drummond and slid in beside them.

'Where's he hit, Charlie?' Hawke asked Drummond.

'In the shoulder. Help me hold him down, will you? We need to get his clobber off him.'

Hawke gripped Foxton's shoulder as Drummond carefully pulled off his webbing. The wounded man cried out again, arching his back with pain.

'Keep still, Foxy, damn you!' exclaimed Drummond. 'We've got to get this stuff off you.'

'Arghh!' screamed Foxton.

With the lieutenant at the far right of the platoon's position, Hebden was calling out to Spears, and by the time Drummond had carefully pulled back Foxton's battle blouse, eased off the white braces, now stained deep red, and torn the shirt clear, Spears was crouching above them. Foxton was still grimacing in agony, his brow feverish with sweat. A large piece of jagged metal stuck out of his shoulder.

'Nasty,' said Spears.

'Isn't it a bit risky squatting there, Sarge?' said Drummond.

Spears glanced around him. 'I'm pretty sure the Jerry MG crews have moved on,' he replied.

'There's still incoming mortar, though,' said Drummond. 'Look what it did to Foxy.'

Spears sighed, then pulled out his hip flask and put it to Foxton's lips. Some went in his mouth, the rest running down his chin. 'Foxy,' said Spears, 'I can't pull that out because I don't know how deep it is inside you. So what we're going to do is try to get you to the MO straight away.' Foxton groaned. Spears looked at Drummond and Hawke, and took a deep breath. 'All right, we're just going to have to take a chance. We'll pull him out, then carry him on to the ramparts and through the garden and house and then one of us can get the

MO.' He glanced at Hawke. 'You stay here. Drummond and I can manage.'

'Can we?' said Drummond. 'It would be a lot easier with Johnny, Sarge.' Another mortar whistled down towards them and Spears flattened himself on the ground. The missile landed near the wrecked tank, which absorbed much of the blast.

'They're not mortaring as much now,' said Hawke.

'They might once they see us struggling with Foxton,' muttered Spears.

'Maybe we should get Bert to help too,' suggested Hawke.

'Good friend you are,' said Drummond. 'Bert's been trying to keep his head down.'

'No, you're right,' said Spears. He called out to Hebden. 'Come and help,' he said.

Foxton was whimpering, the wound glistening around the protruding metal. His chest was streaked with blood and as Spears and Hebden hoisted their hands under his arms, the flesh moved, blood pulsed from the gash and Foxton cried out again.

'Right, let's drag him away,' snapped Spears, 'then, Hawke and Drummond, you jump out and grab his legs.'

Clambering out, Hawke glanced anxiously behind him, then with Drummond grabbed Foxton's legs and together they dashed the fifty yards towards the ramparts. Almost immediately a burst of machine-gun fire rang out, but the bullets were high, then they heard the whistle of incoming mortars, and having placed Foxton flat on the rampart path, each dived on to the ground. Hawke clutched his hands over his head as four mortar shells fell among their positions, bursting huge clods of earth into the air.

'Everyone all right?' called out Spears as the blast subsided.

'Yes, Sarge,' said Hawke, lifting his head. Drummond and Hebden also grunted their presence.

'Good, then let's get him inside.'

Clambering on to the ramparts, Hawke was surprised by how calm he now felt. The panic of earlier had gone. His senses seemed alert once more. The Brens and their own mortars were offering some covering fire, while the wrecked tank seemed to be providing them with protection from the enemy machine-gunner – a piece of unexpected fortune. Without hesitation, Hawke stood over Foxton, and when the others were ready, lifted. Through the open doorway, up the walled garden and in through the back of the building – safe from the next round of mortars that now crashed down outside.

The house was still fully furnished although covered in dust and fallen plaster, and with a musty smell, but the front of the building, facing Grand Place, was in better condition than the rear, and so they placed him on a chaise in the drawing room off the front hall.

'Drummond, you and Hebden stay with him,' said Spears. 'Hawke, you run to Battalion and get the MO or some medical orderlies. I'm going to head upstairs and have a dekko.'

'Yes, Sarge,' said Hawke. He hurried out into the hall, found the front door unlocked and then stepped out on to Grand Place. Even more buildings had been destroyed since they had last been there a few hours earlier, the rubble spilling out on to the square. The noise of battle was sharper again – he could hear small-arms and cannon fire coming from the long street that led towards Dead Horse Corner and from the north. A group of exhausted soldiers was crossing the square from the north-east corner.

'We're surrounded!' one of them called out. 'Jerry's got us surrounded.'

The sound of battle certainly seemed to support the claim, but could that really be the case? *Already?* Hawke ran on, his mind reeling from the news. He wanted to believe it wasn't true, and yet he knew it must be. Ahead stood the burnt-out carrier and upturned car, the piles of rubble, the stench of smoke. Destruction.

Reaching Battalion Headquarters, he struggled to make his presence felt, as officers and clerks appeared to be deeply embroiled in writing and receiving messages, strained expressions on their faces. A young captain was cursing a telephone whose line had been cut yet again. As a shell whistled over and crashed somewhere on Mount Cassel, the building shook and dust fell from the ceilings.

'Excuse me,' said Hawke, 'excuse me, but I'm looking for the MO.'

'You and half the battalion,' said the captain. He turned to one of the clerks, a lance corporal. 'Hoskins,' he said, 'see if you can get a couple of medical orderlies for this fellow, will you?'

Hoskins nodded, pushed back his chair noisily and said to Hawke, 'Follow me.'

He led him back out of the building to the house next door, where the ground floor had been made into a makeshift hospital. Hawke could hear the coughing and groaning from the hallway, but was shocked by what he saw as he entered the main living room. The furniture had been cleared, and mattresses, presumably collected from a number of houses, had been laid out on the floor. Already most were occupied by men in various states of undress and covered in bloody bandages. The doctor was stitching up the head wound of one man who was unconscious, while orderlies were moving around between the others.

Hoskins coughed, then said, 'This man here needs help.'

'What's wrong with you?' the medical officer asked, turning to look at Hawke.

'It's not me, sir,' Hawke explained. 'It's one of my mates. He's got a bit of shrapnel stuck in his shoulder.'

'Well, where is he, then?' snapped the MO.

'Just down the other end of the square, sir. We managed to get him on to a couch.'

'Very well,' the doctor nodded, then called out, 'I need a stretcher to go with this fellow here. Matherson and Spencer – can you go?'

'Sir,' said one of the men. The two men disappeared briefly, then returned carrying a canvas stretcher. Hawke saw that it was bloodstained.

'So,' said one of the orderlies. 'Where is he?'

Hawke led them back to the house where Foxton had slipped out of consciousness. 'That's good in one way,' said Matherson. 'There's no anaesthetic here, so it'll hurt less.'

'But not so good in another,' said Spencer, the taller of the two.

'Just do your best for him, will you?' said Drummond as the orderlies placed Foxton on the stretcher. 'He's our mate. A good lad, is Foxy.'

'We'll do what we can,' said Spencer. 'The MO's a good sort. If anyone can save him, it's the doc.'

When Foxton had gone, Hawke said, 'I saw some men. Ox and Bucks, I think. They said we're surrounded.'

'Then how the hell are we ever going to get out of here?' asked Drummond.

Hebden said, 'Let's go and find the sarge.'

Reaching the first floor, and with no sign of Spears, they then took a narrow wooden staircase that wound its way up to the attic. Still peering out of an open dormer window, field glasses to his eyes, was the sergeant.

'Foxy's been taken off,' said Hebden. 'He's unconscious, though.'

Spears lowered his binoculars. 'We've got off lightly, all things considered.'

'And Johnny here has heard that we're now surrounded.'

Spears paused, then moved away from the window. 'You can pretty much see that for yourselves.' He offered his binoculars to Hebden. 'You can see their field artillery to the south beyond the woods, but then look to the east and west.

'Blimey,' muttered Hebden. After a short while, he passed the binoculars in turn to Hawke, who peered out. All the roads to the south seemed to be full of enemy traffic, dust clouds marking their progress. A field gun, perhaps two miles away, flashed and moments later he heard the shell whooshing towards the town. For a moment, Hawke thought it was heading straight for them, but it exploded some two hundred yards away to their right.

To the east of the town, moving in a wide arc, he saw a large number of tanks, half-tracks, trucks and motorcycles gathering at an assembly point, while to the west of the town, a column of tanks and trucks was steadily moving forward. Hawke was speechless.

'Now you know what a Jerry armoured division looks like

on the move,' said Spears, as Hawke passed the binoculars to Drummond.

'What the hell are we going to do?' said Drummond.

Spears shrugged. 'It's a bit late to pull back.'

Drummond gave the sergeant the binoculars then, clenching his fists, kicked the wall twice.

'No!' he exclaimed. 'No! This can't be happening. We've been left here, haven't we? What, to die? Or to spend the rest of the bleeding war as Jerry prisoners?' He glared at the others, his eyes watery with tears. 'I shouldn't be here. I should never have joined up. Should have stayed at home and played football.' He kicked the wall again. 'I could have been a professional footballer by now, and instead I'm stuck here, in this bomb-blasted hole, watching my mates get knocked over and surrounded by bleedin' Jerries.'

'Easy, Charlie,' said Spears.

'Anything could happen,' said Hebden. 'Maybe our lads will counter-attack. Maybe we'll be able to make our way out of here after all. The Germans can't be everywhere, can they? You can't give up hope yet.'

'Bert's right,' said Spears. 'But now we need to get back to the platoon. We've been away too long already.'

Spears led them down to the ground floor, but as they stood by the rear of the garden, waiting to move out on to the ramparts, he turned to them and said, 'Remember this. We're all alive. We've made it through some tough fighting so far today, despite the odds. If we can do it today, we can do it tomorrow.' He patted Drummond on the arm. 'Don't give up yet.'

## 18

## SILENT NIGHT

The Germans did not attack again that day, 27 May. Desultory shelling continued until evening, but the mortars had gone and so had the machine-gunners. Firing could be heard to the south-east and to the north, but as the sun began to set towards the west, so a strange stillness descended on Cassel. From his slit trench, Hawke watched the thinning wisps of smoke in the plain below, but further away, on the roads to the south and west, clouds of smoke continued to show an enemy army on the move.

At eight o'clock, the platoon was stood down. A prowler guard was established of two riflemen and a Bren crew, but the rest of the platoon moved back to the walled garden and the house they had taken over as their own. All the men were exhausted – exhausted and hungry, although there was more bad news: there were no more rations. Somer Force would have to survive on what food it could scrounge from the town.

Some wine had already been found in the cellars as well as a larder of pots of jam and honey and some tinned food, but it was not enough to feed the platoon, so Lieutenant Farrish asked for a group of volunteers to see what could be found. For once, Hawke felt in no mood for volunteering.

'I'll go,' Spears offered. 'That way I can make sure they don't get themselves drunk and that they behave themselves. You know what these Frogs are like – there's bound to be wine in all the cellars.' He took Miller, White and Fletcher.

No sooner had they gone, however, than a truck pulled up outside the front of the building on Grand Place and two medical orderlies, one of whom was Matherson, clambered down and announced that they had come to collect the dead.

'Of course,' Farrish said, as the two men were brought to him in the garden at the back. 'You'll need some help.'

'Thank you, sir,' said Matherson, who was carrying a bundle of blankets in his arms. 'We want to get it done before the light fades completely, so any help would be much appreciated.'

Farrish looked around, saw Ibbotson, Hawke, Drummond and Hebden standing around the Primus. 'You four,' he said, 'help these men with burial detail.'

Hawke groaned inwardly and cursed himself for not offering to help scavenge for food.

'Haven't we done more than our fair share today?' muttered Drummond as they followed the men out on to the ramparts.

'How many are out here?' asked Matherson as he began laying out the blankets on the ground.

'Three mortar men,' said Hebden, 'a couple of Jerries. Do you want them too?'

'Yes. We'll take the lot. Don't want them rotting in front of us, do we?'

'Were there any others in A Company?' Hebden said, looking at Miller. 'Dusty, you were a bit further along from us, weren't you?'

'One slit trench got a direct hit, but there's not much left there,' he said.

'We've got to collect all the bits,' said Matherson, matter-of-factly. 'They like to have something to bury where possible.'

'And what about O'Connell?' said Drummond. 'And Collier?'

'Where were they?' said Matherson.

'Further over. On the track we came up earlier.'

'In A Company's sector?'

'No – they were Glosters, come to think of it.'

'Then they're not our problem,' said Matherson. 'Now let's get to it.'

'We'll get the Jerries,' said Drummond quickly. 'Come on, lads.'

Matherson gave them a wry grin. 'That's all right,' he said, 'we'll get the mortar men and the bits.' He patted his stomach. 'It's made of steel.'

There were just two Germans to collect, both lying face down on the ground a few yards from their tank, but as they reached the panzer, Hawke paused to look at it, running his hands along the smooth, cool metal, and the black cross painted on its side below the turret.

'It's not so intimidating up close like this, is it?' said Hebden. 'Look, you're almost as tall.'

'What size gun is that, do you think, Bert?' Hawke asked.

Hebden rubbed his chin and then peered at the barrel. 'I'm not sure. Not much more than an inch, is it? No wonder they never managed to knock out our two-pounders. It's just a small cannon.' He looked at the smaller, perforated barrel protruding next to it. 'And a machine gun too.' He patted the turret. 'No, I'm very glad I don't have to sit inside one of these things. Three men in there! Blimey! I bet it gets horrible hot and there's barely enough room inside to scratch your backside.'

'Get a move on!' Matherson called out.

'Who does he think he is, ordering us around?' said Drummond, who was rummaging through one of the dead men's kit.

'Found anything, Charlie?' asked Hebden.

'Got a nice little pistol,' said Drummond, holding up a small black leather case.

'Come on, Charlie,' said Ibbotson, standing over the dead man. 'Let's get this over with.'

'We don't want to be too keen,' said Drummond, 'or they'll start making us pick up body parts.' He now held up a small horseshoe-shaped ring of metal, which had a cross-piece on to which were attached a screwdriver end, a corkscrew and a pick, folded back into the ring. 'Here, what do you make of that? Ingenious. I reckon that'll come in handy, that will.'

'Perks of the job, eh, Charlie?' Hebden grinned as he and Hawke stood over the second dead man.

'You got to take them when you can,' Drummond replied.

'Come on, Johnny,' said Hebden, 'let's get to it. I haven't quite got the same urge to scrounge off this poor chap, have you?'

'No,' said Hawke, bending down and grabbing the man's ankles. 'I just want to get back and have something to eat. I'm starving, but this is putting me off my food.'

'Don't go throwing up on us again, Johnny,' said Drummond.

Hawke smiled. 'I won't. I think I've become hardened.'

'There speaks the voice of experience,' said Hebden. 'Sixteen years old and already a battle-hardened veteran.'

Hawke grinned bashfully. But what Spears had told him had

been true – the first sight of death had been the worst. A couple of days of hard fighting and his stomach had become lined with steel. When they reached Matherson, the dead Rangers had already been laid on a rug each and the wool wrapped around them and pinned together. They now laid down the Germans and watched the stretcher bearers reach down and find the dead men's identity tags. Unlike the British ones, which were cardboard, the Germans' were aluminium, and oval shaped with a perforated line across the middle. Matherson snapped both, pocketing the two halves and leaving the remainder on their chains. Then he deftly wrapped and pinned them.

'All right,' he said, 'let's get them out to the truck.'

A short while later, they were back in the walled garden, sitting around the Primus.

'We should have taken some of that beef with us,' said Hebden. A billy can of water and tea leaves was already beginning to boil.

'What, and have large chunks of bloody meat stuffed into our packs? No, thanks,' said Drummond. 'I've seen enough raw flesh for one day. Anyway, we hardly had the time to start hacking up bits of cow before we left.'

'I can't believe we only left the farm this morning,' said Hawke. 'Seems like days ago.'

'Don't it just,' said Hebden. 'Sad to think it's all burned down. It makes me think of our own place, back home. I'd hate for anything to happen to it.'

'What did you farm?' asked Hawke as Hebden gave the tea a stir with his bayonet.

'A bit of everything. Sheep, a bit of arable, and a few dairy cows. It's not big – a couple of hundred acres, but we did all right. Never went hungry, anyway.'

'Didn't you? Blimey, I did,' said Drummond. 'I was starving nearly all the time – well, not starving, but hungry.'

'Me too,' said Ibbotson. 'There was only the three of us – my mum and my sister, Betty, but it was hard. With Dad gone, my mum had to go out and work in the mill, but they didn't pay her much, the thieving swines.'

'We didn't have much by way of money either,' added Drummond, 'not with five of us kids to feed. Didn't even eat meat that often. At least me being here makes a bit of a difference at home. Not only do I save them food, I can send them home some of my pay too.'

'For what it's worth,' grinned Hebden.

'Yeah – not much. But I tell you I've eaten better since I joined the army than I ever did in civvie life.'

'Apart from now,' said Hawke.

'Yes.' Drummond rolled his eyes.

The tea began to boil.

'Brew's up,' said Hebden, calling out to the rest of the section. Pouring hot, sweet tea into the outstretched tin mugs, he said, 'We'll all feel better for this – although what we'll do if we run out of tea and sugar, God only knows. Then we will have a calamity on our hands.'

'Frogs don't really drink tea, do they?' said Drummond.

'No,' said McLaren, now standing with them. 'No wonder they're struggling.'

'I wonder what'll happen to the people who lived here,' said Hawke. A fair few had remained when they'd first reached the town – people who had since been ordered to leave. The town, until the war had erupted, must have been a thriving, busy market town, Hawke guessed. Now it was a desolate war zone.

'I suppose eventually they'll come back,' suggested Hebden. 'Even if the Jerries take it over. Once the battle stops, people will feel it's safe to return.'

'And they'll find their homes burnt and ruined,' said Drummond.

'And their cellars cleaned out,' said McLaren. '*Zut alors, les Anglais* have stolen *les vins*!' Everyone laughed.

'It is sad, though, isn't it?' said Hebden, echoing Hawke's own thoughts. 'I mean, right now, we're just thinking about ourselves and making sure we're all right, but this is some French bloke's house we're in. We haven't asked his permission or anything.' He smiled. 'I'm still grateful to him, though. Might even get some decent kip in here tonight.'

'I hope so,' said Ibbotson. 'I feel dead to the world.' He sat down next to Hawke, his hands clasped round his enamel mug.

'Your mother never remarried, then?' Hawke asked him.

Ibbotson shook his head. 'No. They were childhood sweethearts. I was only three when he died – it was at Arras. April 1918.'

'Near where we were before here,' said Hawke.

Ibbotson nodded. 'Yes, it's made me start thinking about him a bit, to be honest. I saw all those cemeteries around the town. He's buried in one of them – which, though, God only knows.'

'You've never seen his grave?'

'Don't sound so surprised, Johnny. We didn't have money for trips to France. Not even my mum. We were sent a photograph of it, though. One day I'll make sure she gets out here. I know it broke her heart. She'd want to see where Dad's lying now.' They were silent a moment and then Ibbotson said, 'Your dad died too, didn't he?'

'But not in the war. A few years later.'

'But if it weren't for the war, he'd still be alive?'

Hawke nodded. 'I suppose so.'

Ibbotson sighed. 'I missed him, growing up. I don't really remember him. I like to tell myself I do, but I don't really. I wish I had. I wish I could just have – I don't know . . . I wish I could have had a chance to talk to him properly, ask him a few things.'

'I know what you mean,' said Hawke. 'I think that all the time.'

Ibbotson looked at him. 'Do you?' He sighed. 'I also worry about Mum. She hated the idea of me joining up.'

'I didn't tell mine.'

Ibbotson grinned. 'You don't say.'

Hawke felt himself flush.

'But I just felt I had to,' Ibbotson continued. 'I wanted to know what Dad had gone through. I suppose I wanted to be closer to him in a way.'

'That's how I felt,' admitted Hawke.

Ibbotson sighed again. 'But now . . . I don't know. I worry what would happen to her if anything happened to me.'

'I can't even think about it.'

Ibbotson looked at him again, then picked up a stone and lobbed it gently away. 'No,' he said at length. 'It's probably best not to.'

Spears and his gang of foragers returned not long after. They had not been the only ones looking for food, but despite the competition had brought back a couple of cured hams, some old bread, plenty of cheese, some more wine and several dry boxes of last season's apples, as well as an assortment of other supplies. Food was carefully divided up into sections, with enough held back for the following day.

Having eaten, and knowing that he was on prowler guard from midnight until three, Hawke took Hebden's advice and went into the house to find himself a place to sleep. Remembering the cupboard he had seen in the attic, he climbed the stairs, found a wool rug and a quilt and made a rough bed for himself on the floor. Outside, it was almost dark, the stars just beginning to twinkle through the open window. Hawke closed his eyes, and in moments was fast asleep.

Spears had insisted that Lieutenant Farrish should get some sleep – and in one of the beds still made up on the first floor. The lieutenant had half-heartedly resisted, but soon gave in. 'If you're absolutely sure, Spears,' he said.

'I am, sir,' Spears told him. 'You look knackered, if you don't mind me saying so.' It was true. Dark rings lined Farrish's eyes, while his lean face looked gaunt and smudged with dirt.

'I think we're all pretty done in.' He smiled. 'I don't mind saying, Spears, I had never really imagined finding myself in a situation like this.'

'It was hard fighting today, sir.'

'Yes – and the men did magnificently. I'm only sorry that we've lost so many. They were my responsibility.'

'It could have been a lot worse, sir. But you're right – they did do well. They kept their heads.'

'You know, I'm proud of them. All of them. I really couldn't have asked for more.' Farrish ran his hands through his hair. 'I wonder what will happen tomorrow. I know we're surrounded now, but do you think we'll ever get away from here? The future suddenly seems so . . . so damned bleak, and yet it's our job to try and keep their morale up.'

'Best not to think too hard about these things, sir. All we can do is whatever's asked of us to the best of our ability. We're not the generals. We get given a line to defend and we do it. But don't worry about the lads. They'll be all right.'

'I hope you're right. Some of them have lost close friends.'

'Try not to worry about it, sir. Get some kip and you'll feel a lot better.'

Farrish nodded. 'All right, Spears. But make sure you get some sleep as well. I'm going to need you tomorrow – and fit and fresh too.'

Farrish left him alone in the kitchen – the only room in the house not heavy with already resting Rangers. Spears had found another bottle of Calvados and, taking a tumbler from a cupboard, he poured himself a generous measure, then filled up his hip flask, and sat down at the table. On the wall, an old clock ticked rhythmically. Leaning his elbows on the table, he drank the Calvados and rubbed his face, and thought of Maddie. He wondered what she had been doing that day and was glad that she had not witnessed what he had seen. That lad at the mortars. Jenkins had been his name – he'd seen him about a bit before the balloon had gone up. He'd even shared a drink with him once or twice, but to see him lying there, his guts in his hands, the look of terror on his face.

Spears shook his head and poured himself another large drink, and prayed that when it was his turn he would go quickly.

Shooting Jenkins had not been easy, but it had been the right thing to do.

He remembered a time when he had been young, no more than ten or so, when one of the farm horses had become ill. Those horses had been like pets – beloved by them all, part of the working team of the farm. But Chester was in pain and not going to live, so his father had asked him to steady the horse and put a pistol to the big fellow's head and shot him.

Now, some fifteen years later, Spears had done the same thing, but not to a horse, to a man, a human being. It *had* been the right thing to do, he told himself again – Jenkins would never have lived – but that had not made it any easier. Jenkins's face – the sheer terror – would haunt him until his dying days. Of that he was certain.

He wished he could tell Maddie – she was the one person who might be able to help, who would understand, but he knew he could never inflict such a memory on her. Maddie was an innocent, and he loved her for it. No, he thought, whatever images of Jenkins remained would have to stay his, and his only. That was a burden he would simply have to carry himself.

He drank again and then pulled out his pad of pale blue writing paper, mercifully still clean despite the mud and bloodstains on his battle blouse.

*My darling Maddie*, he began, then thought of the half-dozen letters he had written and never sent and wondered whether he ever would and whether they'd ever reach her. *I hope you are well and enjoying as warm an early summer as we are over here. The blossom is out, the hedgerows full of green and the birdsong incessant – although less so today. The Germans attacked us but we managed to beat them off.* That was true, he thought, although he could not say the enemy now had them surrounded. *We lost a few good lads, but fortunately both Johnny and myself are fine and still in good heart.* He paused again, then added, *Your brother is a brave fellow – he's always the first to volunteer, even though I keep telling him not to. Today he came to help me and then ran to help a wounded man in his section. I keep saying to him that he has nothing to prove, but I think he does these things on instinct. From what you and your family have told me of your father, it seems as though he must be a chip off the old block.*

Spears paused again. The figure of John Hawke, Maddie's father, was a big presence in the family. He had not been forgotten over the passing years. There was that photograph of him on the mantelpiece above the grate in the drawing room – his gentle brown eyes gazing out at them all, and Spears could not remember a visit to their Headingley house when their father had not come up in conversation. To begin with, he had wondered how Richard Mallaby had felt having to listen to endless references and tales about his wife's first husband, but then realized that Richard spoke of him just as often. The two had been best friends – close mates since they were little. Spears got the impression that Richard missed him as much as anyone.

And it had been Richard who had told Spears about John Hawke's heroism in the last war. It had been one night the previous summer, when the two of them had stayed up, at Richard's instigation. Lucy and the girls had left them to it and over a bottle of whisky the whole story had come out. There had been the storming of the German trenches at Loos in 1915, when officers had all been cut down and the company had found itself leaderless. He had won the Military Medal – the MM –

for that. At the Somme, John Hawke had rescued their lieutenant, carrying him back from a shell-hole to their lines, across no-man's-land, despite being hit twice himself in doing so.

He had been given the Distinguished Conduct Medal for that one. The bullets had been pulled out and he had been patched up and back at the front by April the following year, in time for the spring offensive at Arras, where he had once again shown both extreme bravery and considerable leadership skills. And finally there had been Passchendaele. With the company commander wounded, John Hawke had again taken over command, leading the men in an attack that had seen them reach the third line of German trenches and in the process capture more than two hundred of the enemy. That had gained him a bar to his MM, although if Richard was to be believed – and he had been there, at John Hawke's side – had he been an officer he would have been given a Victoria Cross. Later in the battle, as the rain had fallen and the ground turned to slurry, the Germans had used mustard gas and it was this that had finally brought John Hawke's war to an end. He had recovered, had fathered three more children in Molly, Joan and Johnny, but the wounds he had suffered and the gas that had damaged his lungs had left him weak. In the November of 1923, five years after the armistice, John had caught the flu, which had then become pneumonia. And that had killed him.

It had been Richard Mallaby who had saved the family from destitution. Richard, who had solemnly promised as John had lain sweating and dying, that he would look after his friend's family. So he had, and in time he and Lucy had come to an understanding and married.

Spears remembered that evening vividly, despite the whisky. 'Don't you feel as though you're living in the shadow of another man?' he'd asked Richard.

'He'd have done the same for me,' Richard replied. 'How could I let my best friend's family face destitution?'

John Hawke might have died, but his spirit remained. Spears had felt even more keenly that he had to live up to that reputation, that he had to prove he was every bit the soldier Maddie's father had been. Perhaps that was why he had been so ready to tell Johnny stories of fighting Pashtuns in the North-West Frontier, and of subduing the Arabs in Palestine. He had been careful not to mention the crippling fear he'd felt as a boy soldier, heading overseas for the first time, or the terror he'd felt when he'd faced a sword-wielding tribesman in the Swat Valley. He cursed now – cursed John Hawke, cursed his own bragging, and cursed the fact that now he was sitting in a house somewhere in Flanders, not so very far from where Maddie's father had performed such feats more than twenty years earlier. Because they were now surrounded and he honestly did not know how he was ever going to get himself or the boy Johnny out of there.

# 19

## TEA RATION

All morning, the men had stood to, watching from their trenches, farm buildings, houses in the town and from behind the piles of rubble and sandbags barring all routes into Cassel. Yet despite steady, regular shelling, there had been no sign so far of any enemy attack.

At Somer Force Headquarters, there was concern about the dwindling supplies of ammunition and the shortage of food. The latter had been partially resolved by authorizing looting of the town. It had sat uneasily with the brigadier, but had been considered a necessity. The shortage of ammunition, although not yet critical, could not be so readily resolved. Instructions had been sent round to unit commanders telling them to ensure their men fired only when strictly necessary, an order that was easier to uphold when the enemy was doing little other than lobbing shells towards them. It was why every passing minute and hour that the enemy did not make an all-out attack was something of a godsend.

Even so, this respite did little to lift Brigadier Somerset's mood. At around eleven, he and his chief of staff strode up to the windmill at the top of Mount Cassel. The old mill was miraculously still in one piece, but all around the evidence of the past two days of shelling was all too clear to see. A large number of buildings had been hit, several had caught fire, the stench of which, even now the flames had subsided, still hung heavy on the air. Around the town, many of the trees had been blasted, jagged stumps remaining where just the day before they had been proudly standing in full bloom. Blackened vehicles stood mangled and burnt out on every street. It was raining too, the brightness of the day before replaced by leaden skies and low cloud.

Both men peered through their field glasses, the brigadier facing north.

'Enemy columns to the north,' he muttered. 'And to the west.'

'There are more to the south too, I'm afraid, sir,' said Bullmore. 'But there's no sign of them attacking. It's strange. I can't work out what Jerry's playing at.'

Somerset lowered his binoculars and turned to his chief of staff. 'I can,' he said. 'He hammered us from all sides yesterday, and now he's cutting off all our lines of retreat and stabilizing his front to the north. God knows what's going on with the rest of the BEF, but no doubt the enemy's still pressing forward. Closing the ring. He knows that the more ground he secures, the more hopeless is our situation here.'

Bullmore sighed. 'Does he still need Cassel?'

'I think so, yes. It's the apex of five major roads and it's still the best vantage point in all of Flanders.'

'If only we knew what was happening at Dunkirk.'

Somerset rubbed his mouth, deep in thought, then said, 'Bully, do you think we should try to pull out tonight? We've held up the Huns for more than a day, but is there anything more to be achieved by staying here?'

'Our orders are to stay, sir. To fight and hold off the enemy until thirty May.'

'Yes, but they were also to hold up the enemy for as long as possible in an effort to give the rest of the BEF a chance to escape. Are we still holding up the enemy?'

Bullmore thought for a moment. 'Yes, sir, I think we are. They're still shelling us, so that's tying up artillery pieces, and as you pointed out a moment ago Jerry still needs to take Cassel. The harder we make it for him, the better.'

Somerset breathed in heavily. 'All these men,' he said. 'I don't want to be the one that throws them to the lions.'

'You're not, sir. It's GHQ who ordered us here. We're just carrying out our orders.'

'It doesn't feel that way.' He sighed. 'So you think we should stay put until we receive instructions to the contrary, or for a further two days – or until such a point that we can no longer continue?'

'It seems bleak, I know,' said Bullmore.

'No, you're right, Bully.' Somerset sighed again, then looked up at the sky and felt the light rain patter down upon his face. 'Come on,' he said, 'let's get back. No point getting soaked as well as shelled.'

Hawke did not know it, but Captain Astell had been of rather the same opinion as the brigadier. With the rain falling and with no sign of any massing enemy to the south, he had given orders to his platoon commanders that picquets should continue keeping watch from the forward positions just as they had through the night, but that the rest of the men could keep watch from the buildings behind.

Hawke had spent the morning cleaning his rifle, packing and repacking his kit and staring out of the ground-floor window at the rain. Shelling had continued, but none had landed near them. Hawke barely flinched at all now when the missiles screamed over, their dark shapes scything through the sky towards them.

At noon, he and Hebden had taken their turn on picquet duty. The farm where they had been stationed for three days was still smouldering, thin wisps of smoke rising through the rain. Both Hawke and Hebden had put on their gas capes, designed to protect them against any possible gas attack, but more use against the wet. They still felt damp, however. The rain pattered against their steel helmets.

'I've got drips running off the edge,' said Hebden.

'Me too,' said Hawke. 'Imagine having to live in trenches all the time like they did in the last war.'

'They had dug-outs, though,' said Hebden. 'And they were rotated, weren't they? They weren't in the front line all the time. But I know what you mean. I've got great big clods of earth on my boots and my backside's getting wet.'

They were silent for a moment, and then Hawke said, 'All that fighting yesterday and now look at it. Oxelaëre seems pretty quiet today.'

'What's left of it. I wonder what's happened to those cows and chickens. I hate to think of animals being in distress.'

'I was wondering what's happened to the rest of the company. Over a hundred men moved into the village the other day, and how many came out? Our lot plus a dozen others. That's less than forty men.'

'It's sad. The company's gone. I've always been in B Company.

Mind you, I've always been in Sixth Platoon too, and at least that's still living and breathing.'

'But what do you think has happened to them?' said Hawke. 'All those blokes?'

Hebden shrugged. 'I suppose Jerry took their rifles away, then marched them off somewhere. Eventually, they'll probably be sent to Germany, to some POW camp. How they'll be treated, I wouldn't know.'

'Well, I'm not going to be taken prisoner,' said Hawke.

'What if we're all surrounded and there's no alternative?'

'I don't know. I'll run, or hide, or something until they've gone, then sneak out at night.' He turned to look at Hebden. 'I'd rather die, Bert! All I know is that I'm not going to spend the rest of the war in POW camp.'

'All right, Johnny,' said Hebden, 'all right. But remember we've hopefully both got a lot of life left yet. I don't want to be a Jerry prisoner either, but given the choice I think I'd rather live than be killed for no good reason.'

'We shouldn't even talk of such things,' said Hawke. 'Somehow we'll get out of here. I can't believe we won't.'

Hebden grinned at him. 'That's the spirit. You know, I'm glad you joined us, Johnny. Don't get me wrong, Charlie's a great bloke, and so are the other lads, but it's good to have a bit of optimism about the place. Good for morale, I reckon.'

The afternoon wore on, and the rain began to ease, although low cloud covered the skies. Hawke found himself becoming increasingly restless. There was too much waiting – waiting for an enemy that would not attack, and yet even though Hawke was only a private, he was keenly aware – as they were all aware – that their situation was hardly good, isolated as they were, completely cut off from the rest of the BEF. Food was running low and so too was ammunition. Hawke had forty-five rounds – nine five-round clips – and that was it. The stash of tins of Bren magazines was also getting low: just thirteen remained. That was one hundred and fifty-six for all three Brens in the platoon, each containing thirty rounds. For a light machine gun that had an effective rate of fire of 120 rounds per minute, that was not a great deal. He wondered how many rounds the gunners and mortar men had left. One thing was certain: they could not last here for too much longer. Another day? Maybe two? Three, perhaps, if the Germans left them alone for a while longer.

It was all so uncertain, but the previous day, when so much had happened, Hawke had not thought about such things. Now, however, he had time to brood and to worry. It wasn't death that was troubling him – that was simply too impossible to imagine – but, rather, the thought of being taken prisoner, and of being dragged into Germany. It made him feel an overwhelming sense of claustrophobia just to think of it. He'd meant what he'd told Hebden, and the more the afternoon wore on the more he was determined that no German would make him his captive.

Hawke was conscious that he was not the only one finding the tension increasingly difficult to stomach. The men were all subdued. All were hungry, all were filthy. There was still running water in both houses, but none that was hot, and although they could wash there was no point in being too thorough because their clothes were all soiled and dirty and there was nothing they could do about that. The single lavatories in each house had long since become blocked, and the stench pervaded the buildings, mingling with the smoke and dust and sweat and stale tobacco.

By mid-afternoon, Hawke had begun to itch again. Removing his battledress and shirt he had burned off several lice from the seams, as had most of the rest of the section. Yet it was not the growing number of lice that was worrying Hebden, but the dwindling rations of tea.

'I can live without milk in my char,' he said, 'but I do need a regular brew.'

'You're being ridiculous, Bert,' McLaren told him. 'We've got bigger things to worry about here than the lack of tea.'

'I don't think so, Corp,' Hebden replied as they stood on the ground floor watching the south from the now smashed windows. The glass had been cleared up, but there were still shards lingering between the dust and dirt on the floor. 'It's what keeps me going.'

'It's only a bleedin' cup of tea,' said McLaren.

'No it's not. It's the looking forward to the next one, the lighting of the stove, the brewing it and adding the sugar, then the drinking of it. If I can't brew up, I might as well hand myself in to Jerry now.'

'Then you'll be even less likely to get a brew,' said Drummond.

'When we're stood down tonight, I'm going on a scrounge,' said Hebden. 'There must be tea lurking about the place somewhere.'

'Can I come with you?' asked Hawke.

'And me,' said Drummond. 'I'm sick of this place. Anything for a change of scene.'

'You'll need permission from the lieutenant or the sarge,'

said McLaren. 'But, if you do go, for God's sake don't just bring back tea. It's grub we need more than char. That small square of Froggie cheese and thin slice of ham we had for tiffin has left me feeling starving. My stomach's grumbling something rotten.'

The platoon was stood down at 7 p.m., and Lieutenant Farrish gave Hebden permission to look for rations with Drummond and Hawke, but ordered Spears to go with them.

'Where do you think we should try, then, Sarge?' asked Hebden as they emptied their sacks and haversacks into an empty cupboard in the kitchen.

'There's a number of houses up around Mount Cassel, near the windmill,' said Spears. 'I reckon we should head there. It's near Brigade HQ so I'm hoping they'll have had less need to loot. Also, there's quite a lot of rubble to clamber over, which might have put off some others.'

Outside on Grand Place, the town looked even more desolate. Another day of shelling had taken its toll. Several more houses had been hit and now lay partly strewn across the cobbles. There were other troops out and about, all looking tired and drawn, their uniforms dirty and torn. As they turned off the square, they saw a telegraph pole had been knocked over and that wire now lay limply across the road. A group of sappers were in the process of clearing it, but since their way was still blocked Spears led them down a narrow lane and then up some steps to the foot of the windmill at the summit of Mount Cassel.

Too late, they saw the brigadier with two of his staff officers approaching from the right, from the direction of Somer Force

Headquarters. Immediately, Spears brought the other three to attention and saluted.

The brigadier saluted back. 'At ease, at ease,' he said, pausing beside them. 'How are you chaps?'

'Fine, thank you, sir,' said Spears. A sudden rumble from the sky made them all look up. Overhead, just below the cloud cover, a dozen enemy fighter planes roared over.

'All right for some, eh?' said the brigadier. He smiled. 'You're Rangers. What company are you in?'

'B Company, sir,' said Spears, 'or rather, we were, sir. Now we're attached to A Company.'

'Good Lord!' said Somerset. 'You weren't the fellows I watched take out those panzers yesterday were you?'

Spears allowed himself a faint smile. 'Possibly, sir. We managed to successfully pull out of the farm at Oxelaëre and then saw the enemy tanks approaching as we were trying to reach the town, sir.'

'What's your name, sergeant?'

'Spears, sir.'

'Well, it was a damn good show, Spears, and right in front of everyone too – gave everyone a lift, I can tell you. I know it did me.' He shook their hands all in turn, then, seeing Hawke, his eyes narrowed in recognition. 'Now I remember bumping into you the other day. What was the name again?'

'Hawke, sir. And you met Privates Hebden and Drummond too, sir.' Spears glared at him.

Somerset smiled. 'So I did, so I did. Good to see you men. Now, are you here for any reason?'

Spears cleared his throat. 'We're looking for some rations, sir.'

'We're getting low on tea, sir,' added Hebden.

'Well, we can't have that. I'm sure I can help you on that score,' said Somerset.

'We've plenty of tea at Headquarters,' said the captain standing beside him.

'Thank you, sir,' said Hebden, his face brightening.

Somerset raised a hand. 'It's the very least I can do after what you chaps did yesterday.'

He glanced at the captain. 'Robson, take these men back to Headquarters, give them some tea and do whatever else you can.'

'Of course, sir.'

'Thank you, sir,' said Spears. 'And, sir? Do you know how much longer we'll be here?'

Somerset glanced at his chief of staff. 'I wish I could say, Sergeant, but I hope not much longer. We have been playing a vital role, however. That much I can say. Good luck, and keep up the excellent work.'

Spears saluted again. 'Thank you, sir.'

'Follow me,' said Captain Robson.

They followed, Hebden wearing a big grin on his face and punching one hand with the other in delight. At the entrance to Headquarters, Robson asked them to wait. 'I won't be long,' he said.

'You're a jammy beggar, Bert,' said Spears once Robson had disappeared inside.

'I thought we were going to get a rollocking at first,' said Hawke.

'Me an' all,' said Drummond.

'He's a good bloke, is the brigadier,' Hebden grinned. 'As I've always said, it's not what you know, but who you know.'

'It's the sarge here who got us the tea ration, Bert,' said Drummond. 'He was the one who took out them panzers, not you. That's why the brig helped us out.'

'I was joking, Charlie, only joking.'

'Yes, well, maybe I'm just not feeling in much of a jokey mood,' muttered Drummond. 'The only thing that's going to perk me up is getting out of this hole. You heard the brig. We're not going anywhere any time soon and he knows it.'

'Look,' said Spears, 'feeling sorry for yourself isn't going to help. We don't know what's going to happen – we really don't, so there's no point worrying about what we don't know. Now, let's get our tea ration, then find some scoff, and when we get back we can have a brew and something to eat. Tomorrow's another day. Let's worry about it then.' He patted Drummond on the back. 'Come on, Charlie, we've survived another day, haven't we? At least we're all alive, eh?'

'For now,' muttered Drummond, 'but for how much longer?'

# 20

## BLITZ

They had eaten well the previous evening thanks to the food that had been found among the shattered remains of a row of houses not far from Somer Force Headquarters. The amount of rubble and the precarious state of the damaged buildings had clearly deterred other scavengers. But in return for the risks taken, they had been rewarded with half a dozen cured sausages, a couple of plucked chickens and three ducks, more cheese, as well as several bottles of Armagnac. And, of course, there had been the generous tea ration handed over by Captain Robson. It had meant that at first light, on Wednesday 29 May, the men of 6th Platoon had all been able to have a warming mug or two. Even Drummond had been grateful for that.

Hawke and Hebden had been on prowler guard, as picquet duty was known, from six in the morning – one of the best slots and recompense for having had the worst the previous evening. The rain had stayed away during the night, but patchy grey cloud still covered the sky, and just before six, as Hawke and Hebden sipped mugs of hot, sweet tea, it had still been cold, so that Hawke had fastened the top clip of his battle blouse and turned up his collar, and clutched his enamel mug with both hands.

At six, they clambered down over the ramparts and made their way back to their slit trench. The soil was still damp from the previous day's rain, while out to the south a grey light covered the endless flat plain of Flanders.

'It still seems quiet, doesn't it?' said Hawke.

'Very,' agreed Hebden. He glanced across at Merryweather and Grimshaw, the Bren crew from 2 Section, also keeping watch, and gave them a brief wave. 'They've lost a few of their mates in this fight,' he said. Merryweather waved back, and Hebden added, 'But they seem all right. We've been lucky so far. I hope it lasts. I'm sure it will.'

'I can't really imagine it,' said Hawke. 'Dying, I mean. I can't imagine any of our lot getting themselves killed. Even the other day, in all that fighting, I couldn't really think about anything happening to me. It's strange.'

'Did you feel scared?'

'Did you?'

Hebden nodded. 'At times. At times I was bleedin' petrified. Not all the time, though. Not when we were busy firing down at the farm. I was concentrating on shooting and making sure my aim was good – I didn't have time to feel scared.'

'I felt scared at times,' Hawke admitted. He smiled, wondering whether he was admitting too much, and said, 'My hands kept shaking.'

Hebden laughed. 'Mine too. And that horrible feeling in the stomach?'

'Yes!'

They were silent a moment, then Hawke said, 'Do you think about home much?'

Hebden scratched his cheek. 'I did yesterday. There was too

much time to think about things, wasn't there? You can't help it sometimes, though. My dad and my brother will be thinking about cutting the hay around now, and I used to love hay-making. It meant the start of summer, and that smell – warm and sweet and fresh. Not like the horrible stink here. I miss that and I wish I could be there, but feeling homesick isn't the answer. We're here and that's all there is to it.'

'I've been trying to write,' said Hawke. 'I keep getting out my paper and starting and then putting it down again.' He took his pads from the inside of his battle blouse. 'There's so much I'd like to say, but I can't.' He read the first few lines to himself.

*Dear All,*

*I hope you are all well. I am doing fine. The weather has been warm although it's raining now, which is not very nice. We're a bit short of food, but I went out into the town this evening with Tom, Bert and Charlie and we found enough. It was a good meal in the end. Bert and Charlie are in my section and are good friends. Bert always manages to look on the bright side, but I think Charlie wishes he was back home. He is a brilliant footballer and could have played for Sheffield United if it weren't for the war. Jerry seems to have gone to ground today.*

He had stopped there.

'It's tricky,' said Hebden as Hawke took out his pen and held it poised. 'We can't say much because the censors will get jumpy, and you can hardly write about those poor mortar lads getting blown up, and nor do you want to say that you've been shelled and shot at all day, because you don't want to worry them. And if you can't say any of that there's not much you can say, is there?'

'No, just a few lines about the weather and how you hope they're doing all right.' Hawke sighed. 'I don't know why I'm bothering anyway. It'll probably never reach them now.'

'You could always keep a diary, or a journal,' suggested Hebden.

'I thought we weren't allowed to.'

'Who would ever know? Some of the lads are keeping diaries. The corp is.'

Hawke thought for a moment. 'Maybe I will, then.' He held his pen still poised, but then they heard the distant thrum of aero engines and both looked up, scanning the skies.

'Theirs,' said Hawke.

'I think you're right. Jerry planes sound different. You're getting good at this, Johnny.'

'There!' said Hawke, pointing to the south-east. 'See. Tiny dots.'

'Got them,' said Hebden. 'On their way to the coast, probably.'

The aircraft disappeared into cloud, then emerged once more, drawing ever nearer. Hawke began counting them. 'Twenty,' he said. 'I can see twenty,' and then as they drew even closer, he said, 'They're not Stukas. They're twin-engine bombers. Ju Eighty-eights, I think.'

The aircraft were quite low in the sky, no more than four or five thousand feet, their bulbous noses and twin engines now clearly visible. Suddenly, they began to drop height, not as dramatically as a Stuka, and with no screaming siren, but diving all the same.

'God help us,' muttered Hebden, 'but I think they're heading for the town. They're heading straight for us, Johnny.'

All along A Company's front, those on watch were calling out and pointing frantically. From the building behind them, Hawke could hear shouting, a crash of something being flung hastily to one side, and then Spears yelling out for the men to take cover.

Hawke looked at Hebden. His eyes were wide, fear etched across his face.

'Got that feeling in your stomach?' Hebden asked.

Hawke could only nod. And not just his stomach. His whole body had tensed rigid. He looked back up at the sky, saw the Junkers hurtling towards them, their engines screaming and then the bombers were over them and clusters of dark shapes were tumbling from their bellies, innocuous looking, but whistling towards them. One load, then two, then three, four, five bombs screaming towards them. Hawke braced himself. He wanted to grab Hebden's hand, but instead clutched his rifle to him, hugging it, his teeth clenched.

And then the bombs began to explode.

The noise was deafening, an enormous rippling roar of high explosives detonating, of tumbling stone and rock and timber. The ground shook and juddered, the soil in their slit trench crumbling around them. Hawke clutched his hands over his head and clenched his teeth as first one, then another Junkers roared almost directly over his head, the pale blue undersides streaked with oil, the black crosses stark and menacing.

Merryweather was firing, but the bombers roared onwards, banking south of the town and beginning to climb once more. Yet more bombs fell, the whistling even closer now, and then there was an ear-splitting crash as a bomb struck the house behind them while several more fell in a row that cut across A Company's front.

Hawke could no longer hear. His head had gone numb, but he was vaguely aware of seeing huge fountains of soil and stone erupting into the sky. He wanted to scream and to yell, but no sound came out. Earth was crashing down upon him, clattering on to his helmet, peppering his shoulders and filling the slit trench. Bits of mud were in his mouth, he could hardly move, and the ground was convulsing even more. Another bomber thundered overhead and then from behind them came another sudden crash and Hawke hunched his shoulders ever more tightly, curling himself as small as he could.

It was all over in just a few minutes. As the last bombs exploded, the enemy planes flew on, and Hawke looked up through the swirling clouds of dust and smoke to see their ghostly shapes rapidly turn from giant terror machines to innocuous gnats in the sky, and then disappear altogether. His ears were ringing shrilly. He moved an arm, and then another, and looked across at Hebden, half buried. Hebden glanced back, disbelief across his face, then began easing himself out of the loose soil and earth. Hawke did the same, and as the dust and smoke began to settle he stood up, looked around him and saw what devastation had been caused in just those brief minutes.

Part of the roof had collapsed, while much of the adjoining building had gone entirely. Where before there had been a building several hundred years old there was now just a gaping hole from the first floor upwards. Hawke's ears still rang, but his hearing was returning.

'My God,' said Hebden, shaking his head in disbelief. 'Are you all right, Johnny? I can't believe we're still alive.'

'I'm fine,' mumbled Hawke. He patted himself down again.

'We need to dig out our slit trench,' said Hebden.

Hawke nodded and began tugging at his entrenching tool. He still felt dazed, his senses disorientated, but then he heard voices – shouts – from the house and so stopped and clambered out of the trench. 'We should see if they need help,' he said, then stumbled and fell.

'Yes, yes, of course,' said Hebden, climbing out too, and helping Hawke back to his feet. For a moment they stood and stared – at the rubble, at the smoke, at the buildings beyond in the town that were on fire and billowing smoke – and then as they staggered towards the ramparts, they saw Spears at the doorway into the walled garden.

He was covered in dust and there was a cut on his face below his right eye.

'Sarge!' Hawke called out.

'You two are all right, then?' he said.

'Somehow,' said Hebden. 'We were coming to help. What about everyone else?'

'Not sure yet,' said Spears. 'But stay where you are. I'm going to send some of the others out. We need to keep watching our front. Remember last time their bombers came over, Jerry attacked soon after.'

What Spears did not told them was that he had already seen enemy troops moving into their assembly areas. Just before the bombers came over he had been watching with Lieutenant Farrish from the attic window. Large formations of tanks, armoured cars, motorcycles and lorried infantry had been gathering to the south and east. At the sound of the approaching aircraft, he had turned to Farrish and suggested they move quickly. Kicking Miller and Ashworth, who had been on midnight watch, awake he and Farrish then hurried downstairs and ordered everyone to take cover in the cellar.

They all knew a bomb had hit the building. They had heard it whistling down, had felt the whole building judder as it hit and heard the crash of falling brick and stone. Once the raiders had passed, Spears had been the first to climb the cellars stairs to see how much damage had been caused.

He'd been able to open the door into the hallway, which had been a good start, and after briefly looking around and seeing nothing but dust and large chunks of fallen plaster, had climbed the stairs to the first floor. There Spears discovered that only the roof and attic rooms had been hit. Clouds of choking dust still filled the corridors, but the staircase to the attic had gone. It occurred to him that he had not seen either Ashworth or Miller in the cellar.

Spears approached the wrecked staircase carefully, but there was suddenly another cascade of rubble. Stepping back just in time, he was nonetheless showered with dust and plaster and a piece of falling wood gashed his face. Cursing, he then thought of Hawke, and ran back down to call into the cellar that the ground floor appeared to be safe. Then he hurried out through the walled garden and to the door, where, *thank God*, he saw Hawke and Hebden, both apparently in one piece.

Standing in the doorway now, he glanced across at the Bren pit. The bombs had cratered and churned up the platoon's front, but to his relief Merryweather and Grimshaw were now busily dusting themselves down and checking the Bren.

'Dig out your trenches,' Spears called out after Hawke and Hebden, 'but keeping watching the front. And jump to it too. We've no time to waste.'

Lieutenant Farrish and the rest of the men were now emerging from the house, dazed expressions on their faces. Then one of the men pointed to the pile of rubble that had spewed out into the garden. Others followed, and hurried over to where an outstretched arm was sticking up from under the brick and stone.

*Damn it, damn it*, thought Spears, running forward. Reaching the pile of debris, he began moving the rubble away from the dust-covered arm.

'Oh no,' muttered Farrish, standing beside him. 'Miller or Ashworth?'

Spears nodded. 'I think so, sir.'

Farrish turned and looked to the south. 'We need to get the men to stand to, Spears,' he said. 'And we should also send a runner to Captain Astell, don't you think? In case he hasn't had word that the enemy might be about to attack.'

'Good idea, sir. Send someone along the ramparts.'

As Farrish took out his notebook, Spears shouted out, 'One Section, get moving this rubble, Two and Three Sections stand to below the ramparts! At the double!'

Men stumbled forward, the section leaders urging their men on. Spears turned back to Farrish. The lieutenant's hands were shaking so much he could barely write. 'Damn it all,' he cursed. 'I'm fine, I know I'm fine. Just a bit disorientated, that's all.'

Spears took out his hip flask and offered it to the lieutenant. 'Here, sir.'

Farrish looked at it, paused a brief moment, then took it

and had a swig. 'Calvados,' he said. 'Thank you, Spears.' He gasped, then smiled faintly. 'That's better.' Handing back the flask, he began to scribble his note. 'Enemy massing to south and south-east,' Farrish said as he wrote. 'Imminent attack seems likely.' A moment later, both Ashworth and Miller were discovered lying on top of each other under the rubble. Both were quite dead.

'That means we've now lost nine dead and two wounded in three days,' said Farrish as the bodies were pulled clear. Apart from the vivid streaks of blood, both were covered in chalky dust, as though a bag of flour had been dropped on them. So crushed were their bones, it took three men each to lift them.

'That's a third of our men,' said Farrish. He took off his tin helmet and ran his hands through his hair. 'And down below we've got God only knows how many Germans getting ready to attack.'

Guns suddenly rang out from the plain below, followed by a volley of screaming shells, scything through the air towards them. Farrish flinched and hastily put his helmet back on his head. As the first shells crashed into the town behind them, more guns opened fire, pulses throbbing through the ground below them, the noise of shells screaming over and exploding ear-splittingly loud.

The battle had begun.

# 21

## AN ORDER TOO LATE

The men of 6th Platoon were not the only ones who had taken refuge in one of the town's many cellars. Late the previous evening, Somerset had moved his headquarters to a more protected building near Mount Cassel, formerly a casino, and the moment the first bombs began to fall, the brigadier and his staff had hurried down into the large, musty underground vaults, and then, when the raiders had passed, they brought down tables, chairs and even cabinets. From now on, the cellars would play host to the brigadier's command post.

The shelling had only just begun when a dusty and exhausted despatch rider arrived and was hastily brought before the brigadier.

'This fellow's come from GHQ, sir,' said Captain Robson as the despatch rider descended the steps behind him.

The man saluted and passed Somerset a note.

'You managed to get through,' said Somerset.

'Yes, sir,' said the despatch rider, lifting his goggles on to his helmet and wiping his face.

Somerset read the note.

*1445, 28.5.40*
*Evacuate Cassel soonest. Dunkirk evacuation well underway.*
*You have achieved your mission. Good work.*
*Gort, OC BEF*

The brigadier read it again, as above more shells crashed into the town. Sprinkles of grit and dust fell from the roof as one shell exploded not far way. Somerset knew he should be feeling a sense of enormous relief and pride, and yet it was with anger and frustration that he said, 'This is dated yesterday afternoon.'

'I'm sorry, sir,' said the despatch rider. 'I couldn't get through. To the north of here it's thick with Jerries. I had to spend most of the night in a ditch. I got here as soon as I could.'

Somerset nodded. 'It's not your fault.' He clenched his fist, swallowed hard, and turned to Captain Robson. 'Get this man a drink, will you?'

'Of course, sir,' said Robson.

As the despatch rider followed Robson, Somerset led Bullmore back to the map table.

'It's ridiculous,' he hissed. 'It's taken nearly eighteen hours to get here. We could have been gone last night.' He sighed heavily. 'Damn communications. We're all fumbling around in the dark.' He shook his head. 'How could those fools send us into war without enough radios? I mean, damn it all, Bully, how many men are we going to lose today as result?'

'Will you tell the commanding officers, sir?' asked Bullmore.

'Yes. But no one else. I don't want the men to know. They need to concentrate on getting through today.'

'Clearly we've got to wait until the cover of darkness, sir,' said

Bullmore, 'but I just wonder whether perhaps we could speak to the despatch rider. If he got through this morning, maybe we could send some men out to recce the best route out of here.'

'We can talk to him, certainly.' He called the despatch rider back over. 'What's your name?'

'Corporal Brand, sir.'

'And which way did you come, Brand?'

'I zigzagged all over the place, sir,' said Brand.

'And did you see many Germans? Are they everywhere or concentrated in certain places?'

'It's hard to say, sir, because the enemy's on the move, but they're mostly sticking to the main roads. I got through by weaving my way along tracks and back roads.'

'Show me on the map.'

Brand leaned over, his finger to his mouth. 'Here, sir,' he said after a moment's pause. 'I came through Winnezeele, Le Temple and Le Riveld. Small little villages and I didn't see any Jerries in any of them.'

'Winnezeele,' said Somerset. 'That's about six miles to the north-east.'

A commotion at the top of the stairs caused the brigadier to pause and look up.

'Sir,' said Robson, hurrying back down into the cellar with another officer behind him. 'Major Farrell, sir, from the Ox and Bucks.'

'Brigadier,' gasped Farrell as he reached the bottom of the steps. 'I'm sorry, sir.'

'What is it, man?' barked Somerset. As Farrell emerged into the light, he saw the major was covered in blood and small globs of flesh.

'The Gendarmerie,' he said, 'the cellar took a direct hit. Everyone there has been killed.'

'How many?'

'I'm not sure. The commander, most of Battalion Headquarters.'

Somerset sighed then ordered one of the clerks to help Farrell get cleaned up.

'A lucky escape, sir,' said Bullmore as Farrell staggered back up the steps. 'Could have been us.'

'Yes,' said Somerset, rubbing his brow. He cursed then brought a fist down hard on the table. 'We've got to do all we can to escape from here,' he said. 'I think you're right, Bully. Let's send out a troop now from the East Riding Yeomanry. Brief them to try to reach Winnezeele and see whether there's an escape route still open. The Huns can't be everywhere all at once. There must be a chance. There must be.' He sighed again. 'There *has* to be.'

Along A Company's front, Captain Astell had made some adjustments to the way his men were positioned. Half the men were placed in slit trenches on the forward ground, while the rest were positioned behind the garden walls that ran along the edge of the ramparts. Visiting 6th Platoon shortly after the aerial attack, he'd suggested that the men hastily build sangars behind them, to protect them from any shell blast that might hit the buildings. 'After all,' he said, looking at the piles of rubble, 'there's no shortage of stone.'

Much to Hawke and Hebden's annoyance, no sooner had they finished excavating their slit trench than they were recalled to the garden and immediately employed with the rest of

1 Section building sangars, which involved lugging stone, brick and any other bits of loose rubble to create a makeshift wall a few yards back inside the garden.

They worked quickly, the shelling continuing around them, so that by the time the sangars were completed the men were exhausted. Hawke stood at his post, his rifle by his side, peering through the loophole in the wall. His eyes stung with fatigue, his arms and shoulders ached, while his hands, covered in dust and dirt, were raw and sore. He leaned his arm against the brickwork and momentarily closed his eyes.

'Not falling asleep on us, are you, Hawke?' said Spears, behind him.

Hawke started. 'No, sir – I mean, Sergeant.'

'Get a grip on yourself,' said Spears.

Hawke turned and looked at him. Spears's face looked so hard. The jaw was clenched, his forehead creased in a frown, the eyes narrowed. He wondered what had happened to the person he had met the previous summer. He blinked and lowered his eyes, then Spears turned away.

In the next moment, another shell screamed over. This time, Hawke thought the sound and tone were different somehow. He was standing there thinking this, when Spears grabbed him and shouted, 'Everyone down!'

Pulled to the ground by Spears, Hawke fell just as the shell landed like an express train, striking the building behind. The ground shook, his ears rang and for a few seconds thousands of shards of grit and stone were blasted into the air, hissing and whizzing above his head, clattering on to his helmet as more of the house collapsed in a cascade of smoke and swirling dust.

As the debris settled, Hawke felt a hand on his shoulder once more and looked up to see Spears lying beside him.

'All right?' rasped the sergeant.

Hawke nodded. 'Thank you.'

And then Spears gave a flicker of a smile – just a faint one, but in that brief moment those hard features seemed to soften.

A second later, Spears was standing up and looking around. Men were coughing and spluttering and slowly getting to their feet once more. Hawke got up too, dusting himself down and through watery, squinting eyes saw that not only had the rest of the roof and most of the second floor gone, but the back door was now almost completely blocked. Next to him, Ibbotson was holding his helmet aloft and staring at it incredulously.

'Will you look at that!' he said. A neat V had been cut clear from the front rim. 'I had it on the back of my head,' he said, 'and felt this whoosh right over me, but I never realized it had done that.' He shook his head.

'A close one, Jack,' said McLaren. 'Those sangars were worth a few cut hands, then, weren't they?'

'Too bleedin' right,' said Ibbotson. 'I'll never complain again, I promise.'

The others laughed.

'I'll hold you to that,' grinned McLaren.

Suddenly a Bren sputtered to their front, and the men hastily stood to their posts. More Brens were firing, the air sharp with the reports of the machine guns as bullets spat forth. Hawke peered through his loophole and saw movement down below as men and tanks emerged from the woods. Return fire began fizzing towards them, fortunately too high, the bullets spattering into the chestnut still standing just to the left of their position.

Hawke instinctively jerked backwards then cautiously peered again. He could see the enemy clearly now, about five hundred yards away. Tanks were heading up the tree-lined track that ran almost across their front away to their left – a road that led up to the eastern end of the town and eventually to Dead Horse Corner. Infantry were crouch-running, trying to make the most of the tanks' protection. A rifle cracked nearby and then another. Spears, standing beside the edge of the doorway out on to the ramparts, turned and shouted, 'Hold your fire! Don't waste ammo. Only shoot if you've got a clear shot.'

Hawke looked out again and with a lurch in his stomach saw four tanks veer off the road and start trundling towards them, the now familiar squeak and rattle of tracks clearly audible above the din of battle.

Immediately the two-pounder in the alleyway to their left opened fire, but the shot was too long. The mortar teams also fired off several shells, while the Brens chattered. Hawke watched as small explosions of earth and smoke burst into the air around them, but moments later the panzers reappeared. Two of the larger tanks stopped and fired their cannons, while the two smaller tanks hurried forward either side of them firing their machine guns. Bullets spat up the already soft ground of the Rangers' forward positions, then, raising their aim, a series of bullets clattered along the wall. Hawke flinched, jerking himself clear of the loophole, but Ibbotson, on the Bren, was too late. With a gasp, he was flung backwards against the sangar.

'Jack!' cried out McLaren, dropping to his knees beside him. Hawke hurried over with Hebden, and Brens and rifles were now firing furiously at the enemy tanks.

'Stop firing!' shouted out Spears. 'Save your ammo. Keep your heads down and wait until they're closer.'

McLaren was frantically ripping open field-dressing packs and stuffing them into Ibbotson's neck.

'Come on, Jack, come on, mate,' he muttered as Hawke pulled out a field dressing of his own. Ibbotson was lying back, his eyes blinking, his face already drained of colour. His mouth frothed with blood, incomprehensible words gurgling from his now crimson lips.

McLaren snatched the field dressing from Hawke, but then Spears was beside them. 'Damn it!' he cursed, then glancing at Hawke said, 'Get back to your post.'

Hawke did as he was told as another burst of machine-gun fire rattled along the wall. Flinching, he stood there, his eyes closed, that nauseous feeling once more stirring heavily in his stomach.

'Johnny!' said Hebden, a few yards away. 'Are you all right?'

Hawke nodded. 'I can't believe it. Jack was only talking a moment ago.'

They both looked over towards their stricken comrade. Ibbotson had begun to convulse, his legs and body jerking as Spears and McLaren kneeled beside him.

'Poor devil,' said Hebden.

Hawke had to look away. He liked Jack Ibbotson – he'd liked him a lot – and now there he was, lying there against their hastily built stone wall, a gash like a cave in his throat, the lifeblood draining out of him, and his body thrashing as though he were possessed. He thought of what Ibbotson had said about his mother – how he was worried should anything happen to him. And now it had – the very worst.

The enemy machine-gunning had stopped, so cautiously Hawke peered out of his loophole. To his surprise, the enemy tanks seemed to be pulling back towards the tree-lined road.

'What are they doing?' he muttered quietly to himself and then, peeping through the hole in the brickwork again, realized most of the column that had been moving forward across their view had disappeared. Suddenly, he understood: the panzers had been a diversion, drawing fire while the rest advanced safely behind them.

He glanced back at Ibbotson. The jerking had stopped and Spears now looked up.

'Hawke,' he said, 'and Hebden. We need to move Jack.'

'How is he, Sarge?' asked Hebden, slinging his rifle back on to his shoulder.'

'He's dead, Bert,' said Spears.

Hawke realized his mouth had gone dry. A renewed wave of nausea had settled inside him like a lump of lead. An image of home flashed across his mind and not for the first time he wondered whether he would ever see any of his family again.

# 22

## THE GUNNERS

The afternoon wore on. Across the southern front of the town, the battle was quiet – a bit of shelling, the occasional burst of enemy machine-gun fire, but that was all. Elsewhere, though, the sound of fierce fighting could be heard: first, to the west of the Rangers' position, where the Glosters held the western approach from Bavinchove, and to the north, now held by the Ox and Bucks. Then the fighting seemed to shift to their left, to the east, as had seemed inevitable from the movement of troops they had seen earlier. Small-arms, guns, the rumble and squeak of tanks, and smoke – lots of smoke rising up through the trees – told of heavy fighting along their own C Company's front.

Hawke found the minutes passed slowly. At around three o'clock, Hebden took advantage of Lieutenant Farrish's appearance from the forward positions to ask permission to make some tea.

'All right, Hebden,' said Farrish. 'You can always hurry back, after all.'

'Thank you, sir,' said Hebden. 'It's sod's law that the moment the water boils Jerry will show his ugly face.'

'Then get on with it, Bert,' said Drummond. 'I'd rather Jerry did come. All this hanging about waiting is getting on my nerves.'

Hawke felt much the same way. It was, he had discovered, the thought of action that bothered him. Waiting, but knowing that at some point soon the enemy *would* appear. That was what brought the terror in the pit of his stomach. Once the fighting began, it was different. In the brief engagements he'd had so far, he had not had time to feel afraid. Rather, his body and mind had felt alert, as though some other, completely unfamiliar, part of his brain was taking control.

Hebden had made the tea, and they had all drunk it, and been grateful for it too, but still there was no attack. Not until just after four o'clock did they begin to suspect the battleground might at last be shifting. The fighting had lessened to the west, but the sound of battle was suddenly getting noticeably louder away to their left, and then they could hear shouting and shots from the street behind.

'Stay here,' said Spears, hurrying back to the remains of the house. The rear doorway had been cleared, and he now disappeared inside only to reappear a few moments later.

'Get ready,' he said as he ran past them and headed through the door on to the ramparts.

'What the hell's going on?' said Chalkie from his position with the Bren. More shots could be heard behind them, followed by a burst of machine-gun fire.

'D'you think Jerry's broken through?' said Drummond, his face ashen.

'Panzers in the town already?' said Hebden.

There was another burst of machine-gun fire from away

behind them. 'Ruddy heck,' said McLaren. 'I don't like the sound of this. Where's the sarge got to?'

'I'm here,' said Spears, now standing the doorway. 'Chalkie, and you, Fletch, you stay here on the Bren. Sid and you other three, come with me.'

Clutching his rifle, Hawke followed. Spears was running along the ramparts towards the gunners manning the two-pounder. As they clambered over the rubble and sandbags protecting the gun, one of the gunners nodded his head behind him and said, 'What's the trouble back there?'

'Jerry tank,' said Spears, hurrying on down the alleyway.

'Get the beggar,' said one of the gunners, patting Hawke on the back. Hawke's mind raced. *So they have broken through*, he thought to himself. *Just one? Or more?* They ran on down the narrow alleyway, their boots stamping loudly in that narrow space. Spears halted them a yard from the end of the alley.

'Shhh!' he said, standing still and listening. Rifle shots were cracking from Grand Place and then there was a louder shot, followed by another loud splutter of a machine gun. An engine revved and then they heard the telltale clatter and chink of tank tracks.

'No one even so much as peep their head out on to the street,' said Spears. 'We're going to wait until it reaches us.'

'Then do what we did last time?' said McLaren.

'Yes. We keep nice and low, then I'll jump out and drop the grenade in.'

'What about us?' said McLaren.

'You cover me. Move out into the street and make sure we

don't get hit by our own boys or any other Jerries coming down the street.'

The tank was moving closer, rumbling down the road, the squeaking of the tracks getting ever louder. Hawke watched the empty road in front of them intently, his heart thumping in his chest. He gripped his rifle, the wood warm in his clammy hands. *How far now?* Another burst of the tank's machine gun, louder than ever in the confines of the narrow street. There was now little return fire. One crack of a rifle, but Hawke guessed the men in the square would be nervous of exposing themselves to the panzer's machine guns. The squeaking was even closer now – a rolling, thundering beast inching towards them. Hawke swallowed, saw Spears hold out his grenade, ready to pounce and then there it was, filling the view directly in front of them, trundling forward at no more than walking pace.

Spears leaped forward and Hawke followed. A quick scan either side – no Tommies in the square, but figures at the end of the long, straight street. A glance at the tank and Hawke cursed – the side vent was closed – *what now?* – but Spears was now jumping on to the side of the tank. He gripped a bar on the side, his legs swinging dangerously close to the rolling tracks, then hoisted himself on to the side. Hawke watched open-mouthed and ran after the tank. Spears was trying to hoist himself up and had just gripped the turret when the panzer hit a small mound of rubble, jolting the side of the beast upwards. The force made Spears lose his grip and he was thrown clear, but as he fell, he threw up the grenade and, dropping his rifle, Hawke snatched it with both hands. Everything was happening very quickly and yet the world seemed to have slowed down. All noise had gone. It was just Hawke and the tank. Running a few paces, he leaped on to the back, gripped a box that was fastened on to the hull behind the turret and pulled himself up. Now firmly on the rear of the panzer, he clambered up behind the turret, saw the hatch, then momentarily looked at the grenade, breathed in deeply, and pulled the pin, and yanked at the hatch. Voices in German, a release of foul hot air, and Hawke dropped the grenade and rolled off the back, landing painfully on the road just as the grenade exploded. He gasped, lying on the cobbles as a second explosion erupted, flame and smoke bursting from the turret. The tank slewed, trundled slowly forward and crashed into the side of a house. There were cheers from the direction of Grand Place and he gasped again, grimaced and looked up to see Hebden and Spears beside him, then pulling him to his feet.

'Good work, Johnny,' said Hebden.

Tommies from Grand Place were running towards them and towards the knocked-out panzer – Rangers, Hawke saw from the familiar green on black shoulder tabs.

'Well done, lads,' said a sergeant. There was a gash across his eye and a face etched with fatigue. He called his men away from the tank. 'Come on, lads,' he shouted. 'We need to get back.'

'Wait,' said Spears. 'What's going on down there?' Hawke followed his gaze. The men at the end of the street were Tommies, their helmets silhouetted against the smoke. The sound of frenetic small-arms firing rang out, not only from the end of the road, but from beyond the houses that lined the right-hand side of the street.

'Jerry's been attacking since noon,' said the sergeant. 'The Ox and Bucks boys have been holding his main assault from around Dead Horse Corner, but how this lad got through, God only knows. We'd taken some wounded up and been scrounging for ammo. Came back and there's this ruddy great panzer trundling down the street towards us. Thank God you boys were there. I don't know what happened – how he got through.'

'There're Tommies down the street now,' said Spears.

'Hopefully any gap's been closed, although how much longer we can hold on I'm not at all sure. The boys are getting very low on ammo.' Another fusillade of fire rang out. 'We really should get back. Are you A Company?'

'Yes,' said Spears.

'Well, good luck.' He gripped Spears's hand, patted Hawke on the back, then ran on with his men.

Thick smoke from the burning tank now filled the street, and Hawke began to cough, his throat raw.

'Come on,' said Spears. 'Let's go.'

Hawke's shoulder and upper arm hurt where he had fallen, and as they hurried back across the street towards the alleyway he clutched it with his hand and winced in pain. He saw now that his battle blouse had torn and he cursed to himself. Both the rip and his badly grazed arm were forgotten, however, the moment they stepped back into the narrow passageway. From the far end, the two-pounder boomed, but immediately a tank gun responded, the shell screaming down the alleyway and crashing into the walls just above them. Hawke jumped in surprise, ducking instinctively as bits of shrapnel and shattered brick clattered down on him.

Through the dust and smoke he saw Spears running on, McLaren just behind, so Hawke followed, stumbling and nearly falling as he did so. A heavy burst of machine-gun fire stopped them, and then they saw the gun crew sprawled by their two-pounder.

'Damn it!' cursed Spears, signalling to the rest to crouch down.

'Are they all dead?' said McLaren.

'No – but their firing days are over,' Spears replied.

'Where the hell is that Jerry tank?' said McLaren.

'We'd better find out, and quick,' said Spears. They were just fifteen yards from the gun, and he scampered forward, then beckoned the others. Hawke was suddenly conscious of how heavy his breathing sounded. His ears were playing tricks on him. Three of the men were dead, their chests a bloody mess. A fourth sat slumped behind the gun shield, a gash across his head, his right arm hanging limply.

'I can't fire,' he mumbled. 'I can't get my hand up to fire.'

'You're all right, mate,' said Spears. 'We'll get you sorted.' He turned to the others. 'But you need to tell us how to fire this thing.'

'Is it still working?' asked Drummond.

'I reckon so,' said McLaren. 'Iron is a bit stronger than flesh and bones. Everything looks to be in order.'

'Well,' said Spears, 'there's one way to find out.'

Hawke peered round the edge of the gun shield. One of the larger German panzers was just ahead, and firing towards the A Company positions. A little further away to the left he could hear several more panzers – the boom of the cannon and the staccato chatter of the machine gun different from the light machine guns the infantry seemed to use. He was getting used to the varying sounds different weapons made. The tanks were out of sight, because just away to their left the ramparts dropped a short way and curved round towards the east end of the town. But he was sure the panzers were close.

'What can you see, Johnny?' asked McLaren, as Hebden and Drummond pulled the two dead men clear.

'A Jerry tank a hundred and fifty yards dead in front,' he said, 'but there are at least a couple more behind him out of sight to our left.'

'Let's sort this beggar out first, then,' said Spears. 'Hopefully we might be able to catch the others too when they appear.' He looked around and Hawke followed his gaze. There was rubble and debris everywhere, and a large number of empty brass shell casings, but there were still a few wooden boxes of ammunition. That was something.

'Why isn't that Jerry tank firing at us any more?' said Drummond.

'He thinks he's taken this gun out. And your field of vision isn't great in a tank, is it? So let's clobber him before he cottons on. *Jaldi*, lads, *iggery*, as we used to say in India.'

They moved the wounded gunner carefully, Hebden apologizing as the man cried out in pain.

'Bandage him up, will you, Bert?' said Spears, 'but we need him close by.' He felt in the side pocket of his battle blouse and pulled out his hip flask. 'And give him some of this.'

Squatting beside Spears, Hawke looked at the two-pounder. Ahead the tank was still firing, and so stationary, but any moment it might move on. They needed to knock it out quickly, before it was too late, but they were riflemen, not gunners, and to fire without taking proper aim risked revealing their position. He breathed in heavily. At every turn, it seemed, the odds were stacked against them. But there were small wheels beside the breech, which, he guessed, enabled the barrel to traverse up and down and even left and right. To the left, in the gun shield, was the sight. Spears was peering through it.

'How is he, Bert?' demanded Spears. 'We need to fire this lad quickly.'

'The range is close,' rasped the wounded man, 'so look through the site and aim just below the turret.'

Spears did so. 'Got it,' he said, 'perfect shot.'

'Good,' said the man. 'I had him in my sights before we were hit. The breech is already closed ready. All you need to do is fire. But move your head clear of the sights. The recoil could take your eye out.'

'How?' said Spears. 'How do I fire?'

The man started to cough. Hawke saw the expression of exasperation on Spears's face – an anxiety he felt himself. 'Come on, come on,' he muttered to himself.

The wounded man recovered. 'To the right of the breech is the operating lever. Can you see it?'

Spears put his hand on the small metal rod. 'Yes.'

'Pull it towards you. But again, make sure you're clear of the breech. The recoil is twenty inches.'

Spears looked through the sights again, then turning to Hawke said, 'All right, you'd better pull the operating lever.'

'When, Sarge?' said Hawke, gripping the cold metal with his left hand.

In front of them, the tank was firing again, then revved its engines.

'Now!' said Spears.

Hawke pulled the lever, the gun fired with a resounding crack and the breech flew backwards, but Hawke was watching ahead of him. To his utter amazement, the two-pound shell smacked in between the turret and the hull precisely where they had been aiming. But although sparks flew off the metal there was no explosion.

'Quick!' gurgled the wounded man, 'load another shell!'

The panzer was motionless for a moment, then opened fire again with its machine gun, tracer bullets pouring towards A Company lines.

'Pull down the cocking handle!' spluttered the gunner, straining to sit up with his one good arm. 'The empty casing will flip out and then you can shove in another.'

Spears found the cocking handle, pushed it down and out came the brass casing. McLaren hastily handed him another, Spears rammed it in and closed the vertical sliding block over the breech, then peered through the sights once more.

'Quick, Sarge, he's moving!' called out Hawke.

Against the left-hand side of the breech was a shoulder pad. Pushing against it, Spears now traversed the barrel slightly across, then said, 'Fire!'

Again, Hawke pulled the lever, and this time the shell shot out of the gun and hit the panzer in the wheels near its front. Immediately, the nearside tracks sprang loose, unravelling like the crack of a whip, the forward wheels jammed, and after rolling backwards a few yards the tank ground to a halt.

'Good shooting, lads!' croaked the gunner.

'And now we can hit the beggar at leisure,' said Spears. He looked at Hawke and grinned. 'Reckon I could get the hang of this.'

Hawke now pulled back the cocking handle, and McLaren was ready with another shell.

'Sarge, look!' said Hawke. On the top of the tank, the turret was now opening and first one and then another of the crew frantically clambered out and leaped over the side.

'Well, shoot them someone!' said Spears. 'Come on, Bert, Sid, where are you?'

A third German began climbing out and then suddenly there was a volley of Bren and rifle fire and all three fell, the first two sprawling on to the ground, the third dropping back inside the turret.

'Killing tank crews is the infantry's job,' said the gunner. 'You're too busy on the gun to start firing rifles.' He fell backwards with a gasp. 'Good riddance to them. They killed my mates.'

Spears looked around. 'Right – Sid, you're the loader. Charlie, you keep a good lookout and have your rifle ready. Bert, keep an eye out too and with Charlie get this poor bloke clear and out of the way. Johnny, you're on breech opening and firing. Got it?'

Hawke nodded, aware that it was the first time Spears had used his Christian name since he joined the battalion. He smiled to himself, but then he heard the sound of approaching tanks. Tensing, he opened the cocking handle and McLaren rammed in another shell.

'All right, boys,' said Spears. 'Get ready. Let's try to do this quickly. Load, aim, fire. Load, aim, fire.'

The sound of the approaching tanks got nearer and nearer. Hawke glanced across at Spears, squinting through the sights. His heart was hammering again, and his mouth was as dry as chalk, but although he was desperate for a drink of water he did not dare reach for his bottle. A clatter of Bren fire from A

Company made him glance forward, and then suddenly there it was, a machine-gun-firing German tank, lurching round the corner, just thirty yards away. Spears pushed hard against the shoulder pad, then cursed.

'Damn it! He's not in shot!'

'Quick, Sarge, do something!' called out Drummond.

Hawke was watching the tank as it continued to rumble forward.

'Come on, come on!' muttered Spears. There was more firing from the direction of A Company. Hawke heard the hollow *thwack* of a mortar firing and moments later saw a column of earth erupt just ten yards from the tank.

'Come on!' urged Spears. 'Just a few more yards!'

'Sarge, he's spotted us!' called out Hawke, now watching the turret of the panzer turning towards them.

'Just a few more yards!' called out Spears. The tank opened fire, orange flashes spurting from its twin-mounted guns. Bullets hissed over their heads, pinging and zipping off the brickwork behind them. Hawke crouched behind the shield, ducking his head, but then Spears shouted, 'Fire!'

Fumbling for the lever, Hawke grabbed it and yanked, the gun blasting out its shell as the breech lurched backwards.

Hawke heard the crash and looked up to see a large gash ripped out of the front of the turret. German voices were shouting and smoke had begun to gush from the hole.

'We got him!' yelled McLaren.

'Could hardly miss at that range,' said Spears. 'Just getting the beggar into the sights that was the problem.'

The Germans were still shouting and then suddenly machine-gun ammunition started firing manically from inside, the bullets pinging madly as they ricocheted around the inside of the tank. The shouting stopped. More smoke gushed from the tank and away to their right they heard the men of A Company cheering.

'Two down,' said Spears, 'and one to go.'

# 23

## THE LAST ASSAULT

None of them spoke for a moment, as they tried to listen. Another burst of Bren fire rang out, but then the men held their fire. The battle still raged elsewhere, somewhere to the north of the town, but Hawke could hear another tank squeaking nearby.

'He's coming, Sarge,' he said.

'I know. And at least we've got a dead panzer right in front of us barring our way.'

He was right, and Hawke felt his spirits lift. This third enemy tank would have to go past the knocked-out panzer in front of them and then turn. Hopefully, it would give them a chance to fire off a round or two as it emerged into their line of sight.

'Where is he?' said Spears, then stood up, and clambering over the makeshift sangar in front of the gun he scampered forward towards the knocked-out tank in front of them. A burst of enemy MG fire sputtered, bullets rattling against the tank. Spears dived on to the ground, but then they saw him crawl forward again, until he had reached the tank.

'I've got to admit it,' said Hebden, 'he's a brave fellow, our sarge.'

'Or mad,' said Drummond. 'Flipping heck, what's he thinking?'

Hawke watched Spears as he lay there, peering from between the two tracks of the German tank. He knew Tom Spears was not mad. The previous summer, when he'd first met his oldest sister's new man, it had not once occurred to him that Tom might be anything other than a brave and fearless soldier. Nothing he had seen in the past few days had given him any reason to doubt that his initial assumption had been right.

After a minute or so, Spears began inching clear of the tank, then sped back. Another burst of machine-gun fire followed, but it was once again wide of its mark, and he jumped back over the mound of rubble unscathed.

'Blimey, Sarge,' said McLaren. 'You had us going there. I hope it was worth it.'

'It was,' said Spears.

'What did you see?' asked Hawke.

'It's a Jerry panzer with a cannon – one of the bigger ones. Infantry are trying to move up. Our boys have got them pinned down at the moment, but they're working their way beneath the ramparts away to our left – the trees there are giving them some cover. If I was them, I'd be trying to clear this gun position and then I think their infantry will try to infiltrate round here and up the alleyway. It was a good job we knocked out the other two, or else they'd already be here.'

'How come they haven't been spotted already?'

Spears shrugged. 'There must be a blind spot on C Company's front. Maybe they were distracted by that Jerry tank breaking through. I don't know, but there are more trees around there and there's a greater drop below the ramparts.' He pushed his helmet back. 'Charlie,' he said looking at Drummond, 'I want you to run back to the platoon. Get the lieutenant and get Fletch and Chalkie with their Bren – and as many mags as they can get their hands on.'

Drummond nodded. 'What if I can't find Mr Farrish, Sarge?'

'Just get Fletch and Chalkie anyway. Now get going. I want you back right away.'

As Drummond hurried off, Spears turned to the others. 'The tank is about two hundred yards off at the moment, but it could fire at us between the panzer in front of us and the rampart walls. So we're going to cut that option out.'

'How?' said Hawke.

'We're going to move the two-pounder back down the alley. That way the panzer will have to come round this dead tank before it can get a clear shot at us. We'll be ready and we can hit it in the tracks and disable it.'

'What if we don't?' said McLaren.

'Then we'll be in trouble. But we've got to knock it out, boys. We knock it out and then we nobble their infantry. Do that, and we can stop their assault in its tracks. If we don't, Jerry's going to get into the town. And then . . .' He let the sentence trail. Hawke breathed in deeply. They all knew what that would mean. The battle would be lost.

Having hastily cleared away the debris of spent shells and bits of rubble, they discovered the two-pounder was quite easy to move. With McLaren and Hebden pulling on the trail, and Hawke and Spears pushing behind the shield, they were able to shift it quite easily, pulling it back ten yards within the narrow confines of the alleyway. No sooner had they finished than a breathless Drummond reappeared with White and Fletcher and the Bren gun.

'I didn't see the lieutenant, I'm afraid,' Drummond said. 'He's still forward.'

'No matter,' said Spears. 'How many mags have you got?'

'Six each,' said Fletcher.

'We didn't realize it was you lot knocking out those tanks,' grinned White. 'Good on you, lads.'

'Now that you're here,' said Spears, 'do you want the good news or the bad news?'

'I don't like the sound of this,' said White.

Fletcher sighed and rubbed his brow, his grin gone. 'Go on then, Sarge. Let's have the bad news.'

'I want you two to run over to that dead tank, lie underneath and set up your Bren.'

'And the good?' asked White.

'When you're there, you'll see a nice lot of juicy Jerries round this corner. Once we've got the next tank that's coming, give 'em hell.'

'If we don't get killed getting there,' said Fletcher.

'You won't. There's still a bit of smoke coming from the tank and if you're quick they won't be able to reach quickly enough. The tank will give you plenty of cover.'

'The things you make us do, Sarge,' groaned White. 'When do we move?'

'Now. That panzer's getting close.'

White and Fletcher did as they were ordered. Clambering over the old gun position, they crouched down low then sped across the open thirty yards. Spears was right: a gentle breeze had wafted the smoke their way, giving them some extra cover. This time, no enemy responded. Diving down by the tank, White looked back and raised his thumb towards them.

'Told them it'd be a piece of cake,' said Spears.

Hawke glanced across at the sergeant. The frown had gone, his face free of the obvious anxiety of earlier. He found Spears's newfound confidence was raising his own spirits. The dull weight in his stomach had left him and a different sensation, almost one of exhilaration, was sweeping over him. He could hear the tank, close now, but quickly took a glug from his water bottle, the water soothing his parched mouth and throat. *Come on, then*, he thought, *let's see you*.

The rumbling and squeaking increased and then they heard the tank stop and a moment later a shot rang out. The shell was high, crashing into the wall to the right of the alleyway, but then it fired again and this time blasted the sangar where they had been just a few minutes before. Then it revved and rumbled forward.

Spears was crouched by the sights, the gun loaded and ready. Hawke placed his fingers on the lever, waiting, waiting . . .

The tank crept into view, inching forward, first one wheel then another. It was just fifty yards away. Hawke could see White and Fletcher shift position anxiously. *Come on, Sarge*, he thought. There was the barrel, and then the turret. *Come on, come on*.

'Fire!' said Spears.

The gun rocked, the breech flung back and the shell whooshed across the open ground, over White's and Fletcher's heads and smashed into the panzer's side. The track whipped free, two wheels spun into the air and the tank shuddered to a halt.

At the same time, Hawke had yanked down the cocking lever, the spent casing spat free and McLaren rammed home another shell. But now the turret was traversing, the barrel swinging steadily towards them. Hawke shot a glance at Spears, who was frantically elevating the gun. He caught Hawke's eye, then peered through the sight and shouted, 'Fire!' A spurt of orange spat from the panzer's cannon barrel at the same moment as their two-pounder blasted out a second shell. Hawke ducked instinctively as the enemy shell whooshed over their heads and exploded a short distance behind them, but already their own charge had hit the tank's turret, ripping open another hole in the ironwork.

'Quick!' shouted Spears. 'Another shot!'

Again, Hawke yanked down on the cocking lever, McLaren thrust in a further shell and without further adjustment Spears gave the order to fire. The shot smashed into the turret again, knocking it clear. A moment later, there was a boom and the tank erupted into flames, thick black smoke billowing out and rolling back towards the town. Now the Bren opened fire, White giving a series of short, sharp bursts. Then, once Fletcher had whipped off one magazine and slotted in another, White gave one long continuous burst, firing in a wide arc, so that Hawke could see his shoulders and helmet shuddering with the rapid recoil of the gun. Another magazine was taken out and replaced, and White continued firing, and now mortars and small-arms were ringing out from A Company's lines, a sharp, deafening fusillade that sang of the Rangers' defiance and a spirit that, so far, had proved unbreakable.

White now stopped firing and Hawke saw him turn towards them and raise his fist in triumph, followed by loud cheers from the ramparts away to their right. And, for that brief moment, the fatigue, the despair, the terrible sights he had witnessed in the past few days were all forgotten and Hawke was consumed by a wave of exultation and relief.

# 24

## BREAK OUT

By half past seven that evening, 29 May, the shelling had at last appeared to have stopped.

'It's now been twenty minutes, sir,' said Major Bullmore, as he and Brigadier Somerset stood on the veranda at the rear of Somer Force Headquarters. The patchy cloud from earlier had largely dispersed, so that above them was a clear, blue sky. Around the shattered town, however, an acrid pall hung heavily, so that with the evening sun bearing down it looked as though a giant yellow veil had been draped across it.

Somerset lit a small cigar he had found in the house and took a sip of his brandy. 'Good God, look at this place,' he said. 'A few days' fighting and look what's become of it. Smashed houses, rubble everywhere, telegraph wires strewn across the streets.'

'Cassel has served us well, sir,' said Bullmore. 'We wouldn't have held on without this position.'

'It's a miracle we've kept going this long. An absolute miracle. This morning – well, I don't mind admitting, Bully, I thought we'd not make it through the day. I take my hat off to every single one of our chaps. That the Hun has been unable to make a single sustained breach anywhere, with all their weight of arms and fire-power, has been an extraordinary effort on our part.'

'I agree, sir.'

'And they deserve their chance for freedom now that the task set them has been faithfully carried out.'

Bullmore remained silent, but eyed the brigadier carefully.

'Well?' said Somerset at length. 'You don't suppose we should just stay here, do you?'

'There's been no sign of the troop we sent out earlier, sir,' said Bullmore.

'That doesn't necessarily mean they've been stopped. They might have reached Winnezeele, then not been able to get back – not in daylight at any rate. Their absence is no reason not to give our boys a *chance*. Don't forget, Bully, that this morning you agreed that if we were still here this evening we should break out.'

'I know, sir, but I can't feel so optimistic about those Yeomanry we sent off. Odds are they've come a cropper. If we surrendered now, at least we would be saving the lives of all the men. The town is surrounded after all. Is it worth risking any more lives when the chances of us getting away are so slight? It took that courier half a day and all night to get here and by all accounts he was lucky to make it. And there was just him, not all the men of Somer Force.'

Somerset turned to face his chief of staff. 'No, Bully, my mind's made up. These boys have fought heroically here. To throw in the towel now, without trying to break out would be unfair to them. At twenty-one thirty, we will begin leaving the town. We can tell the unit commanders that there is no longer any need to fight to the last man. If they encounter heavy enemy numbers, then they must know there is no dishonour in giving themselves up. But we will try, Bully, we will try.' He paused and drew on his cheroot, clouds of blue-grey smoke wafting into the air. 'The Ox and Bucks hold the north of the town. Send them out first. Then the Glosters, and then the Rangers.'

'And when do we leave, sir?'

'With the vanguard. We will leave at the head of our men.'

A few hundred yards away, along the southern edge of the town, four Rangers still stood to by the two-pounder gun that had performed such great service over the past few days. Sergeant Spears was no longer with them – he had returned to 6th Platoon's positions on the ramparts – but McLaren, and three of his section – Drummond, Hebden and Hawke – had remained by their new post.

After the German attack had been repulsed, they had moved the gun forward again, and the wounded gunner had been stretchered away. Since then, a strange eerie calm had descended over the battleground. The frenetic firing of earlier, the intense noise, had gradually died, until at last the enemy gunners had even stopped shelling for the night. The earlier euphoria had quickly worn off as adrenalin subsided and exhaustion consumed them. Hawke had sat with the other three, perched uncomfortably on a piece of rock that just a few days before had been part of a building, staring out at the still smouldering German tanks. His eyes stung with fatigue, and his young body ached. His upper arm and shoulder, particularly, throbbed painfully. He'd been so proud of his smart appearance when he had first joined the battalion, but now his battle dress was filthy and, on the shoulder, even torn. Lice lived in the seams. He'd not had a proper wash for more days than he could remember. Dark arcs of grime lined the end of his fingernails, while his hair was so thick even a metal comb would have struggled to untangle the knots.

It was just after eight when Spears reappeared, walking casually towards them along the ramparts.

'All right, boys,' he said, 'we're being stood down.'

'At last,' said Drummond.

'Brew-time,' said Hebden, perking up and rubbing his hands together.

'And we're leaving tonight too.'

'What?' exclaimed Hawke.

'We're leaving,' said Spears. 'The whole garrison. It seems that while we've been holding off Jerry, the rest of the BEF have been pulling back to Dunkirk.'

'Dunkirk?' said Hebden. 'Bleedin' heck. That doesn't sound good.'

'We're being evacuated,' said Spears. 'They're trying to get us all out.'

'Can't they use any other ports?' asked Hebden.

Spears shook his head. 'Jerry's got the lot. Calais, Boulogne, Gravelines – you name it.'

Hawke had taken off his helmet and now scratched his head. 'But, Sarge, if we're surrounded here, how are we all supposed to get to Dunkirk?'

'With a great deal of luck, I reckon,' said Spears. 'Now hop it. Go and get your kit together and find something to eat. They're brewing up something back there and there's some beer too. I'd have thought even you might deserve a drink this evening, Johnny.' He winked at him.

Relief and happiness at this simple gesture suddenly welled together with his intense exhaustion, and for a moment Hawke thought he might ruin everything because he knew he could easily break down and cry.

Getting to his feet, he had to turn and look away, feeling the tears pricking at the edge of his eyes, and so walked forward a few yards, to the blackened hulks of the tanks they had destroyed earlier. Four panzers – four they had knocked out that day in all! He could hardly believe it had happened. There was a sharp stench across the battlefield – of smoke and cordite and something else, a rather rich, sweet smell. For three days they had fought here at Cassel – first down by the farm and since then here, along this southern edge of the old town. The number of bullets and shells that had been fired in that time was incredible, and yet he was still alive – alive when so many were not. Now they were leaving it all behind and venturing out into the unknown Flanders plain beyond. He was glad it was over and yet he instinctively knew that more trials lay ahead. The Germans could not be everywhere, but how could an entire brigade slip through the net? Even he, a young soldier, knew that the chances of success were slim.

'Johnny!' called out Hebden. 'Come on!'

Hawke waved in acknowledgement and looked out a moment longer at the battlefield. *Don't think about it*, he told himself. Soon they would be heading out of Cassel for good. What would happen then, he had no idea. But there was no point, he realized, wasting any energy worrying about it. He would need every last scrap of that just to keep going at all.

Brigadier Somerset left the wreck of the town in the staff car that had brought him to Cassel five days earlier, although, as he turned through the northern gate at around 9.30 p.m. that evening, it seemed to him like a lifetime ago. Behind him, the remaining men of the Ox and Bucks Battalion were beginning their march, lined up in a long column and heading, as he and his staff were, for the road to Winnezeele.

He had wondered whether he and his Somer Force staff should have been marching along with the rest of the men, but the brigade was already now split up and breaking out in its different units. Somer Force was no more, and there was nothing he could do for them other than wish them all the very best of luck. Pretending otherwise would have been pointless.

Even so, he felt a sharp pang of guilt as the car trundled down the cobbled hill and the column of men gradually disappeared from view. He was also overcome by a sense of helplessness. Bullmore had been right: these men didn't stand a chance. There was no way they could disguise themselves from the enemy – not that number. He sighed heavily and looked out of the window. The sky was still not completely dark – a faint, milky glow shrouded the countryside, so that he could see the outline of passing woods, farms and houses.

And yet, for several miles, the car quietly rumbled on, with not a German in sight. Skirting around Le Coucou, they rejoined the Winnezeele road, passing undetected through the small villages of Le Riveld and Le Temple. Somerset was astounded. Not a soul stirred. Incredible though it seemed, the enemy who had been pressing the town so hard all day appeared to have simply melted away.

'This is extraordinary, sir,' said Bullmore, sitting in the back seat beside him. 'I'm beginning to think you were right. Perhaps that yeomanry troop did get clear away after all.'

Somerset chuckled. 'It does seem blissfully empty of Huns, I agree.'

Another half-mile passed and Somerset felt his spirits rise further. He had always expected the first few miles to be the most treacherous, yet they had gone five at least already.

'That's Winnezeele up ahead, sir,' said Robson from the front seat. Somerset moved so he could see through the windscreen. Faintly, in the deepening darkness, the silhouette of a church and a number of houses could be seen. Somerset tapped his knuckles on his knee. As they reached the village, he heard an owl hoot and somewhere not far away a dog barked. The place seemed empty, just like the other villages they had passed through.

As the last of the houses slid behind them, Somerset leaned back and closed his eyes. There was still a long way to go, he knew, but there was always confusion in war, and perhaps a car could weave its way through undetected – after all, the Germans had plenty else to think about. Perhaps a lone car would be assumed to be one of theirs. Perhaps even a column of troops, marching at night, would be assumed to be German. Perhaps, perhaps . . .

'Sir,' said Robson, his voice urgent.

Somerset opened his eyes, his heart sinking.

A torch was flashing up ahead and was now turned towards them. The driver rolled the car to a halt and then more torch-light was being flashed through the windows towards them. Somerset squinted and raised his hand to shield his eyes as the doors were opened one by one.

'*Aus!*' one of the men shouted. '*Machen Sie schnell!*' Out. And be quick about it.

Behind the glare, Somerset could see the outline of a German helmet.

'I'm sorry,' he said to the others. 'We've been caught after all.' He clambered out of the car. Rough hands pushed him forward. '*Hände hoch!*' Somerset raised his hands as a rifle barrel was pressed into his back.

A torch shone in his face. 'I hope you enjoyed your quiet evening drive, Herr Brigadier,' said the man in heavily accented English. 'You are from Cassel, are you not?'

Somerset said nothing.

'Well, we've been expecting you. First your panzer men, now you and, before long, I should not wonder, the rest of the garrison of Cassel.'

Somerset cursed inwardly.

Another torch flashed nearby. He saw several vehicles further on and was conscious of being surrounded by a number of enemy troops. Then he saw the face of the man beside him – a lean face, caught in shadow, and with the shoulder tabs, he saw, of a colonel.

'I must congratulate you on your defence of the town, but it is all over for you now, Herr Brigadier. For you and all your men.'

# 25

## THE AMBUSH

As Brigadier Somerset had planned, the Yorks Rangers were the last battalion to leave. The 2nd Battalion had begun the month with nearly eight hundred men, but were now down to just two hundred and twelve with two of their companies gone altogether. The last ten days of fighting had taken its toll. Even so, a little over two hundred men was still a large number to try to conceal, and Spears had been angered by the decision to break out in company formation.

'It's madness, sir,' he'd said after Farrish had returned from a briefing at Battalion Headquarters. 'We were barely strong enough to fight when we had the town to help our defence. Out in the open, with no artillery at all and next to no ammo left, we've got no chance.'

'I'm sorry, Spears,' said Farrish, 'but those are the orders. The brigadier's orders, I might hasten to add.'

'But I thought you said each battalion had been left to its own devices, sir,' said Spears. 'If we're allowed to make our own way as platoons, we might be able to get somewhere.'

'Spears,' said Farrish, his irritation mounting, 'it's no good having it out with me. Orders are orders. We march out as a battalion and that's that.'

And so they had, passing through the now silent Grand Place with its stench of burning and decay, the ruined buildings eerily silhouetted against the night sky. It was around half past ten when they finally headed back down the long, narrow street where earlier Hawke had knocked out the enemy tank, and not long after that they had tramped back around Dead Horse Corner, still strewn with rubble, empty casings, smashed wagons and vehicles.

Once down at the foot of the town, where earlier that morning Spears had seen the Germans moving up to attack, they had begun their tramp across country, trekking briskly through fields, down narrow tracks, over dykes and streams and along the thickening hedgerows that marked the Flanders plain. They skirted round a couple of villages and by several farms. Cows lowed, occasionally dogs barked at the sound of the men passing by, but otherwise the night seemed still.

At around 3 a.m., the long column paused at a crossroads of tracks. A company was at the head of the column, behind Battalion Headquarters, with 6th Platoon in the middle, ahead of C Company. The platoon was now just sixteen strong, the notion of sections abandoned now that they were on the march.

The sky was clear and Hawke saw Spears look up at the stars. He followed the sergeant's gaze – there were hundreds of thousands, twinkling benignly.

Hebden had evidently also seen Spears look up because he said, 'They're like old friends, aren't they? Look, there's the Plough.'

Hawke looked up. 'Which one's that, Bert?' he asked.

Spears shook his head. 'Don't you know?'

Hawke felt a stab of shame and embarrassment. 'No. I was never taught them.'

'Shouldn't have to be taught them,' said Spears in a low voice. 'You should want to learn them.'

'It's townsfolk, Sarge,' said Hebden. 'In the country you're brought up knowing things like this.' He patted Hawke on the back.

'I'm a towny,' said McLaren, 'but I know them all right.'

'Yes, but you've been in longer than most of these greenhorns. Look,' said Spears pointing. 'The Plough looks like a plough – or like a saucepan to some.'

'Also known as the Big Dipper,' added Hebden.

'Yes,' said Spears. 'Those three there are the handle, if you like, and those four in a rough rectangle are the plough or the pan.'

'Yes, I see it,' said Hawke.

'Then move your eyes right a bit,' added Spears. 'There's Cassiopeia. Like a W turned on its side.'

'Got it!' said Hawke with a bit more enthusiasm than he'd intended.

'Right,' said Spears. 'Then you run an imaginary line westwards from the centre star of Cassiopeia to the outer lip of the Plough. Then halfway along that line you'll see Polaris.'

'Yes, I can see it,' said Hawke.

'That's the North Star, Johnny,' said Hebden.

'Follow that and you'll be heading due north,' added Spears. 'Which is what we're doing. It's a brilliant natural compass.'

'Thanks, Sarge,' said Hawke.

'Yes, thank you, Sergeant,' added Farrish. 'Very interesting.'

'Don't mention it, sir,' said Spears.

'Of course, it's no good when it's cloudy,' said McLaren.

'That's why I keep an ordinary compass in my haversack,' said Spears.

Up ahead in the faint starlight, Hawke could see a huddle of officers discussing which way to turn.

Spears had seen them too. 'They need to go left, sir,' he told Farrish. 'Dunkirk is only a little to the west of due north.'

'I'm sure there are other considerations, Spears.'

They turned right. Spears groaned to himself, wishing they could separate from the rest of the column. It crossed his mind that perhaps he should grab Hawke and one or two others and slip away, but he dismissed such thoughts. *For the moment, at any rate*, he thought.

However, the column had not been travelling more than five minutes down the track when they suddenly heard furious small-arms and mortar fire half a mile or so up ahead. Faint lines of tracer could be seen.

'What's going on, Sarge?' Fletcher asked him. 'Do you think that's some of our lads?'

'I'd put good money on it,' Spears replied.

The column halted again, the men chattering agitatedly, then a minute later the head of the column came back down the track. In the faint milky light, Spears saw the battalion commander. Back they went, turning left back at the crossroads of tracks as Spears had originally suggested.

Half an hour later, with no let-up in the fighting going on away to their right, the first grey streaks of dawn were lighting the horizon in the east. In an hour, Spears knew, it would be quite light. His unease began to grow. Two hundred men, tramping across the north France countryside behind enemy lines . . . What were they thinking? His thoughts turned to Maddie. He pictured her face – so innocent, so gentle. The possibility that he might not see her again made his heart lurch. Somehow, he had to get back. He and Maddie's little brother.

Drummond had a blister.

'You should've taken more care over those dykes,' said McLaren.

'I didn't meant to slip,' he grumbled. 'I thought I'd jumped clear.' Instead, as he'd cursed out loud at the time, his whole foot had got soaked and both his foot and the boot it was in had swollen and started rubbing.

'You'll just have to put up with it for the time being, Charlie,' said McLaren.

'I'm hardly going to throw in the towel because of a blister,' he muttered. 'But it still hurts. And we've barely started.'

'Think of Blighty,' said Hebden. 'Think of playing your first match for Sheffield United.'

'Not with this foot,' grumbled Drummond.

'Just imagine it,' continued Hebden. 'It's a full crowd – a local derby against Leeds. You've only been on the pitch a few minutes, and the ball is passed to you. Suddenly you see that up ahead there's a man out of position. It's a wonderful opportunity. You sidestep round the first player, dummy your way past a second and now the goal is only thirty-five yards away and, although two defenders are converging towards you, you know you have a chance. You kick the ball with all your might. It arcs through the air like a bullet. The crowd watches, open mouthed, barely daring to breathe. The keeper stretches, but the shot's too good – the ball whistles past his outstretched fingers and finds the back of the net. You've scored and the crowd rises to its feet and cheers.' He hoisted his arms.

Hawke laughed, and even Drummond began to chuckle.

'"This new lad, Drummond," the old men say to themselves, "I like the look of him. And apparently he marched all the way to Dunkirk with a fiendish blister. Shows determination that does. And you need determination to make it big in football. Determination and guts."'

They were all laughing now, even Spears.

Then suddenly machine guns and small-arms were firing at them, lines of tracer zipping across the open fields to their right and front. Men cried out and fell and now mortar shells were raining down too. Hawke felt a hand push him hard to the ground and turned to see Spears beside him as they lay on the grassy bank at the edge of the track. A flare fizzed into the sky, burst and crackled, bright magnesium lighting up the sky around them.

Hawke frantically pulled his rifle to his shoulder, his body tense and his heart drumming. Two hundred yards away, to the north-east, stood the outline of a farm and he could now see the outline of several armoured cars, trucks and other vehicles. Machine-gun tracer was coming in short, sharp bursts from the farm and from behind the hedgerow either side of the house and outbuildings.

The track was lower than the level of the field in front of them, the grassy bank offering some cover, but a number of men had been cut down by the first murderous enemy salvo. Beside Hawke, Spears was cursing furiously. Men were returning fire, but the column had been thrown into confusion.

'What do we do now?' Drummond cried out.

'Keep our heads,' muttered Spears. He was looking around him. Behind them, the other side of the track, the ground continued to fall away gently towards a wood, no more than a couple of hundred yards away. 'That's where we need to be,' he said. 'In there.'

'Spears!' called out Farrish. 'Is anyone down your end?'

'No, sir,' Spears replied. 'We should get to that wood, sir.'

'Let me find Captain Astell,' came the reply. No sooner had he said this, however, than to their left they saw that men were already crawling away from the track and scurrying towards the wood, and then a captain from Battalion Headquarters was among them, crouched low, and saying, 'Fall back to the wood! Colonel's orders are to fall back!'

Another flare fizzed into the sky and burst, prompting a further furious tirade of enemy fire. A number of men clambering clear of the track were caught, bodies jerking forward.

'All right, chaps!' called out Farrish. 'Sixth Platoon, let's move!'

'Keep low!' hissed Spears, 'And stick near me!'

Hawke nodded. The sky was continuing to lighten, but still only faintly, and as the flare died they crawled across the track, rolled over into the field and not until they had gone twenty yards or more did they get on to their knees and feet and then begin to run.

Hawke was conscious of some figures running beside him. 'Bert! Charlie!' he called out.

'Just run, Johnny!' Hebden replied.

Hawke did so. A mortar shell landed not far behind him, earth and grit pattering into his back. Above his head, bullets fizzed and hissed, but the edge of the wood was close now.

Glancing either side of him, he saw other men running furiously. One fell – *did he trip or was he hit?* – and Hawke faltered and stumbled himself, but as he hit the ground he felt a hand grip his webbing and pull him back up to his feet, and turning he saw Spears.

'Go on!' urged Spears, and Hawke ran on, his lungs tight in his chest, his legs aching and sweat running down the side of his face, until at last he reached the trees. Bullets crackled through the branches and leaves above but as he hid behind a fat beech, he gasped, bent over, his hands on his knees.

'My God!' spluttered Hebden. Hawke saw that he and Drummond were both sheltering behind another beech a few yards away, then he spotted McLaren and Fletcher and White. *We've all made it*, he thought. So too had Lieutenant Farrish and Merryweather and Grimshaw and several others from the platoon. Farrish began to carry out a head count. Only one man was missing: Collins, from 3 Section.

'Anyone see Collins?' asked Farrish.

No one had. Farrish cursed. 'Damn it!' he muttered, looking back out towards the field they had just crossed. 'Collins!' he called. 'Collins!'

There was no answer, but now someone was calling out, 'A Company to me! A Company to me!' from deeper inside the wood.

'Sir?' said Spears.

Farrish looked one last time out across the field, then nodded. 'Come on, then.'

They found Captain Astell and a number of A Company men in a small clearing a short way inside the wood. Hawke looked up through the dense canopy of branches and saw the lightening sky, although within the wood the early morning light remained murky. The firing had died down but the Germans were mortaring the wood, the missiles crashing into the trees and exploding with violent bursts of orange light.

'The situation's obviously not very good,' said Astell, then flinched as a mortar shell exploded not more than fifty yards away. 'I'm going to try to find out what orders are from Battalion, but my instinct is that for the time being we should keep in our platoons. We're not going to be able to move out of here until the Germans scoot off and that seems unlikely to happen while they know we're all hiding in these woods.' He pulled out a whistle from his breast pocket and held it up. 'When I blow this three times, that's the signal for us to form up together again, all right?' Heads nodded. 'Good. In the meantime, try to find a good place to hide. I'm afraid it may be a long day. Good luck to you all.'

Farrish led the remnants of 6th Platoon deeper into the wood. Several times they bumped into other groups of Rangers, but eventually they stopped among some oaks. A large beech tree had fallen and lay sprawled between the aged oaks, its underside offering a screen from any hunters and incoming shells. There was a good covering of undergrowth too – bracken, newly in leaf, and brambles.

'This is a good hideout,' said Hebden, sitting crouched beside Hawke. 'We did well to find this.' Around the wood, the mortaring continued.

'I wish it wasn't so damp underneath, though,' muttered Drummond.

'Better to have a wet backside than to be blasted to hell by Jerry,' said McLaren, 'so stop moaning.'

An hour later, the sun had risen, so that at last they could see the size of the wood. It was, Hebden reckoned, risking getting up and looking around, about twelve acres.

'Not big enough,' muttered Spears.

Soon after, the mortaring stopped and German troops began calling out, '*Kamerad! Kamerad!*'

Hawke brought his knees closer into his chest and huddled tightly next to the rest of the men. Crouching there, it was hard to tell whether the Germans were venturing deep into the wood, but it was clear enough that they were rounding up a number of the men. Occasionally, shots rang out, and once there was a sustained drum of machine-gun fire.

'Do you think they're shooting the men they've taken prisoner?' asked Fletcher, his face ashen.

Spears shrugged. 'Keep quiet, Fletch, and you might never have to find out.'

Nearby, there was movement and they froze, but then whoever it was scurried away again. Germans were still shouting out and then, a little distance away, they heard a single voice call out clearly, in English. 'Come out! Come out, Tommies! Hitler is winning the war. You are beaten. Come out, or we will shell this wood and you will all be killed. Lay down your arms and come out!' There was a pause and then they heard him call out the same words again, further away this time.

Hawke looked at the others, anxious to see in their faces what they were thinking. The lieutenant seemed to be wrestling with his conscience, knotting his hands together, his face taut. Spears had closed his eyes, while others looked around.

'Maybe we should chuck it in,' said Merryweather. He looked around at the others. 'I mean, let's face it. We're surrounded. We've not even gone ten miles from Cassel yet, and we'll never get to Dunkirk in time, even if we do get out of here.'

Hawke saw that a couple of the men were nodding in agreement.

'What do you all think?' said Farrish.

'They're bluffing,' said Spears. 'I'm not surrendering. Not to a bunch of goose-stepping Nazis.'

Farrish cleared his throat. 'And I'm not going to either. But I think if anyone feels strongly that their best chance of survival is to throw in the towel, then it would be unfair of me to stop you. You've all fought damn well these past few days. You would have nothing to feel ashamed about.'

For a moment there was silence. Hawke looked at the others, but no one moved. Not even Merryweather.

'Bleedin' heck,' muttered Merryweather at last. 'All right, I'll stay too.'

For about twenty minutes there was silence. No birdsong, despite the time of year, no shouts, no firing of enemy guns. Just the rustle of leaves above them as a gentle breeze blew.

And then the shelling began.

# 26

## ESCAPE FROM THE WOOD

The shelling continued all morning and on into the afternoon: mortars and field guns, lobbing shells of various sizes. To begin with, the barrage was intense, branches tumbling to the ground, lethal shards of wood flying through the air, and a choking, acrid smell of smoke. The men of 6th Platoon huddled tightly, placed handkerchiefs made damp with water over their mouths and felt the vibrations and pulses of the detonating shells shimmer through their bodies. A nearby oak was hit, and with a loud snap and groaning tear, a large branch thundered down. Hawke saw it falling and closed his eyes, tucking his head further towards his chest, but to their relief it landed across the fallen beech without touching a single one of the platoon. Its branches had since provided them with even greater protection.

The Germans did not keep up the intensity of shelling, however, and soon the whistle of incoming shells became more sporadic, so that by early afternoon the men had begun picking at the few rations they'd managed to bring with them and even move out briefly in order to relieve themselves. Occasionally, they heard engines revving from the direction of the farm, but, otherwise, enemy activity seemed to be lessening, and by mid-afternoon, the shelling had stopped altogether. At around four o'clock, Spears volunteered to carry out a quick reconnoitre, and returned soon after.

'I don't reckon there's that many of us left in here,' he said. 'I only saw a handful of men.'

'What about Captain Astell?'

Spears shook his head. 'I didn't see him, sir.'

Farrish scratched his face. He had scrupulously shaved every single day while they had been at Cassel, but now, for the first time, a thin shadow of a beard was starting to show. 'So, to all intents and purposes, we're now on our own.'

'If you ask me, it's better that way, sir. The fewer there are of us, the easier it will be to avoid capture.'

'Yes, I suppose you're right. God only knows what would have happened if we'd not been ambushed last night, but it was hard to see how we could have ever got very far.'

Spears said nothing.

'What about Huns? See any movement?'

'No, sir. I reckon they've packed up. Got bigger fish to fry.'

'Should we try to make a move, then?'

'Perhaps we should wait until dusk. From now on, I think we should move by night and rest up by day. And now the shelling's stopped we'd all do well to try and get some kip first.'

Farrish agreed and for the first time that day Hawke moved from the tight space beneath the fallen beech, and with his greatcoat taken out of his pack and draped over him, lay down and closed his eyes. He had felt tense and anxious all day, which had helped keep him alert, but now that the shelling had stopped extreme exhaustion descended over him once more. The ground was far from smooth, the damp of the forest floor filled his nostrils, and the lice in his uniform were beginning to bother him again. Yet, despite these discomforts, he had barely closed his eyes before he was fast asleep.

A hand on his shoulder, shaking him awake. Hawke opened his eyes, momentarily disorientated. The wood was darker now.

'Time to get going,' said Spears.

'Yes, Sarge,' said Hawke sitting up. His whole body seemed to ache, but his shoulder especially. He rubbed it, then his eyes, and got to his feet, rolling up his greatcoat and putting it back in his pack. He felt better for the sleep, but his stomach groaned with hunger. All he had left was a packet of hard biscuits, which he retrieved from his haversack and began to chew slowly. Hard, dry and largely tasteless, but food, nonetheless.

It was nearly nine o'clock. Hawke had been asleep for almost five hours, he realized – almost the longest stretch of continuous sleep he'd had since arriving at Cassel. He yawned as the men stood around waiting to move.

'So what are the odds of us surviving the night?' said Drummond.

'Good,' said Hebden. 'I've got a good feeling about it.'

'Really?' said McLaren. 'Why's that?'

'A sixth sense. We deserve a bit of good fortune.' Hawke could see his smiling teeth in the dim light.

'Well, let's stop talking about it and get a move on,' said Spears.

They moved off but at the wood's edge met another small party of five men. Hawke immediately recognized Matherson and Spencer, the two stretcher bearers.

'Where have you lot appeared from?' Farrish asked them.

'We were with Battalion Headquarters,' said Matherson.

'Where are they now?'

'In the bag. Jerry picked them up this morning.'

'You saw this?'

'With my own eyes. We were hiding. Jerries walked right past, but they didn't see us, thank God. Colonel Beamish and most of his staff were taken away.'

Farrish shook his head and sighed heavily. 'Then we really are on our own.'

Hawke glanced around at the rest of the men. They were all looking at the lieutenant, expressions of uncertainty and anxiety etched on their faces. Farrish breathed in deeply again. 'And have you seen anyone else?'

'No, sir,' said Matherson. 'But they captured a lot of our lads. We moved around all morning dodging the shells and the Jerry soldiers. We've just been wondering what to do next, and now you lot turn up, sir.'

'Then you'd better come with us.' Farrish shot a glance at Spears.

Hawke felt himself tense as they stepped clear of the wood and began walking across an open field, heading north. It was still not entirely dark and with every pace Hawke's heart seemed to thump harder. They were stretched out in a line, abreast, and any enemy troops lying in wait would have a perfect target, the men silhouetted against the sky. Hawke gripped his rifle. Spears, he saw, was holding his rifle in his hands. Unlike some of the men, who preferred to keep theirs slung over their shoulders, Hawke had kept his in his hands, like Spears. He gripped it tightly now, scanning the darkening world around him with keen eyes.

But there was no sudden burst of enemy fire, no tracer criss-crossing lethally towards them. Spears's hunch, it seemed, had been right. For several hours they pressed on, heading north, crossing fields and following tracks. Every so often, Farrish would halt them and look at his map, an old Michelin road map he had bought before the war and which he had had the good sense to bring out to France with him.

'I can't see how the lieutenant can use that map,' said Drummond after one of Farrish's brief halts. 'It's too dark and, anyway, I had a peek at it once before. It's the whole of northern France. The scale's way too large.'

'I just hope we're going in the right direction,' said Fletcher.

'We are,' said Spears behind them.

'How do you know, Sarge?' asked Drummond.

'Because Dunkirk is north-north-east of Cassel and that's the way we've been headed.' He pointed out the North Star up in the sky. 'Didn't they teach you anything in training, Charlie?'

'Not that, Sarge.'

'What do we do when there's cloud, Sarge,' asked Hebden, 'and we can't see the stars?'

'We use my compass.'

The men laughed.

They walked on, one step after another. Drummond's blister was getting worse, but he was no longer the only one suffering from sore feet – many of the others were too. Hawke's feet were not rubbing, but his legs were beginning to ache once more and his whole body itched. And his shoulder hurt, the straps of his webbing rubbing painfully where he had fallen from the tank. He was hungry too. Thoughts of food kept running through his mind. He tried to dismiss them but an image of his family sitting down together and eating the Sunday roast kept creeping back into his mind no matter how hard he tried to banish it: the smell of hot chicken, his mother's rich gravy and then a pudding of baked apples smothered in raisins and melted syrup. His stomach groaned painfully, but they had all finished their rations – Hawke had just two hard tack biscuits left.

He was still struggling to banish such thoughts as they crossed a road near a farmhouse. His vigilance of earlier had gone. The world seemed so quiet, so peaceful. On the other side of the road was an open field of young corn, and away to the left another small wood. They marched on, in silence, but with the sound of their boots crunching against the thick shoots of green corn. A dog barked from the direction of the farm and then, faintly, but quite distinctly, Hawke heard voices. He froze immediately.

'What is it?' hissed Spears.

'Voices, Sarge – I thought I heard voices.'

'Get down!' said Spears, now running along their line towards Farrish.

Hawke dropped to the ground as a machine gun suddenly opened fire from somewhere near the farm. Several men near the front cried out as the scythe of lethal fire cut into them. Hawke thought he saw Spears fall and, his heart racing, he began crawling along through the corn. Another burst of fire, bullets whipping over their heads. One man was groaning, and another breathing heavily, each breath a rasping gurgle.

'Sarge! Sarge!' whispered Hawke. 'Are you all right?'

'I'm fine. Just start moving towards the wood. Tell the rest of the men – get moving towards the wood. Now, and as quietly as possible.'

'Yes, Sarge,' said Hawke. He crawled back down the line of prostrate men. 'Sarge says we're to make for the wood,' he whispered. 'Make for the wood.'

'Who's been hit?' whispered Hebden.

'Not sure,' Hawke told him. 'Not the sarge, though.'

'Mr Farrish was up front,' said Hebden. 'Hope he's all right.'

But Lieutenant Farrish was far from all right, as Spears was keenly aware. Three men had been killed: two of the stretcher bearers and Grimshaw. But the lieutenant would not be alive much longer. Spears also had another problem on his hands. He had told Hawke that he was all right. He had lied. A bullet had caught him in his left arm. At the moment, he felt no pain, only a lot of blood, and he had no idea how bad it was, but the job of reaching Dunkirk was formidable enough without carrying a wound. He cursed and crawled towards Farrish.

'Sir,' he whispered. 'Sir.'

'Spears,' Farrish rasped, his voice thick with blood.

'We'll get you out, sir,' he said. 'You'll be all right.'

'No,' gurgled Farrish. 'I'm done for.' He tried to reach something. 'My map,' he spluttered. 'Take my map.'

Spears took it from the large pocket on the front of his trousers.

'I'm sorry,' rasped Farrish. 'I've not been much good. Been far too dependent on you, Spears.'

'No, sir, you're a grand platoon commander. One of the best I've known.'

'Really? Do you mean that?'

'Yes, sir,' said Spears.

Farrish's breathing grew heavier, more laboured. 'What a place to die,' he said. 'I had such hopes.' He sighed, then spluttered.

'All right, sir,' said Spears. 'You take it easy.' In the faint starlight he could see the whites of Farrish's eyes. The lieutenant looked at him, gasped again, then his head fell back.

'Damn! Damn! Damn!' mouthed Spears to himself. He felt for Farrish's dog-tags and tugged hard at the string so that it snapped, then took the lieutenant's Webley revolver and spare rounds and put them in his pack. A pistol would be all he could manage from now on. From the farm, he could hear voices, then there was another burst of machine gun, followed by the hiss of a flare.

Spears scrambled to his feet and ran, then as the flare burst, crackling as it began its slow descent, he dived, just yards from the edge of the wood, more machine-gun fire following him. Bullets fizzed into the trees and branches beyond.

'Sarge!' he heard Hawke whisper loudly a few yards to his left. 'Sarge! We're over here!' For the first time since Hawke had first joined the company, Spears was glad to hear his voice.

# 27

## TALKING WITH THE ENEMY

It was only at first light, and having pushed on further north without further incident, that Hawke realized Spears had been wounded. The sergeant looked pale, even in the early morning light, and from the state of his battle dress it looked as though he had lost a fair amount of blood.

'Blimey, Sarge,' said McLaren as they emerged from a wood and began walking down a sunken track. 'What the hell happened to your arm?'

'Got caught by one of those Jerry bullets,' muttered Spears. He had tied a field dressing around it, but the thin gauze was now dark with dried and fresher blood. 'We needed to press on,' he added. 'Get away from that place.'

'That needs seeing to,' said Matherson.

'We need to find a place to lie up for the day first,' said Spears. He looked at his wristwatch. 'We've got another twenty minutes before sunrise.'

'What about trying to find a barn?' said McLaren. 'There's a farm up ahead. It might be deserted.'

'We'd be better off in a wood,' said Spears.

'Let's have a look,' said McLaren. 'If there's any sign of life, we'll move on to the next wood we see.'

But there were signs of life: a barking dog, chickens pecking in the yard, cattle that seemed in no way distressed, and an open window on the first floor.

'Food, Sarge,' whispered McLaren, pointing towards the chickens.

'No, Sid,' said Spears. 'Too risky.'

So they kept walking, halting not in a wood, but among the long grass beneath a plantation of poplars that ran alongside a narrow dyke. There was no track leading to it, while the nearest road was some way away to their right.

'What about picquets?' McLaren asked Spears as the sergeant collapsed on the soft ground, his head against the base of a tall, straight poplar.

Spears sighed. 'Not much point really. If anyone catches us here, there's nowhere to escape to, is there?'

'No, I suppose not.'

'Might as well try to get some sleep.'

'Not before I've looked at your arm,' said Matherson.

Hawke watched as Spears carefully took off his battle blouse, and then his shirt, then let Matherson carefully undo the sodden bandage. Spears grimaced with pain.

'What a mess,' muttered Matherson, who took out another field dressing from his pack and sluicing it in water, began to try and clean the wound.

'I hope you know what you're doing,' gasped Spears.

'I may not be a doctor,' retorted Matherson, 'but I am a medical orderly. We are given plenty of training, you know.'

The bullet, it seemed, had missed the bone in his upper arm, but had passed right through the muscle, taking with it a chunk of flesh and leaving a bloody mess. Stitches were needed.

'I'm sorry, I don't have any morphine left,' said Matherson, 'but it needs doing, otherwise it won't be able to heal and you'll be at further risk of infection.'

Spears took his hip flask from his pocket and drank the rest of the brandy.

'Go on, then,' he said. 'Let's get it over with.'

Wrapping a tight tourniquet round the top of Spears's arm, Matherson began the surgery, Spears clenching his teeth tightly with the pain. When it was done, and the newly closed wound smothered in antiseptic gentian-violet cream, Matherson bandaged the arm with fresh dressings, then made a sling and, after cutting holes in both Spears's shirt and battle blouse, allowed him to dress once more.

'Thank you, Matherson,' gasped Spears when it was done.

'Let's hope that will last until you get some proper help,' Matherson replied. 'But you'd do well to get as much rest as you can today. We're relying on you, Sarge. Now that the lieutenant's dead we're going to need you to lead us.'

The day passed without incident but slowly – too slowly as far as Hawke was concerned. He'd slept a little in the morning but then had woken, consumed once more with hunger. Apart from his biscuits, he'd not eaten a thing for the best part of thirty-six hours. Nor was he alone in struggling to contain his hunger. All the men were feeling the pain in their stomachs.

Along the road, away to their right, they saw traffic moving, but who and what it was they could not tell with the naked eye. The only man with field glasses was Spears, but he had been asleep. No one wanted to risk disturbing him. Overhead, enemy planes had passed regularly and away to the north they heard the dull boom of guns and of bombs and shells exploding. That was something at least. The battle was not over yet.

In the late afternoon, he returned once more to his unfinished letter home. *We are now in open country*, he wrote, *which is nice, but completely flat. You can see for miles on a clear day – it's very different from Yorkshire. I am doing fine and so is Tom, although he has hurt his arm. He seems to be all right, though*. He paused, struck by the ridiculousness of what he had written. He chuckled to himself.

'What are you laughing about?' Hebden asked him.

'If only my family really knew,' he said. 'All I've done is told them that I am fine and then written about the countryside. It reads more like I'm on a walking tour rather than in the middle of a war.'

'We are in a way,' said Hebden. 'A walking tour of Flanders.' He smiled to himself then said out loud, '*Dear Mother and Father, Flanders is a perfectly pleasant part of the world to look at, although the accommodation is not as comfortable as one might have expected. Our party is suffering from an infestation of lice, which is making us scratch like the devil, and I fear our footwear is perhaps not ideal for the long miles we have already walked*.'

'You can say that again,' muttered Drummond, who had taken off his boots and whose ruddy feet looked swollen and livid with blisters.

'*Nor have we always had the best reception at the places we have visited*,' Hebden continued, '*while the general supply of food has also been disappointing. I shall certainly be complaining to Messrs Thomas Cook and Son on my return*.'

'Damn you, Bert,' groaned McLaren. 'I'd just managed to stop thinking about food and now you start up again.'

'Sorry, Sid, but I must finish my letter home. *However, we are certainly enjoying seeing this wonderful part of northern France by night and getting to know some of its many woods and plantations well by day. Best love, Bert.*'

'My letter is pretty much like that,' said Hawke. He thought for a moment, then remembered what Hebden had suggested a few days before. Folding the letter and putting it at the back of the pad, he turned to a clean sheet and began to write.

I can't believe Lieutenant Farrish has been killed. I never really knew him that well, but he seemed like a good sort and was always fair and led by example. Nor was he too proud – everyone knew he leaned heavily on Tom who has by far the most experience in the platoon. We just had to leave him in the field where we were caught – him and three others. I hope Jerry gives them a proper burial. No one talks any more about whether we will or won't reach Dunkirk. We're all hoping we will, but it's not a good idea to think ahead too much. I'm just taking each minute and each hour as it comes. Hoping for the best. Thank God Tom is all right. It's a nasty wound, but I think he will be fine. It was a stroke of luck picking up Matherson like that.

He paused a moment, thinking. Above in the trees, a bird was singing: a strange, almost haunting whistle, followed by a small flourish of song, then that eerie whistle again.

'What kind of bird is that?' he asked.

Lying beside him, his hands behind his head, Hebden smiled. 'That's a nightingale, that is. Lovely sound, isn't it.'

'Yes, but sad, somehow.'

'Some folk think they're singing a lament,' he said.

'Maybe that's true,' said McLaren. 'Maybe he's singing it for Mr Farrish and all the other lads we've lost.'

'Maybe,' said Hebden, 'but the nightingale's always been lucky for me. First time I heard it, I got picked for the village team the next day. Another time I heard him, I kissed Elsie Addison that very night.'

They all laughed. Hebden sighed. 'She were lovely. A rose. An absolute rose, she was.'

'What happened to her?' asked Drummond.

'Well, there's a tragedy.'

'What?'

'She decided she preferred Stan Wilkinson instead. Near broke my heart.'

'Poor Bert,' said McLaren with mock sincerity.

'Ah, well. That little chap singing above us has cheered me up.' He grinned.

Hawke listened again.

There's a bird singing above us, *he scribbled.* Bert says it's a nightingale and he should know, living on a farm all his life. He says it's lucky. I hope he's right. I don't know why, but I have a feeling he might be. We've made it this far. Another night, maybe two, and Tom reckons we might make Dunkirk. In Cassel it sometimes seemed impossible to think we would ever get away. But we did and we can make Dunkirk too. I know we can.

That night they waited until it was dark. The countryside around was now so flat that there were fewer folds in the land. The sunken tracks and the softly undulating ground around Cassel had gone, replaced by endless level fields, a few villages and farmsteads, and long, straight dykes and streams.

They continued north, at first struggling to adjust to the darkness. With plenty of cloud, and no stars to guide them, the only light came from the moon, which was also frequently hidden by cloud. However, slowly they adjusted. As Spears pointed out, it was never pitch dark at night, not in the countryside.

They were not the only men moving that night. A little way from the road they paused to watch a column of horse-drawn artillery that was moving forward, the occasional braying of the horses and the gentle squeak and rumble of wheels quite distinct on the still night air. They saw the guns too, barrels pointing behind them.

'I think they might be French, Sarge,' said McLaren.

'Really?' said Spears.

'Jerry doesn't have horse-drawn artillery, I'm sure he doesn't. They've got all the M/T they could wish for.'

'Certainly the lads we saw at Cassel seemed to,' agreed Spears. 'All right – let's take a closer look, then. Anyone speak French?'

No one did. 'I'll go,' said Spears, getting to his feet. 'You lot wait here.'

'Sarge,' said Hawke, 'what if they're not French?'

'It's a risk worth taking. If they are, it means we've probably crossed back over Allied lines. And that means we can use the roads and get to Dunkirk quicker.'

Spears got to his feet. His arm still hurt like hell and he had a splitting headache, but he knew his wound might easily have been much worse. Really, he'd been lucky. And maybe that nightingale *had* been a good omen. He preferred not to read into things too much – what would be, would be – but his yearning to get back home, to see Maddie once more, was so strong, he was prepared to take any sign of hope and grab it greedily with both hands.

Leaving his helmet behind, he moved up calmly to the road and then stepped in alongside some troops marching on foot beside the wagons. His intention had been to walk with them and listen, then act accordingly, but no one spoke at all, and Spears was conscious that every step was taking him further from the rest of the men.

Eventually he coughed loudly and the man next to him said something, not in French, but German, and as he spoke the moon slipped out from behind a cloud and Spears saw the familiar shape of the German helmet and even the faint contours of the man's face. Spears felt his body tense, but no matter how much he wanted to turn and run he knew that would be the worst thing he could do.

Instead he murmured, '*Ja, ja*,' softly, and carried on walking a few yards beside the man. It must have been a reasonable response, because the German said no more, but just kept walking onwards. Lessening his pace, Spears allowed himself to fall behind and then, when the moon disappeared again behind the cloud, he quickly sidestepped into the field and ran back to the others.

'They're not French,' he said. 'They're German. I've just been talking with the enemy. Fortunately, they must be even more dog-tired than we are because they didn't bat an eye.'

'Told you that nightingale was lucky,' said Hebden.

'Not lucky enough,' said Spears. 'We're still behind enemy lines.'

There was silence for a moment as the platoon digested this piece of news.

'I'm sorry, boys,' said Spears eventually.

'Where do you reckon we are, Sarge?' said McLaren. 'How many miles have we done tonight?

'About three. I think that makes us about fifteen miles south of Dunkirk,' he said.

'Not so far, then,' said Hebden.

'No. We should get there tomorrow night.'

'If only it didn't get light so damn early,' said McLaren, 'we could have pushed on through tonight.'

'Come on,' said Spears. 'We're almost within shouting distance. Let's keep going.'

They trudged on. The ground was flat and easy to walk over, but there were also innumerable dykes and streams, which had to be crossed. None of them remained dry, their feet swelled, and even Spears was beginning to feel sore with blisters. His arm also hurt like hell. On top of that, there was the lack of food. All of them were struggling. Hunger was severely affecting their energy levels. It made them less spry when crossing the dykes, and more likely to fall in the water. It made it harder to keep spirits up, even when they were now so close.

As they tramped on, Spears came to a decision. They needed to try to find a farmhouse where they could stop until the following evening. A farmhouse with some food. A farmhouse with some hay they could stuff into their boots to help dry them. A farmhouse where they could rest and get some strength back before the final stretch to the port. It would be a risk, of course, but it was going to be a risk hiding in a wood too. Although he had no real idea what was going on, it was clear the Germans were closing in around the port. The closer they got to Dunkirk, the more enemy there would be. And the more there were, the harder it would be to hide. A Frenchman's barn was as good a place to hole up as any.

It was nearing three thirty in the morning when he spotted the farmhouse. Since his escape from the German artillery column, the cloud had been gradually clearing, and now the moon was high and bright, revealing a lone farmstead, not so very different from the one they had occupied at Oxelaëre. He paused them all for a moment at the edge of a field beside a farm track. The air smelled fresh and crisp, as he looked around. There was a village a couple of miles to the north-east and another about the same distance to the west – he could see the spires of their respective churches outlined darkly against the sky, but no obvious road linking the two, just the rough track in front of them.

'What are you thinking, Sarge?' asked McLaren.

Spears explained. 'I'm going to go forward and have a dekko at the farm. If I see any sign of Jerries I'll beat it, but just in case something happens to me I want you to lie low then keep heading north and try to find somewhere else to lie up.'

'Sarge,' said Hawke. 'Let me go and look. You've got your arm.'

'No,' he said. 'No, I'll go. If anything, the wound will help.' He turned to McLaren. 'Sid – you're in charge until I get back. If you think something's wrong, get going, all right?'

'Yes, Sarge,' said McLaren.

'Good.'

'Here's hoping,' added McLaren.

Spears left behind his tin hat once again and turned on to the track, his feet scrunching loudly on the stone, then headed up the lane to the farm. He could see no obvious vehicle tracks on the dusty ground, but as he neared the farm he began to walk more slowly, more cautiously. With no sign of life in the yard, he gently stepped forward, skirting round the edge of one of the outbuildings towards the house. Suddenly something jumped on to the low barn roof and then down in front of him and he reeled backwards with a start, only to see a cat scamper across the moonlit yard.

Cursing, Spears now approached the front door of the house. For a moment, he stood there, listening. Not a thing stirred. With his good hand, he pulled the revolver from his belt and cocked it, then knocked on the door, cringing at the sound, which seemed to resound clearly around the entire farm.

Spears waited, then eventually heard movement from inside. A lamp was lit – he could see it flickering through the windows to the side – and then he heard footsteps. Spears breathed in deeply, offering a silent prayer that whoever it was who opened the door would be friendly.

Another light flickered from within, and Spears heard muffled talking. Then a bolt was drawn, a lock turned and at last the front door opened.

# 28

## THE HAYLOFT

A middle-aged man, with short, greying hair, squinted at Spears, a shotgun at his hip, and wearing trousers hastily pulled on over his nightshirt.

'*Oui?*' he said, then seeing Spears's uniform said, '*Vous êtes Anglais*. You are British.'

'Yes,' said Spears. 'We have come from Cassel. We're trying to get to Dunkirk, but we need help.'

The man eyed him suspiciously. 'What kind of help?'

'I have thirteen men. We have not eaten for two days. We need some food and somewhere to hide during the day.'

'*Les Allemands*,' he said, 'they are everywhere now. Attacking Dunkirk.'

'I know,' said Spears. 'But with your help we can still reach safety.'

The farmer sighed and rubbed his eyes. Behind the door, out of view, Spears heard a woman's voice. The Frenchman turned to her and spoke rapidly, then turned back to him and rubbed his chin, then sighed heavily again.

'Where are *les autres*? Your men?' He had lowered the shotgun and now took a step out into the yard and looked around.

'A little way back. Waiting for me on the track.'

'*D'accord*,' he nodded. 'All right. But not in the house. I have a barn. You can hide there. We will bring you some food.'

'Thank you,' said Spears, relief coursing through him. 'My name is Sergeant Tom Spears. We are from the King's Own Yorkshire Rangers.' He held out his hand and the farmer took it and gripped it firmly.

'Gaston Batiste.' His wife now appeared, a small, pretty woman, younger than Batiste. 'My wife, Lucie,' he said.

'Thank you,' Spears said again. '*Merci beaucoup*.'

'We do not like the Germans,' said Batiste. 'My wife lost her father at Verdun, and I lost my brother. The last war destroyed this part of France. All because of those stupid Boches, and *encore*, here they are all over again.' He spat the word *Boches*. 'If you get your men, I will meet you here in the yard.'

The men were all cheered by Spears's news, and followed him back to the yard where Batiste was waiting for them.

'Come with me,' he said, carrying a paraffin lamp. He led them to a barn on the far side of the yard. Old farming machinery and several carts filled the ground floor, but covering half the building was a hayloft with a rickety wooden ladder leading to it. From the old beams hung ropes and chains, while the roof struts sagged from age and the weight of the tiles.

'Up there,' said Batiste. 'The men will be well hidden and can use the hay. There is still enough from last year. We will create a kind of wall with the bales, a barricade of hay, and the men can hide behind it. From below or even from the ladder, it will just look like a solid stack of hay and straw.' He glanced at Spears's arm. 'Will you be able to make it up the ladder?'

'Yes – I've still one good arm.'

Batiste nodded. 'Good. I will see to the food, then when you have eaten you and I will talk. You will want to know about the Boches, yes?'

The thought of food and rest and chance to dry their sodden feet and legs had lifted the spirits of them all. Once in the hayloft, they had eagerly begun pulling off their boots and stuffing them with dry hay, and laying out their wet socks.

It was dark up there, only a faint, milky light coming through a small rectangular open window at the end of the barn, yet once their eyes became accustomed even this gave them just enough to see by. Sitting against the barn's wall next to Hebden and Drummond, Hawke took a small handful of hay and rubbed it over his feet as though it were a towel. Suddenly released from the wet, warm encasement of his socks and boots, his feet were massaged by the dry dust and gentle scratch of the stalks. He had never before realized that such a simple thing could cause so much soothing pleasure.

Beside him, Hebden breathed in deeply and sighed contentedly. 'Ahh,' he said, 'that's the smell of home. Dust and hay and wood. I'm going to sleep well here.'

'Especially if there's something in our bellies,' agreed Drummond. 'I'm so hungry, I could eat anything, even frogs' legs.'

'Even snails,' added Hebden.

'Do they really eat those things in France?' asked Hawke.

'So they say. Fried in garlic.' Hebden grinned. 'I'd even put up with bad breath I'm so hungry.'

'You've already got bad breath,' retorted Drummond. 'When did you last use any tooth powder?'

'In Cassel,' said Hebden. 'I used some then, which I bet is

more than can be said for you.' He cupped his hands under his nose and breathed heavily. 'I think I'm all right.'

Hawke did the same, but all he could smell was the musty, sweaty odour of his clothes. 'I can't wait to be clean again,' he said. 'When I joined up, it was all about looking as clean as a whistle, with shiny buttons and boots you could see your face in. I never thought that I'd ever be this filthy as a soldier.'

'Filthy with swollen feet and lice,' said Drummond. 'At this rate, I'm not sure I'll ever be able to kick a football again. My ruddy feet are knackered.'

'A few hours off from those boots will make a big difference,' said Hebden. 'Keep rubbing them with hay.'

Batiste brought them cheese and apples, and ham and some cider, as well as bread, gratefully taken by the men and brought back up to the hayloft.

'Ah,' sighed Hebden, biting into an apple. 'I really would have eaten frog's legs, but this is much better. I honestly don't think I have ever tasted a finer meal.'

'Me neither,' agreed Hawke. It was not the largest meal he had ever eaten, but he still felt full. It made him realize just how little they had eaten in the past few days. His stomach had shrunk. He thought of home and his mother. '*You've got hollow legs the amount you eat, Johnny*,' she used to say, and then there would always be the same last word: '*You're a growing lad. You'll be big, just like your father.*' Hawke smiled to himself. Drummond passed him the earthenware jar of cider and he drank thirstily. The cider had a rough, sharp taste, but was delicious.

'Good, isn't it?' said Hebden.

Hawke nodded, took another gulp and in doing so lifted the

jar too much, and sweet cider ran down his chin and on to his battledress.

Hebden smiled. 'It's strong stuff. It'll put hairs on your chest, Johnny.'

Hawke passed on the flagon, then suddenly felt overcome with fatigue.

'I don't know about that,' he said to Hebden, 'but it's certainly made me sleepy.' He lay down on the wooden floor, his greatcoat behind his head.

'Ahhh,' said Drummond. 'Little Johnny's had too much cider.'

'He's only a kid,' laughed Hebden. 'A tank killer, maybe, but still just a little kid.'

Ignoring them, Hawke smiled to himself, closed his eyes and in moments was fast asleep.

Dawn was breaking as Spears descended the ladder. Like the others, he felt better for the food, but his wound was shooting stabs of pain through his body, and exhaustion was beginning to consume him like a wave. Staggering across the yard, he paused and listened. To the north, he heard the faint dull thud of guns – or was it bombs falling? Above the distant sound of war, however, there was birdsong – a dawn chorus bursting with life.

Inside the house, Batiste led him to the farmhouse kitchen, where the range had already been lit. His wife, he explained, had returned to bed. 'But she will take a look at your wound shortly,' he said, taking up a bottle of Calvados from the dresser and pouring two glasses.

'We have a medic with us,' said Spears. 'He has stitched and bandaged it. Although sometimes I think a glass of this is the best medicine.'

Batiste smiled. 'I understand. But my wife will make you a poultice. You should let her help.'

'Thank you – and again for all your help.'

Batiste raised a hand. *It's nothing.*

'You said you have information,' said Spears.

'Only what I have picked up or heard on the radio.' He sighed. 'France is finished, and the British are evacuating, but you know that much.'

'Are they still evacuating?'

'*Oui*. British and French troops were flooding through here a few days ago but now it is only the Boches. Our troops have been holding a line around Dunkirk behind the Bergues-Furnes Canal. That has been the front line, but more and more German troops are moving up. You must be quick.'

'We can't move again until dark.'

'I know. But you must get there tomorrow night. Rest here then hurry. You have a map?'

Spears took it out, embarrassed by its large scale.

'Pah!' said Batiste. 'This is no good. I will find you a better one, and show you a route away from the roads.' He drained his glass. 'And now let us sleep.'

When Hawke awoke, bright sunlight was pouring through the window and between cracks in the tiles above, casting sharp beams of light in which many dust particles lazily swirled. He was lying alone on the wooden floorboards and felt momentarily confused until he saw the mound of hay and straw sheaves and realized that the rest of the men must be sleeping out of sight behind it.

To the north he could hear the guns but a little way away he could hear something else – something that had somehow caused him to wake. Engines. Vehicle engines.

Hastily getting to his feet he hurried round the side of the wall of straw and hay and saw the men all fast asleep. Seeing Spears, he crouched down beside him.

'Sarge! Sarge! Wake up!'

Spears rolled his head, then opened his eyes. Hawke saw there were beads of perspiration on his forehead.

'What is it?' he murmured.

'I can hear vehicles.'

Spears eased himself up, wincing with pain. 'All right. Wake the rest.'

The others were already stirring, yawning and rubbing eyes, but then as sound of vehicles drew closer any vestiges of sleep vanished and they became instantly alert.

'Everyone – keep behind this barricade and don't say a word,' said Spears. 'A single cough will give us away.'

Hawke sat down beside Spears, leaning against the back wall of the barn and staring at the wall of bales in front of them. Outside, what sounded like a motorcycle and a heavy truck were pulling into the yard.

The engines were cut, then a few orders barked. Sounds of men clambering from the truck, boots heavy on the yard. Hawke hardly dared breathe. He suddenly wondered whether they had left any prints from their own boots – but it had been dark and he had no idea whether they had or not.

Now he could hear Batiste. He strained to hear. What was the tone of his voice, of the conversation between him and the Germans? He couldn't tell. Hawke glanced around at the others.

Fletcher and White looked scared, eyes blinking repeatedly. Hebden was biting at a fingernail, Drummond sitting with his head lowered and eyes closed. Spears stared straight ahead, but, Hawke saw, the beads of perspiration still pricked his brow and upper lip.

The great wooden door of the barn was pushed open, the ageing hinges creaking loudly, and Hawke flinched. A fly was buzzing around them and then it settled on his face, tickling him. He desperately wanted to whisk it away but did not dare to. Then it moved, flying off, its wings buzzing noisily.

Several Germans were talking, then one laughed. Now they were moving something – yanking something heavy and muttering with the strain. *So they're not looking for us*, Hawke thought to himself, but then they heard someone climbing the ladder. *No*, thought Hawke, *please no*. And he felt a bead of sweat on his own head, running down his temple and on to his cheek. Again, he had an overwhelming urge to move and wipe it away, but he just sat there, rigid, his heart hammering, desperately trying not to move a single muscle.

A thump as the soldier clambered on to the hayloft, then steps across the wooden floorboards. He spoke something, then took a few more steps. He was just a couple of yards away now. Hawke closed his eyes. Surely this was it. For a moment – just a brief moment – there was silence, absolute silence. Then the fly buzzed somewhere and the floorboards creaked as the soldier shifted his weight.

'*Es gibt hier nichts – nur ein paar Heuballen*,' he called down to his comrades. And then he stepped back towards the ladder and Hawke heard him clamber on and begin to climb back down, but then Matherson suddenly clenched his teeth in agony and began rubbing his leg. Spears glared at him as the floorboards creaked again. On the ladder, the soldier stopped and, once again, Hawke froze. Across from him, Matherson was still gripping his leg, his face contorted with pain.

*Stop moving! Please stop moving!* Hawke wanted to shout.

The ladder creaked as the German began climbing back up towards the hayloft. *No!* thought Hawke. *No!* Steps back across the floorboards, slow, steady. *Cautious.*

Hawke held his breath, and prayed.

# 29

## THE CANAL

Seconds passed. Matherson was still struggling, his face red with the effort of keeping pain under control, but then suddenly he relaxed, breathed out silently and closed his eyes with relief. Behind their makeshift barricade of hay and straw bales, the floorboards creaked again and then they heard the German step backwards, and clamber back on to the ladder. One of his comrades called up to him, but he replied, '*Es war nichts*,' and continued on down the ladder.

Someone else came into the barn, called the men out and they all headed back into the yard.

'Sorry,' whispered Matherson. 'Cramp. The pain was terrible.'

'Shh!' said Spears.

For a further half hour they heard the men chatting out in the yard. Smells of cooking wafted up into the barn, which made Hawke's stomach groan with renewed hunger. Still no one spoke, and no one dared move. Hawke's backside was aching and he desperately wanted move but he remained sitting there rigidly, as did the rest of them. He wondered about Spears. The sergeant did not look well. The perspiration was getting worse, while the colour had drained from his normally tanned and healthy-looking face.

Eventually, about an hour after they had first arrived, engines started up again, shouts rang out around the yard and with a revving of engines and the grinding of gears they drove back out of the yard and rumbled away down the track.

'Thank God,' said McLaren, grimacing as he stood up. He looked at Matherson. 'Blimey, you nearly blew it, didn't you? What a time to get cramp. And you being a medic an' all.'

'I thought you did well to keep it under control,' said Hebden.

Matherson shook his head. 'That was terrible,' he said. 'Honestly, I thought I was going to blow it for you all.'

Hawke turned to Spears. 'Are you all right, Sarge?'

'I'm fine,' muttered Spears, wiping his brow.

'Why do you think that German stopped? I was certain he was going to look around the bales and find us.'

'I think he was scared,' said Spears. 'You're always frightened about what you don't know. He must have known there was something behind the barricade – maybe he even guessed – but maybe he was scared to find out.' He shrugged. 'Anyway, we got away with it.'

'Maybe the nightingale was a good omen after all,' said Hebden.

Spears smiled weakly. 'Maybe.'

A few minutes later, Batiste clambered up the ladder with his teenage son.

'I'll be glad when you men are on your way,' he said with a wry grin. 'That was a bad hour.'

'What did they want?' asked McLaren.

'Nothing. They were a bit lost. They wanted to buy some food and to stop and eat.'

'I'm sorry we have not been able to pay for ours,' said Spears.

'No matter.'

'They found something in the barn,' said Hawke. 'We heard them pulling it out.'

'A bicycle,' said Batiste. 'But then they left it.' He turned to Spears. 'My wife has that poultice ready. Will you let her look at your arm?'

Spears glanced at Matherson, then nodded. 'Yes,' he said. 'I'll come down now.'

Despite the poultice, Spears's condition did not improve. Throughout the rest of the afternoon he remained feverish. Matherson insisted the sergeant try to sleep and so he did, although fitfully. The hours passed slowly. Hawke knew they could not leave until nightfall, but it did not stop him feeling increasingly impatient to get going, and he quickly tired of playing cards. He cleaned his rifle twice, thought about writing his journal, then put pen and paper away again, and glanced across at Spears. The sergeant was asleep – Matherson had said that was the best thing Spears could do. To the north, the guns had barely let up all day. Hawke worried that they'd reach Dunkirk only to find they were too late, that the evacuation was over and the port in enemy hands.

At six, Batiste brought them some more bread and cheese, although less than before. He was not used to feeding such numbers, he explained, but was giving them all that he could. Hawke ate his portion wondering when they might next see any food. He was still hungry when he licked the last bread-crumbs from his hand.

Finally, as darkness began to fall, they began putting their kit back together. Drummond struggled to get his boots back on.

'My feet are still swollen,' he said.

'You've got trench foot,' Matherson told him. 'It's not severe, but that's what it is.'

'Well, it hurts enough,' complained Drummond. He took out his clasp knife and cut slits along the sides of his boots. 'It's the only way I'm going to get them back on.'

'Let's hope we don't run into too many more canals and dykes,' said McLaren.

A little before half past nine, they were all back down in the yard and bidding Batiste goodbye.

'Thank you,' said Spears. 'Really, we can't thank you enough.'

'*Bon chance*,' said Batiste. 'Good luck. One day come back and kick these Boches back out of France.'

To begin with, they made steady progress, and after a couple of hours were, Spears reckoned, nearing the Bergues-Furnes Canal that Batiste had mentioned and marked on the map, but as they were about to cross a road, they heard vehicles approaching, and quickly ducked into a ditch behind a row of poplars. Moments later, a column of heavy artillery, the guns towed by trucks, rumbled past them, the lorries' headlights reduced to dim, narrow slits.

'There go the big boys,' whispered Hebden as the last one passed.

'It's not over yet, then,' said McLaren.

They crossed the road, walking on, keeping to hedgerows

or the numerous long lines of poplars wherever they could. Reaching a track, Spears halted them again.

'What is it, Sarge?' said McLaren.

'Shh!' hissed Spears. 'Listen.'

They all listened and then faintly, on the breeze, they could hear voices. Enemy voices.

'All right,' said Spears, Batiste's map in his hand. 'We're going to rest here a bit.'

'Shouldn't we keep going, Sarge?' asked McLaren. Hawke was thinking the same. He wondered whether it was Spears who needed the rest. The moon suddenly emerged from behind a cloud, bathing the surrounding countryside in that strange, milky monochrome light that was now so familiar.

'Look,' said Spears, 'a mile or so to our left is the village of Warhem. You can see the church. And away to our right is Honschoote. That means the canal is no more than half a mile up ahead. We're nearly there.'

'Then the sooner we get over, the better,' said McLaren.

'Just listen, Sid,' said Spears. 'This area is teeming with Jerries. If we wait an hour or so, there's a greater chance that most of them will be kipping by then.' He nodded in the direction of the voices. 'You don't really want to walk through that lot, do you?'

Hawke smiled to himself, relieved. Spears was all right after all. As usual, he was just thinking more clearly than any of the rest of them.

They crouched down on the bank of the narrow dyke that ran northwards towards the canal. Up ahead, the horizon glowed a faint orange. At first Hawke could not understand what was causing the glow, but then he realized it was Dunkirk, burning. He swallowed hard and realized how right Spears was to be cautious. They might be close, but there was much that could still go wrong.

It was nearing one o'clock in the morning when Spears told them they should get moving again.

'But get rid of any excess kit,' he told them. 'You don't need entrenching tools now, or enamel mugs, or half the stuff we've been lugging around in our packs. Let's make our lives easier, and discard anything we don't need – anything that may chink or knock together and give the game away.'

They spent a few minutes lightening their loads. Hawke took off his entire pack, which included his gas cape, greatcoat, housewife, mug, gas-mask bag, as well as his entrenching tool. All that was left round his waist was his pack and sword bayonet – his water bottle he put in his half-empty haversack. He rolled his shoulders, glad to discover how much lighter they now felt.

They set off again, crossing the track and moving forward in single file, hugging the bank of the dyke, until it veered off to their left. Ahead there was now a stretch of open fields, with no trees and no hedgerows. Spears signalled to them to spread out. Hawke was next to Spears on the far right of the platoon, but as he looked across towards the others he saw the upper halves of their bodies were all clearly silhouetted against the moonlit sky. He was wondering whether he should point this out when Spears signalled to them to crouch. Immediately, the others all disappeared from view.

It was difficult crouching and walking like that, but at least the soil beneath them was soft after the recent rain. Hawke could barely hear either Spears on his right or Drummond to his left as they carefully moved forward over the field. On the horizon, the glow of fire seemed to be getting closer and Hawke felt his hopes rise.

Suddenly he stopped dead in his tracks. He'd been looking around him, but had just glanced at the ground and not a yard in front he realized there was a slit trench with two men curled up inside, snoring very gently.

Hawke breathed deeply, gripped his rifle tightly, then stepped across to Spears.

'There's a Jerry slit trench just there,' he whispered.

'All right,' hissed Spears, 'let's just keep walking.'

Hawke kept moving forward, putting down each foot carefully in front of him, his heart hammering in his chest, expecting any number of enemy troops to suddenly wake and start firing.

'Just keep going,' whispered Spears beside him.

'Yes,' he replied. On they went, one foot after the other, Hawke offering silent prayers, his body tense. He wondered whether any of the others had seen similar enemy positions. Somewhere there had to be picquets – or perhaps those two men had been the picquets, but had fallen asleep on their watch . . . Hawke glanced back into the inky darkness. Away to his left he could still see Warhem outlined faintly against the sky. *Where was the canal?* he wondered It couldn't be far now. His back was aching from crouching and then someone stumbled, the sound of the man falling forward painfully loud in the otherwise still night air. Again, Hawke froze, his body tensed for the worst, but there was nothing. No sound of waking Germans, no cocking of rifles or machine guns. And then there they were: at the road beside the canal and, beyond, the canal itself, still and silvery in the moonlight.

For a moment they stood together on the canal's bank, looking down at the water.

'So how do we get across?' whispered McLaren. 'All the bridges will be blown.'

'We'll have to swim,' said Spears. 'Is there anyone who can't swim?'

'I can't,' said Matherson.

'Nor can I,' said Merryweather.

'You can't swim, Sarge,' said McLaren.

'Course I can,' snapped Spears. 'It's only a few yards.'

'Look!' said Hawke, pointing to the far bank. 'Isn't that a boat?' He stood at the water's edge, peering towards the other side.

'I think it is,' said Spears. 'Whether it's water-worthy is another matter, though.'

'Let me swim over and have a look,' said McLaren.

'Yes, all right,' agreed Spears.

McLaren stripped and then slipped into the water. Hawke watched him as he carefully swam the fifteen yards that separated the two banks. It was hard to see clearly, but he heard McLaren clamber into the boat. A few minutes later, he slipped back into the water and once halfway across could be seen, one arm bringing the small dinghy safely across.

'No oars, I'm afraid,' he said, treading water beside the little vessel. 'It looked half submerged when I got to it, but although there's a bit of water in the bottom I think it's all right.'

'Good work, Sid,' said Spears, then turning to the others

said, 'Right, those who can swim, get your kit into the boat and get swimming. Merryweather and Matherson, you can get your ride once we've got the rest across.' He kneeled down beside McLaren. 'Happy to make a couple more trips, Sid?'

'Yes, Sarge,' said McLaren, then said, 'Sarge, take the boat.'

'You should, Sergeant,' said Matherson. 'It's not worth getting that wound infected with dirty water.'

'All right,' said Spears. 'But we need to be quick here. It'll be dawn before we know it.'

'What's it like in, Sid?' asked Hebden, as he took off his belt and webbing. 'Is it freezing?'

'Nah, it's lovely.'

Hawke stripped down to his underwear then slid down the bank and eased himself into the water. His feet sank into soft, silty mud and for a moment he felt a flash of panic, but as he lunged forward, his feet moved free and he was swimming, the water icy cold but invigorating after the long days without washing and wearing an increasingly filthy uniform. On the far side, his feet once again sank into the soft mud, but then he thought it would be better to help McLaren, so he remained in the water as the rifles and webbing and stinking uniforms were passed back on to dry land.

Five minutes later, and with Merryweather, Matherson and Spears safely brought across, Hawke clambered on to the bank, shivering but strangely refreshed. Away to the east, dawn was once again breaking, the first hint of morning light turning the horizon a faint grey.

As Hawke dried himself down with his shirt, then began putting his battledress back on, he recoiled at the itchiness of the serge against his still wet skin, and at the grime and filth engrained in the wool. The men stood on the bank, forcing raw and swollen feet back into heavy boots, hoisting webbing over their shoulders and clipping belts together. A thin light was spreading over the flat countryside, so that features that had been hidden a few moments before were now revealing themselves.

'My God,' said McLaren, looking back at the road on the far side. 'Look at that.'

Hawke turned and saw that a little further up the road towards Warhem there was a seemingly endless line of abandoned and wrecked vehicles.

'Blimey,' muttered Drummond. 'And they're all British. That's our kit. It's all been abandoned.'

'But where are the lads defending this stretch of the canal?' asked Hebden. 'I thought this was the front line?'

Hawke immediately looked to Spears for the answer.

'Where's the sarge?' he said.

'I'm here,' murmured Spears, and Hawke looked down and saw that the figure shivering on the ground beside him was the sergeant.

'Sarge?' he said, crouching down.

'I'll be all right,' he said.

'You're shivering, Sarge,' he said, then remembered that Spears had not swum across but had been ferried in the dinghy.

'Yes, I know that, thank you,' he snapped, then, with shaking hands, delved into his battledress and pulled out his hip flask. Fumbling with the lid, he cursed, then brought it to his lips. He gasped. 'Damn it, I'm cold.'

'What's up with the sergeant?' said Matherson, now standing over both of them.

'Nothing,' snarled Spears, shakily getting himself to his feet. 'I don't know what you're all standing around for. Are you waiting to be shot?'

'Just getting our kit together, Sarge,' said McLaren, a hint of indignation in his voice.

'We need to get moving,' muttered Spears. 'Time is running out.' The banks of the canal were raised, but behind, as the ground dropped away, many of the fields appeared to be flooded. A short distance to their right, emerging spectrally in the dim early dawn light, there was a badly damaged farmhouse and, beyond that, the remains of a blown bridge. Leading from the bridge was a road, raised either side of the flooded fields.

'There,' said Spears.

They headed round the back of the farm, stumbling past abandoned slit trenches strewn with empty ammunition boxes, discarded tins of food, cigarette boxes and even several tin helmets. They saw the roof of the farmhouse had suffered several hits, while half on the road lay a knocked-out carrier.

Hawke remembered Hebden's unanswered question: if the canal marked the Dunkirk perimeter, then where were all the defenders? He was about to ask Spears when from behind them a machine gun suddenly chattered, and bullets fizzed over their heads.

'Quick!' said Spears, urging them all on. 'Keep your heads down and keep running!'

Hawke ran. Bullets continued to fizz and whip over their heads, but a thin mist had risen from the flooded fields and, glancing back, Hawke saw the farmhouse and the canal melt away. The shooting stopped and, gasping, the men stopped.

'Thank God,' said McLaren. 'Another close escape. The sarge was right – we got over that canal in the nick of time.'

'Where is the sarge?' said Hawke, frantically looking around him.

'Oh no,' said McLaren. 'Where the hell is he?'

'Tom,' mouthed Hawke to himself. 'Where are you, Tom?'

# 30

## DUNKIRK

Hawke hurried back a few yards and saw, faintly through the mist, a prostrate figure lying on the road.

'No!' he said out loud, and ran towards him. Reaching him, he crouched down and turned him over.

'Careful, Johnny,' said a voice, and he glanced up to see Hebden and McLaren standing over him, and Drummond and Matherson running towards them. 'We're almost in view again here – look!'

But Hawke just stared down at Spears. 'Sarge! Sarge!' he said, shaking him by the collar.

'Mind out,' said Matherson, squatting down beside him. He pressed his fingers to Spears's neck. 'He's still breathing.'

'He's got a hip flask,' said Hawke.

'Then get it out,' snapped Matherson.

Hawke delved into Spears's jacket and pulled out the battered silver flask, then, having unscrewed the lid, put it to Spears's lips. The brandy ran down his chin, but then Spears spluttered, his head lolled and slowly his eyes flickered open.

'Sarge!' said Hawke. 'Wake up!'

'Arghh,' muttered Spears. 'My head.' Beads of perspiration were forming on his forehead again, as he tried to lift himself up on his elbows.

'Steady,' said Matherson as Spears dropped back down again.

'Leave me,' he mumbled. 'Just get to the port.'

'No!' said Hawke. 'No one's leaving you, Sarge.' He looked up at the others. 'We're not leaving him here?'

'Course we're not,' said McLaren. 'But we need to make up a stretcher and we've got rid of all our greatcoats.'

'Then we'll have to use our battle blouses,' said Hawke. He began taking off the straps of his webbing.

'Yes, all right,' said McLaren. 'Three battle blouses buttoned up around a couple of rifles might do the trick.'

The mist was beginning to thin and suddenly the farmhouse and the canal came into full view again, with the row of abandoned vehicles clearly visible on the far side. Moments later, a machine gun opened fire, tracer hissing over their heads.

'Quick!' said McLaren. 'Let's just get him out of here.' Crouching beside Spears, he put one of the sergeant's arms round his shoulder then said to Hebden, 'Here, Bert, you do the same on the other side. Matherson, Johnny, you grab a leg each.'

Half crouching, they scampered back down the track, gasping with the effort, but only stopping once they were a safe distance away and finally out of range of the enemy machine gun. By the time they got back their breath and loaded Spears on to a makeshift stretcher, the sergeant had lost consciousness again.

'What's the matter with him?' Hawke asked Matherson as they moved off once more.

'I'm not sure,' Matherson told him. 'But he's hot and feverish. It could be anything. The wound will have weakened him.

I'm hoping it's just a fever and nothing more, but it could be septicaemia.'

'What's that?'

'Blood poisoning. It can be very bad.'

'How bad?'

'The worst.'

Dawn spread over the flat landscape around Dunkirk and, as the sun began to rise, so they saw the huge cloud of thick smoke that rose thousands of feet into the sky and hung heavily over the port. Enemy shelling had begun, but most of it seemed to be directed towards the port itself and away to their left. On they plodded, seeing no one until at last, up ahead, they saw a barricade across the road beside a battered house, and some Tommies appeared.

As they neared, a young subaltern stepped out from the house and began walking towards them.

'Cutting it a bit fine, aren't you?' he said.

McLaren saluted. 'I'm not sure, sir. To be honest, we're not quite certain what the situation is.'

'I can tell you that in one word,' said the lieutenant. 'Dire. Where have you come from?'

'Cassel, sir.'

'Cassel. Good God. We thought you'd all been put in the bag. How on earth did you get through?'

'We walked, sir. By night, sir, and holed up during the day. We were told that the canal back there was the perimeter. What's happened?'

'It was until nightfall last night, then we all pulled back. The evacuation's nearly over. We're all pulling out tonight.' He looked at Spears. 'He looks in a bad way.'

'He's got a fever,' said Matherson. 'He was shot in the arm.'

'Oh,' said the lieutenant. 'I'm afraid he'll have to stay behind. They're not letting any more wounded on. There's a makeshift hospital behind Malo-les-Bains. Take him there. They have medical staff staying behind. It's hard, I know, but there it is. The rest of you better get to the port. They're lifting the last ones from the east mole tonight after dark.'

Hawke listened with mounting anger. 'We can't leave him,' he whispered to Hebden. 'We can't!'

'All right, Johnny,' said Hebden. 'Let's not worry about that just yet. The rules might have changed.'

'Damn the rules,' said Hawke, 'we can't leave him here.'

'How far have we got to go?' McLaren now asked the lieutenant.

'Oh, not far.' He turned his head and pointed. 'This track leads up to the dunes. They're about a mile away. If you get to the beaches, then turn to your left, you'll soon reach Malo-les-Bains. And, of course, you'll see the port itself.' He chuckled. 'Impossible to miss. It's quite a sight, I can promise you.'

'Thank you, sir,' said McLaren.

'Oh, one other thing before I let you get on your way. If you need something to eat, we've got plenty here.'

He led them into the house and there, in the kitchen, were boxes of rations. 'Help yourself,' he said, 'although I wouldn't loiter too long. We're expecting Jerry to attack any moment.'

'Where are the rest of your men, sir?' Hebden asked as he helped himself to several tins of bully beef and fruit.

'Well, we've some here in the house, and a few more spread out either side of the road. There's only twenty-seven left in the entire company and I'm acting company commander. All the rest are dead or wounded.'

It was just after 7 a.m. on Sunday 2 June, when the survivors of 6th Platoon stumbled through the dunes and finally reached the sea.

'My God,' muttered McLaren.

They laid Spears down on the sand and stood there, staring at the scene before them. Hawke sank to his knees.

The beaches were littered with wrecked vehicles, abandoned guns, boxes and the dead. There was debris everywhere. Even the sea was littered with wrecks. Directly in front of them lay a sunken ship, tilted to one side and still smouldering. Further along were yet more abandoned vehicles and even a long line of trucks, toe to tail, snaking out into the water like an oddly shaped jetty. Other wrecks stood out above the water, while not far away the skeletal remains of a fighter plane lay half submerged in the sand.

Away to their left, the battered port of Dunkirk continued to burn. Hawke could see figures now, soldiers huddled on the far end of the beach near the town, but clearly there had been many, many thousands more during the previous days. Nearby, something fluttered in the wind. Hawke looked, then got up to see what it was. Behind a tuft of dune grass lay a dead British soldier, but caught in the grass was a map. Hawke took it and saw that it was of Dunkirk and the surrounding area. In pencil, various lines and positions had been marked.

'Here,' he said, passing it to McLaren.

'A bit late for that,' said McLaren, taking it, then standing up and kicking the sand, said, 'Why the hell couldn't we have had maps like that earlier?' He turned and looked at them. 'Come on,' he said. 'Let's head down the beach and see if we can get that lift home.'

They trudged on in silence, Hawke, with Hebden, Drummond and McLaren, carrying Spears. The tide was out, and had left behind a number of dead. Shells were exploding around the port and behind them to their left, where the last troops were making their final stand. A strange smell hung over the beaches: a stench of oily smoke, the sea and something else – something sweeter and more sickly. Hawke recognized it at once. He glanced down at the bloated figure of a dead Guardsman, his arm outstretched and half buried in the damp sand. Just a few days earlier, he would have recoiled from such a sight, but now he walked straight past, strangely unmoved.

As they neared the end of the beach, a naval officer hurried towards them.

'What unit are you?' he enquired as he reached them. He was wearing a tin helmet, his normal black uniform and a worn, harassed expression.

'We're Second Battalion, King's Own Yorkshire Rangers,' said McLaren.

'Yorks Rangers,' said the officer, 'we've not had many. Just a handful.'

'Really?' said McLaren, brightening. 'We thought we might be the only ones left.'

'There're no ships sailing until tonight, I'm afraid, but we're planning to get every last man lifted tonight. This is to be the end of the evacuation.'

'That's good, sir,' said McLaren.

'It's a miracle. When I was first sent over here six days ago, we thought we'd be lucky if we got forty thousand home. Now it's over three hundred thousand.'

McLaren whistled.

'The weather's helped – lots of low cloud – and of course Jerry hit the oil depots on the far side of town. That was something of an own-goal.'

'Lots of smoke,' said Hebden.

'Exactly. It's pretty much covered the town. Jerry's been bombing blind much of the time.' He looked at Spears. 'I'm afraid he'll have to stay behind, though.'

'He'll be all right by then, sir,' said McLaren. 'We'll look after him.'

'It's not as simple as that. We've had a devil of a job getting everyone off and the wounded take up more space and, more to the point, take up precious time. Getting you fit ones away safely is the priority. The longer it takes to load and unload a ship, the more dangerous it is and the harder the task. So, I'm sorry, but you need to take him to the field hospital.' He looked up at the row of battered houses overlooking the beach. 'It's up there, behind the houses of Malo-les-Bains. You'll find it, I'm sure.'

'Yes, sir,' said McLaren. 'And what should we do until tonight?'

'Keep your heads down if I were you. Find somewhere to shelter. A lot of the chaps have been taking cover in the cellars of the houses in town. Our friends in the Luftwaffe haven't been over yet, but I'm sure it won't be long. Just make sure you're on the east mole by twenty-one hundred.'

He left them and hurried off.

'So,' said Matherson. 'We'd better take Sergeant Spears to hospital.'

'No,' said Hawke. 'We've got to try to get him on board.'

'How are we going to do that? You heard what he said. It's orders. There's nothing we can do about it.'

McLaren stood for a moment, scratching his cheek thoughtfully. 'Look, tell you what,' he said eventually. 'There's no point in us all taking the sarge to this hospital. We're all done in. Us four will take him there. The rest of you, do what you like. We'll find you later, or on the mole this evening.'

Merryweather and Corporal Bristow looked at each other and then at the others. 'All right,' said Bristow at length. 'If you're sure.'

'Hold on, Sid,' said Chalkie White. 'We'll come with you. Our section has stuck together so far – we'll stick with you now too.' He turned to Fletcher. 'Won't we, Fletch?'

Fletcher nodded.

'That's settled, then,' said McLaren. 'The rest of you, try to get some rest, and, like that navy bloke said, keep your heads down.'

They shook hands, and McLaren said, 'Right, then, let's get you to hospital, Sarge.'

Spears stirred and opened his eyes as they lifted him again. 'Have we made it to Dunkirk?' he asked softly.

'Yes, Sarge,' said Hawke. 'We've got here.'

'You take it steady, Sarge,' said McLaren.

As soon as they were out of earshot of the others, Hawke turned to McLaren. 'I'm sorry, Corp,' he said in a loud whisper, 'but I'm not letting him be taken to any hospital.'

'Neither am I,' grinned McLaren.

'You're not?' said Hawke, confused.

'Course not.'

'None of us want to abandon the sarge,' said Hebden. 'He might be a bit hard sometimes, but he's a good bloke really.'

'If it weren't for the sarge,' added McLaren, 'we wouldn't be here. I just didn't want the hassle from Bristow and Matherson. Somehow, we'll get him on board tonight. We just need to find a place to lie up for the day and where we can keep an eye on him.'

Hawke smiled. 'Good,' he said. 'For a moment, I thought I might have to try getting him on board on my own. And I'm not sure how I'd have managed that.'

'We've still got to get through today,' said Drummond. 'We're not on that ship yet. You're all talking as though we've made it, but I'm not going to get too ahead of myself until I can see Blighty again.'

They climbed off the beach and on to the promenade that ran along the front of Malo-les-Bains. A number of the houses had been hit. Carefully they stepped around some smashed glass and then had to walk over a number of collapsed telegraph wires that lay snake-like across the road. More vehicles stood abandoned. Up ahead, several soldiers were leaning on the balustrade clutching bottles and singing drunkenly.

'Blimey,' said McLaren, 'so this is what defeat really looks like.'

'That lieutenant warned us,' said White. 'He said it wasn't pretty and he was right.'

'Where are we going, Sid?' asked Drummond. 'My feet are agony. Can't we lie up in the dunes somewhere? I'm sure this was a lovely seaside town once, but it's horrible now. It's making me feel depressed.'

McLaren nodded. 'Yes, all right, Charlie.'

They doubled back, picking their way through the debris and past other exhausted and filthy troops until they reached the dunes. There were other soldiers hiding there, but they soon found a quiet patch – a little hollow surrounded by thick clumps of dune grass. Lowering Spears carefully, they lifted him off the makeshift stretcher and propped him up against a mound of sand and tufty grass.

It was now around eight in the morning and, as the naval officer had warned, they soon heard the drone of planes overhead. The smoke cloud still covered much of the town and bombs began whistling down before they could see any aircraft.

'Here we go,' said Drummond, crouching low, his hands over his ears.

Most of the bombs fell behind them and on the town itself, although several landed a short way out at sea, sending huge plumes of water high into the air. As the rain of bombs stopped, they could hear machine-gun fire high above.

'Do you think that's our boys?' said Hawke.

'Who knows?' said McLaren.

'Hold on, look up there!' said Hebden. Away to their right, heading north away from the town where the sky was clearer, two single engine fighters were chasing after a German bomber, smoke trailing from one of the wings. The fighters were firing away, and then the bomber seemed to be dropping out of the sky. They watched a long trail of smoke follow it down and then it finally disappeared from view.

'One less to worry about,' said Drummond.

Spears was awake again, his eyes flickering open.

'How are you feeling, Sarge?' asked Hebden.

'I've felt better,' he mumbled.

'Do you want anything?' asked Hawke.

'Water,' he murmured. 'Water. I'm parched.'

Hawke took out his bottle, which was still half full. 'Here,' he said, putting it to Spears's lips.

Spears drank, then lay back and sighed. 'Thanks.'

'Sarge, we've just got to get through today,' said McLaren. 'Get through today and we'll be going home.'

'You'll see Maddie again,' said Hawke.

'Maddie . . .' Spears felt for his breast pocket and, fumbling with the button, managed to undo it and feel inside. He pulled out a bundle of letters and a photograph, and held them up in front of his eyes. 'Maddie,' he mumbled again.

'You'll see her soon, Sarge,' said Hebden.

Spears smiled weakly. 'We've come this far,' he said. 'I'm not giving up now.' He looked at Hawke. 'Johnny,' he said. 'I promised Maddie I'd get you back.'

'And you have, Sarge,' said McLaren. 'Johnny's in better shape than any of us.'

Spears lay his head back again and closed his eyes.

Hawke shot a glance at McLaren and Hebden. 'Do you think he's going to be all right? He is, isn't he? Tell me he is.'

'I don't know, Johnny,' said McLaren. 'I just don't know.'

# 31

## THE MOLE

The shelling continued all day, and behind them, a short way inland, they could hear the fighting intensifying. The Luftwaffe bombed the town twice more, but none fell dangerously close to the small group of Rangers hiding in the dunes. In any case, the sand would have absorbed much of the blast. Unless they received a direct hit, they reckoned they were as safe as in any cellar.

About midday, Spears took a turn for the worse, his brow heavy with perspiration, his body writhing and his breathing increasingly heavy. For a while, McLaren thought they should take him to the hospital after all, but Hawke pleaded with him.

'We can't abandon him,' he said. 'We can't.'

'But he might die if we don't get help,' said McLaren.

'They won't be able to help him there,' said Drummond. 'That place will be heaving with sick and wounded. I reckon he's got a better chance with us.' That had settled the matter. Hawke had felt profoundly grateful to Drummond. And then, as the afternoon had worn on, so Spears's condition seemed to improve. The fever abated and he became calmer. By six, he was fully conscious once more. They continued to ply him with water, until the last of it was gone, and even gave him some food, breaking into the last of their tins of bully beef and mixed fruit.

By eight o'clock, the shelling had stopped and the fighting had died down. More troops appeared on the beach, British and French, and began moving up towards the sea wall that led back to Dunkirk and to the mole that stretched out from the harbour.

'We should move,' said McLaren. He turned to Spears. 'Are you strong enough, Sarge?'

'I do feel much better,' he admitted. 'I suppose there's only one way to find out.'

'That's the spirit, Sarge,' grinned Hebden.

McLaren cleared his throat. 'Er, Sarge, there is one thing we should warn you about.'

'What's that?'

'There's an order that no wounded are to be taken back. We were supposed to take you to a field hospital here and leave you.'

'But you didn't.'

'No. But we can't carry you on to the mole. You're going to have to try to walk.'

Spears nodded. 'Thank you,' he said quietly. 'It's not far to the mole, is it?'

'About half a mile.'

'All right,' said Spears. 'Let's go, then.'

He stood up, stumbled, then clutched his head and leaned forward a moment, his hands on his knees. Hawke tried to help him, but Spears waved him away. 'I'll be all right.'

'We'll take it steady, Sarge,' said McLaren, slinging his rifle over his shoulder.

Slowly, carefully, they moved back through the dunes and down to the sea wall. A number of other troops were also heading towards the mole, most looking equally exhausted and staggering rather than marching briskly. No one so much as glanced at Spears, despite his sling. Eventually, they reached the edge of the port. From the far side, smoke was still billowing skywards from the burning oil tanks on the far side of the harbour, so that although it was now not even nine o'clock it was already nearly dark. Sunken and wrecked ships littered the inner harbour, while behind, towards the town, the quaysides were filled with abandoned vehicles.

'Just how many vehicles did we have?' asked Drummond. 'I never knew it was this many.'

'Such a waste,' said McLaren. 'We might have got most of the BEF back home, but an army can't fight without kit.' He shook his head. 'What a mess.'

They were now being shuffled slowly forward along the stone outer quay. Beyond that, stretching out into the sea, was the east mole, little more than a narrow wooden jetty. Already the outer quay and mole were thick with troops.

'Where are the ships?' said Drummond.

'They'll be waiting until it's dark,' said McLaren. 'What worries me is that mole. It doesn't look strong enough, does it?'

'Seems to have worked so far,' said Hebden.

McLaren cursed under his breath. 'I'm beginning to agree with Charlie. I'm not sure I'm going to relax until we're back home safe and sound.'

Hawke turned to Spears, who was resting against the jetty wall. 'How are you feeling?'

Spears breathed in heavily. 'All right.'

'There's no wounded allowed on,' said a soldier behind them. 'Passage on ship is saved for the fit and able.'

'Shut your trap,' snarled McLaren.

'What unit are you?' asked Hawke.

'RASC,' said the man.

'Well, we're Rangers,' snapped McLaren, 'and we've been defending you lot in Cassel. We've gone through a hell of lot here, and if you think we're going to leave our sergeant behind, you can think again.'

'All right, all right,' said the man, 'no need to be so testy. Just pointing out the orders, that's all.'

'You let us worry about that,' said Drummond.

Spears turned to the man. 'So long as I'm standing, I'm not taking up any more space am I?'

'No, I suppose not,' the soldier replied.

'We'll all get on tonight. They're not going to leave any of us behind. Not now.'

Soon after, the first of the ships arrived, a Royal Navy destroyer, which gently edged alongside the mole. Two more followed, one lashing itself alongside the first ship. The line began to move, shuffling forward once more as the loading of men began. Spears held on to the jetty wall and then, as they inched on to the mole itself, he clutched the wooden railings. He was keenly aware of Hawke looking at him repeatedly, checking on how he was. The boy had done well, really well. He was proud of him – proud of all his men in the platoon. They had suffered so much and now, at long last, salvation was within reach. Against all the odds, they had so nearly made it.

But Spears knew that he was not a well man. It was true that he had felt better earlier that evening, but the walk to the mole had taken more out of him than he cared to admit or let on to the others. His arm hurt like hell – a persistent stabbing pain that coursed all the way to his fingers and across his chest. He was weak, his strength sapped by his wound and by his fever and by long days of battle. His head felt light and his balance unsure. He desperately wanted to lie down, but he knew he could not. Water, that was what he needed, because his mouth was parched, his throat dry. Spears gripped the railing and briefly closed his eyes, and then they shuffled forward once more, small steps along the wooden walkway, a mass of men to the front and behind. The end of the evacuation.

His thoughts turned to Maddie once more. *Just hold on*, Spears told himself, *just keep going. One foot in front of the other.* A few days earlier, he'd not really thought it possible that he would ever see her again, and yet now that reunion was tantalizingly close. *And yet, and yet* . . . He was weak, he was ill, his wound, he sensed, was going bad. He brought his hand to his brow. *Be strong*, he told himself. *Not long now* . . .

It was around half past eleven when it was, at long last, their turn to board a ship home. Two more destroyers had pulled alongside the mole and, after waiting such long hours, the three-man-wide line of troops stumbled forward with a surge.

'Move along, move along,' called out one of the naval officers, 'quickly now.'

For Spears, who had been gripping the wooden railing, his mouth as dry as sand and his head spinning, for the past two hours, the sudden movement was too much. Stumbling, he fell, collapsing on the wooden walkway.

'Sarge!' called out Hawke, and immediately crouched down to help him with the other Rangers. Behind, men, impatient and exhausted, began to shout out.

'For God's sake,' cried out a naval officer, hurrying towards them. 'Who let this man on?' He looked at the Rangers angrily. 'Don't you know the orders? Wounded to be left behind. Now look! Get him up, and quickly!'

As McLaren and Hebden tried to hoist Spears to his feet, the mass of men behind began getting increasingly restless.

'Get a move on!' shouted one.

'Get him out of the way!' yelled another.

Hawke now stood up and turned to face the angry line of men.

'This man,' he hissed, 'this man – he – he's the bravest man I ever met. This man helped defend Cassel while the rest of the BEF fell back to Dunkirk. He helped us find our way here. He saved us. We're all that's left of our entire company – all that's left of our battalion. And we are *not* leaving him behind. He stays here over my dead body.'

For a moment, no one spoke. Hawke blinked, his anger suddenly spent.

'Well said, lad,' said one of the men at last, then turned to the others and held out his arms. 'Give this man a bit of space. Come on, lads, let them get their sergeant aboard.' Hawke saw others nodding in agreement.

'Yes,' said the naval officer, 'you're quite right. Let's get him aboard. I'm sorry, it's easy to lose sight of . . .' He let the sentence trail.

With an arm round Hebden and McLaren, Spears was carried forward to the gangway, then two sailors were hurrying forward to help, taking Spears's legs. Hawke followed behind, stepping from the mole on to the gangway, and from the gangway on to the ship, the destroyer, HMS *Winchester.*

'Well done, Johnny,' said Hebden, as they clambered across the deck towards the prow of the ship.

Hawke smiled. 'I don't know what came over me.'

'A new side of Johnny Hawke,' chuckled Hebden. 'You don't want to cross him when he's angry.'

Spears was propped against the bulkhead of A Gun, the most forward of the ship's four guns, with the rest of the Rangers gathering around him.

'Sorry, lads,' he mumbled.

'Don't be, Sarge,' said McLaren. 'You're on board now. We're nearly home.' He patted Spears on the shoulder. 'We're very nearly home.'

# 32

## SPITFIRE OVER THE CHANNEL

Around 6 a.m., Monday 3 June, Pilot Officer Archie Jackson craned his neck as the CO led them south, the morning sun now thankfully on their port side, and the continental coast stretching away from them. It was their first sortie over to Dunkirk in three days, but already it felt as though it had been a long morning: up before first light, a weary clamber into the blood wagon, rumble down to dispersal, fire up the Spit, then fly to Eastchurch. At Eastchurch, a mug of coffee and a bit of bacon and toast, and then into the Spit again as the whole squadron was ordered to patrol Dunkirk.

They had climbed to eighteen thousand feet, and from that height could see right across the Channel back to southern England. Down below, steaming across the sea were two ships, the lines of their wakes starkly white against the deep blue of the water. As was so often the case with ships returning from Dunkirk, they had taken a wide circuitous route, forced upon them by the number of minefields, and so were well north of Dover and still out at sea. Jackson had been told that the northern route was more than eighty miles long, more than three times the normal distance between the two ports.

Jackson kept his eyes peeled, constantly swivelling his head, looking behind him, then out across the continent, then ahead, and then out across the Channel. He had bought himself a new scarf on his return to England, heading into town with some of the other pilots and choosing a navy blue pattern with small white polka dots. It was, he'd decided, a vast improvement. He wondered what had happened to those Rangers who had rescued him and that young boy to whom he'd given his orange scarf. He hoped they'd got out all right, that they had been rescued in turn.

Suddenly he saw a formation of aircraft crossing the coast. The huge plume of thick oily smoke from Dunkirk still rose some ten thousand feet into the sky, but the formation was to the north of that. Heading for the ships still crossing the Channel, Jackson guessed.

'Nimbus Leader this is Blue Two,' said Jackson. 'Twelve bandits at angels twelve crossing the coast now.'

'Blue Two, this is Nimbus Leader,' crackled the CO's voice in Jackson's ears. 'Good spot. We'll turn back north, dropping height, then attack them out of the sun. All of you keep a close watch out for little jobs. Over.'

Jackson, on the port side of the formation, followed the CO and banked his Spitfire and, opening the boost, surged northwards, once more scanning the skies and praying that no enemy fighters had seen them, and that they wouldn't suddenly arrive out of the sun. A couple of minutes later, they banked again. Jackson had kept a close watch on the enemy formation, but had briefly lost them when the squadron turned once more.

'Where are you?' he muttered to himself, but then saw the wake of the two ships and moments later spotted the enemy machines again, now only a few miles away and just a couple of thousand feet below them. He glanced at his altimeter. They were still losing height, the CO trying to make the most of the sun, which was low in the sky, and which, with luck, would mask their attack.

Jackson strained his eyes, then smiled as he realized the enemy planes were Stukas. To anyone who had seen the newsreels of the German attack on Poland, the Stuka had seemed a terrifying weapon, but as he and his fellow pilots had discovered this past week, they were wonderfully easy to shoot down. The trick was to let them carry out their dive, because as they pulled out again they were moving so slowly they were almost at a standstill and made for a very juicy target indeed. Jackson had already added to his score once since his escape from France. Now he hoped he might add to it again.

The Stukas were now just a mile ahead and only fifteen hundred feet below them and, it seemed, still oblivious to the threat above and behind them. The CO had obviously judged it about right, Jackson thought to himself, because the Stukas had a rear gunner who was presumably there to keep a good lookout as well.

'This is Nimbus Leader,' crackled the CO's voice once more, 'get ready.'

Jackson put his goggles down over his eyes and then switched the gun button to 'fire'. And then the Stukas began to dive.

On board the *Winchester*, the small group of Rangers had met up with the rest of the platoon, all of whom had safely made it on board, and who had apologized profusely for suggesting that Spears should have been left behind. The ship had been full – over a thousand troops were on board – but her MO had found time to examine Spears, clean and re-dress his wound and to give him both some water and medication. At first light, and having slept several hours, he had felt a little better.

His spirits had been lifted further by the sight of the English coast emerging on their starboard side, but no sooner had the men started pointing excitedly than the claxon had sounded, the Stukas were spotted and with orders and shouts ringing out across the deck, the gun crews had prepared for action.

Hawke had followed Hebden and Drummond over to the wire railings near the prow and a few steps away from A Gun, and now, with his hand shielding his eyes, he looked up, squinting into the sky.

'There!' he said, pointing, as above them the first of the Stukas peeled off and began its dive, its siren screaming.

'I don't believe it,' muttered Drummond. 'We survive everything Jerry can throw at us in France, finally get away and are within sight of home and then the ruddy Luftwaffe turns up.'

'I reckon it's quite hard for them to hit a moving ship, though,' said a voice beside them and all three turned to see Sergeant Spears standing next to them, gripping the metal rail tightly with his good arm. 'We're travelling at thirty knots or so.'

Suddenly the guns opened fire as one, a deafening boom that made Hawke clutch his ears. Black smudges of flak peppered the sky. Behind them, beyond the bridge, they could hear the pom-pom pumping shells into the sky. The first of the Stukas was almost on top of them when suddenly the *Winchester* lurched to port. The men gripped the railings and Spears nearly lost his balance, but a split second later a bomb was falling from the Stuka and landing well wide, exploding as it hit the sea. A huge plume of water erupted into the sky like a geyser.

More bombs were dropping as the ship continued to zigzag and swerve across the sea. Again and again the guns rang out as more and more fountains of water spurted high into the sky, but although several bombs landed only thirty or forty yards from them, and although the spray of the explosions lashed the men on deck, not a single bomb hit either *Winchester* or *Venomous*, a short distance behind them and zigzagging out of trouble with every bit as much energy.

Suddenly, Hawke heard another roar, a deeper, more guttural engine, followed by the sound of machine guns. Looking up he now saw a number of aircraft diving down after the Stukas.

'Look!' he grinned, 'Spitfires!'

Jackson had watched the CO flip over and dive down after the Stukas now attacking the second of the two destroyers, but his flight commander, Pip Winters, had led Blue and Green sections down towards the Stukas attacking the lead ship. He saw Pip open fire on one as it emerged from its dive and in the corner of his eye saw smoke burst from its engine, but already his attention was focused on a different Junkers, one that had jettisoned its bomb and was now desperately trying to turn away.

Jackson followed it, watching it fill his sights. *Hold on, hold on*, he told himself, then at about two hundred yards, opened fire. His Spitfire juddered, tracer fizzed in wispy trails across the sky and appeared to strike the cowling of the Stuka. In a split second, however, he was overshooting and his Spitfire roaring past the enemy machine. Craning his neck backwards, he saw there was a puff of grey smoke bursting from the Stuka's engine. But was it enough?

On board the *Winchester*, Hawke and the others watched the Spitfire attack the Stuka.

'BM!' exclaimed Hawke. 'Look, the squadron letters on the side – it's BM. That's Jackson's squadron.'

'Maybe it's Jackson,' said Hebden.

'He certainly owes us one,' said Drummond.

'Here, Johnny,' said Hebden. 'Have you still got that scarf of his?'

Hawke had forgotten all about it, but now felt for his haversack. 'Somewhere,' he said. 'I think so.' He rummaged for a few moments, then pulled it out.

'Looks like he's coming back for another run,' said Spears.

Hawke followed his gaze. 'Yes,' he said. 'I think he is.'

'Well, give it a wave when he comes past, then,' said Hebden. 'You never know.'

Opening the boost once more, Jackson climbed then rolled the Spitfire, the sky and sea swivelling, and dived back down, righting himself as he did so. His target had banked and turned in towards the ship, but although it was now only a few hundred feet off the surface, Jackson was determined not to let his quarry escape.

'You're not getting away from me,' he muttered to himself. Carefully lining himself up behind the Stuka he hurtled towards it and not until he was a hundred and fifty yards away did he open fire. Again, the Spitfire juddered and this time bullets poured towards the stricken dive-bomber. A moment later, Jackson was over it and then past it. He craned his neck to look back, saw a burst of flame and smoke and then the Stuka wobbled briefly and plunged into the sea. Jackson smiled grimly to himself and then streaked past the lead ship on his port side, delighted to have had an audience. As he roared past, something caught his eye – a flash of orange.

'No,' he said out loud. 'It can't be.'

He flew on, then climbed once more and looked round. He could only see a couple of other Spitfires. One was chasing another Stuka. He wasn't sure how many enemy aircraft had been shot down, or how many were now heading back east, across the sea and hidden by the blinding sun. He knew he should climb and try to find the rest of the squadron, but curiosity would not let him just yet. First, he had to fly by the lead ship again. Banking, he pulled back on the throttle and then turned back towards the ship, flying alongside its port side as low as he dared. Jackson lifted his goggles and glanced out and saw one of the soldiers near the front of the ship waving an orange scarf in the air.

Laughing, he waved, then opening the throttle, surged forward, climbing into the sky and rolling the Spitfire. He flew on, quickly scanned the sky to make sure neither any enemy aircraft or the CO were anywhere near, then banked again, turning back towards the ship. He glanced at his altimeter – only a hundred feet off the sea. *Oh well*, he thought, then grinned to himself and yanked the stick over to port.

'It is him!' exclaimed Hawke. 'It has to be!'

They were all laughing and cheering now, Hawke frantically waving the scarf as Jackson hurtled past once more, then rolled the Spitfire and after righting himself waggled his wings and sped on his way.

'Look at that,' sighed Hebden. 'A victory roll. Good old Jackson.' He sighed, then said, 'After all that excitement, I'm going to sit down again, I think.'

'Me too,' said Drummond.

Hawke turned to Spears, but the sergeant was gazing out to sea, and so he waited a moment.

'Sid told me what you did,' said Spears at length. 'Last night, I mean.'

Hawke looked down. 'Oh, well, I just suddenly felt a bit angry.'

Spears smiled. 'I'm glad you did. Thank you.'

'If it weren't for you, Sarge . . .'

'Tom,' he said. 'You can call me Tom. It's all right.'

Hawke swallowed, a flood of emotion welling up deep within him.

'I'm sorry,' Spears added. 'I've been hard on you. Too hard, perhaps. But, you see, Johnny, Maddie asked me to look after you, to keep you safe. I was angry because I didn't think I would able to. It's the youngsters who always get killed first – they don't have the experience, the sixth sense.'

'And you thought she would blame you if anything happened to me?'

Spears nodded.

'She wouldn't. I know she wouldn't.'

'She would have done, Johnny. She might not have admitted it, but deep down she would have done.' He turned to face him. 'I love your sister very much, Johnny, and I couldn't bear the thought of anything coming between us.'

'You mean me.'

'Yes.'

They were silent a moment, and then Spears said, 'But you've done well, Johnny. I'm proud of you. And so would your father be, if he could see you now. But promise me one thing?'

'What?'

'Don't feel you've got anything left to prove. God only knows how long this war will last. Just try your best to get through it.'

Hawke nodded. 'All right, Tom.'

Spears smiled again, and then patted Hawke on the back. 'Look,' he said, pointing towards the coast. The cliffs could be clearly seen, while, above, another squadron of fighter aircraft flew over. 'Nearly home,' he added.

Hawke nodded and grinned. 'Nearly home at last.'

# HISTORICAL NOTE

This book is a novel and entirely fiction, but it is based on very real events that took place in May and early June 1940. The BEF was forced back by the collapse of the French and Belgian forces either side of their part of the front, but because the Germans had simultaneously attacked in the north through Holland and Belgium, and across the River Meuse to the south-east in France, the BEF, plus a large number of French and Belgians, soon found themselves almost completely encircled. The problem for the British was that they had never planned on having to defend themselves at the same time to the north and south, which was why General Gort decided to establish 'strongpoints' such as Cassel, in the process sacrificing the troops holding them, but gaining crucial time for the rest of his men to fall back behind them to the coast at Dunkirk. Thanks to men such as those of Somer Force, the plan largely worked.

Brigadier Somerset was a real person and so were all the units named in this book – with the exception of the Yorks Rangers, who are, I'm afraid, made up. Dead Horse Corner is still there, part of Rue du Maréchal Foch, and is the first turning into town after the cemetery (where some of the defenders of 1940 are buried). Despite the battering Cassel received, it has since been rebuilt and is a very pretty and charming place to visit, with cobbled streets, beautiful buildings, and, of course, commanding views. It is still possible to stand by the windmill on Mount Cassel and on a clear day see a hundred villages dotted around the Flanders plain below. The Battalion HQ of the Yorks Rangers is also a real building, as is the Châtellerie de Schoebeque and most of the other buildings mentioned in the novel. It is also possible to walk down narrow alleyways from Grand Place and on to the ramparts. From there, Bavinchove, Zuytpeene and Oxelaëre can all be clearly seen.

The fighting took place much as described, including several German panzers getting very close to the town and even down one of the streets. The defenders never surrendered and it is one of the great tragedies that the order commanding Somerset to pull out on 28 May did not reach him until the following morning.

As it was, most of those who had defended so gallantly were caught out in the open or surrounded in the many woods that cover the Flanders countryside around Cassel. Brigadier Somerset spent the rest of the war in a German prison camp, as did most of those who had defended the town. Just a handful managed to make their way back to Dunkirk and survive to fight another day.

The meeting between British and French commanders to discuss the defence of Dunkirk described in the book also really did take place in Cassel on that morning of 27 May, and it says much about the muddled thinking between both Allies that such a discussion could have taken place in a town that was right at the front line. The truth is that while the French were all at sea with their strategy and tactics, it was lack of communication that contributed more than any other factor to their defeat. No one had anticipated the roads becoming quite so clogged with traffic and refugees, but there was also a terrible shortage of radios among the British and French, which meant that orders were constantly being lost or delayed, or completely out of date by the time they reached their recipient. It was not a problem faced by the Germans, whose communications were superb.

When the evacuation of Dunkirk began, Operation DYNAMO – as the evacuation was code-named – was expected to bring back around 40,000 troops at best. In the end, all fit and able British troops were lifted and, with a number of French soldiers too, accounted for some 338,226 that were safely ferried across the Channel. Although those on the beaches could rarely see the air fighting going on overhead, the RAF played a crucial role in ensuring the success of the evacuation. Squadrons such as those of Archie Jackson were part of RAF Fighter Command, who would later in the summer defend the country in the Battle of Britain, and they flew many missions over the French coast and the Channel. Although their losses were significant, they were not as high as those of the Luftwaffe.

The kit used was also much as written about in the book, and if anyone is interested they can see pictures and descriptions of it if they go to: *www.dutycallsbooks.com*

James Holland

## ACKNOWLEDGEMENTS

I have a couple of thanks I'd like to make. First, to the boys of Forest Hill School, who told Puffin they would like a book about ordinary soldiers caught up in the Second World War, and second, Shannon Park, Samantha Mackintosh and all the gang at Puffin for all their help, input and enthusiasm. Thank you.

# It all started with a Scarecrow.

**Puffin is seventy years old.**

Sounds ancient, doesn't it? But Puffin has never been so lively. We're always on the lookout for the next big idea, which is how it began all those years ago.

Penguin Books was a big idea from the mind of a man called Allen Lane, who in 1935 invented the quality paperback and changed the world.
**And from great Penguins, great Puffins grew, changing the face of children's books forever.**

The first four Puffin Picture Books were hatched in 1940 and the first Puffin story book featured a man with broomstick arms called Worzel Gummidge. In 1967 Kaye Webb, Puffin Editor, started the Puffin Club, promising to **'make children into readers'**. She kept that promise and over 200,000 children became devoted Puffineers through their quarterly instalments of *Puffin Post*, which is now back for a new generation.

Many years from now, we hope you'll look back and remember Puffin with a smile. **No matter what your age or what you're into, there's a Puffin for everyone.** The possibilities are endless, but one thing is for sure: whether it's a picture book or a paperback, a sticker book or a hardback, **if it's got that little Puffin on it – it's bound to be good.**